A JIM H
DRIFTLESS
NOVEL

M000106483

Driftless
TREASURE

SUE BERG

LITTLE CREEK PRESS
AND BOOK DESIGN

MINERAL POINT, WISCONSIN

Little Creek Press®
A Division of Kristin Mitchell Design, Inc.
5341 Sunny Ridge Road
Mineral Point, Wisconsin 53565

Book Design and Project Coordination:
Little Creek Press and Book Design

First Printing
November 2021

Printed in Wisconsin, United States of America

For more information: downadriftlessroad.com
To contact author: bergsue@hotmail.com
To order books: www.littlecreekpress.com

Library of Congress Control Number: 2021921594

ISBN-13: 978-1-955656-13-9

Cover photo:
Riverside Edge, La Crosse, Wisconsin
© **Phil S Addis**

This is a work of fiction. References to real places, events, establishments and organizations
in the Driftless area are intended only to provide a sense of authenticity. They are used fictitiously
and are drawn from the author's imagination to enhance the story being told.

Don't collect for yourselves treasures on earth, where moth
and rust destroy and where thieves break in and steal. But collect
for yourselves treasures in heaven, where neither moth nor rust
destroys, and where thieves don't break in and steal.

Matthew 6:19–20

PRAISE FOR DRIFTLESS GOLD

What readers are saying about the first book in the Jim Higgins Driftless Mystery Series:

Driftless Gold was a wonderful read, and I look forward to future books in the Driftless series.

~Alexandra Birdy Veglahn,
Birdy's Bookstore, Holmen, Wisconsin

Driftless Gold was so well written—a great page turner. I like how the legend was developed into a great story.

~Lona, Bloomington, Wisconsin

Sue Berg knows the territory. She knows the Driftless Area—its steep hills, limestone outcroppings, meandering valley streams, and unique glacial history. She knows the changing moods of "Old Man River." She knows policemen get beat up, shot, and sometimes killed. But best of all, she knows how to write a compelling story that keeps you guessing.

~Harold Thorpe, author of the *O'Shaughnessy Chronicles*

Driftless Gold is like the Hardy Boys—all grown up!

~Dave, Viroqua

Deeply engaging and absorbing. A thrill of twists, turns, and romance at the same time. When I finished reading *Driftless Gold*, I was ready to read the next book.

~Bill, southwest Wisconsin

Sue Berg's *Driftless Gold* takes us to the bluffs, coulees, and winding roads along the Mississippi River in western Wisconsin. The dramatic landscape is blended into an irresistible tale of lost treasure and the scoundrels who will do anything to get their hands on it—even murder.

~Jeff Nania, author of the best-selling Northern Lakes Mystery series and 2020 Midwest Book Award winner, Portage

Murder, hidden treasure, and a side of good old-fashioned romance make *Driftless Gold* a delightful read.

~Leah Call, freelance writer,
Westby, Wisconsin

THURSDAY
OCTOBER 18

1

MID-AFTERNOON

Where is this guy? He wanted to get this over with. He poured another cup of coffee from his Thermos and dug around in his seat until he found a box of Little Debbie Nutty Buddy Bars. He tore one open, took a big bite and felt the familiar sugar rush flood over him. He opened his window, and as he waited, he threw his cellophane wrapper out the window.

He glanced over at the package on the seat. Looked official. Even had an identification label with a tracking code. All fake. Once he gave it to the driver, it'd be a done deal. As he waited at the wayside on U.S. Highway 14 between Coon Valley and the Ten Mile Hill near La Crosse, Wisconsin, he thought about his pathetic life. Nothing had worked out the way he thought it would. But everything was about to change. Everything *would* change.

The fall trees were mostly bare, but patches of sporadic color appeared here and there. As he waited, his eyes flitted over the naked staghorn sumacs hunched together along the blacktop, their seed cones dark red. *Dark like blood,* he thought. He smiled and slouched in the seat of the gray Mercury Marquis.

Feeling drowsy, the sound of an engine downshifting roused him, and his senses snapped to alert. An MV Series International delivery truck with a blue cab and an unlettered white trailer rolled into the shaded wayside. Brett Hoffman, the driver of the truck, swung his vehicle around the Mercury and parked about twenty feet ahead of the car.

Pulling his brimmed hat further down over his eyes, the driver of the Marquis opened the car door, carefully plucked the package from the seat, and jogged to the passenger side of the truck.

He jumped up on the step and opened the door.

"Hey, sorry about the screw-up. This is fragile. It needs to stay level," he said pleasantly. "Hope you didn't have to go too far out of your way."

Brett Hoffman shrugged his shoulders. "All in a day's work, I guess. I'll be home by five. That's all I care about." He leaned over and took the package, laying it carefully on the front seat. "I'm not going to bother putting it in the back. I'll be delivering it to the south side of La Crosse anyway. That's only a half hour away."

"Whatever," the killer said, shrugging his shoulders. "Have a good one." He stepped down and slammed the door.

The killer walked back to the Mercury Marquis, got in, and started the engine. He drove around the delivery truck to the exit, then turned west. He picked up the cell phone from the seat when he was about a half mile down the road. With shaking fingers, he dialed.

BA-BOOM! He heard the whump of the explosion as he slowed down, listening through the open driver's window. He felt a chill run through his body, and he shuddered from the pleasure of it. A cold smile froze on his upturned lips. In his rearview mirror, he could see pieces of the truck cab disintegrating into the air, creating a cloud of debris that rained down on the surrounding landscape. Engine metal, bumpers, glass, and upholstery blew outward into the frosty October day.

Brett Hoffman no longer existed. Whatever he believed about life after death, eternity for him had just started. *Mission accomplished,* the killer thought, pumping his fist in the air as he stepped on the gas and headed to La Crosse. ◉

2

Jim Higgins, chief investigator for the La Crosse Sheriff's Depart-ment, was replacing a door jamb in his garage on Thursday afternoon. He'd just returned from his ten-day honeymoon in Paris with his second wife, Carol. He tinkered with the wooden sash, scraping it with a plane so the door would fit snugly.

As he worked, he remembered the leisurely breakfasts in Paris on the hotel balcony eating quiche, croissants, and drinking lattes. Hours were spent lazing on a blanket in shady parks lunching on baguettes, cheese, and wine. And the romance of Paris nights—small, dimly lit cafes accompanied by intimate conversation, candlelight, and luxurious food. The Eiffel Tower, the consummate French monument, brilliantly illuminated at night. Days were filled with interesting side trips—the Rodin Museum, strolling down the Rue Cler exploring quaint little shops, biking along the Seine River, and watching parades of Parisians ambling down the Champs-Élysées in practiced nonchalance. And, of course, exploring every inch of each other in their charming room at Hotel Relais Bosquet.

How could it be over so quickly? Jim thought. Now at home in La Crosse, Wisconsin, they were adjusting to domestic life on Chipmunk Coulee Road in the house Jim had lived in for over twenty years. Despite the list of domestic jobs Carol had assigned him, the French buzz was still alive and well, making him feel relaxed and happy. *Wine, the Eiffel Tower, and making love will do that,* he thought. His cell phone beeped in his pocket.

"Jim Higgins."

"Jim, it's Davy. A truck bomb exploded about a half hour ago up on 14 above Ten Mile Hill at the wayside. I need you and your team here, like five minutes ago," Jones said, the stress building in his voice. Jim heard the chaos of the scene snaking through the cell phone. The French glow sputtered and died.

"Right. I'll be there in twenty minutes." Jim ran into the house.

"Carol! Carol!" he shouted down the hall into the kitchen.

"In here," she yelled back.

Jim trotted into the kitchen. "Something's come up at work. I need to leave right away. Probably won't be back until late." He kissed Carol quickly, turned, retraced his steps into the garage, and punched the garage door opener. Before he backed out, he called Leslie Brown, one of his detectives, giving her a brief outline of the bombing.

"I'll meet you at Ten Mile Hill," he ordered brusquely. "Where's Sam?"

"He's prowling around in Onalaska talking to his drug informants. I'll get a hold of him and get him up there," Leslie said.

"See you there," Jim said as he gunned the Suburban down Chipmunk Coulee Road. When Jim got to U.S. Highway 35, he headed north to the junction with U.S. Hwy, 14, which headed southeast. He drove a little crazy, careening around slower vehicles, hitting eighty miles per hour on one stretch. Woods and fields, houses and farms whizzed by as he hurtled toward the bomb site.

Eventually, the Ten Mile Hill flattened out on top. As Jim approached the scene, he saw the flashing red and blue lights of squad cars and an ambulance parked in the middle of the road. TV news vans hunched along the shoulder of the road, reporters scrambling to get their cameras and equipment ready for broadcast. Diverting live traffic to Brinkman Ridge Road, officers from the

SUE BERG

sheriff's department were setting up roadblocks and a detour, sealing off the area. Jim drove closer and stuck his ID badge out the window as a patrolman waved him on. Arriving at the scene, he pulled the Suburban off the highway next to a roadblock and slammed the vehicle into park. He jumped out of the vehicle and then abruptly stopped as he took in the devastation. It felt like the world had stopped spinning. His eyes and nostrils burned from the acrid smell of smoke in the air.

The magnitude of the blast was appalling. The cab of the truck had disintegrated into pieces of metal, glass, and plastic. Debris was blown over a one hundred fifty feet diameter, and a piece of a truck door lay in the middle of the highway. As Jim observed the surreal devastation, he noticed part of a hand lying on the pavement, a finger still adorned with a wedding ring.

He turned at the sound of Leslie's voice. "What the—?"

Jim glanced at her and noticed her frozen expression of horror. She turned her head away, lifting a hand to cover her eyes. Visions of the missions she'd been on in Iraq came flooding back into her memory. She grimaced at the sour taste of bile in her mouth, and for a brief moment, she thought she might vomit.

As the minutes ticked by, Jim retreated into himself. All vestiges of normal life vanished. All the trappings of modernity had been reduced to a pile of rubble. It was as if his carefully constructed world had suddenly been smashed with a wrecking ball by some irreverent bully. The whole scene was fascinating in a horrible way, like a movie scene in some action-packed thriller. Jim knew just being here and experiencing this would change him forever. *What was this world coming to?* He brought himself back to the scene and glanced at Leslie.

"You all right?" he asked.

"No, I'm not," she said hesitantly, "but that's not the main concern right now, sir. Someone is going to have to tell the next of kin what happened." She stopped speaking for a moment. "I'm glad it won't be me."

Jim walked toward Sheriff Davy Jones, standing in the middle of the exploded materials surrounded by first responders. He waved his arms, pointed and directed police officers, listened to their questions, and gave commands. Jim walked up to him.

"What happened? Do we know yet?" Jim asked the sheriff, his blue eyes scanning the barbarity of the scene.

"A medium-sized delivery truck exploded while sitting at the wayside. We haven't positively identified the driver, but the truck was registered to a Brett Hoffman from Sparta. Two officers are on their way to his home in Sparta to talk to his wife. The truck van is not damaged too badly. There's no writing on the side—just a plain white trailer. We found part of a door from the cab labeled Hoffman Trucking, and it had a partial interstate DOT number. The bomb squad from Madison is on the way. This looks like an act of terrorism of some kind. My God, what a disaster," Jones said, wiping his hand across his eyes.

"What do you need from us?" Jim asked, watching the crime scene crew arrive to begin the ominous task of collecting physical evidence.

Jones seemed to come out of a momentary trance and said, "I want you to talk to all the neighbors in the immediate vicinity of the wayside. See if anyone can remember any vehicles that might have been parked here today. Anybody that came and went. See that lady over there?" The sheriff pointed toward a young woman in a nurse's uniform. "Her car was about a quarter mile down the road when the bomb went off. Talk to her, take her statement, then start combing the neighborhood for any witnesses."

Sheriff Jones mopped his brow with his forearm. "Good luck," he said with a grunt. "You're gonna need it. It's going to take a while to get on top of this, Jim. We're not sure yet what caused this explosion, but if this was intentional and planned, we've got a big problem on our hands." His face reflected disbelief and disgust. After a moment, he whispered, "What a friggin' disaster."

SUE BERG

"Right. We'll get started. I have Leslie Brown with me," Jim said, turning away from the scene.

"What about Saner and Birkstein?" Jones asked.

"I haven't been able to reach Saner yet," Jim said over his shoulder as he started back toward Leslie, "but Sam's up in Onalaska. I'll get him down here as soon as I can," he yelled as he jogged toward the nurse.

"You do that. I'll talk to you in a while," Davy said. The sheriff had turned another shade of pale. Little rivulets of sweat were running down the sides of his face. The beginnings of a migraine had started somewhere in his brain, and the pain was like fireflies flickering in a field of neural synapses. He squeezed his eyes shut as the discomfort began exploding in his head.

Jim veered away from the sheriff, spotting Leslie near the edge of the debris field where he'd left her. She looked up, and he caught her eye, pointing in the direction of the nurse. They walked up to a young, rather heavy-set woman. Despite the chaotic scene, she seemed in control of her emotions, watching the workers with perceptive eyes. *She's seen trauma before,* Jim thought.

"Hello. I'm Lt. Jim Higgins, and this is Detective Leslie Brown," Jim said by way of introduction. They flashed their IDs. "We understand you witnessed the explosion. We'd like to ask you a few questions." Leslie pulled a notebook from her backpack, her pen poised above the paper.

The young woman was dressed in blue surgical scrubs, and a hospital lanyard hung loosely across her ample chest. A polar fleece jacket was slung across her shoulders. Her light brown hair cut fashionably short and professionally highlighted, medium hazel eyes, and pert small nose gave her a look of efficient competence.

She sighed. "I'm Shelly Overton. I'm an ER nurse at Gundersen Lutheran. I had just finished my shift at three o'clock and was driving home to Chaseburg. I almost always drive this way, and today was so beautiful. Then this happened." She paused and took a deep breath. "Was this planned by someone? What kind of a nut would do something like this?" Her eyes swept over the scene. Tears began to moisten the corner of her eyes. Then she looked at the two detectives waiting with their questions.

"We don't know yet," Jim began. "Can you recall if you met any cars coming from the direction of the wayside?"

Shelly looked off in the distance, replaying the moment in her mind. "Yeah, I'm sure I met somebody, but you know I had no reason to remember colors or makes or models of the vehicles. When I drive home from work, I unwind, and I'm not very observant. I'm thinking about my family and what I'm going to make for supper. It just wasn't on my radar. Sorry," she apologized, shaking her head.

"I understand. I've done that myself," Jim said, his voice detached and professional. "So, can you describe what happened when the truck exploded?"

She turned and pointed west. "I was just rounding the corner up there. See that Packers mailbox?

The green and gold one? That's about where I was when the explosion happened." She paused, frowning. Jim thought the distance was about the length of a football field, maybe a hundred yards.

"Okay. Go on," he encouraged, looking in the distance at the mailbox. Leslie continued to take notes.

"I was going about fifty-five, and then I felt something, almost like an ocean wave hit me, and then I heard this terrible boom. The next thing I knew, the whole truck exploded, pieces of stuff flying everywhere. It was shocking. Unbelievable, really." She looked at Jim and then Leslie. "This whole thing is crazy. It's just crazy."

I've seen that look before, Leslie thought. For a brief moment, she was back in Iraq with Paco, her military working dog. Images of shattered debris, dust and bedlam briefly passed through her mind. "Anything else you remember?" she gently asked the nurse.

"No, not really. When I got closer, I could smell the explosive in the air. And then I thought about that driver. I called 911 as soon as

Deeply engaging and absorbing. A thrill of twists, turns, and romance at the same time. When I finished reading *Driftless Gold*, I was ready to read the next book.

~Bill, southwest Wisconsin

Sue Berg's *Driftless Gold* takes us to the bluffs, coulees, and winding roads along the Mississippi River in western Wisconsin. The dramatic landscape is blended into an irresistible tale of lost treasure and the scoundrels who will do anything to get their hands on it—even murder.

~Jeff Nania, author of the best-selling Northern Lakes Mystery series and 2020 Midwest Book Award winner, Portage

Murder, hidden treasure, and a side of good old-fashioned romance make *Driftless Gold* a delightful read.

~Leah Call, freelance writer,
Westby, Wisconsin

PRAISE FOR
DRIFTLESS TREASURE

Upon return from a ten-day romantic Paris honeymoon, Lt. Jim Higgins, still feeling relaxed and happy from those exotic days—and nights—is jolted back into an investigator's world. A well-liked delivery man with a wife and three young children is disintegrated by a bomb placed in his truck.

Higgins and his courageous crew systematically work their way toward an ever-eluding solution. Sue Berg skillfully weaves a story of avarice, revenge, and Middle East intrigue into a setting of charming riverfront villages, friendly people, and the steep, rugged landscape of Wisconsin's Driftless Region.

~Harold William Thorpe, Wisconsin author

Once you've read *Driftless Treasure*, you'll never look at the Driftless Area the same again. Your mind will associate Sue's unforgettable characters and story with each landmark you pass. Sue breathes life into each and every character. She expertly weaves their plights into a clever, suspenseful novel that you won't want to put down. I found myself thinking about each character when I wasn't reading the book—that's how much I endeared myself to them. Romance, love, faith, history, suspense, crime, shock, resolution—it's all here. Sue did a fabulous job, and I can't wait for her next story!

~Heidi Overson, Driftless Area writer, www.heidioverson.com

Driftless Treasure, the second Jim Higgins mystery, is a must-read! In these pages, Berg submerges you in the beautiful Driftless Area and pulls you in with murder and stolen treasure. This page-turning mystery will captivate you until the very end.

~Alexandra Birdy Veglahn, owner of Birdy's Bookstore,
Holmen, Wisconsin

Some authors take you on a journey, while some have a way of taking you back home. Sue Berg somehow does both in this exciting, yet somehow familiar, tale. The journey takes you through the rolling hills and valleys of the Coulee Region, where you can almost see the views through Berg's illustrative writing. You will appreciate what home feels like in the warmth of the words and flow of the *Driftless Treasure* story. You'll root for the good guys and admonish the bad guys, but you'll feel a connection with all of the vibrant and well-established characters. The book may be called *Driftless Treasure* but we've found a gem to be cherished in the author, as well.

~Stacey, a reader from Prairie du Chien

AUTHOR'S NOTE

In the foreword to *The Doctor Stories* written by Atul Guwande, he says that the author, William Carlos Williams, "came to believe writing should have specificity and locality, and favor the domestic over the grand. He wanted to capture the voices of ordinary people …"

Throughout the summer of 2021, I was humbled by the number of people who enjoyed the specific localities in the Coulee region that I used in my story—the Freighthouse, Piggy's, Leo & Leona's, Rudy's Drive-in, and, of course. the geographical features of La Crosse like Grandad Bluff and the peaceful trout streams along Spring Coulee Road near Coon Valley.

Thank you for confirming in me the belief that writers should write about what they know. Even though most locals would still consider me an import even after living fifty years in the Coulee Region, you made me feel as if I belonged here all along. My deepest thanks! ⊙

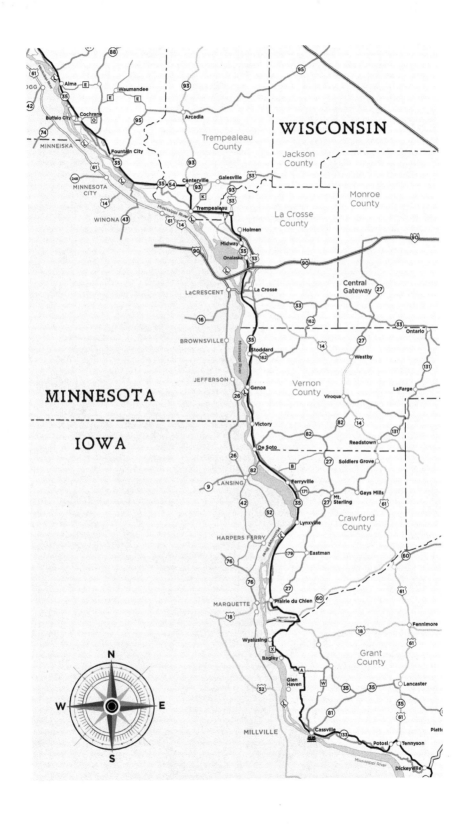

I pulled my car off the road."

They talked a while longer, and Leslie took the nurse's contact information. Jim handed her his card. "If you remember anything later, just call. My cell number is on the back."

"I'm sorry I couldn't be more helpful," she said. Her eyes were sad, and her shoulders slumped with discouragement.

"You did fine. You've been very helpful," Jim replied. "You're free to go, and thank you."

Jim turned to Leslie. Her face was pale, but underneath he could see the anger building in her eyes. *Give her something to do.*

Near the wayside, several houses, perhaps fifteen or so, had been built along the highway strung out two or three acres apart in an era of construction that Jim guessed had happened thirty years ago. It was basically an unnamed community, the wayside being the single most memorable detail that people recalled about this section of highway leading to La Crosse.

"Listen, Lez," he said. "You take the houses from the Packers mailbox west, and I'll take the ones closer to the wayside. We'll meet back at the car when we finish, okay?" His blue eyes focused on her.

"Got it, Chief," Leslie said, her voice tight. *She's on a mission,* Jim thought. He flipped open his phone and called Sam Birkstein.

"I need you up above Ten Mile Hill at the wayside on Highway 14 as soon as you can get here. I want you to check in with Leslie and help her go from house to house to see if anyone noticed anything this afternoon."

"I'm already on my way. Comin' through the south side. I should be there in ten minutes or so," Sam said.

Moving through the neighborhood area, the team questioned the residents who lived in close proximity to the wayside. By seven o'clock that evening, Leslie and Sam had finished canvassing the assigned houses and were standing on the shoulder of the road in the growing darkness watching the Dane County Bomb Squad set up their lights and equipment.

Jim covered a total of five homes. Three of the residents hadn't noticed anything unusual, and at the next house, no one was home. Now Jim was sitting at the kitchen table with Mrs. Evelyn Terwilliger who lived right next to the wayside. She was a petite sixty-year-old with brown hair streaked with gray, friendly eyes and a long, slender nose. She poured two cups of freshly brewed coffee and sat down. Without prompts from Jim, she began reciting her narrative of the afternoon's events.

"I was sitting in my recliner watching *Masterpiece* on PBS," she began, her voice high and lilting. "Usually I take a little catnap around three o'clock. I had just drifted off when I felt the house shake, like a shudder almost. Then I heard glass breaking. That must have been the garage windows, I guess. I jumped out of my chair and looked toward the wayside. I ran out on my lawn. I saw a lot of smoke, and there was stuff scattered all over the road. I couldn't believe the mess. There were pieces of stuff all over the place. I ran back inside and called 911, but apparently, someone had already called it in." She stopped briefly.

"Did you notice anyone parked at the wayside this morning or early this afternoon?" Jim asked, taking a sip of coffee.

"Well, you might have noticed the privacy fence on the west side of the house," she said as she pointed toward the garage. "We put that up a couple of years ago because we didn't want everyone gawking over here. We don't pay attention to who comes and goes from the wayside. Besides, I wouldn't know them anyway," she said, shrugging her bird-like shoulders up and down.

"Sure, I get that," Jim commented. "Anything else you can remember?"

"No, not really," Mrs. Terwilliger commented. "Did I tell you that my husband is a salesman for Snap-on Tools, and he's on his southern Wisconsin run today and tomorrow? He'll be mad that he missed this," she said, looking worried. "Are we going to be compensated for the damage to our property?"

"Well, the sheriff's office will be in contact with you. But you should report it to your insurance company the first chance you get. If you remember anything else ..." Jim put his memo pad into his coat pocket and slid his card toward her. He took another sip of coffee.

"Wait a minute," Mrs. Terwilliger said suddenly, snapping her fingers. Her eyes drifted to Jim's face. "I just thought of something." Jim leaned forward, listening intently. "My grandson had one of those motion cameras back here in the woods behind the wayside. Scoutin' for deer. You know, hunting season's coming up." Jim nodded in understanding, feeling a little chill run over his arms. "Maybe there would be something recorded on that," she said.

"Can you show me where it is?" Jim asked. *This could be good.*

"No, I don't know where it is, but my grandson lives just down the road. I'll call him," she said as she hurried to the phone.

Mrs. Terwilliger's grandson, Austin, arrived on his four-wheeler ten minutes later. Armed with a heavy-duty flashlight, Jim walked through the woods behind the wayside with Austin until they came to a large gnarled oak tree. Austin pointed to the camera. It was aimed in the direction of the wayside, but Jim doubted that they would be able to see much through all the trees and brush.

Jim studied the position of the camera, then reached up and opened the side. "I'm going to take the chip, but I'll make sure you get it back. I'll see if there's anything helpful on it," Jim said. "If there is a record of the explosion, I'll have to keep it as evidence."

Austin nodded. "That's okay. I've got more cards for the camera. Don't worry about it," he said.

"Thanks. This could be helpful," Jim said as he slipped the chip into an evidence bag and then into his jacket pocket. They walked back to the house, talking about bucks, deer rifles, and the upcoming hunting season. *Nice kid,* Jim thought.

Standing on the front porch, he thanked Mrs. Terwilliger, returned her flashlight, and walked toward the wayside parking lot. The dark October evening was closing in. The stars were just beginning to peek through the black curtain of sky. The cold air was crisp, Jim's footsteps crunched the shoulder gravel underfoot, and his breath came in wispy puffs of white condensation. *Hard frost tonight,* he thought.

He worked his way along the perimeter of the yellow caution tape, sidling up to Leslie and Sam. Jim stood quietly next to them as they conversed softly. They all watched the bomb squad gathering and sorting evidence. Leslie glanced over at him.

"I saw a lot of this type of thing in Iraq. Boy, none of those memories are good." She shuddered, her face a reflection of hard times.

"Find out anything interesting?" Jim asked, his voice serious and flat.

"We talked to all seven households on that end," Sam began, waving his hand in the general area of the homes, "and basically, they didn't see anything worth remembering. Most of them don't really keep track of the wayside. It's not something they waste their time on. Besides, most of them can't even see the wayside from their house."

"Yeah, I hear ya," Jim said. He pulled out the bag with the chip from the motion camera. "I might have something here. A kid down the road had a wildlife camera mounted on a tree aimed toward the wayside. But there's a lot of brush and tree trunks in the line of the camera, so I'm not holding my breath."

They stood in silence for a few more moments, then Jim's cell chirped.

"Jim Higgins."

"Jim. Mike Leland here. We're up at the Hoffmans' in Sparta. Mrs. Hoffman has no clue why her husband, Brett, was at that wayside. That's not his usual route. As far as she knows, his trucking business is on the up and up. She does all the dispatching and billing and is willing to share the financial aspects of the business as long as her attorney is present."

"Where was he coming from, and where was he going? We're going to need to know that to get started," Jim said. "Tell Mrs. Hoffman I'd like to talk to her tomorrow around ten o'clock."

"I'll run it by her," Mike said. "If you don't hear back from me, it's a go."

"Sounds good."

Sam looked at Jim, an expression of curiosity on his face. "So, the way I see it, this truck was blown up for one of two reasons."

"Let's hear it," Jim said, zipping his insulated windbreaker.

"Someone wanted to get rid of the driver, or someone wanted to get rid of the cargo," Sam theorized.

"Or both, driver and cargo," Leslie added, folding her arms across her chest. She went on. "Another possibility ... Brett Hoffman is the collateral damage of someone's basement demolition project, in which case we could have a serial bomber on our hands."

"Right now, they're all possible," Jim said. "My gut feeling is this was done to cover something up or distract from some other illegal activity. Or it's a statement by some radical political group. I know one thing—it's going to terrorize our community. That might be a possible motive, too. But we won't know anything until we get more information," Jim concluded. "It's all conjecture right now. We might as well head out. We can't do much else tonight." Jim put the chip back in his coat pocket, hoping something might come from it. ◉

3

LATER THAT EVENING

Paco, Leslie's black Lab, had been cooped up in the apartment all day. He'd been obedient and used the doggie door to do his business throughout the day, letting himself in and out to the fenced backyard. But his canine energy had been stifled all day, and now he was chomping at the bit and anxious for his nighttime stroll.

He heard Leslie's footsteps in the garage, and he began to pant. His nose was telling him she had someone with her. He went to the door and stood, whining and cocking his head to one side. The black Lab could detect the explosive residue from the truck bomb on her clothing, and he grunted and puffed with anxiety. Turning the key in the lock, Leslie burst through the door. Kneeling down beside Paco, she hugged him. He kissed her face with slobbering enthusiasm.

"Must be nice to get a hello like that every day after work," Sam commented, watching the affectionate interplay between Paco and Leslie. "What am I doing wrong?"

"Plenty of dogs at the pound who need a home," she commented.

"Who says I was talkin' about dogs?"

"Soda, beer, or coffee?" she asked, ignoring his remark, throwing her coat over a chair. She went in the direction of the small kitchen and opened cupboard doors, found some glasses, and filled a bowl with corn chips and another with salsa. Paco sized up Sam, circling him, sniffing and investigating.

Peeking around the corner, she said, "Just give him the top of your hand to smell. He's trying to decide whether to accept you or pee on your leg." She grinned to herself in the kitchen.

"Are you kidding me right now?" Sam asked, letting Paco sniff his hand. "I'll have a Pepsi if you have one."

Leslie bustled around in the kitchen, filling glasses with ice. "Let's go out to the living room. It's more comfortable there," she said as she brushed by him. Carrying the drinks and the chips into the room, she handed a Pepsi to Sam. He plopped into a used overstuffed recliner. Leslie went back to the kitchen and got the salsa.

"Thanks," Sam said, taking a sip of soda. "How'd you ever get interested in becoming a military dog trainer?" he asked. "I never would've guessed that when I first met you." He grabbed a chip from the bowl and crunched on it, then took another and dipped it in the salsa.

"When I joined up, I thought I would end up in the medical field, probably as a nurse," Leslie began. "My mom's a registered nurse, and my dad teaches biology and human physiology at the tech school in Decorah. Medical training runs deep in our family, and I enjoyed science in school. But one day, the dog people came around and put on a demonstration. I was hooked the minute I saw the bond between the dog and handler. It was absolutely fascinating." By now, Leslie had propped her feet up on a battered, scratched coffee table. Her features relaxed; her eyes were less wary. *It's good to see her unwind,* Sam thought.

"Didn't you have to leave your dog behind when you left the military?" he asked. Leslie noticed his talent for getting people to talk.

"Paco was wounded in battle—took some shrapnel in his hip. He would have been taken out of service anyway, so they let me adopt him when I retired," Leslie explained, dipping a chip in the salsa. "I've never regretted it. He's my best friend. I can't tell you how many times he probably saved my life. He understands me." Her voice had gotten quiet. Paco looked up at Leslie from where he'd been lying at her feet. He acted like he knew what they were saying. "His loyalty to me is unquestioned," Leslie finished. Those words seemed to hang in the air.

After a moment, Sam said, "So he's trained to smell explosives, right?" The questions kept coming.

"Yep. And he's one of the best. Only three other army dogs have beaten his record for the number of IEDs located by a military working dog. His sense of smell is phenomenal. He has seventy times more olfactory receptors than the average human." She reached down and stroked Paco's silken fur, caressing his warm ears. Sam could see they were nuts about each other.

"Still doesn't replace the love of a human, does it?" he asked, hoping she'd look at him. He got his wish. Leslie locked eyes with Sam and stared at him until he began to get uncomfortable. But he resisted the temptation to look away or squirm. She finally broke the silence.

"Are you talking about romantic love?" Her eyebrows lifted, but her blue eyes remained steadfast, sizing him up. Sam's stomach lurched. *You asked for that,* he thought.

Running a hand through his long dark hair in a nervous gesture, he said after a moment, "Yeah, I guess I am."

"Nothing can replace that," she said firmly. Sam suddenly felt hot and slightly embarrassed.

"More Pepsi?" Leslie asked coyly, watching him squirm.

"No. I probably better get going. Work tomorrow," Sam replied. *You are such a chicken shit,* he thought. He got up to leave. Paco walked him to the door. "Why do I feel like I'm being followed?"

"Because you are being followed by my number one protector."

"Did I pass the Paco test?"

Leslie shrugged. "Maybe. He's a pretty tough critic."

"What about the Leslie test?" His eyes roamed around the room, finally coming back to her.

"The jury's still out on that one," she said, her mouth twitching with the beginning of a grin.

"Alrighty, then." Sam turned to go. Leslie grabbed his hand and placed a soft kiss on his cheek.

"Don't give up too soon," she warned, noticing his hazel eyes and the way his dark hair flopped softly over his forehead. His skin smelled like pine and sky.

"I hadn't planned on giving up." He squeezed her hand. "See you tomorrow. 'Night, Paco."

Paco growled softly.

"I think you're in for it," Leslie said with a tender laugh.

"Very funny." Sam let himself out. As he walked to his Jeep, he thought, *She has a lot of scars and a truckload of baggage, but who doesn't?* ⊙

4

As Jim left the scene of the bombing and drove back home to Chipmunk Coulee, he wondered about the perpetrator. Practically anybody with access to the internet, twenty dollars worth of supplies, and a disposable phone could make a bomb. They still didn't know what kind of cargo the truck was carrying. That might tell them more about the bomber's motive, but there were too many unknowns yet to begin building a theory or constructing a profile of the killer.

Chipmunk Coulee Road was quiet. Jim braked when he saw the reflection of a set of eyes glowing from the ditch. A white-tailed buck jumped out and pranced provocatively across the blacktop, his hormones zeroing in on a mate. Five minutes later, Jim drove down his driveway and parked the Suburban in the garage. He walked into the house, kicked off his shoes, and hung his insulated jacket on a hook in the back hallway. Smells of pork roast and onions made his stomach cramp in hunger.

"Jim, is that you?" Carol said, her voice sounding muffled.

"Yeah, babe."

"There's supper on a plate in the fridge. Just nuke it," she said.

Jim opened the refrigerator, saw the plate, placed it in the microwave, and set the timer for two minutes. He wandered down

SUE BERG

the hallway in his stocking feet toward the bedroom, where he found Carol tucked inside a closet digging through cardboard boxes. She looked up with a smile, and he leaned down to kiss her.

"Hey, whatcha doin'?" he asked.

"Well, I was cleaning out this closet, and I found some of your family pictures. I thought about making a nice display in the hallway with yours and mine. Maybe buy some coordinating frames to tie it all together," she explained. "Whaddya think about that?"

"Fine by me," he said. He heard the ding of the microwave and walked back to the kitchen. Carol stood up and followed him.

"So, I hear you had quite an incident up at the Ten Mile wayside," Carol said. Jim's eyebrows shot up.

"How'd you know about that?" he asked gruffly.

"I called Emily, and I kinda squeezed it out of her," Carol said, looking guilty. "You're not mad, are you?" Carol was still getting a feel for the boundaries of Jim's professional work in their relationship. It was hard to keep the professional and personal parameters fixed. It seemed they were always shifting, creating murky situations.

"I don't mind as long as you don't post it on Facebook," he said sourly, turning to retrieve his dinner from the microwave. Jim sat down at the table with his plate and began wolfing down pork roast, stuffing, and roasted autumn vegetables.

"Mmm, this is so good. I was starving," he mumbled between bites. "Hot, though." He took a drink of cold milk. "Never dealt with a bombing before, but I've heard catching bombers is a hell of a challenge. We don't know enough yet to even get started."

"Boy, when I think of bombings, I think of larger cities and nut jobs who live up in the mountains somewhere. Isn't that where these incidents usually happen?" Carol asked, looking worried.

Jim kept eating. Between bites, he said, "You mean like Ted Kaczynski, the Unabomber?"

"Yeah, or Timothy McVeigh."

Jim grimaced at the memory of the two infamous bombers. "With today's access to explosive components, it's surprising it hasn't happened here before this." His fork was poised in midair, and he jabbed it occasionally as they talked. Discussing what they knew about bombs, Jim finished eating and put his plate in the dishwasher. Grabbing the teapot, he asked, "Want some tea?"

"Sure, and a piece of that apple pie on the counter," Carol said. "You need to come look at the living room." She walked in that direction.

"Okay. I'll be there in a minute," Jim said.

He fussed around in the kitchen, boiled water, and filled two mugs with water, teabags, and honey. He placed two slices of pie on a tray along with napkins and forks. Carrying it to the living room, he stopped in his tracks when he got to the doorway.

"Holy moly, Carol," he said softly. Jim's eyes swept over the room.

"Do you like it, hon?" she asked, wanting his approval.

"What's not to like?" he said.

Gone were the beige overtones and out-of-date overstuffed furniture. Carol had selected light steel gray for the paint on the walls. Along the windows that faced the backyard, she had placed an L-shaped pale blue velvet sofa. Its contours were sleek, and it was trimmed with nail heads along the arms. Blue and white floral pillows were thrown casually on the couch. A swoopy black leather chair and a club chair in shades of brown and blue sat on either side of a round side table stained a dark gray. A slab of rich natural live-edge walnut was formed into a coffee table that sat in front of the sofa. A wool floral print rug in cream, blue, and gray was arranged over the oak flooring. All of it worked together to suggest a chic, modern style that created a relaxed ambiance.

"Wow. I can't believe it's the same place," Jim commented, his eyes still traveling around the room as he held the tray with the tea and pie. *I wonder how much this cost me?*

"It isn't the same place, Jim. That's the point. I still have to get some art on the walls, but I'm going minimal, I think. Not too busy. Simple but elegant," Carol replied. "Maybe a river scene. Sandy Lateman does some fabulous Mississippi River oils. She has a show down at the Pumphouse in November. I might go and see her work at the show."

Jim set the tray down on the walnut coffee table. He felt the surface and admired the rough bark edge. "I love this," he said.

They ate pie and drank tea. Jim filled Carol in on his first day back at work, and Carol bemoaned the fact that she had to return to work in a few days. They also discussed Paul and Ruby's baby, Sam's slip back into his homeless look, and Jim's twins, Sara and John, from his first marriage to Margie. An hour passed.

"I'm going to bed," Carol said after a wide yawn. "I'm going to try and finish up the house this week before I go back to work. Coming soon?" she asked, her brown eyes inviting.

"Yeah, I'll be there in a few minutes." Jim was getting better at interpreting Carol's nuanced invitations. "First, I've gotta take a look at a chip from a motion camera we discovered at the crime scene," he explained as he returned the tray to the kitchen.

Jim walked into his study, fired up his laptop, and popped the chip in. He moaned when he thought he'd have to search for the bombing footage, but then he noticed the dates and times were in the lower right-hand corner just below the recorded images. He rapidly scanned through them until he found the morning's recording.

The images were clear. To the right, in the distance, he could see the two toilets. A few scraggly skinny oaks and some scruffy bushes were in the camera's range, but the camera had been mounted high enough on the tree that the view was unobstructed except for a few mature trees and some stunted brush. As Jim watched, he realized the view was the west end of the wayside.

He continued watching the video. The action unfolded. The delivery truck rolled into the wayside, parked, and waited. In about fifteen seconds, a man approached the truck carrying a box. *The bomber's vehicle must be east, so it's out of the camera's range*, Jim thought. A man with a baseball hat pulled down low carried what appeared to be a standard shipping box.

"There's the bomb," Jim said softly to himself. The man opened the passenger door of the truck, and after a brief conversation with the driver, slammed the door and disappeared off screen. Then a gray car pulled around the truck, turning right out of the wayside lot. Jim backed up the tape to see if he could see the license plate. It was very small, but with enhancement, they might be able to decipher the number. About one minute later, the truck exploded.

Jim shuddered as he watched another human being literally going up in smoke, blown to bits. *Must have been a phone-activated bomb,* he thought. Groaning, he pulled the chip from his laptop and slipped it back into the small envelope. *God, this is awful.* But the chip and the findings of the bomb squad would help them get started. Plus, they had an image of the suspect.

Jim tiptoed into the bedroom, undressed down to his boxers, and slipped into bed beside Carol. He snuggled up to her, pulling her close to his chest. Wrapping his arm around her, he cradled her breast in his hand.

"Mmm. Night, love," Carol murmured.

Jim kissed her shoulder. "Love you," Jim whispered back, burying his face in her hair. It was a while before he could get the explosion out of his mind. *This is gonna be a long haul,* he thought, before he finally drifted off to sleep. ◉

FRIDAY
OCTOBER 19

5

Wade Bennett sat on the peak of his barn roof in Rockland, Wisconsin, enjoying the warm October sunshine. The wooded hills in the distance were like a Monet mosaic of smudged gold, red, and orange trees. He tipped his face upward in a worshipful pose. Since his retirement from the U.S. Army in January 2017, he'd changed his appearance from military regulations to something resembling a progressive hippie.

His buzz cut was gone. Now he sported a long, brown ponytail. His deep-set gray eyes looked out from a sculpted face, and a trimmed beard and mustache gave the impression of a tough, seasoned ex-soldier, which is what he was. On his left bicep was a U.S. flag tattoo. Blue jeans, Carhartt shirts, and camo jackets were his favorite clothes now. His six-foot frame was hard and chiseled thanks to a rigorous jogging and weightlifting regimen.

Coming back to Wisconsin after his military service, Wade purchased a twenty-acre farmette near Rockland, about fifteen miles northeast of La Crosse. When he bought it, the place was dilapidated and needed some serious repairs. He dove into the remodeling with enthusiasm. Sitting on the top of his barn roof, he gazed with pride at the changes he'd already made to the property. He'd replaced the broken-down fences with steel fence posts and four-strand barbed wire. Wade bought five beef heifers to graze and clean up the overgrown weeds and pasture, enriching it with their manure to replenish the depleted soil.

The clapboard farmhouse was a classic two-story affair. The driveway curved through a couple of acres of pasture dotted with clumps of large soft maples and a few pin oaks. The kitchen and bathroom needed some serious updating, but Wade could get by for now. After all, he'd lived out of a pack in the desert and mountains of Iraq and Afghanistan, so owning a house was a privilege when compared with life in military barracks and tents.

The barn was the next improvement project on his list. Carrying a tool belt and hammer, he expertly removed the old shingles, throwing them down to a flat rack wagon below. He wouldn't be a very savvy businessman if he let the treasures stored in the barn become wet and moldy, ruined by moisture. After all, some of them were as old as civilization itself. Getting them out of the Middle East had been a long, difficult process, fraught with danger, intrigue, and money—lots of money.

He thought back to the day in 2003 when his unit, commanded by Colonel Michael Bogdonovich, had rolled into Baghdad and driven up to the National Museum. The whole scene came back to him in living color as he sat on the barn roof.

By the time U.S. troops arrived in Baghdad, the famous landmark was in shambles. Insurgents had looted the museum of its most precious possessions in one fell swoop of bedlam. Iraqi soldiers who were supposed to protect the museum had strewn their uniforms in careless abandon on the marble floors. Precious vases lay crushed and broken underfoot. Wade could still hear the broken glass crunching under his boots. Gold jewelry, amulets, cylinder seals, and ancient coins were tossed on the floor in reckless abandon. Desert air currents moved through the vast structure, creating paper tornadoes of documents and microfiche.

Wade had made invaluable connections during the restoration of security forces at the museum—friendships with dealers in the lucrative antiquities black market. Those relationships had made him a very rich man, and now he was free to capitalize on it. The antiquities he'd purchased overseas were snugly tucked in his barn, waiting for buyers throughout the Midwest.

Once he had the barn fixed, he intended to get reacquainted with his old girlfriend. He let out a contemplative sigh. Leslie Brown, his beautiful Nordic dream girl, was as intelligent as she was beautiful. They'd parted on difficult terms, certainly less than affectionate. But that was about to change. He'd done his homework. Leslie worked for the La Crosse Sheriff's Department now. He could imagine the shock on her face when he appeared on her doorstep. As Gomer Pyle used to say:

"Surprise, surprise, surprise!" ◉

6

Jim Higgins stood in his bedroom Friday in the early dawn admiring the shapely leg of his wife, Carol, visualizing her nude body beneath the sheets. *Beauty is all around you. You just have to know where to look,* Jim thought. As if she knew Jim was watching her, Carol rolled over and stretched her hands over her head in a catlike pose.

"Mornin'. What time is it?" she asked sleepily, the sheets tangled between her legs.

"Five-thirty."

"Ugh. I'm still on Paris time," she mumbled. She rolled over and buried her head in her pillow, her dark brunette hair falling gently over her face.

"In that case, I'm just getting started," Jim said. He scooted next to her and pulled her on top of him. Kissing her, he ran his hands down her back.

"Jim, at some point in time, we're going to have to come down from cloud nine and rejoin the human race," Carol whispered. She studied Jim's face, running her fingers through his graying hair. "You do know that, don't you, honey?" His blue eyes sparkled with humor. She gave him a languid kiss.

"Yeah, I know, but don't remind me now," he said. He buried

his hand in her mussed hair, pulled her close, and nuzzled her neck. Carol's breath quickened, and she eagerly kissed him again.

Later, while Jim shaved, Carol stepped from the shower and wrapped herself in a thick towel.

"Remembering Paris?" she asked, her eyebrows arched in curiosity as she watched Jim in the bathroom mirror.

"Mm-hmm. Remembering all those moments with you," Jim said, his intense blue eyes traveling over her bare shoulders and up to her warm brown eyes. "From now on, Paris is my go-to happy place." He held his razor mid-air, half his face still covered in shaving cream.

"Me too," Carol answered coyly, giving his butt a little slap as she headed for the bedroom.

After coffee and toast, Jim backed his Suburban out of the garage and headed down the driveway. He rolled the window down slightly and inhaled deeply. The air had that brisk autumn snap that he loved. As he drove north on U.S. Highway 35 toward La Crosse, he noticed the scarlet heads of the sumac at the edge of the woods standing at attention like soldiers on parade. Crimson, orange, and gold deciduous trees blazed in a late riot of color, their trunks rigid and dark brown. Along the Great River Road, leaves floated and fluttered in the air. Perched in a dead oak tree, a bald eagle watched the water with hooded yellow eyes. Just above the surface of the Mississippi, wispy currents of fog created eerie columns and otherworldly shapes. Later the sun would burn it off, leaving the surface of the river like a mirror, reflecting a million glittering sparkles.

The harbors at Stoddard and Pettibone Parks were already busy this morning with fishermen getting in some last days of casting and trolling before the winter season. Jim wished he could join them. It was a perfect day for a boat trip on the *Little Eddy*, the craft he'd inherited from his dad.

Instead, he left his daydreams behind and maneuvered his car into the south side Kwik Trip on Mormon Coulee Road. After purchasing a coffee and a cinnamon crunch bagel, he cruised through town on his way to the law enforcement center on Vine Street. At fifty-two, he was still reveling in his recent marriage to Carol Olstad, secretary of the La Crosse County Morgue and personal assistant to Luke Evers, the La Crosse County coroner and medical examiner. Finding a parking space, he walked to the entrance of the law enforcement center and scanned his ID through the secure entry. Inside the law enforcement complex, he was greeted with congratulations from long-time friends and colleagues.

Stepping out of the elevator on the third floor, Jim heard the subdued hubbub of a well-run office—the subtle ring of phones, the pecking of word processors, the gentle hum of secretaries performing their duties. Everything felt like a well-oiled machine, whirring with productive activity. Had he really been gone two weeks? It seemed like a lot longer, but here he was, back at it.

Jim's secretary, Emily Warehauser, sat behind her desk concentrating on her administrative obligations. Her auburn hair was cut in a short, stylish bob, her clothing immaculate and fashionably up to date, and her green eyes simmered with curiosity and an insatiable desire to please. Emily had been with him for over ten years. Consistent, dependable, and loyal, Jim had complete confidence in her ability to keep the clerical side of his investigative team running on all cylinders. Besides that, she had been a faithful friend during the illness and death of his first wife from breast cancer. Jim couldn't count the times Emily had provided support when his world was falling apart.

When Jim walked off the elevator, the pool of secretaries paused in their morning activities as if they were inhaling a breath of air. Jim and Carol's whirlwind romance had been the fodder of law enforcement gossip for the past three months. He smiled to himself. The office personnel were always hungry for new tidbits to add to their continuing rumor mill of love affairs going on throughout the law enforcement community.

"Good morning, Chief!" Emily chirped enthusiastically. "How was Paris?"

Leaning over the counter, he grinned and said softly, "Paris was fabulous, thanks to all of our planning and preparation." Jim smiled wider, a dimple denting his cheek. "I appreciate your help, and I owe you big time. You'll have to come by my office later, and I'll give you the lowdown." He winked conspiratorially.

"Will do, Chief!" Emily flashed a dazzling smile.

"Any news while I was away?" Jim asked, glancing down the hall to his office door.

"Not much," Emily remarked. She stopped and held up her index finger. "Oh, I almost forgot. Paul and Ruby had their baby, Melody Ann Saner, six pounds, seven ounces on September 28. Everything went fine. Paul is on paternity leave for a few weeks until they get a schedule going." Emily looked up at Jim and shrugged. "You know, bonding and all of that." She gave Jim a long stare, looking him up and down for any signs of stress. "You look good, Chief," she said enthusiastically.

"Thanks," Jim turned toward his office, balancing his bagel on top of his coffee cup.

"Your mail's on your desk," Emily informed him, swiveling back to her computer.

"Gottcha," Jim said. Opening his office door, he hung up his coat, sat down at the computer, logged on, and began perusing emails.

Carol hadn't returned to work yet. She was redecorating the home that he'd shared for twenty-six years with his first wife, Margie. Jim's worn-out surroundings had been replaced with new furnishings and a fresh coat of paint. Jim couldn't believe how a few simple updates made everything seem new and exciting. The makeover in the living room made him wonder what else she had up her sleeve before she was done.

The contents of Carol's condo had been moved to Chipmunk Coulee Road. After sorting through everything, they consolidated their stuff and took a huge load to Goodwill and The Salvation Army. Their recent conversation reminded him of the adjustments coming down the pike.

"Jim, are you sure you're okay with the changes I'm making?" she asked, her eyebrows crinkling with a frown. "I know it's a lot to deal with." She was studying paint chip cards from the hardware store in the morning light. "Yeah, this light sage color would be nice in the bathroom."

Jim lowered the *Wisconsin State Journal* a few inches, his blue eyes peering at her over the top of the paper. "I'm fine with it. You want to make this house your own—put your stamp on it. Go for it, sweetheart. The only thing you can't touch is my study, but you already know that." He raised the paper again and continued reading.

"Yeah, I'll be sure to leave that alone," she said smiling, holding up the paint samples with an outstretched arm. "There might be a few more boxes to sort in the garage," she finished in a distracted tone.

"Probably won't get to it 'til the weekend," said Jim, his voice muffled behind the paper.

A faint tapping on his office door startled him, bringing him back to the present. Sam Birkstein and Leslie Brown strolled into his office. New investigators in Jim's department, their boundless enthusiasm more than made up for their inexperience. Jim waved them in, then leaned back in his chair and took a good look at them.

Leslie was dressed in black business slacks with a burnt orange pullover sweater and a fashionable scarf draped around her neck. *Elegant*, Jim thought. Her minimal makeup and blonde, shimmering hair hinted at her Nordic genetics and gave most of the guys in the department a good reason to pause and soak in her beauty.

His eyes shifted to Sam. Jim scanned him from head to toe. Red high-top sneakers hid beneath a pair of saggy gray sweatpants. A red and black hoodie that read PIKE'S PEAK – Only Real Men Do It completed the look. His dark hair fell over his forehead, his handsome features punctuated by a pair of curious hazel eyes.

"What's with the duds?" Jim asked, frowning at Sam's get-up. "Our officers shouldn't look like they just spent the night under a bridge somewhere." He felt a twinge of regret at his comment when Sam's friendly smile disappeared.

"I was going to do some undercover stuff up on the north side today—" he began explaining but Jim interrupted.

"No, you're not. Not with this bombing thing. That takes priority over your drug perps," Jim reminded him gruffly.

"Just ignore him. It's good to have you back, sir. You look rested," Leslie said, trying to redirect Jim's attention to his homecoming and away from Sam's homeless vibe.

"You don't have to apologize for me," Sam said grumpily to Leslie.

"I didn't, did I?" Leslie asked, looking surprised.

"Sounded like it," Sam said peevishly, barely hiding a teasing grin. Jim looked from Sam back to Leslie, wondering at the barbed exchange.

Leslie noticed a contented happiness that seemed to radiate from Jim despite the grave circumstances of the bombing last night. He had a distinguished look that set him apart from other men his age. His gray-blonde hair was a little odd but not unpleasant. Maybe it was his rugged face with those piercing, self-confident blue eyes and dimpled smile. Leslie couldn't remember seeing her boss like this before. When she joined the staff a year ago, he was still grieving the death of his lovely wife. *This might be the first time I've ever seen him truly happy,* she thought.

"Well, I was feeling great until this mess last night," he said, his smile fading. "But Carol and I did have a fabulous time in Paris. It's definitely a city that caters to lovers," he said frankly, looking over at them.

"That's wonderful, sir," Leslie said, embarrassed, looking at her shoes. "We'll just leave it at that."

Jim pointed them to two chairs. "So, how're our perps doing in jail?" he asked in a brisk tone.

"Well, they've lawyered up, sir. We're just hoping that all of our evidence will stand up in court." Leslie answered.

"You can never have enough evidence," Jim said seriously.

"While you were gone," Sam interrupted, "we arrested a ring of prostitutes last week who were operating out of an apartment complex on 25th Street over by the bluffs. You should have seen my drag outfit. I even got invited to a party and got propositioned. The sting was a classic. The look on the faces of those gals when we slammed the cuffs on them is something I'll never forget."

Jim noticed Leslie watching Sam. She wore an expression that bordered on disapproval, but her eyes revealed a subtle hint of admiration.

"What?" Sam said, staring at Leslie, his arms crossed defiantly across his chest.

"Don't brag," she said. "After all, you're supposed to be the big drug and sex crime expert, remember?" She tipped her nose in the air with a superior flourish.

"What's your problem, huh?" Sam complained. "Must be that time—"

Jim interrupted. "What about the charges facing Amy?" he asked, trying to get the conversation back on track. "Are they going to stick?"

"We can only hope, sir," Leslie reiterated.

"And just so we're clear," Jim said sternly, pointing a finger at Sam, "I never enjoy seeing people end up in jail. But the alternative of them wandering free after committing serious crimes, especially murder, shouldn't happen either. That's the system for you. What I really prefer is that they'd never committed the wrongdoing in the first place," he said, slitting open envelopes as he stood by the desk. "Can't get away from our depraved human nature."

"That's true, Chief," Sam said. "'The heart is deceitful above all things and desperately wicked. Who can know it?' Jeremiah 17:9." Jim looked taken aback at the familiar verse. Sam shrugged. "It's something my dad would say, being a Lutheran pastor and all," he said, cocking his head at an angle.

"Well, it's a truth all of us should remember, dealing with

miscreants every day. Except for the grace of God, there go I," Jim said. Sam nodded his head in agreement. Jim huffed impatiently and continued. "Okay, let's move on. About the bombing—I want you two to find out what that truck was doing at the wayside. Mrs. Hoffman said Brett never went that way. So why was he there yesterday?"

"Excuse me, sir, but I wanted to tell you about something that happened while you were gone," Leslie said.

"Well, it has nothing to do with the bombing, right?" Jim asked, noticing Leslie's rigid posture. *At ease, soldier,* he thought.

"No, it doesn't, but it may be something that could have national and international ramifications," Leslie said seriously.

Jim stopped what he was doing and locked eyes with Leslie. "Don't you think we have enough on our plates with the truck bombing? What about those implications?"

"Well, I won't argue with that, sir. The bombing does have serious implications, but I really think you should hear what I have to say," she continued staunchly. Sam stared at Leslie as if she'd grown a nose on her chin.

"National and international ramifications? Really, Lez? Another exaggeration?" Sam asked sarcastically.

"I can understand your skepticism—" she began again, throwing Sam a look of disdain.

But Jim interrupted, waving his hand in front of him. "All right, all right. But make it quick."

Leslie began. "While you were on your honeymoon, I spotted some genuine Iraqi vases at Jay's Antique & Curiosities over by that busy strip mall." she said. "At least, I think they're genuine." She hurried on when Jim gave her a brazen stare. "I went in there out of curiosity, and there they were. Are you familiar with that place on Grand River Boulevard?" she asked.

Jim relaxed a little and nodded. "Oh, yeah. Margie and I used to go there looking for Indian arrowheads and stuff like that. She bought quite a few Native American baskets there. What makes you think these vases are real?" he asked, stacking his mail in a pile. Sam slouched in his chair in the corner, studying his fingernails, looking bored.

"I'm not positive they are at this point," she said, shrugging her shoulders. "I looked through my materials at home about the stolen items from the National Museum in Baghdad back in 2003. You might remember when Sadam's insurgents and U.S. troops decided to fight it out using the museum as their battleground. I was stationed in Fallujah at the time. Our troops rushed to Baghdad to try and save what was left of their precious art and antiquities. Some of the guys texted me pictures of the damage. It was horrible. There were over 7,000 Mesopotamian pieces destroyed that had been stored there. It was a great loss for the Iraqi people and for the entire world." She glanced at Jim, who was watching her with a curious look on his face. "Sorry, didn't mean to get on a high horse."

Jim said, "Not a problem. I'm aware of your work in the military with ancient artifacts." Besides being a working dog handler in the U.S. Army, Leslie had been trained as an antiquities specialist by Dr. Rochelle Drummond. Dr. Drummond was well-known in military circles for developing a program in conjunction with the Department of Defense designed to sensitize enlisted soldiers to the cultural and historical artifacts in the countries where they served. Leslie had assisted the professor in expanding the program and had become something of an expert on Middle Eastern antiquities.

"Those vases downtown look very similar to a pair listed in a reference catalog I have," Leslie finished. "The Iraqi government is still trying to recover the stolen items, and according to the catalog, the vases are still missing."

"So, how valuable are these vases?" Jim asked. He stopped rifling through his mail.

"They're worth between $20,000 to $25,000 each, but in the shop, they were marked for $6,500. It's very typical for sellers of these antiquities to lowball the price. Usually, it's because many dealers don't know they're real. They just assume they're replicas. Copies sell very well on the decorative market. But if these vases are authentic, which I think they are, their value is in their cultural and historical relevance, and they need to be returned to the National Museum in Baghdad. Some of those pieces date back to biblical times and have their origins in Mesopotamia," she said passionately, her eyebrows arching. "The Fertile Crescent? Remember your world history lessons, sir?" she asked skeptically, crossing her arms over her chest. Sam continued watching the conversation, his head bouncing back and forth like he was watching a tennis match.

"Absolutely, I remember. I'm old, but I'm not *that* old. You mean Ur of the Chaldees where Abraham lived? The Cradle of Civilization, Hammurabi's Code? The birthplace of Islam, Judaism, and Christianity?" Jim responded, a satisfied look crossing his face. "*That* Mesopotamia?"

Leslie's eyes sparkled with surprise. "Very good, sir. I'm impressed." Sam rolled his eyes.

"So, what's your plan?" Jim asked. He leaned back in his chair and clasped his hands behind his head. He watched her carefully, feeling a little glow that he'd remembered his history.

"I thought I'd keep checking at area antique and art galleries to see if any other Middle Eastern items start appearing. Like everything else, the antiquities market fluctuates. The price on this stuff has gone down recently. Dealers may try to dump what they have before it completely crashes. I'd just like to keep an eye on the situation," she proposed. "Maybe I'll discover who's selling them."

"Sounds good. Use your knowledge. Keep me informed. If you need help, let me know," Jim advised, grabbing his coat. "I'm heading up to Sparta to interview Amanda Hoffman."

"Right, sir. Sam and I will check out the route change for the bombed truck and maybe visit Jay's Antiques & Curiosities again if we have time." Leslie turned to leave.

"One more thing," Jim said, holding up an index finger.

Leslie turned to face him. "Yes, sir?"

"Remember, lost treasure can have strange effects on people. If the wrong person gets hold of these artifacts, things could go south real fast. We've already had that happen once before. Be careful."

Jim's eyes locked on Leslie. There was no mistaking his serious tone.

"Yes, sir. I will," she stammered. ☉

7

Leslie expertly parked her Toyota Prius on Grand River Boulevard in front of Jay's Antiques. Sam stepped out of the car. She joined him on the sidewalk, zipped her insulated blue jacket, and wound a gold scarf around her neck. The October air was invigorating and held a hint of frosty weather that would soon become November. Cars and trucks rumbled by, the sound of their tires amplified in the cold air. Bundled in warm jackets and scarves, people hurried around them like water flowing around a rock in a stream.

Standing on the sidewalk, Leslie thought back to her conversation with Sam when she'd stopped in front of his apartment earlier in the morning.

"Go in and change. Wear some normal clothes. None of this homeless, destitute look. A nice pair of jeans, a dress shirt, and a suit jacket is the order for the day. Maybe even a tie." Her crystal blue eyes held Sam in a serious stare. "I've planned a visit to Jay's Antiques & Curiosities, and I need your help," she finished. She turned and stared out the front window of her Prius. Sam felt his stomach turn over. Sometimes she had a strange effect on him, especially when she talked tough. *Why should she care what I wear? Nobody else seems to,* Sam thought. *Except Higgins.*

"So what's your plan?" he asked.

"A little undercover assignment," she explained, tilting her head, her eyebrows arched. "Right up your alley." A teasing grin played at the corners of her mouth.

Sam's eyes widened, and he grinned back. "Undercover? All right, I'm all in."

Now standing outside the barn shop, Sam wondered what he'd gotten himself into.

"So here's the plan," Leslie explained, her hands gesturing as she talked. "There are a couple of vases in here that I think are stolen booty from the National Museum in Iraq. We're going to pose as a couple looking for decorative items for our new apartment. That way, I can examine them to determine their authenticity."

There was an uncomfortable silence. Sam had an odd look on his face. "Wait a minute. Let me get this straight. I'm posing as your husband?" Sam said quietly.

Leslie shrugged casually. "Husband, lover, whatever. That's not the point. Posing as a couple will make us look more believable. We don't want to tip them off that we're cops. We need to have a look around, and this is the easiest way to do it." She reached in her jacket pocket, pulled out two rings, and handed him one. Sam nodded, slipping the ring on his finger.

"Okay, let's do it." He blushed and held up his hands. "Oh, sorry. I didn't mean *that*."

"Sheesh! Will you get serious?" she said, flustered. "Now, did you do your homework last night?

"Yeah, I did." He rolled his eyes, his voice parroting her serious tone. "*The Treasure from the Royal Tombs of Ur* was stupendous—not. I know as much now about Middle Eastern antiquities as I did two years ago, and that ain't much." He frowned and shifted on his feet. His eyes brightened. "But I'll be a bang-up husband." He grimaced again.

"Sorry."

"Come on," Leslie said. She sidled up to him, entwined her arm in his, and walked toward Jay's. "Let's get this over with. And *pa-lease*, you could at least look like you're enjoying it?" she said, glancing at him sideways, irritated by his insolence.

"You better take your own advice. You're lookin' awfully ornery for such a pretty woman." He smiled disarmingly as he kissed her on the cheek. Her shocked expression filled him with a sense of satisfaction. "Just playin' my part," he said, gaining confidence about this ruse.

Leslie grinned, trying to control a chuckle. "What a putz," she said, her heart suddenly skipping.

Jay's Antiques & Curiosities was located in a worn out two-story warehouse next to a busy strip mall off Exit 4 on I90. The owners had cleverly built a barn facade on the front, reminiscent of ones you might see in the Wisconsin countryside. Inside, two floors and seventy-five booths were packed with collectibles and antiques on consignment.

Walking into the building, Sam and Leslie strolled arm in arm and began meandering around each floor. A musty smell circulated in the old structure when the furnace kicked in. A couple of booths displayed antiquities like copper scrolls, late eighteenth-century vases, Chinese sculptures from the Ming dynasty, and fourteenth-century Iranian tapestries.

"Is there something I can help you with?" A clerk with frizzled gray hair approached Leslie and Sam. Within her wrinkled face, two bright bird-like eyes peered at them, and a pair of half-moon glasses perched on her bulbous nose. Her frumpy clothes were intended to hide the bumps and lumps of an aging body, but it wasn't working.

She looks like an antique, Sam thought.

"Actually, I brought my husband with me today to see those two unique vases you had here last week." Leslie pointed toward the back of the store. "Are they still here? You know, the ones that looked Middle Eastern?" she asked. "We're looking for some interesting pieces for our new apartment, and I wanted Sam to see them."

"Oh, yes, dear. Come with me. They're in a locked showcase," she explained, hobbling into the depths of the store. "I'll have to get the key from the office."

They waited at the glass showcase. Sam studied the vases. Ten inches high, they were a dark ocher color with panels of stylized deer and nude women decorating the sides. They were exquisite if you liked a dull excavated look. Sam was no expert, but their patina looked authentic to him.

"I've seen similar vases at the Smithsonian in Washington from the Abbasid period around the tenth century. Look at that surface! Aren't they wonderful?" she exclaimed quietly, glancing at Sam.

"Wow. You really do know about all this art stuff, don't you?" Sam said, his eyes widening at Leslie's obvious knowledge.

"Oh, I don't know everything," she said modestly, "but I've learned to really love Middle Eastern art. It's such a rich culture, and what was done to the treasures at the National Museum in Baghdad is a national shame," she whispered. She looked over at him, and Sam was surprised to see tears misting at the edge of her eyes. *I'd save my tears for something other than pottery,* he thought.

There was a rustling of fabric and footsteps behind the glass display case. They looked up and saw the clerk approaching the showcase carrying a ring of keys. "Would you like to examine the vases?" she asked politely. A faint scent of violets hovered in the air, and her perceptive gaze stopped briefly at Sam's wedding ring.

"We certainly would, wouldn't we, honey?" Leslie cooed.

"Yes, my wife just loves this stuff. Me? I'm just starting to learn about it," Sam said, looking over at her for approval.

Leslie's eyes softened as the clerk unlocked the showcase and carefully set the vases on the counter. Leslie ran her fingers over the surface decorations, tipped them over, and inspected the marks underneath. To her professional eye, she did not doubt the legitimacy of the vases. The marks and worn spots were authentic to the time period when they were used. They were the real deal.

"May I take a few photos with my cell?" she asked.

The clerk's eyes hardened for a second. Then she smiled and said,

"Only if you're very serious about purchasing them."

"Oh, we are serious. Aren't we, Sam?" Leslie said, looking over at him.

"Whatever makes you happy, darlin'," said Sam, smiling disarmingly. *I'd like to make you happy,* he thought.

Leslie began snapping photos before the clerk could object or change her mind. When she had the photos, she said, "We'll be in touch in the next few days. Do you take debit or credit cards?"

"Either is just fine," the clerk smiled, but her expression had changed. Her eyes had become wary with suspicion.

They exited the store and walked energetically to the car. Sitting in the driver's seat, Leslie rubbed her hands together rapidly after starting the engine. Whether from the cold or the excitement of authenticating the vases, Sam wasn't sure.

"Did you notice the change in the clerk when you started examining the vases?" Sam asked.

"Oh, yeah. The old bitty was suspicious, or at least protective. I wonder what she knows about them."

"Probably not as much as you do. Any other places you want to investigate?" He looked over at Leslie's silhouette. *She is lovely.*

"Yeah. Rossellini's, an art gallery on Pearl Street. Let's take a look there, too, while we're at it. I'm going to send a text to Dr. Drummond and attach a photo of the vases. I need her professional opinion." ◉

8

By noon on Friday, the skies had turned a gunmetal gray. Murky fog obscured the last of the color into an autumnal wash that resembled a Monet painting. Crows cawed raucously back and forth among the partially naked trees at the Highway 14 wayside, the sounds adding a sense of bleakness to the gruesome work that went on below them. The Dane County Bomb Squad was still not prepared to release its findings despite laboring through the night. The crime scene continued to be closed off to local traffic. However, the partially bombed-out shell of the truck and its contents had been moved to the impound center in La Crosse and was being checked for more explosives. Then it would be analyzed by local CSI personnel.

Bomb Squad Coordinator Stephan Wiles had worked through the night, taking a few hours toward morning to catch a nap in his truck. His assistants continued the collection of evidence which would be turned over to the La Crosse Sheriff's Department later in the afternoon with a report updating investigators about what they'd discovered. What little body parts they'd recovered had been bagged and given to the La Crosse County Coroner's Office to be returned to the victim's family. *Glad that's not my job,* Wiles thought. He sighed, and as he looked up, he noticed Lt. Jim Higgins walking steadfastly toward him, his shoulders hunched and his head bowed deep in thought.

Higgins' reputation preceded him. He was thorough, moral, determined, and somewhat priggish. *Well, that might be a bit unfair,* thought Wiles. *After all, not everything on social media had validity, especially when it came to reputations.*

"Hey, Lt. Higgins," Wiles said, holding out his gloved hand, noticing Jim's odd hair color—a combination of sandy blonde flecked with gray.

"Sorry. Think I'll pass on the handshake," Jim said casually, pointing to the latex glove. Wiles shrugged nonchalantly and withdrew his hand. "So what's standing out so far? Anything unusual or memorable?" Jim asked.

Wiles had a head of thick, sandy hair, perceptive hazel eyes, and a nose that was a little too pointed sitting above a full expressive mouth. Overall, the man exuded self-confidence, but it was balanced with modesty.

"We're still gathering evidence, but we did find something interesting that might give us DNA. A Nutty Bar wrapper was blown into the grass where we think the car might have been parked. Not sure if we'll get a hit, but it was intact, anyway."

"Huh. That's interesting," Jim commented. "Anything else?"

"There's a ton of debris," Wiles continued. "We've found some of the device, but you'll get all of that when we have a briefing later today. Most of the explosive materials will be analyzed by the ATF office in Madison next week. They'll probably assign an operations investigator to the case. So there's no sense repeating that now, and it'd be presumptive on my part to try and guess what they'll find. Too early yet," he finished.

"Right. I understand," Jim said, disappointed. "Well, I was on my way to an interview and thought I'd check on the progress."

"No problem. See you about four o'clock," Wiles said, turning back to the scene.

Jim walked to the Suburban and left the bombing scene. Weaving through valleys and ridges on a series of county roads that headed northeast, he finally hooked up with State Highway 27 to Sparta.

His interview with Amanda Hoffman at one o'clock would be crucial to understanding the possible reasons for the bombing. From what Officer Mike Leland had told Jim last night, she had no idea about motives. That wasn't a surprise. Most people Jim knew would be puzzled and shocked by an event like this.

Jim drove to 608 Myrtle Street. A two-story gray saltbox home with matching four-by-four windows sat on a large city lot along the shaded street. The front door was painted cherry red and a fall wreath hung in the center of it. Pumpkins sat in a cluster on the doorstep. A three-car garage in the same shade of gray was positioned behind the house. Carefully spaced white pines defined the back border of the property. Maple trees were scattered around the acre lot, and a clump of white birch sat within a flower bed near the sidewalk.

Jim got out of the car, walked to the house, and rang the doorbell. He heard footsteps approaching, and the door opened cautiously. Amanda Hoffman appeared dry-eyed but looked haggard. Cinnamon highlights set off her smartly styled brown hair. She was subdued, her ivory skin especially pale, her green eyes filled with pain and sorrow.

"Hello," Jim said politely, holding out his credentials. "I'm so sorry about what's happened." His blue eyes focused on her, and the threat of tears was just below the surface.

"Thank you," she said quietly. She stepped aside to make room for Jim. "Please come in. I think we'll go in the kitchen if that's all right with you." She led the way.

"Perfect. Whatever is most comfortable for you is fine with me," Jim said, following her.

They entered the immaculate kitchen with its gleaming chrome appliances. Seated at the table, Amanda's lawyer had been waiting. He stood.

"Gus Kramer," he said brusquely, extending his hand.

They shook hands and sat down. Amanda bustled around, getting each man a freshly brewed cup of coffee. It tasted good to Jim, brisk and hot. He noticed a pile of folders next to Gus. *Must be the books from the trucking business,* he thought. He pulled out his memo pad and wrote as Amanda recited information—years of marriage, number of children, business ventures, and civic and church involvement. Jim dutifully jotted down the framework of the Hoffmans' life together. Then he began his formal questioning.

"So, did you have any contact with Brett yesterday after he left home?" Jim began.

"No. He left for Galena to pick up a load of merchandise at about seven o'clock," Amanda said. "We had breakfast and coffee, reviewed the day's pickups and deliveries, got the kids up and off to school, and that's the last time I saw him," she said, tears forming at the corners of her eyes.

"Where did he go in Galena for the pickup you mentioned?" Jim asked.

Amanda reached for a manila folder, opened it, and plucked a slip from inside. "He went to a warehouse on Galena River Road. The order that was supposed to be picked up was from Import Specialties, a Chicago-based firm. They have a store and warehouse in Galena. We've hauled for them before. Quite a bit, actually," Amanda said, more in control now, dabbing tears from her cheeks.

"How did he end up at the wayside? Do you have any ideas about that?" Jim asked.

"No. When I heard he was there, I just couldn't figure it out. That's not his usual route, so someone must have called him and changed the order. I don't know. That's never happened before," Amanda said with a puzzled expression.

Jim could see she was confused. He asked, "Do you do all the phone work? You know, arranging the trucking, pickups, drop-offs, that sort of thing?"

"Yes. Brett and I have worked together in the business for about three years now," she told Jim. "Things were going well. We weren't getting rich or anything, but we made a comfortable living." Looking out the window, she stopped talking for a moment. Her shoulder-length hair shone in the light. Then she turned her attention back to Jim.

"I don't know what's going to happen now." Her voice wavered as she bit her upper lip. "Brett was a wonderful person. A good Catholic, involved in the Knights of Columbus, coached our kids' soccer teams. We had a good marriage. I don't know how I'm going to go on. There's no instruction manual for something like this, is there?" Her eyes were question marks, and she seemed to expect Jim to know what to say.

Jim shook his head but maintained eye contact with her. "No, I'm sorry, there's not," he said sympathetically. He remembered the sense of loss and bewilderment he'd experienced when Margie died. "Were you aware of any problems Brett might have had with anyone in his trucking business? You know, hard feelings over a business deal, that kind of thing?" he asked.

"Well, Brett was usually very laid back. He could get mad, but it took a lot. He had a very long fuse," she replied. Jim raised his eyebrows, not sure of her meaning. When she hurried on, Jim chalked it up to the trauma of the moment. "But no, I don't know of any problems with our customer base." "Okay. What I'd like are copies of your business transactions for the last year. If you're wondering about our right to see them, we can confiscate them through a law called civil forfeiture. It's just to ensure that your assets have not been used in any criminal activity, especially drug trafficking. I hope you understand," Jim informed her.

Amanda glanced at Gus for approval. "It's standard procedure in a criminal investigation," Gus said. "You have nothing to hide that I can see." Looking at Jim, he continued, "These are the business transactions from the last two years." The lawyer pushed them across the table to Jim.

Jim grasped them and then asked, "Is there anything else you want to ask me?"

Amanda nodded her head. "Who's going to coach the soccer

team now?" she asked softly. Her face crumpled, and her quiet sobs filled the kitchen. Jim covered her hand with his and waited. Finally, he said, "I'll let myself out. Thanks, Amanda. I'm so sorry." ◉

9

Later Friday afternoon over in Rockland, Wade Bennett was hard at it, pounding new shingles onto his barn roof. His phone chirped.

"Wade Bennett," he answered brusquely. Despite the cool October temperatures, the sun was hot. He was sweating from the physical activity, and he mopped his forehead on his sleeve while he listened.

"We've got a problem," an unfriendly voice said.

"Who is this?" Wade asked, his stomach lurching with suspicion. *Probably Girabaldi,* he thought.

"That's not important. Someone has looked twice at the Iraqi vases for sale down at Jay's Antiques in La Crosse. They may be undercover police. You need to get over there and remove the vases—immediately. They're attracting too much attention."

"Tough. I need to sell them. It's part of my business now, and I need that income. Besides, unless you identify yourself, this conversation is over," he said sternly.

"Don't threaten me. You know who this is, so cut the bullshit. I decide what antiquities are sold and where. That's the way our cartel works. I'm warning you for the last time. Remove them from Jay's."

"Buzz off—" but the line had gone dead. "Hello? Hello?" Wade repeated.

A cold thread of fear snaked up his back and sent chills down his arms. He'd been afraid this might happen, but he had no one else he could count on. Most of the members of the cartel remained anonymous to each other. It was safer that way if one of them was discovered by law enforcement. Besides, he'd already burned his bridges with his former army buddies. He was out on a limb, and it felt like the limb was breaking. He began pounding more nails, attaching shingles to the roof. Despite the brilliant sunshine, a frozen dread had fallen over him that made him shiver with apprehension.

◉

10

E arly Friday afternoon, Leslie Brown and Sam Birkstein were at the impound center on Vine Street getting their first up-close look at the partially exploded truck box. The damaged packages toward the back of the ravaged van were still in the same position as when the bomb had detonated. The crew had removed the large blue plastic tarp that had covered the blasted opening in the front. Surprisingly, the heavy front panel of the van had absorbed much of the impact of the explosion, protecting the cargo toward the back.

Paco was sitting next to Leslie, alert and anticipating orders. His intense brown eyes were fixated on his master, waiting for her commands. With his bulletproof vest in place, he was ready for action.

Leslie turned to Sam and said, "I'm way too familiar with this whole procedure. The only difference is that at least in this van, there are no body parts," she said, her eyes taking on a steely, determined look. Turning to the black Lab, she unclipped his leash. "Paco, find fish," she said in a firm, uncompromising tone.

Paco stood, his nose quivering, each nostril working independently to pick up the most minute smells of undetonated explosive materials. He padded toward the van, and when he reached the back, Leslie gave him a boost up into the truck. She watched him as he began to work. Sam stood aside, observing, gaining a new respect for the fine animal's incredible sense of smell and intense focus.

"Boy, he's pretty serious," Sam said in an undertone. "What does 'find fish' mean?"

"It's our code phrase for finding bombs and explosive material," Leslie answered. "He's amazing. When he's done, we'll know one way or another if it's safe to unload and open the boxes on the truck."

"What about the vest? What's that do?" Sam asked.

Questions. Always questions, Leslie thought. "When I put on Paco's vest, it's a physical reminder that it's time to go to work," Leslie explained. "And the vest is bulletproof, in case someone wants to take a pot shot at him."

"You don't have to worry about that here," Sam said.

"Yeah, I know, but I did in Iraq," Leslie reminded him.

Paco sniffed the entire cargo of the van, working his way from side to side, front to back. His poking and prodding among the shipping boxes continued for a half hour. Finally, he came to the back of the van and stared at Leslie.

"Come, boy," she said, patting her leg. Paco jumped down, and Leslie pulled out his gray kangaroo chew toy. She tossed it in the air. He leaped like an acrobat and caught it expertly in his teeth. Leslie leaned over Paco, her blonde hair hiding her face.

Praising him, she whispered, "Good boy. Good work, Paco." He returned her admiration with ardent kisses and whines. Lying down on the cement floor, he joyously chewed on his kangaroo.

"It's safe now," Leslie announced to Sam, who was standing close by, leaning against the wall. Leslie gave a thumbs up, and the technicians began unloading the undamaged boxes, taking photos of everything, dusting for fingerprints, hoping for DNA evidence. Then they began cutting the packaging tape and removing the bubble wrap inside each parcel.

Sam watched Leslie's profile. "Do you think they'll let us examine the contents of the boxes if we use gloves?"

"I don't know. Let's ask," she said as she strolled over to one of the techs near a table that had been set up for the packages. They stood there watching her work until she looked up.

"Now what?" she asked, her arched eyebrows emphasizing her question.

"We need to see what this trucker was hauling. Is there any way we can take a look inside the undamaged boxes?" Sam asked.

"The packages are evidence, aren't they?" the tech asked.

"Yes, they are. Don't worry. Leslie's experienced at this type of thing," Sam said.

"Oh, yeah?" she said, giving Leslie the once-over. She shrugged her shoulders. "Whatever. You'll have to wear gloves, and nothing can leave here. You can work here," she instructed, pointing to two long white plastic tables. "You have to leave as much of the box intact as possible. All the shipping labels need to be preserved, and any bubble wrap needs to be saved."

"Got it. We'll be very careful," Leslie said.

Hovering over the tables, Sam and Leslie began the tedious task of inspecting the contents of the undamaged boxes, logging the descriptions of the articles inside, and saving the packaging materials. Sam held his breath as Leslie lifted the flaps of the first box and leaned in to see the contents. Bubble wrap concealed the object inside. She carefully lifted it from the box and cradled it in her hands. She laid it on the table. Unwrapping the packing materials, she gasped at what she saw. Sam gave her a puzzled look.

"What? What is it? Is it important?" he asked in rapid succession, his head poised over the object, his shoulders touching Leslie's.

"It's a Middle Eastern relief scene. Look, a marketplace tableau with merchants and traders," Leslie said, bending over to examine the piece. "We'll have to use either argon dating or thermoluminescence to analyze it and determine its age, but I think it's old—really old."

"Well, if anyone would know, you would," Sam said, peering at the artifact.

"I'll take that as a compliment … I think," she replied, crinkling her nose.

Sam and Leslie began to unpack the contents of each undamaged box, recording the details of the objects and Leslie's best estimate as to country of origin and approximate historical dates. They continued creating a record of the items until Leslie's phone beeped.

"Leslie Brown."

"Leslie, Jim here. I'm on my way into the office. What have you got on your end?"

"We're at the impound center. Paco just went through the van and cleared it. No more explosives there. But the cargo in the van is interesting, to put it mildly."

"Whaddya mean?"

"Looks like we have some artifacts from the Middle East. Some specifically from Iraq, but others from Egypt and Syria. You need to come down here and take a look at them," Leslie concluded, her voice trailing off. Jim heard some mumbling in the background.

"Okay, I'm just coming into La Crosse from interviewing Amanda Hoffman. I'll be there in fifteen minutes. But I won't be much help when it comes to identifying where the stuff came from. That's more your department."

"Well, I have a hinky feeling some of it is illegal—probably smuggled in. But if you could get down here, you can give us your ideas," Leslie said.

"Be there soon." Jim shut his phone.

By the time Jim arrived at the impound center, Sam had gone upstairs and retrieved his laptop. He scrolled through a University of Chicago website that had photos of Iraqi museum antiquities. Leslie recognized some of the pieces from her research with Dr. Drummond. Sam was taking pictures of the artifacts with his phone while Leslie continued recording descriptions.

"So, how's it going?" Jim asked, speaking into Leslie's ear. She jumped, clasping her hand to her chest.

"Oh my lord, you scared me! I didn't hear you come in," she gasped, her breathing coming in little puffs. She stood to one side, her hand gripping her shirt.

"Sorry," Jim apologized, noticing Leslie's breathing, stepping back a few feet. Focusing his attention on the table, he asked, "So what am I looking at?"

Recovering, Leslie took a deep breath and began reciting facts about the pieces as she walked the length of the tables, pointing to each one. Jim and Sam followed her, listening carefully to her analysis.

"Well, here we have a limestone vase with some relief carvings dating from around 3,000 BC. See the lion motifs on the handles?" She pointed to a vase as she listed its characteristics. "There are a number of bowls with inlaid mosaics in some kind of gray stone, possibly granite or limestone, from about 2,500 BC."

She continued walking the length of the tables, with Jim and Sam following closely behind.

"Here's a fantastic gold dagger with a lapis lazuli handle and sheath," she said. "Probably from Ur, dating from about 2,000 BC. These are similar to the ones Sam found on the University of Chicago website. Those antiquities," she pointed at the laptop screen, "are currently at the Oriental Institute. We're using the site as a reference point to try to identify objects we've found here in the van." The table was lined with other interesting pieces, most of which were ancient. Jim could see they were exquisite in detail and design. He loved Native American artifacts, and the patina on these objects reminded him of the ancient spears and arrowheads in his collection.

"Wow! This is amazing. They aren't replicas?" he asked, looking from Sam to Leslie.

Sam held up his hands in a stick 'em up position. "Don't ask me. I know nothing."

Leslie nodded, "That's true." A grin crept across her lips.

"Hey! A little respect for your partner," Sam said, irritated.

"You want respect, then start doing your homework," Leslie said firmly.

"To quote the late, great Aretha Franklin, 'All I want is a little respect when I get home,'" Sam said triumphantly, his arms crossed over his chest.

"You don't live with me."

"Minor detail. What about respect at work?" Sam grumbled.

Jim wondered at these taunts. *Did I miss something along the way?* he thought. He sensed that things were changing between these two. *I don't have time to babysit a romance. I've got enough to do.*

"Could we get back to the present?" he asked. Turning his gaze to Leslie, Jim waited. Her modesty about her knowledge was admirable, but he didn't have time for modesty right now. What he needed was her expertise.

"All right, you two. Cut the bullshit," Jim ordered sharply. "Leslie? Your professional opinion, please."

"I believe they're authentic Middle Eastern antiquities," she said confidently. "Now the question is, what were they doing in a truck headed for a warehouse in La Crosse?"

"Exactly my thoughts," Jim said as he continued gazing at the relics. They were beautiful. He understood the drawing power the objects could have on someone.

"Black market? Some antiquity cartel?" Sam asked dubiously.

"I feel like I'm in a B-rated Indiana Jones movie right now," Jim mused, still wondering about Sam and Leslie's exchange.

"That would be funny if this wasn't so real—and didn't involve murder," Sam concluded seriously, his eyes scanning the unearthed treasures on the table. "They do kinda get under your skin, don't they?"

"That's part of the problem. The lure they have on someone can easily turn into an obsession," Jim said. He stepped over to the table again and looked at the golden dagger. "Keep working. Catalog this stuff," he instructed, his voice crisp and clean. "We're meeting with the bomb squad on Monday, third floor. Bring as much information about these items as you can to the meeting. See you there." He ran his hand through his hair, turned, and walked briskly back to his truck. ◉

11

Driving her car through downtown traffic late Friday afternoon, Carol found a space across the street from the Grand River Apartments complex. She took a peek in her rearview mirror—brunette hair stylishly cut in a simple bob, warm brown eyes, high defined cheekbones, and a button nose. She whisked lipstick over her full lips. Getting out of the car, she grabbed the baby gift in one hand and her purse in the other. The street was wide and busy with traffic. As she walked across the boulevard, she inhaled the crisp fall air. Red and orange leaves were drifting down on the street like autumn missives reminding everyone that winter was next. Entering the main lobby, Carol heard the whoosh of the heavy door close behind her. She buzzed apartment 315.

"Hi, Carol," Ruby said, her voice friendly. "I've unlocked the elevator, so just come up to the third floor. We're waiting for you."

"Got it. I'll be there in a couple of minutes," Carol answered.

Carol and Ruby had become acquainted through Jim and Paul's work, and they'd had lunch together several times since. Ruby opened the door at the sound of the knock, grabbing Carol's arm and pulling her into the flat. She gave her a generous hug.

"How are you, dear?" Carol asked, smiling, holding her at arm's length.

"Good, now. We had to get a schedule going. Melody is cooperating a little better, so we're all in a friendlier mood, getting more sleep."

"Can I see her?" Carol asked tentatively, setting her brightly colored gift bag on the kitchen island.

"Sure. She's sleeping, but we'll sneak in for a peek," Ruby whispered, waving Carol down the hallway.

The nursery was darkened with blinds. Ruby adjusted them so a little natural light flowed into the room. Smells of baby powder and lotion drifted in the air. Carol felt a stab of regret when she thought about the privilege of being a mom. She'd missed out on that. She crept quietly to the edge of the crib.

"Oh, my. She's so tiny," Carol said under her breath.

Melody's little head protruded from beneath a pink quilted blanket. Her tiny arms were spread out, her fists clasped. Dark brown hair bloomed in profusion, and thick brown lashes lay in perfect formation on her pink cheeks.

"She's beautiful," Carol whispered in a hushed, reverent tone, laying her hand gently on the quilt. Ruby noticed the soft awestruck expression that engulfed Carol's features.

"Come on. We'll have some tea," she said in Carol's ear.

Ruby bustled around the kitchen, flicking on the hotpot and gathering tea and cups. Walking toward the large windows, Carol enjoyed the view of the Mississippi River to the south and the big blue bridge that led to La Crescent, Minnesota. "Nice view you've got here," she commented. Over tea, they caught up on the news and gossip.

"So, how was Paris?" Ruby asked. "When I heard you went there on your honeymoon, I was green with jealousy." She watched Carol over her teacup.

"Oh, it was phenomenal! There was so much to see and do. But it's great to be home, too."

They visited for a while. Ruby shared details of her delivery and the experience of being a new mom. Carol updated her on the decorating renovations that were happening at Chipmunk Coulee Road. Finally, an hour later, Carol excused herself. On the way home, she thought about a comment Ruby had made about older women becoming mothers. Ruby told her it was the new trend. Carol doubted it. She'd have to discuss it with her physician, although Dr. Lockhart had already informed Carol she was entering the menopausal stage of her life. *Would Jim want to start over with another family? Probably not at fifty-two,* she thought.

Besides, the problems facing pregnancy in older women were formidable: pre-eclampsia, miscarriage, and low birth weights. Still, Carol was healthy and in good shape. Immediately, she had doubts that it would ever happen. She was still recovering from the incredulous events that had played out in her life recently, and to hope to start a family at her age was a little over the top. *Best not to tempt fate,* she thought. But the idea of having a child of her own had found a home in Carol's heart and didn't seem to want to leave. ◉

**SATURDAY
OCTOBER 20**

12

Carol lay awake next to Jim in the early morning light, her head resting on her propped-up pillow. She glanced out of the large low window in the bedroom, savoring the beauty of dawn. Last night the wind had whipped the bare trees in a rollicking motion, leaving twigs and branches scattered on the frozen lawn. Now, as the sun pinked the horizon, it was quiet. A doe and her yearling fawn stood on the edge of the grass and looked toward the house. Then they leaped into the high brush on the border of the property, disappearing in silent panic.

Watching Jim's peaceful whiskered face slack in sleep, she noticed he was getting grayer, but it added a maturity that Carol found very appealing. She got up quietly, slipped into her robe, and tiptoed out into the hallway. In the kitchen, she started her morning coffee concoction, consisting of hazelnut vanilla and breakfast blend. Gurgling and steaming, the fragrant liquid slowly distilled into the pot, filling the kitchen with an enticing aroma.

How'd I get so lucky? she thought, leaning against the granite countertop. Getting to know someone like Jim at her age and falling madly in love did not just happen. God must have looked down and decided to bless her beyond anything she deserved. Jim was so good to her and so good for her. *And to think it had all started with a sexual assault.* Whenever she recalled that event, she thanked God for his protection and Jim's steady presence. She could still conjure the image of him leaning against the living room wall of her condo, listening to the sordid details when Gordy Wilson assaulted her at Goose Island Park. She'd been in such a pathetic state that night she couldn't imagine anyone would be attracted to her. Maybe that's why this whole romance with Jim never ceased to amaze her.

Late last night, after an extended conversation about the gruesome details of the bombing and the depressing interview with Amanda Hoffman, they'd climbed into bed, exhausted and spent.

"I think my endorphins need a shot in the arm," Jim commented as he turned out the light. "All this gore and sadness is heartbreaking. You'd think I'd be used to it by now."

Carol cuddled up to him, laying her head on his chest. "You better hope you never get used to it. You'd be a pretty poor police officer if you did. How 'bout a back rub?"

"Is that the best you can do?" Jim asked with a low chuckle, kissing the top of her head.

"You might not be able to handle anything else tonight."

"You're probably right. A back rub would be great."

He rolled over, lying flat on his stomach in bed while Carol expertly massaged his back. She kneaded the tight muscles, working her hands over the muscles in his back until she heard him softly snoring. Carol slipped over on her side of the bed, pulled the quilt up over them both, and fell asleep. Now she crept into the bedroom and tried to sneak back into bed, but it didn't work. Jim reached for her and pulled her on top of him.

"My endorphins never got recharged," he complained gruffly, brushing his whiskered face against her neck. "But my back feels great."

She kissed him and purred, "Well, you just let me work on those endorphins."

Nibbling on her shoulder, Jim whispered, "Oh, yeah. It's working."

Later, as they lay tangled together, Jim said, "My endorphins are charged up." He smiled. They lay quietly for a few moments. "Hey, it's supposed to be a beautiful Indian summer day," he said. "How about taking *The Little Eddy* out on the river? We could stay overnight on one of the islands if you're up to it."

"Would this proposition include necking by a fire?" Carol asked.

"Absolutely. Although I don't think it's called 'necking' anymore. I think the kids call it 'hooking up.'"

"Whatever. You know what I mean. I'll throw together some food. What time do you want to leave?"

"Maybe around three?" Jim suggested.

"Perfect."

By mid-afternoon, they had packed the Suburban with a cooler of food and drinks, a couple of sleeping bags, a feed sack of firewood, and some extra warm clothes. The temperature had hit the low seventies, and everything glowed with a golden, ethereal light. Leaves swirled in lazy paths onto the highway as they zipped down U.S. 35. The road banks and hills popped with late fall colors. Dark and inviting, the river was crowded with boats taking advantage of one last cruising opportunity.

As they motored out of Pettibone Harbor, Jim navigated the houseboat downstream, giving a wide berth to the low riding barges loaded with grain, moving their cargo downriver to New Orleans. By four o'clock, Jim had found a small, uninhabited island about fifteen miles south of La Crosse. The weather was amazing—a gift that just kept on giving. Jim and Carol unloaded the boat, cleared a place for a campfire, and explored the nooks and crannies of the island.

At dusk, Jim grilled steaks and fried potatoes in a cast iron pan. Carol fixed a salad, and they ate a relaxed meal on plastic plates. Later still, under a sky punctuated with stars, they cuddled together on a blanket and stared at the glowing coals, mesmerized by their amazing good fortune.

"I don't know about you, but this might be right up there with Paris," Jim drawled lazily, sipping on a beer.

"Never. Paris is in a category all by itself," Carol answered, smiling with the memories of the famous city. "But this is about as good as it gets in Wisconsin." She watched Jim's profile. The light from the fire lit up his handsome features. "Have I told you how much I love you?"

"Yeah, you showed me this morning, remember?"

"Oh, yeah. How could I forget that?"

They laid back on the blanket, warm in their jeans, sweatshirts, and thick socks. The velvety darkness of the October night sky was pierced with pinprick points of light. Watching the stars flicker, Jim and Carol pointed to the constellations they knew.

"The old North Star keeps everything anchored and steady," Jim said softly, pointing to the end of the handle of the Little Dipper. "Kinda like you keep me anchored." Carol's brown eyes drifted to his face.

"Do you know how precious you are to me?" he asked, rolling on his side looking at her. His blue eyes were glowing. Carol touched his cheek tenderly. "For a while after Margie died, I thought I was going to drift off into old age and become a bitter old man, worn out before my time. God knew how lonely I was—no prospects for the future. Then you came along, and everything changed."

"You know what I love about you?" Carol asked.

"That's easy—everything," Jim joked. His dimple dented his cheek, and a wide smile spread across his face.

"No, don't joke," Carol said seriously. "I love how vulnerable you are when you're with me."

Jim sighed and rolled on his back, staring into space. "Well, I learned that the hard way—through suffering. Going through tough times teaches you how to be vulnerable and in the moment like nothing else. My dad always said, 'Don't let your suffering be wasted. Learn from it. It can make you a better person.'" A comfortable silence fell between them.

Jim leaned over and gave Carol a tender kiss. "So tell me again how much you love me."

SUE BERG

"I think it's time we zipped our sleeping bags together, and I'll *show* you how much I love you," Carol said softly, returning his kiss.

He pulled her close. "Mmm, I like that idea." ◉

13

Saturday's weather was one of those fall gifts filled with summer reminders—unseasonably warm temperatures, musky scents of woods and water, and nagging to-do lists relegated to another day.

Leslie returned to her apartment about eleven o'clock from a brisk run with Paco. Pushing the vacuum around, the tasks of cleaning and decluttering had lifted her mood considerably from yesterday. Paco hid like he always did when she ran the vacuum with its incessant whine and terrifying suction. Grinning, Leslie searched for him and found him buried in a heap of clothes on the closet floor in the bedroom. Coaxing him out with a doggie treat, Paco chewed the liver-flavored biscuit with slobbering enthusiasm. Her phone buzzed.

"Hello. Leslie Brown," she answered formally, sitting on her bed, absentmindedly stroking Paco's fur.

"Hey, it's Sam."

"Oh, hi. What's up?" Leslie asked, hoping the call wasn't work related. She was trying to follow Lt. Higgins' suggestion to relax and decompress.

"Wondering if you want to go for a hike up to the Van Loon Wildlife Area this afternoon. It's such a gorgeous day. We aren't going to get too many more of these. After the hike, maybe we could go to the Trempealeau Hotel for some dinner?"

"Wow! That sounds great. I'm just finishing some cleaning. What time?"

"Between two and three?"

"Sounds good. Can I bring Paco?" Leslie asked. "He'd love it."

"Sure, we'll make it a threesome. I'll pick you up about two-thirty."

By three o'clock, they were on their way, driving north on Highway 53. It was gorgeous. Undulating fields of corn rustling in the wind reminded Sam of waves on the ocean. Ripe, orange pumpkins and bushels of red apples were displayed at roadside stands, and weathered red barns peeked out of wooded lots. Paco panted over the front seat of Sam's Jeep, leaving drool and slobber everywhere. Finding a deserted gravel lot in the Van Loon area, Sam pulled over and parked. They piled out.

"This is gonna be great," Sam commented, reaching down to pat Paco's head.

The threesome headed down a trail bordered by pine forest, which eventually opened into sand prairies, interspersed with oak savannas punctuated with prickly ash and winterberry shrubs. Paco dived into the landscape, his nose to the ground, running and leaping over fallen logs. Squirrels scampered just out of reach, sending the black Lab into fits of barking. They came to a trussed timber frame bridge that crossed the Black River. A yellow-crowned night heron was poised at the edge of the water, sitting on a dead branch like a statue, watching the shoreline for minnows or frogs.

Sam and Leslie took their time hiking, their strides easy and relaxed. The sights, smells, and sunshine soothed the tension they'd experienced from the bombing. Stopping on a bridge, they watched Paco frolicking in the cold water. Throwing her head back, Leslie soaked up the rays of sunshine. "This sunshine feels so good," she said. Sam noticed the light playing on her golden hair.

He looked at her cautiously, then turned back to admire Paco's graceful athleticism. "I was wondering how you're doing with all of this bombing business."

She huffed and stomped her foot. Her blue eyes flashed with indignation. "Well, as you can probably guess, it brings back some pretty gruesome memories," she said, her irritation prickled by the question.

"It's a simple question, Lez. You don't have to answer if you don't want to. But avoiding an answer will tell me what I want to know," Sam said, raising his eyebrows, tilting his head slightly.

"Listen, I don't need a knight in shining armor ... or a psychoanalyst. I already have one of those." Sam noticed her grip on the bridge timber tightening, her knuckles turning white. Her voice had a panicked edge to it.

"Okay, okay," he said, in a soothing voice, backing up a couple of steps. "Not a problem." The conversation slipped into an uncomfortable silence. After several minutes, he held out his hand and said, "Come on. We better start back."

Leslie turned, hesitated, and then grasped his hand. She called for Paco. As they walked back to the Jeep in the late afternoon shadows, she thought about how good it felt to be with someone. *Was this a date?* she wondered. She supposed it was, although it just seemed like good friends enjoying some time together. Sam's expectations were casual at this point, and despite not sharing her thoughts with him about the week's events, he had a nonthreatening way about him that made her feel safe.

When they reached the Jeep, she stopped walking and dropped his hand.

"I really appreciate this. It's been a beautiful day. Thanks." She noticed his hazel eyes studying her, the soft curling locks of his hair gently framing his kind face. They climbed in the Jeep.

"That was fun, wasn't it?" he asked as he leaned over and put the key in the ignition. "Hungry?"

"Starving."

"Good. Trempealeau Hotel—here we come," he said with a smile. "Not you, Paco." He looked at the black Lab in the rearview mirror. "You get kibble in the car."

Paco yawned as if to say, *We both know who's top dog around here, buddy.* ☉

.

MONDAY
OCTOBER 22

14

By four o'clock Monday afternoon, the sheriff's entire investigative team, CSI technicians, and the Dane County Bomb Squad had convened in a third-floor room in the La Crosse County Law Enforcement Center on Vine Street. The room held an assortment of metal folding chairs and white plastic rectangular tables. A whiteboard on the front wall had a tray filled with colorful markers, and a coffee pot off to the side on a black metal cart did nothing to warm up the cold atmosphere, although the smell of the brew did lift spirits a little. Jim circulated among the personnel, chatting, cajoling, and listening to various theories about the bombing incident. Finally, he moved toward the front of the room, a signal that the meeting was starting. A hush fell over the room as Jim began speaking in his clear baritone voice.

"By now, you're all aware that Brent Hoffman, an independent trucker from Sparta, was killed in a bomb blast at the Ten Mile wayside on Tuesday afternoon. We're going to begin our meeting today with Stephan Wiles, the lead member of the Dane County Bomb Squad. The team has been working the scene at the Highway 14 wayside. Mr. Wiles—" Jim waved to Stephan at the back of the room and moved off to the side, standing in his familiar listening pose—arms crossed, head down, one foot crossed over the other.

Wiles walked briskly to the front and began disseminating the information collected at the scene. "I'm Stephan Wiles, Dane County Bomb Squad. If you have any questions during my presentation, please ask." He waited a moment, then cleared his throat and began his report.

"Yesterday, a cell phone bomb was detonated at the wayside on U.S. Highway 14 above Ten Mile Hill. It killed the driver of a truck, Brett Hoffman, and did considerable damage to the vehicle. We know from fragments we've recovered from the scene that the bomb was constructed of typical parts, including a blasting cap, wires, and explosive material. In this case, it was black powder—a combination of charcoal, potassium nitrate or saltpeter, and sulfur. You can buy any of these components at a home improvement or farm supply store or online to make your own bomb. We believe the bomber was inexperienced. This may have been his first bomb because he used a small amount of blasting material, so the explosion was not as powerful as it could have been. This accounts for some of the packages toward the back of the van remaining intact during the explosion. The bomb was triggered by a cell phone which sent the signal via radio waves. Whoever detonated the bomb was nearby when it exploded. Frequently these individuals enjoy seeing or hearing the bomb detonate, which leads us to think it may be a domestic terrorist. It's a possibility anyway."

"Could the bomber be a lone wolf?" Sam asked.

Wiles nodded. "Yes, that's very possible. In fact, that's more probable than a coordinated attack by some extremist group. Lithium batteries are easily available nowadays and have a known chemical instability, making them attractive to those who build battery bombs. We think the bomber either waited to watch the bomb explode or waited to hear it explode when he was down the road. But it also could be a kid who used the internet to construct the bomb in his basement." Wiles turned to Higgins. "Jim, what about the time factor from the wildlife video?" he asked. Jim spoke from where he was and relayed the information to the group.

SUE BERG

"Fifty-six seconds elapsed from the time the bomber walked from his car, placed the bomb on the front seat of the truck, and returned to the car. He drove out of the wayside and down the road, where he dialed his cell. The bomb exploded a split second later, so he was still in the vicinity when the bomb went off. If anyone wants to view the video, it's in the evidence room."

Wiles took over again. "We know that many terrorists not only enjoy seeing or hearing the bomb explode, but they also get a high from the pandemonium that ensues after a bombing. It's the recognition they get that motivates them to strike again. They get a thrill from it," he explained dryly.

Leslie was listening carefully. None of this was news to her. Her experiences in Iraq had cemented the gruesome facts about roadside bombs in her brain. As the report went on, she could feel her stomach tightening into a hard ball. Sweat broke out along her neck and back, and a wave of nausea passed over her. *Stop it. You're fine. Breathe,* she silently told herself.

Sam glanced at Leslie and noticed her pale color. "Are you all right?" he whispered, leaning toward her. She nodded, but her color didn't improve.

Wiles continued. "Many bombers experience a vicarious gratification and sometimes a sexual thrill when they watch the victims vaporize at the time of the explosion. I know it's gruesome and sick, but that's the hard truth of it. On another note, Brett Hoffman's remains have been given to the La Crosse County morgue. They will be returned to the family for burial. The Madison ATF office will analyze any information about the other materials. That will probably take about a week. I know it doesn't seem like much yet, but a more comprehensive report will come later after our Madison lab techs have a look at the evidence. Questions?" He waited, answered a few questions succinctly, then gathered his crew and left. Jim scanned the current evidence, interviews, and timeline that had been recorded on the whiteboard. When the meeting broke up, he waved Sam and Leslie down the hall to his office.

Jim got settled behind his desk. Sam and Leslie grabbed chairs and positioned themselves in front of him. The atmosphere felt tense and claustrophobic. They were all sickened by what they'd heard.

"Stuffy in here," Jim commented, moving to open the window slightly. A whiff of fresh air briefly revived them.

"Well, what'd you think of that?" Jim asked, staring out the window, noticing the early onset of darkness that signaled fall. The gory details of the bombing had made him queasy.

"Whoever did it is a damned pervert!" Sam said with an air of righteous anger. Leslie remained quiet.

"I'd agree with that," Jim said, nodding his head. "One thing still strikes me as odd. Why did the trucker bypass his regular route and end up at the wayside? Leslie, I want you to work on that aspect of the investigation." He noticed the frozen expression stamped on her face, but he moved on.

"Sam, I want you to visit the warehouse here in La Crosse where the shipment was supposed to be delivered." He handed him a slip of paper. "See what kind of merchandise is there and also interview the owner. And you guys need to keep categorizing those antiquities found on the truck. We need to figure out if they've been smuggled into the area. How did they get here to the Midwest? Maybe there's a black market antiquities cartel operating somewhere around here. If they're legitimate artifacts, we need to know who's purchasing them." He stopped and leaned his elbows on his desk.

"Right, Chief," Sam said, shuffling in his seat, rolling his shoulders. "How'd the interview go with Brett's wife?"

"About like you'd expect. She's devastated. *Like a bug crushed underfoot,* he thought. "They've got three beautiful kids who are without a father now," Jim said, his voice edged in sadness. "I didn't get the feeling that she was involved in any way. I'm going to start going through the company's business records today. Two years worth," he said as his shoulders slumped. "By the way, Leslie, have you heard back from Dr. Drummond about the other vases you found downtown at Jay's Antiques?" Jim asked, looking over at her.

Leslie nodded. "Yes, she texted me. She's on a dig in Basra, Iraq, but she was very interested in our find and promised to get back to me in a few days. I haven't heard anything more yet, but when I do, I'll let you know." She pushed a wedge of blonde hair away from her face, then held up her index finger and pointed to the ceiling. "Back to the bomber. What about the gray Mercury he drove? Is somebody checking on that?"

"We've put out a description to law enforcement in the surrounding counties, but do you know how many people drive a gray Mercury Marquis? A lot of people," he said, answering his own question. "The license plate is being looked at by the people downstairs. We might get lucky if they can enhance it." Jim paused. "And Wiles said they found an intact Nutty Bar wrapper at the scene of the bombing. It hadn't gone through the blast, so Madison may be able to get some DNA and fingerprints from it. We'll see."

Jim leaned back in his chair and studied the ceiling as if answers were written on the tiles. Everyone remained quiet and deep in thought about the task ahead of them. Finally, Jim said, "Well, let's call it a day. I'll see you tomorrow as long as nothing else catastrophic happens." Jim got up and put on his sport coat. Sam and Leslie replaced their chairs against the wall and shuffled toward the door.

"Leslie, can I talk to you for a minute?" Jim asked. Sam waved and left the office.

"Sure," she replied, turning back from the door. Her blue eyes studied Jim carefully.

"I'm wondering how you're doing with all this stuff. The bomb and all," he said, staring at Leslie intently. Her face was a mask of control, but she didn't fool him. He'd observed her pale complexion, the light sheen of perspiration on her forehead around her hairline, and her shaking hands during the meeting with Wiles.

Leslie thought about lying but decided it wouldn't work with Higgins. "Truthfully, not so good," she said. The tears that filled her eyes embarrassed and angered her. "I lost some of my best friends—" but by now, she couldn't go on, and she began crying earnestly.

Jim quickly came around his desk and enfolded her in his arms, drawing her close. "Hey, it's horrible stuff. None of it's easy. It's okay," he said, feeling guilty he'd made her cry. After a minute, she untangled herself, and he grabbed a couple of Kleenex, handing them to her.

"I'm sorry. I'm not being very professional," she whimpered, wiping her cheeks and blowing her nose with a loud honk.

"Professional has nothing to do with it. We're human. These horrible situations should bother us. If they don't, we're in the wrong profession. Besides, we're entitled to some emotion," Jim said, smiling at her. He placed a hand lightly on her shoulder. "Better?"

"Not really." She smiled weakly. "You can't understand it unless you've been through it." She wiped away more tears. Jim recalled the devastation he witnessed at the Ten Mile Hill. He understood better now, but it was something he wished he'd never experienced. And he couldn't imagine what Leslie had seen and experienced in her military service in Iraq.

"I don't mean to minimize your suffering by suggesting a good cry will cure it all," Jim said. "It's way too complicated for that. I get that." He waited a minute, then said, "Listen. Go home, hug Paco, take a run, get outside, do something fun. And that means not reading your catalog from the Baghdad Museum," Jim ordered, pointing a finger at her.

"Right, I can do that," Leslie said quietly. "I'll be all right, sir. Really, I will," she said, still sniffling. She took a few deep breaths and straightened her back, the military bearing coming through.

"We have people on staff who can help, you know," Jim said. He dipped his chin and looked into her eyes.

"You've helped me more than you know." She paused, gathering her thoughts. "I'm very proud of my military service, but I've been changed by it. Sometimes I wish I'd never seen those horrible things over there," she said, her eyes meeting Jim's gaze.

"Thank you for your service. And it's no problem, really," Jim said sincerely. Leslie turned and waved and then was gone.

SUE BERG

As Jim exited the building that evening and walked to his truck in the parking lot, he thought about his daughter, Sara. Intelligent, energetic, spunky, sensitive. She was a wonderful daughter, but she had never experienced the horrors of warfare like Leslie, although they were almost the same age. Jim was glad Sara was still innocent and optimistic about life.

He hoped Leslie understood her changed outlook on life was more out of necessity rather than choice. That wasn't a bad thing; it was just different. Jim knew from experience the trauma police officers absorbed couldn't be minimized or ignored. It had to be acknowledged and understood. Only then would real healing happen. He thought back to what his mom had told him years ago. "Just when you think you have everything figured out, life happens, and you have to start all over again." ◉

15

Wade Bennett stood inside the cool shade of the hip-roofed barn near Rockland and admired his new locked cabinets. Inside them were Iraqi treasures, precious antiquities from a variety of sources overseas, which he hoped to unload throughout the Tri-state area in the next few months.

The anonymous phone call he'd received as a warning was all but forgotten. His focus now was selling his Middle Eastern treasures for the best price he could get minus a small percentage to the shops where they were displayed. He'd already sold the two tenth-century vases at Jay's Antiques & Curiosities in La Crosse. Now he needed to find homes for his other antique treasures—places like Rochester, Minnesota or Hudson, Wisconsin—upscale establishments where white-collar professionals were willing to pay exorbitant sticker prices for a piece of culture and history that could impress their professional, ladder-climbing, snobbish friends.

Wade had discovered you had to capitalize on conceit and self-importance, and when you appealed to those baser instincts, the objets d'art flew off the shelves. It was all about one-upmanship, self-importance, and upward social mobility.

Wade walked out into the pallid sunlight. He'd forgotten what winters could be like in Wisconsin. The cold season might come early, blowing in with a vengeance and overstaying its welcome into April with surprise ice and snowstorms. Let the wind blow. He was ready. His treasures were secure. He tipped his head back and admired his shingling job. Damn square. He'd done it right. He was ready for more than winter. He was ready for life. ◉

TUESDAY
OCTOBER 23

16

The fabulous weather held through Tuesday, giving everyone a reprieve from thoughts about November. Paul Saner whistled softly as he walked across the parking lot of the law enforcement center. Around the office, he was affectionately called Piano Man. He'd been on a career path as a concert pianist when a run-in with a chainsaw mangled his right hand. He'd come out on the other side emotionally crushed after enduring multiple surgeries. Ruby had been a major factor in his recovery. Her insight and evaluation of his natural gifts led him into a career in law enforcement. It had worked out well. Paul loved his job, and he still played piano, often entertaining the staff at holiday or fundraising events—The Piano Playing Policeman.

"When are you going back to work, hon?" Ruby asked on Monday evening, looking up from Melody, who was nursing.

"I don't know. We haven't talked about that yet." Paul was banging around in the kitchen, clearing the table and loading the dishwasher. "Why? Do you think it's time?"

"Time? Are you kidding?" Ruby's eyes danced with humor. Paul gave her a deer-in-the-headlights look, a couple of dirty glasses poised in midair.

"You need to go back. You're driving me nuts," she said, a grin wrinkling the corners of her mouth. "If you clean one more inch of this apartment, we'll be able to eat off the floor." Paul's mouth fell open. "Don't give me that innocent look like you haven't thought about it. You're losing your mind sitting around here, especially when there's a bomber running loose," she said.

"It's scary how well you know me," Paul confessed, arranging the glasses in the dishwasher and adding detergent. He pushed a few buttons to start the cycle. "Are you really comfortable with me going back? Because I'm entitled to six full weeks of paternity leave, you know," Paul explained.

"We'll be fine," Ruby continued. Gazing at Melody cradled in her arms, she said, "We are women of great strength and endurance, aren't we, Melody?" She kissed her baby's cheek. Ruby looked over at Paul, her smile wide. "Women defy the odds all the time."

Paul rolled his eyes. "Femi-Nazis," he said under his breath.

"What was that?" Ruby asked, frowning.

"Nothing," Paul laughed. "I'll be out of here tomorrow morning. Is it really that bad?"

"It's close," Ruby said, grinning.

Paul smiled as he recalled the comic exchange. Taking the elevator to the third floor of the law enforcement center on Tuesday morning, he greeted Emily, then regaled her with Melody's latest infant capers.

"She smiled at Ruby the other day, and she's growing like a weed. Higgins in yet?" he asked casually, turning to go down the hall.

"Yep. He got here fifteen minutes ago. Go on in. He'll be glad to see you," Emily said, turning back to her keyboard, pecking away enthusiastically.

Paul walked down the hall and knocked quietly on Jim's office door.

"Hey, Chief."

"Paul! You visiting, or are you back on duty?" Jim asked, smiling.

"I'm back—and glad to be."

"Good, although after you read this file," Jim pushed a manila folder at him, "your mood may change from being glad to another more appropriate adjective." Jim's smile disappeared. "It's pretty bad," he continued, shifting his shoulders as if to lessen an invisible burden. "A truck bombing that left a widow and three fatherless kids behind, antiquities that appear to be smuggled from the Middle East, no identification of the bomber's car, and no idea who the bomber is. We've got a lot on our plate."

Paul picked up the folder. "Anything specific you want me to focus on?"

"Yeah, call downstairs and see if they've been able to enhance the license plate on the bomber's car. Read through that stuff," he said as he pointed to the folder, "and let's have lunch at noon. You can give me your thoughts."

"Right," Paul said curtly. He turned and left Jim's office, feeling his heartbeat quicken as he thought about the challenges facing them in this new case. *Were criminal activities supposed to energize you?* he thought. *If they do, I better not tell anybody.* ◉

17

Sam was still feeling an inner glow from being with Leslie on Saturday. The memory of the hike and dinner filled him with a radiant flush that warmed his chest and traveled down his limbs. He wondered if this was what love felt like. He'd never loved a girl before, and the realization that he might be falling for Leslie created a dichotomy of feelings—a fierce, protective urge that made him want to fix all of her problems balanced with a tender, wistful affection charged with an intense sexual attraction.

Things were certainly changing between them, but Sam knew he had to keep those feelings at bay for a while, especially at work. He thought Lt. Higgins was already suspicious, and Sam didn't want to endure his scrutinizing blue-eyed gaze. He was sure Higgins wouldn't approve of a relationship between them, even though there was no specific policy against it in the department's handbook.

He pulled out the slip of paper that Higgins had given him Friday evening—Capital Innovations, 7098 30th Street. Sam punched the address into his GPS and followed the directions heading southeast from his apartment even though he had a pretty good idea where it was. Ten minutes later, he pulled into an empty, paved parking lot. A low, gray metal-sided warehouse squatted unceremoniously on the blacktop parking lot. Sam studied the building. In the northwest corner of the warehouse, an office displayed a CLOSED sign that hung crookedly in the entry door window. Sam walked up to the door and looked in. Dark, dusty, deserted.

He began strolling around the perimeter of the building until he reached a five-foot retaining wall that defined the back of the warehouse lot. The rear of the warehouse had an oversized garage door with an unloading dock. It was quiet here, and the sounds from the street seemed hushed and muffled. Smells of musty leaves and diesel fuel wafted in the air. Sam looked up toward the roof for surveillance cameras, but there were none. He noticed a service door. Approaching it quietly, he tried the knob. It turned easily in his hand.

He stepped into the building, which was dark except for the faraway light of the single office window in the front. The diffused light made it challenging to see the layout of the building's interior. As his eyes adjusted, he noticed that both of the outer walls had huge sections of shelving reaching almost to the ceiling. A forklift was parked in the center of the floor. Packages and cardboard boxes of various sizes were stacked here and there, but Sam thought about half the shelving was empty. Was the inventory down, or did someone take off with some of it since the bombing? Did the owner sense someone would be coming around to ask questions? Where was everybody? Why was the back service door unlocked?

Pondering those questions and feeling apprehensive, Sam heard a low-pitched growl somewhere behind him. He froze. His heart moved up into his throat. As he stood there, the growling sounded a little closer and a little louder. Something was moving toward him. *What would Leslie do?* he thought. *Where's the dog expert when you really need her?*

Without a plan in mind, Sam stupidly began to whistle a mindless tune—whether out of blatant tomfoolery or a misguided sense of danger, he wasn't sure. He trilled his tune softly at first, then a little louder until he became more confident. With exaggerated slowness, he turned around and came face to face with a huge beast of a dog. Its dark eyes reflected an eerie red glow from the ambient light. Sam could see its teeth glistening with moisture and a pink tongue dripping with saliva. *I'm going to be killed, and my body will look like one of those deer that gets smucked on the highway,* he thought. His heart was banging in his rib cage, and his scalp prickled with fear.

His whistling dried up. He stared at the humongous dog, transfixed with terror. He suddenly remembered something he'd read that you should never make eye contact with an animal that is threatening you. He looked away. *Stay calm. Move slowly but confidently,* he thought. He took one step, then another, all in melodramatic slow motion. The beast growled and barked a deep-throated warning.

Sam continued to take steps, moving at a deliberate snail's pace. The dog circled around behind him. Breathing its hot foul breath on his pant leg, the animal refused to give up, but he was confused by Sam's steady, calm advance. Sam was almost to the door when his panic overwhelmed him. Frantically, he grabbed the doorknob.

In an instant, the dog leaped through the air, gripping Sam's right buttock in his huge jaws, pinning him against the service door. The teeth sank in, and Sam heard himself scream. The growling was louder now, the excruciating pain building. Sam batted unsuccessfully at the dog's jaws to no avail. He cursed loudly and continued to hit the dog. Then he remembered he had a beef stick in his jacket pocket. With shaking hands, he ripped it out and tore off the plastic.

"Here, boy. Here," he said, waving the stick near the dog's nose. He threw it a few feet away. The dog released his grip, lunging after the treat. Sam turned the handle and slipped out the door, slamming it behind him. He stood there nauseated, trembling, and shaking. He leaned over and puked up his breakfast.

Wiping his mouth on his sleeve, he started to walk back around the building. As he walked, the reality of the bite sideswiped him with sharp, throbbing waves of pain. He could feel the blood running down his leg into his sock. Staggering like a drunk, he finally reached his car. *I must be in shock,* he thought.

When he sat down in the driver's seat, his buttock felt like it was on fire. He started the car and aimed it out to Losey Boulevard and then toward Gundersen Lutheran's emergency room. He hoped he wouldn't pass out. *I just survived the beast from hell,* he thought. *How embarrassing would it be to kill myself in a car accident on the way to the hospital?*

Jim had spent the first few hours of the day poring over the Hoffman Trucking business records. Although he wasn't a bookkeeper, he knew enough about accounts receivable and billing to see that the business was in good financial shape on the surface. As he studied, he tapped his pencil rhythmically on the desk.

Amanda Hoffman had been meticulous in her monthly entries, recording Brett's pick-ups and deliveries, making deposits at the bank, and paying bills. Not seeing any financial inconsistencies, Jim reviewed what he did know. Brett had driven to Galena, Illinois, just over the southwestern border of Wisconsin on Thursday morning, October 18. He'd picked up a load of packages at Import Specialties that were supposed to be delivered to Capital Innovations on 30th Street in La Crosse later that day. The pick-up receipt simply said "decorative items." Somewhere between Galena and La Crosse, Brett had been redirected to the wayside for unknown reasons. That fact still bothered Jim. *Why was he at that wayside?* His phone buzzed.

"Higgins."

"Hello. Is this Lt. Jim Higgins of the La Crosse Sheriff's Department?" a female voice asked politely.

"Yes, it is. Can I help you?"

"I hope so. This is Cossette Myers. I'm the admitting nurse at the Gundersen ER. Sam Birkstein asked us to contact you. He's one of your detectives, right?"

"Yes." Jim felt a dull thud in his stomach, a feeling of dread coming over him. "What's happened?" he demanded. "What's wrong?"

"He's here in the ER because apparently he's been attacked by a dog. Could you possibly come down here?"

Jim stood quickly, continuing to talk on his phone as he walked across the room. "I'll be there in fifteen minutes," he said. He flicked his phone shut, grabbed his jacket, and headed for the door. Running down the hall, he poked his head around the door to Paul's cubicle. "Come on, grab your coat. I'll explain on the way," he yelled.

In twenty minutes, Jim and Paul had fought through downtown traffic and roared to the south end of La Crosse into the ER parking lot. Jim threw his sheriff's department sign on the dash, and they hurried into the emergency area, holding up their IDs to the admitting nurse behind the desk.

"One of my officers is here—Sam Birkstein?" Jim said, a little out of breath.

"Oh, yes, come through here. They're just preparing him for some minor surgery." She motioned them through the swinging door and then into a private examination room.

"Oh, boy. That doesn't look good," Paul whispered, his eyes traveling down Sam's muscular back to his buttocks. Sam's left side was covered with part of his gown. For once, Paul understood why hospital gowns were slit up the back. It made perfect sense as he gaped at Sam's wounds. He noticed a pile of bloody clothes on a chair in the corner.

Sam's dark hair was splayed across a white sheet as he laid on his stomach on a gurney. His eyes were closed, and he seemed to be oblivious to the activities around him. The ER physician was probing a huge set of teeth marks on his right buttock with gloved fingers. Already the muscles around the bites were turning angry shades of red, blue, and dark purple, the teeth wounds oozing red fluid. A nurse was cleaning up the blood that had run down Sam's right leg. Sam continued dozing.

"We gave him a shot of morphine, so he's pretty sleepy, and we numbed up the wounded area." the nurse explained.

Jim stood against the wall while Paul inched closer to get a better look. Grimacing, Jim asked, "How bad is it?"

The doctor glanced over at the two detectives and began giving them a detailed report.

"Oh, he got nailed big time by a large, aggressive dog who clamped down and hung on. Someone should try and find the dog and check for rabies. Mr. Birkstein will have a lot of impressive bruising and a good amount of sutures. We'll stitch him up, give him a shot of antibiotics for infection, and something for pain. But he's gonna be hurtin' for a while. You'll have to watch him for signs of septicemia and get someone to help him change his bandages every day."

Jim and Paul looked at each other. "Leslie," they both said at the same time.

Sam stirred when he heard their voices.

"Chief, that you?" he asked sleepily.

"Yeah, it's me. What happened?" Jim asked, walking around to the front of the gurney.

"I went to that warehouse over on 30th Street and went in the back door. It was unlocked, and I walked in to look around." He drifted off in a morphine haze, then started again. "Some huge beast of a dog crept up behind me and bit me in the ass, as you can see," he mumbled, getting sleepy again.

Jim patted Sam's shoulder. "Don't worry. We'll get you home. Of all the stupid things," he said, shaking his head. He watched the nurse swab the wounded area with iodine.

"Boy, that's gonna hurt for a while," Paul mumbled, frowning.

"Better call Leslie. Let her know what happened," Jim instructed, stepping away a few feet. "I'll call animal control and have them go over and get the dog."

"I don't know if you're aware of it, Chief," Paul said softly, their eyes meeting across the gurney, "but I think Sam is pretty attracted to Leslie. Things kinda heated up while you were away on your honeymoon."

Jim gave Paul a sideways glance. "I've got eyes. I'm not sure I like it, but they're free and twenty-one. Trying to discourage them will only add to the attraction. They'll have to figure it out. They are adults, after all." Jim looked back at Sam's wounds and winced as the doctor began stitching.

"Just saying. If Leslie gets a look at those tight little buns, things might intensify," Paul whispered. He leaned over the doctor's shoulder. The doctor looked up at Paul, and he backed up a few feet.

"Like I said, they're adults," Jim reiterated in a serious tone. "Of course, you could always go over and assist with the bandages." He looked at Paul, lifting his eyebrows in a telling stare.

"Yeah, I guess I might have to run interference when you put it like that," Paul sighed, shrugging in resignation. "And this is just my first day back. What else is gonna happen?" ◉

18

Leslie was on Skype conversing with Dr. Rochelle Drummond, U.S. Army archaeologist and antiquities recovery expert. Dr. Drummond was calling from Fort Hamilton, New York.

"So you just got back from Basra?" Leslie asked, leaning closer to her computer screen. She picked up her sub sandwich and took a bite, mayo squeezing out the side. She swiped her mouth with a napkin as she listened.

"Yeah, the army needed some consultation done on a newly discovered site there. They were having some issues with protection, and the location needed shoring up before our troops arrived."

"So, changing the subject … I filled you in on my situation here in La Crosse. What do you think?" Leslie queried, getting to the point of the phone call.

"In my opinion, you definitely have some smuggled treasures. Do you have any idea how they're filtering into your area?" Dr. Drummond asked.

"No, we're still trying to track down the sources of the artifacts, but it's early in the case, and we're just getting started. Personally, I think someone is fencing them as facsimiles of the real things. But in reality, they are the real thing."

"And they would be doing that ... why?" Dr. Drummond looked confused.

"Well, if the items are real and have been smuggled into the country," Leslie began explaining, "then they run the risk of someone recognizing them as authentic antiquities. If they get caught with them, the artifacts will be returned to the country of origin, and the seller gets nothing, except maybe some jail time, although the way the laws are now, it would probably be just a fine and a slap on the wrist."

She took a drink of soda and continued. "Also, they can't be advertised as genuine artifacts because it's illegal to own them. So they're passing them off as copies and still collecting a reasonably good price for them," Leslie explained. "That's my theory at this point, anyway. Whether it's accurate or not, time will tell."

"What are you going to do with the ones you found?" Dr. Drummond asked.

"I don't know. What should we do with them?" Leslie leaned back in her chair, watching the archaeologist's reactions carefully. She took another bite of sandwich. "I was hoping you could give us some direction."

"Well, looting has been happening throughout history right up to the present. Think of Solomon's temple plundering in biblical times and the ransacking of our capitol during the War of 1812. Traditionally and historically, plunder is the privilege of the victor. Hopefully, we've moved beyond that attitude, but from the looks of your situation, the practice has followed us right into our modern day and age."

Leslie smiled at the context of her comments. Dr. Drummond was a wealth of historical information.

Dr. Drummond continued. "Sorry. Didn't mean to get on my soapbox. To answer your question about your artifacts, I would contact the nearest ICE office. For you, that's probably in Chicago. Tell them what you've found and go from there."

"OK. Thanks for your help. Hey, where can I get some testing done on these pieces to date them more precisely?" Leslie asked.

"Trust your eyeball at this point. You've seen enough artifacts that you should have a pretty good idea of what's real and what isn't. Assume they're real and go from there. ICE has the technical equipment to make a better judgment once they examine the treasures."

"Sounds good. Thanks for the help."

"No problem. Let me know how it ends up," Dr. Drummond said, smiling. "Good luck. Take care." She disappeared from the screen. Just as Leslie ended her Skype connection, her phone chirped. "Leslie Brown."

"Leslie, it's Paul."

"Oh, hi. How are things going at home?"

"Ruby and Melody are fine, but I'm not at home. I came back to work today, but right now, I'm over at Sam's apartment," Paul explained.

"You are? Why?" Leslie asked, puzzled.

"Well, it's a long story. Sam was investigating a warehouse over on 30th Street, and he had a run-in with a big dog who bit him—

"What?" Leslie interrupted, sounding slightly alarmed. "When did this happen?"

"A couple hours ago. Can you come over here?" Paul asked.

Leslie hesitated. "I'll be there in ten minutes if you really think I'm needed."

"Of course, you're needed."

"I'm on my way," Leslie said, swinging into action.

Back at the apartment, Jim looked down at Sam, who was comfortably tucked in his bed, despite the pain which had intensified in the car. Jim gave him more pain meds, and he drifted off to sleep.

"Leslie coming?" Jim asked as Paul walked back into Sam's bedroom.

"She's on her way," Paul answered as he placed his phone in his coat pocket.

Jim looked relieved. "When she gets here," he said, "we're gonna find the owner of this warehouse. Something's screwy. I got a bad feeling about this. Looks like you came back to work in the nick of time."

Paul grinned. "None too soon from the looks of it." ◉

19

By mid-afternoon, Jim and Paul had tracked down the owner of the warehouse. Standing on the front steps of a craftsman bungalow at 1672 Losey Boulevard, Jim impatiently rang the doorbell a second time. He was about to give up when heavy footsteps echoed in the hall, and a middle-aged man flung the door open.

Dressed in skin-tight jeans and a paisley shirt with bouffant sleeves, the man looked Jim up and down. His dark brown hair was curled around his fleshy face. Pushing his locks away from his face in a feminine gesture, he leaned around Jim to get a good look at Paul standing on the sidewalk. He carried a teacup Yorkie terrier under his arm. The dog looked at Jim with liquid brown eyes, its tiny pink tongue dripping with saliva.

"Yes? Can I help you?" the man said in a tone flecked with irritation. The little dog let out a few yaps.

"I hope so," Jim commented, trying to keep his voice professional. After giving the man's outfit the once over, Jim couldn't help but wonder where the hell some of these people shopped. Must be secondhand or resale places. He'd have to ask Sam. Jim didn't even think they made paisley fabric anymore. "We're looking for a Mr. Rod Girabaldi who owns a warehouse on 30th Street over on the south side?"

"Oh, that's my partner," the man informed Jim, toning down his voice to a normal range.

"Is he here?" Jim asked politely.

"I think he's back in the garage, doing some woodworking. Just walk down the driveway. The garage is back there," he pointed vaguely behind himself. He turned and slammed the door in Jim's face.

"Thanks," Jim said after the fact, staring at the closed door. Turning, he noticed Paul's ridiculous grin.

"Don't say another word," Jim snarled, pushing past him. "If this day gets any weirder, I'm hanging it up and going home."

They walked down the cement driveway, which curved to the right. A tuck-under garage was located beneath the house's second story, and the garage door was wide open. A man was using a drill, boring holes in a long piece of wood. Other woodworking tools were laid out on a bench nearby.

As Jim and Paul approached the garage, the man laid down the drill and looked up. Paul noticed his cool gray eyes. Spiked, dark hair framed a face with a strong, square jaw and aristocratic nose. He was well-built with broad shoulders, huge biceps, and the beginning of a middle-aged gut. He looked them over with disdain. *An attitude?* Paul thought as he locked eyes with the man.

"Something you want?" the man asked rudely, his eyes shifting from Paul to Jim. *Cops,* he thought.

"Are you Mr. Girabaldi?" Paul asked with a slight edge in his voice, flipping open his ID.

"Yeah, that's me." The answer was a short bark of impatience slicked over with disdain.

Jim flashed his ID. "Do you own a warehouse over on 30th Street?" he asked, keeping his voice neutral.

"Yeah, I do. So what?"

"What kind of materials do you receive and store there?" Jim asked, trying to control his irritation at the rudeness of the man.

"I'm a jobber for a bunch of companies who deal in decorative housewares. Why do you want to know?"

"Today, one of my detectives went to your warehouse. No one was in the office, so he went around back and found an unlocked service door. When he went in, he was attacked by a vicious dog and ended up in the hospital." Jim waited, carefully watching the man's tense face.

"Why are you snooping around my warehouse?" Girabaldi asked, jumping down Jim's throat. "If you had called first, you would know we're usually closed on Mondays," he explained, "and besides, it's private property. I keep the dog there because some teenage kids were breaking in and stealing stuff. I've got a right to protect my property," he finished, curling his lip in defiance.

"You certainly do," Jim agreed, taking note of his hostility.

"We're investigating some antiquities that were supposed to be delivered to your facility on Friday, but a bomb blew them up. Do you know anything about that?" Paul asked.

A sudden tremor of indecision passed over Mr. Girabaldi's face, and he looked away. But he quickly composed himself, barely hiding his contempt for the two detectives. "I'm sorry, but I don't. Anything else?"

"So, you're not aware that the cargo in the bombed truck was priceless Middle Eastern antiquities that cannot legally be sold in the United States?" Paul asked.

"My job is to make sure the packages are delivered to the customers in the area. Most of the time, I don't even know what's in the boxes," Girabaldi said, feigning ignorance, his tone slightly more cooperative.

"Well, I'd like you to come down to the sheriff's department tomorrow for more questioning. Ten o'clock. My detective who was attacked would like to ask you a few questions," Jim said, his blue eyes boring into the man.

"Don't you ever get tired of hassling people?" Mr. Giribaldi sneered, returning a steely glare.

"Tomorrow. Ten o'clock," Jim demanded, his voice stern.

"Yeah, whatever."

"Tell that to my guy who has thirty-two stitches in his butt," Jim snapped, straightening his tie as he spun around and stomped down the driveway. Paul hurried to keep up. ◉

WEDNESDAY
OCTOBER 24

20

Sitting on the side of the bed in her nightie, Leslie stared at the text in disbelief. Was this really possible? How had Wade found her after all this time? *Maybe I should just ignore it,* she thought. But she knew she could never do that. If Wade was texting her, then he also knew where she lived and worked. She let out a long sigh, her anxiety ramping up. *I thought this was all behind me.*

Lying at her feet, Paco lifted his head from his paws as if he sensed trouble looming on the horizon. His tail thumped a few times on the floor. Reaching down to reassure him, Leslie stroked his ears and began changing her clothes. Finally, she clipped on his leash and stepped out into the brisk morning air.

Now sitting at her desk on the third floor of the law enforcement center, she reread the text.

"Leslie. Just wanted you to know I'm in the area and would love to hook up. When can we get together? Wade"

She closed her eyes and tried to suppress a growing sense of panic. What did he mean by *hook up*? Wasn't that a reference to some kind of sexual activity? Well, *that* wasn't happening. She'd tried to make a clean break with Wade in Iraq. He was being deployed to Afghanistan, and she was being sent home stateside. It was the perfect opportunity to end a relationship that had become shallow, codependent, and too convenient. Besides, after the rough sex the last time she'd been with him, there was no way she was going to risk being alone with him again. He'd apologized profusely after the incident, but Leslie would have none of it. She told him it was over. What part of rape did he not understand?

She leaned back in her office chair and stared at the ceiling. *Just text him and get it over with,* she thought. Sighing despondently, she decided to make an honest attempt at discouraging him. With shaking hands, she thumbed out a text.

"Wade, sorry I can't meet. I'm in the middle of a tough case. What we had is over. I've moved on. Hope you can, too. Best Wishes, Leslie"

She hit send and prayed it would be the end of it, but she doubted it. Her phone buzzed.

"Yeah, Chief."

"Meet me in my office at nine, okay? I'm running a little late."

"Sure, I'll be there."

By nine o'clock Wednesday morning, Jim was seated at his desk, handsome and alert in a crisp cornflower blue dress shirt, navy dress slacks and a Mendeng red and blue plaid tie which created the allusion that his eyes were a darker azure than they really were.

Paul strolled down the hall, rapping on Leslie's door.

"Ready?" he asked.

Leslie shut the cover on her laptop and joined Paul in the hallway.

Paul strolled casually down the hall. "So, how's Sam doin'? Have you been checking on him?" he asked. Leslie thought his question was intrusive. *Some people were so nosy.*

"He was hurting pretty bad last night. I cooked him some homemade chicken soup and made sure he was thoroughly medicated before I left."

"Homemade chicken soup? Really?" he asked, looking doubtful. "I didn't think anyone under the age of thirty knew how to make that."

She stopped walking briefly and stared at him. "What world do you live in? Some alternate universe?" Leslie asked accusingly. She began walking again, picking up the pace as she explained.

"Chicken soup is one of the easiest dishes you can concoct. Just throw some cut-up cooked chicken in a pot and dice some carrots, onions, and celery. Add some broth and cook until the veggies are tender. Throw in some noodles and season with salt, pepper and thyme, and there you go. It's the ultimate comfort food."

"Did you lend any other comfort?" he asked, grinning and ribbing her with his elbow.

"That's none of your business!" Leslie said, her hackles rising. She stopped at Jim's door, knocking politely. Paul hurried in after her, still grinning.

"Morning," Jim said, looking up. "Just talked to Sam. Man, he's sore. Says he can hardly sit. He'll be gone today, but he's going to try to come in tomorrow."

Paul looked at Leslie, raising his eyebrows. "Leslie's in the comfort and chicken soup business."

Leslie frowned and snapped, "Put a sock in it!"

"Did I miss something?" Jim asked, wondering about the exchange, glancing back and forth from Leslie to Paul. Lately, he was feeling more out-of-step than usual.

"Nope, Chief. We're ready for the day," Leslie assured him, giving Paul a dismissive glance.

"In that case, let me hear what you found out yesterday," Jim began, looking at Leslie.

"I Skyped with Dr. Drummond in New York. She's certain that the antiquities on the truck are real. Actually, she said I should trust my judgment. So, for the record, I'm declaring our treasures to be real, but we will need official testing done, which ICE can probably provide."

"ICE?" Paul asked, looking confused.

She paused briefly. Jim smiled, and she went on. "She recommended that we call the Chicago office of Immigration and Customs Enforcement, ICE, which I did. Haven't heard back from them yet, but I'm expecting a call this morning. Most likely, they'll send an agent so we can coordinate our efforts. They'll take possession of the objects, assess their authenticity, and return them to the proper authorities in each country."

"Good work. What about the truck being sent to the wayside?" Jim asked. "How'd it get called off its normal route?"

"Haven't gotten to it yet, but I thought I'd work on that this morning. I'm assuming Brett had a cell phone, and when we know the carrier he used, we should be able to trace calls he made. Probably have to talk to his wife, too. I'll also contact Import Specialties, but I doubt they would have anything to do with planting a bomb."

Paul looked up. "No, but they might be dealing in the stolen antiquities. What about Hoffman's funeral? Is it today?"

"No, the funeral is tomorrow—Thursday," Jim said. "That reminds me. I'd like all of us to attend the funeral and burial. I'll give you the time and place when I find out the specifics. Hoffman's trucking business looks legitimate. The books and records were organized and up to date. I can't find anything suspicious. Paul, did you see anything in the file?"

"Nothing sketchy. By the way, the computer guys were able to enhance the license plate number." Paul looked in the file folder he held in his hand. "When we ran it through the DMV, it came back as belonging to a Regina Lipton from Arcadia. She said her plates were stolen from her car while working the night shift at Beaumont furniture last week. She thought maybe Tuesday or Wednesday. She didn't notice they were gone until Thursday, when she reported it to the DMV. I thought I'd run up there this afternoon and see if they have any security tapes. We put out an APB on the plates. Maybe we'll get something."

Jim leaned back in his desk chair. It creaked ominously, but he didn't notice. Things were happening fast and furious, but they didn't seem to be getting too far. His phone buzzed.

"Higgins."

Jim listened, slowly sat up, and rose from his chair. He ran his hand over his eyes as he listened. "When? Where? Okay. We're on our way. Thanks, Mike." Jim flicked his phone shut. "Get your coats. A runner found Rod Girabaldi shot in the head and thrown on the Three Rivers Bike Trail near the backwaters of the Mississippi over by Menard's on Copeland Avenue. Let's go."

The flashing lights of a city squad car and the presence of the La Crosse County coroner's van added an ominous layer of dread to an already dreary, misty morning. The backwaters of the Mississippi were clogged with dying vegetation, and the smells of moist earth, decaying fish, and car exhaust floated together in the air. Someone honked and a biker whizzed by. Traffic on Copeland Avenue rolled by in a kind of noisy parade, everyone oblivious to the tragedy playing out a few hundred feet away. Three orange caution cones blocked off the Three Rivers Bike Trail nearby.

La Crosse police officer Mike Leland was unrolling yellow police tape around the victim, attaching the tape to posts stuck in the ground creating a perimeter around the crime scene. A small crowd had gathered on the corner of the Menard's parking lot. They stretched their necks, trying to assess the situation. Among the soggy flock, a couple of girls who looked to be about fifteen were smoking and talking, animated by the gruesome scene, pointing to it now and then.

Jim, Paul, and Leslie approached Luke Evers, the La Crosse County coroner. Crouching next to the victim in his white coveralls and blue latex gloves, he was taking photos with his cell, shifting back and forth from one knee to the other. He stopped moving—still scrunched down—and looked up at the trio standing near the trail.

"Bad deal," Luke began, resting his arms on his knees. "Execution-style murder. One shot to the head. Bullet entered the left side near the temple, exiting above the right ear. He was shot somewhere else, then dumped here. Looks like a professional hit. Probably happened

SUE BERG

around midnight last night. That's all I can say for sure right now. I'll have to do more tests at the lab."

Jim stood with his hands in his pockets, a pensive gaze emanating from his blue eyes as he took in the dead man's flat stare into oblivion. He glanced at Leslie, her face impassive and pale.

"Paul and I interviewed the victim yesterday. I'm starting to think he may be tied somehow to the bombing up on Highway 14 last Friday and the antiquities we discovered in the truck. This whole thing is looking like some kind of organized crime activity. Maybe some kind of cartel business."

Jim stared off into space for a minute, thinking. Then he turned and retraced his steps back to the Suburban. Before he got to the truck, he stopped, pivoted, and yelled back to Luke, "Let me know when you have the results of the autopsy." Luke waved and continued to work. Jim threw the keys to Leslie.

"You drive," he ordered quietly. Leslie followed Jim and climbed in the driver's seat of the Suburban.

"Paul, I want you to head up to Arcadia and try to secure those parking lot surveillance tapes. While you're doing that, we're going back to Rod's partner and see what he's got to say," Jim said.

"Drop me at my truck, Leslie," Paul instructed.

Jim slumped in the passenger seat as Leslie drove back to the law enforcement center on Vine. They dropped off Paul, then headed to Girabaldi's residence on Losey Boulevard. During the drive over, Jim reviewed everything they'd learned about the case. Leslie maneuvered in and out of traffic, her thoughts fixated on Wade. The telltale signs of Girabaldi's murder pointed to someone efficient and effective—someone with skills like Wade. She shivered at the implications of her thoughts.

"This afternoon, we need to organize our information—motives, suspects, and evidence. We need to get on top of this. Man, I wish Sam was back. We could use his help." The murky weather drifted by their windows as they moved across the city to the south side.

The residence on Losey looked the same as it had yesterday—

quiet, unassuming, well-kept. Leslie pushed the doorbell while they waited on the front stoop. When no one answered, she rang the bell again. Eventually, the same large man answered the door. But today, he was a study in grief. His face was crestfallen and lined with worry. He had retreated behind a mask of sadness. He wore a maroon silk smoking jacket and black silk pants, and his teacup Yorkie was tucked under his arm. He petted her absentmindedly as he peered at Leslie and Jim through the screen door.

"Hello again," Jim said, looking around Leslie. He displayed his ID. "I'm so sorry for your loss. We realize this is a difficult time, but we really need to ask you a few questions. Would you be up for that?"

"I suppose I don't have much of a choice. Come in." He moved aside gracefully, opened the door, and pointed toward the living room area, a handkerchief wadded in his hand. They stepped inside, walked into the room, and found a place on the couch.

"I'm Emery Bushnell. Rod Girabaldi was my partner for over twenty years." His voice cracked. "Sorry," he said, wiping his eyes. After a moment, he regained control. Sitting in a recliner, he began rocking, his little dog's head bobbing with the motion.

Jim took a moment to introduce Leslie, and when he was done, he began the formal interview. "We're very sorry about what's happened. But I'm sure you'll understand that we need to ask you where you were between nine last night and six this morning."

Emery leaned back, patting the terrier's head, stroking its silky ears. "I was right here. Rod and I had dinner about six-thirty, and we watched the news on PBS. He got a phone call around nine-thirty. He'd been working out in the garage, and he told me he was running over to Menard's for a few special screws he needed for a project he was working on. I waited a while, but when he didn't come home, I finally went to bed about ten-thirty." He looked at Jim and Leslie and shrugged. "And no, I have no one who can testify to that."

"How'd you know he got a phone call if he was in the garage?" Jim asked.

"He left his cell lying here on the coffee table. I answered it and took it out to him," Emery recited wearily.

"Did you recognize the caller?" Leslie probed.

"No, but I assumed it was some business dealing. Rod has ... had a variety of business operations, and he got calls at all hours of the day and night. I really didn't pay too much attention to all that."

"Could you explain what you mean by a variety of business operations?" Leslie leaned back against the couch, listening carefully, taking notes.

"Well, Rod owned a number of warehouses. The warehouses led him into building storage units all over the south side. He was a middle man in the decorative market. Some of it was high-end stuff. Then he built some car washes. And he owned two McDonald's and a Subway on this end of town. So he was a very busy guy, and I might add, a good provider." With this reference, Emery's face buckled. His shoulders shook, and he cried noisily and sincerely into his crumpled handkerchief. Jim and Leslie waited out the sorrow. When Emery calmed down, Jim pitched another question.

"Were you aware of anyone who might have wanted to kill Rod?"

"Oh, no. No!" Emery said empathically. "I admit that Rod could be moody and argumentative. Sometimes he was a downright asshole. But I can't think of anyone who would go to that length." For a few minutes, Emery became quiet and contemplative. "Then again, I suppose someone might have hated him or wanted some of his money. Maybe one of his associates tried to blackmail him?"

"Why do you say that?" Leslie asked.

"Well, he's pretty wealthy, and I've met some of his so-called associates. They weren't very friendly."

"When you say wealthy, could you attach a dollar figure to that?" Leslie asked.

Emery looked off in the distance with a furrowed brow, then brought his eyes back to her. "I couldn't give you a dollar figure. Most of his wealth is tied up in real estate. But this house is paid for, and he's only thirty-five. He had a significant amount of life insurance, too. A policy for $500,000." They all thought about that for a minute. "And no, I didn't kill him to get the insurance money," Emery said, "although I am the beneficiary. I have plenty of my own money already. Inheritance," he said as if that was enough of an explanation.

"Did you ever see any of these high-end decorative arts that Rod dealt in?" Jim asked.

Emery paused. "No, but he told me some of the items looked like real ancient works of art. He said they had great patina—whatever that is. But I never actually saw any of it." Jim recalled Girabaldi's adamant denial that he'd ever seen the contents in the packages he stored and delivered. Apparently, that was a bold-faced lie.

"What we're going to want from you," Jim explained, "are copies of the financial records for all of Rod's businesses. Profits, losses, that kind of thing. You may want to contact your accountant and have him prepare copies, including income tax records for the past three years. And I want permission to look at the merchandise in the warehouse, too."

"No problem. Permission granted," Emery said as he wrote Jim's request on a pad.

Jim continued. "I can pick them up later, say Thursday afternoon, or you can bring them to the sheriff's department. Be assured this is all normal procedure when we're investigating a crime. Also, if you could make a list of his business associates, that could be extremely helpful. It might give us a starting point—something to go on." Jim and Leslie stood, and Emery led them to the door. Leslie turned as they were leaving and said, "We're very sorry about this.

"I believe you," he said with sad eyes as the door softly clicked shut. ◉

21

Mike Walsh had moved to Kreibich Coulee in southern La Crosse County off County Highway M three years ago. The valley was a perfect hideaway for someone with antisocial personality disorder, but even this isolated setting was no guarantee that he could stay out of trouble. Walsh's relationships with people were often punctuated with anger and a vindictive, spiteful attitude. An adequate bankroll of inherited funds had supported Walsh's intense interest in demolitions and explosives. After three tours of duty in the United States Army where he'd learned his trade during the Vietnam conflict, he spent many years in the public sector as an explosives expert, working for private and municipal bridge builders and road construction crews, including the building of several federal dams.

The conflict with his neighbors had escalated in pitch and fervency over the last couple of months. Unfortunately for Walsh, his neighbor Josh Ellefson was not of a friendly persuasion, particularly where his property was concerned. Mike's latest caper with demolitions had left a massive oak tree scattered in the bordering pasture of his neighbor's property. Josh promptly reported him to the sheriff's department. It was one of many complaints lodged against him over the last several months.

A year earlier, Mike had been arrested for disturbing the peace when he set up a series of underground explosions that had been timed to go off at one-minute intervals. As the charges began to detonate, dirt and debris were hurled hundreds of feet in the air. Mike, who was stoned and roaring drunk at the time, rode his ATV through the demolition field, screaming and laughing like a wild banshee. When the sheriff arrived, Mike was lying in the grass, laughing, smoking a joint, enjoying the recognition he'd received, however minuscule, from his furious neighbors. He incurred felony charges of disturbing the peace, causing excessively loud noise, damaging and disfiguring a neighbor's property, cursing, and public drunkenness, which earned him two months in jail and a fine of seven hundred dollars.

Now, after all the recent hoopla had blown over with Josh Ellefson, and his blood pressure had returned from its dizzying elevation, Mike sat in front of his potbellied woodstove, warming his stocking feet on a footstool, reading a short article buried on page ten in the *La Crosse Tribune*. He read it with interest.

La Crosse Sheriff's Department Stumped by Bombing

Chief Investigative Officer Jim Higgins of the La Crosse Sheriff's Department is making inquiries about the truck bombing that occurred on the afternoon of Thursday, October 18. At approximately 3:10 p.m. that afternoon, Brett Hoffman lost his life when a crude homemade bomb was detonated in his truck near the U.S. Highway 14 wayside above Ten Mile Hill. It is believed the bomb was activated by a cell phone.

"We are looking for a medium-sized man, dark hair, about thirty-five years old, and driving a gray Mercury Marquis. Anyone who has any information about the bombing or the perpetrator is asked to call the sheriff's department or the Crime Stopper's Anonymous hotline. It is crucial we find this person. The Hoffman family has lost someone precious to them, and we are determined to provide justice for the family," Higgins said late yesterday.

Brett Hoffman, age 37, was the owner of Hoffman Trucking in Sparta, Wisconsin. He leaves behind a wife and three children. On Thursday, October 25, funeral services will be held at 9:30 a.m. at St. Anthony's Catholic Parish in Sparta.

Mike cracked open his bottle of Leinenkugel's and rocked back in his chair, studying the ceiling. Taking a swig of beer, he carefully re-read the article, then let the newsprint fall to the floor. He had a special affinity for others who shared his interest in munitions. Demolition experts were a rare breed, and Mike believed they had a special bond. An involuntary grimace slipped across his lips.

Bombers of the world unite. ◉

22

At about eleven o'clock on Wednesday, Paul stood in parking lot 4E of Beaumont Industries, a worldwide furniture and decorative arts manufacturing complex in Arcadia, Wisconsin. This was where Regina Lipton's car was parked when her license plates were stolen. The parking lot must have held at least 250 vehicles, a huge lot by small-town standards. But Beaumont Industries defined Arcadia. No, they *were* Arcadia. As Paul thought about that, he looked up at the lights and noticed cameras.

Making his way to the closest entrance of the huge facility, he was told that all security concerns were handled through the main office. He was directed through the building, and after some hassles, he talked to the person in charge of security.

"We can certainly send you the video surveillance for Lot 4E by email. But you'll have to talk to Ms. Lipton to identify her car location in the lot," Chad said.

"Yes, I've already done that," Paul answered. Regina drove a red 2013 Volkswagen Jetta, and she shared the location where she parked on October 16 and 17. Paul wrote his email address on the back of his card, chitchatted a little more, turned down a tour of the plant facility, and headed back to La Crosse.

Arriving at his office an hour later, he opened his email and found a Beaumont message and the attachments of the parking lot videos in his inbox. Paul was watching the surveillance tapes when Jim popped his head around the entrance to his cubicle.

"Hey, I'm goin' down to the morgue to see if Luke has anything more on the Girabaldi shooting, and then Carol and I are going for lunch. Wanna join us?"

"No, thanks. I think I'll try and get through these videos."

Down on the first floor, Carol was back on the throne as secretarial hotshot of the morgue, and she looked comfortable doing it. Jim breezed into her office. Leaning over the counter, he smiled, a dimple appearing in his right cheek.

"Hey, I'm heading back to talk to Luke," he informed her, pointing to the swinging doors. He came around the counter, and seeing no one, he bent down and kissed her. "Jeez, I get to do that now."

"Better watch it. You might be on camera. Jones might bust you for fraternizing during working hours. Besides, I noticed you checking it out to make sure no one was watching," Carol replied.

"Force of habit, but when your hot wife is sitting there, it's hard to resist," Jim grinned.

Carol brushed him aside and waved toward the doors. "He's back in the recesses of his cave, somewhere," she said, rolling her eyes and returning to her keyboard.

Jim entered the morgue and found Luke in full autopsy gear. Jim pointed to the victim on the gurney zipped in a black body bag. Luke shook his head.

"Haven't gotten going yet," he said, lifting the plastic face shield. "Just got back from the scene. But you'll be the first to know if anything stands out."

Disappointed, Jim nodded. "Okay." He turned to go. "One thing." He turned back to face Luke and held up a finger. "What made you think it was a professional hit job?" He crossed his arms. "That's what you said at the scene." His baritone voice echoed off the white walls.

"No signs of a struggle or fight. Close range. I'm guessing the guy didn't see it coming," Luke said, his voice quiet, his analysis succinct. "The killer was probably someone Girabaldi knew well. I'm not expecting to find any fingerprints or hair. Probably used gloves. It was a very clean hit." Luke lifted his hands and shrugged. "Could be ex-military. He was very carefully situated on the bike trail so he'd be found quickly and easily. Why was that? A message? A warning? Don't know, but it was thorough and well planned, which might indicate some reconnaissance beforehand."

Jim nodded, pursing his lips. "That helps a little. Thanks, Luke." He walked out to Carol's office and waited a few minutes for her to finish what she was doing.

Grabbing her purse and coat, she said, "Let's go before the phone rings—again."

The weather outside had turned colder. The wind kicked up leaves, and gusts blew through the nearly bare trees. The sky had turned a dark gray, the clouds heavy with precipitation. Jim swore he could feel ice crystals on his face as he quickly guided Carol to the truck.

"Whoa," Carol said, climbing in the front seat and straightening her windblown hair. "I think October is getting kicked out the door. Hello, November."

Driving downtown, Jim found a parking space outside of Lindy's Subs on Main. The shop's windows were fogged with condensation reminding everyone of the stark contrast between the temperatures indoors and outside. Carol and Jim exchanged work-related news while enjoying their savory hot soup and sandwiches.

"I don't know. This case is looking like some kind of organized crime thing," Jim pondered, taking a bite of his Reuben sandwich. "Could be the work of a cartel, too. Luke thinks Girabaldi's murder was a professional hit job. I'd tend to agree with him." They talked about that for a while as they sipped soup until Jim's cell buzzed.

"Higgins."

"Hi, it's Leslie. Sam's standing here, and I'm arguing with him.

He can hardly walk. He shouldn't be here yet, sir."

"That's not your decision. We need him, so put him to work," Jim said brusquely. Carol eyed him curiously, her eyebrows raised. He softened his voice. "Please."

"Okay. We're meeting at two, right?"

"Absolutely. Catch Sam up in the meantime."

By two o'clock, the team was sitting in a classroom on the third floor of the law enforcement center, except for Sam, who leaned against the wall, pale and subdued, his dark hair brushed away from his face. Leslie continued to send him concerned glances, much to his chagrin.

The facts and evidence were taped on the whiteboard, and they went over the bare bones of the case again. Two victims who seemed to be linked by the artifacts, the unusual discovery of rare antiquities being transported in the back of the bombed-out truck, and guesses as to who the perpetrators of each murder might be.

Animated discussion and exchanges by the team continued. Soon vehement justifications for each theory were raised until arguments broke out, and everyone was shouting. Watching the brouhaha, Jim wondered how this all started. The team volleyed their reasoning back and forth, rudely interrupting each other until he felt like he was watching a fast-paced game of tennis. Or a boxing match.

"Wait a minute, everybody!" Jim yelled loudly over the heated dialogue as he suddenly rose to his feet. His three cohorts stopped, turning their eyes toward him. The irritation in his voice had captured their attention. Their strident arguments sputtered to a stop. Suddenly the classroom was quiet. Jim had the floor, and now he towered over them, his expression dark and troubled.

"We're all on the same team, remember?" he began, his voice echoing off the bare walls. "This isn't a junior high debate contest. All theories at this point are welcome. Each one needs to be evaluated and argued for their merit based on evidence, but let's not reduce ourselves to petty competition. Two people are dead. Let's remember that," he said brusquely, his finger jabbing the air. "We've done this before. Where does the evidence lead us? That's Detecting 101. Your personal opinion does not matter here. So, everybody chill, but keep thinking."

Jim's blue eyes moved from one person to the other. He reached up and straightened his tie, a sure signal his temper was bubbling and had spilled over. He waved at no one in particular. *Was it the sexual tension between Leslie and Sam or the onslaught of parenthood pressures for Paul?* Jim thought. *What in the world was going on?* Whatever it was, it had to stop. One of his favorite quotes by Ambrose Bierce, a journalist from the Civil War period, came to mind. "Speak when you are angry and you will make the best speech you will ever regret." *Old Ambrose would be proud of my speech,* Jim thought, *but I'll probably regret it tomorrow.*

"I think what Lt. Higgins is saying is that we need to think about the outcome instead of the obstacles. Right, sir?" Sam asked softly, feeling like a chastised ten-year-old.

Jim thought about spending yesterday morning in the ER. Sam's butt had to be hurting.

"Yeah, that includes the obstacle of your chewed-up rear end." He smiled. "What's the outcome of that?" he asked.

"I don't know, sir, but it was pain well earned," Sam remarked. The tension in the room seemed to dissipate a little.

Jim waited a few moments, letting the silence find its mark. "Now, to refocus," he said calmly, sitting down again. "Thanks to Paul's work on the parking lot videos, we know the bomber stole the license plates from Regina Lipton's VW on Tuesday night, October 16. By comparing the two tapes from the wayside and the parking lot, we believe the individual in both tapes is the bomber and may still be in the area. Maybe hanging out around Arcadia."

"Agreed. The physical features of the individual on each tape seem to suggest it's the same person," Paul repeated. "Small stature, dark hair, but not enough detail to make out facial features."

"Did you notify the Arcadia police about the make of the bomber's car?" Jim asked, propping his feet on a nearby chair.

"Yep," Paul said in a clipped tone.

Jim continued. "So let's get as good of an image as we can of the bomber and get it out to the public. Paul, get it to the TV stations and the *Tribune*." He looked at the clock. "It's just three-thirty. Maybe you can get it on the six o'clock news and the ten o'clock report. Also, let's schedule a press conference tomorrow at one o'clock."

He continued. "Leslie, did ICE return a call?"

"Yes, someone ..." she glanced down at her notebook, "a Sheila Hayes is driving up from Chicago tomorrow. We're going to meet at the impound center in the afternoon to look at the artifacts."

"Good. You do that." Jim turned to Sam, whose face was pinched with pain, and said, "Sam, if you're here tomorrow, I've got some desk work for you. In the afternoon, we'll get Girabaldi's business records in. You can look at those." Jim felt like they were finally a cohesive team. "And remember, Leslie and Paul, the funeral for Brett Hoffman tomorrow morning. We'll leave at nine."

"Is there a specific reason we're attending the funeral, sir, other than to pay our respects?" Paul asked.

Jim eyed each of his young investigators. *Come on, guys! Figure it out,* he thought.

"Maybe the bomber will show up to see how the family's faring?" Paul guessed. "Maybe he wants to get a rise out of the damage he's done?"

Jim clapped his hands a couple of times. "Atta boy, Paul."

"We better get our act together," Sam said seriously, "before someone else gets whacked." Leslie gave him a weak smile. Jim groaned inwardly. *That's all I need is a romance between those two.*

The temperature plummeted toward evening. Frost warnings

were issued for all of the Coulee Region. Winter was knocking on the door. The river was a current of gray steel, its ebb and flow sluggish and frigid. Paul entertained Melody with some fine piano music while Ruby enjoyed some leisurely personal time. He stood by the window, watching the evening sky turn from smoky gray to charcoal to black velvet. Traffic stopped and started in jerks over the big blue bridge which led to Minnesota. He lifted his arms over his head, stretching backward until he felt his tight muscles relax. He let out a little groan and straightened up.

He'd been rethinking Higgins' premise of the bombing since he'd arrived at home. Was it someone who'd been bullied looking for revenge or someone who'd been relegated to obscurity and searching for fame and notoriety? Whoever the perpetrator was, he was certainly bold and brash. Maybe at the funeral, they'd spot someone who seemed out of place, but he doubted it.

"Paul? Are you okay?" Ruby stood in front of him and wrapped her arms around his waist.

"Yeah, I'm fine," he said, lowering his arms, playing with her hair.

"Melody's down and sleeping. How was work today?" she asked, tilting her head to look into his eyes. "You're not too distracted from your first day back, are you?"

"Distracted? No. Why?" he said, looking confused. He twirled an auburn curl around his finger, noticing Ruby's green eyes. She'd just gotten out of the shower, and she smelled heavenly, like pine and lilacs.

Ruby began unbuttoning his shirt, pulling it out of his trousers.

"What are you doing?" he asked, holding his hands out to the side.

She maneuvered him out of the shirt and dropped it on the floor. Kissing him intensely, she grabbed his hand and led him toward the bedroom.

"I want your full attention to the task at hand," she said over her shoulder, removing the rubber band from her ponytail and shaking her red hair until it cascaded down her back.

"Whoa! You've got it, baby," he said softly, following her with single-minded purpose. Closing the door gently, he whispered, "You've got my full attention." ◉

**THURSDAY
OCTOBER 25**

23

He hadn't planned on attending the funeral. In the final analysis, the bombing was successful. Brett Hoffman had paid the ultimate price, but the bomber was feeling defeated. The buzz from the explosion was fading, and he needed a little boost—a reminder that it had all been worthwhile.

There had been very little attention devoted to the bombing in the newspapers or on television. When he thought about how the news media ignored it, he could feel his rage building like floodwater behind a dam. It was the same feeling he'd had all those years in school when everyone called him "pint" and "squirt." He could still hear their taunts and feel the pushes and shoves he'd endured on the playground, to say nothing of the tripping and kicking that had happened in the bathrooms and hallways. He recalled the smell of the shit in his shoes, and waves of humiliation caused him to tremble with the indignity of it. He remembered how small he'd felt. Invisible. Like a fly on the ceiling. How long did he have to suffer? Where was God's justice now?

Someone might wonder if he had an ax to grind. *Are you kidding?* he thought. *I've got more than one.* But Brett Hoffman was one tyrant whose days of intimidation were over. Poof! The ringleader who'd started the whole bullying campaign against him was contained in a little jar in the front of the church. A life reduced to ashes. *That's what he deserved,* thought the bomber.

The bomber watched Brett's wife and kids from the balcony. He could see their tears and sorrow were real, and that gave him a thrill of satisfaction. *I did that,* he thought proudly.

Suddenly, as he watched the mourners comforting the family, he noticed three people in line. Well dressed, polite, but watchful. *Cops,* he thought. They gave off a particular vibe. *What were they doing here?* Maybe they were hoping to spot him—someone who didn't fit in.

He noticed the older tall one, his odd-colored hair, good-looking, perceptive. Sweeping his eyes over the crowd of mourners, he was looking for some oddity. *Need to be careful—he's dangerous.*

The husky, dark-haired one leaned in and hugged the younger boy while the older man looked on, his serious gaze fixed on Amanda, Brett's wife. The older man took her hand and covered it with his other one. The bomber could see the reassuring, comforting effect it was having.

The blonde woman probably had a military background. Her posture was rigid and uncompromising. She seemed very sure of herself—beautiful hair and fine features. She leaned in, too, talking with each of the children, her hand resting lightly on the young girl's shoulder.

Quietly, the bomber stood and moved toward the entrance. He stumbled over some other people in the pew to get to the stairway, and a little blonde girl began raising a ruckus. "He stepped on my foot!" she cried. Other mourners looked up to see what the commotion was. *Get out. Stay calm,* he thought.

The bomber crept down the spiral staircase, the air filled with the scent of roses and burning candles. Just as he came into the narthex, the three cops were leaving to go to the cemetery. He blended into the crowds at the door, but not before the blonde woman glanced at him. Did he imagine a fleck of suspicion in her eyes?

He walked slowly, forcing himself to look casual, perhaps even a little sad. Turning at the corner, he saw his Mercury parked two blocks away. He forced himself to walk at a normal pace. As he crawled into his car, he drove away from the church, breathing a huge sigh of relief. *That was close. Have to be more careful from now on,* he thought. *Need to get a different car.* ◉

24

Sam Birkstein struggled to get dressed. He was sore, and no amount of pain medication seemed to help much. He'd looked in the mirror and couldn't believe the colorful swath of bruising that covered his right butt cheek—purple, dark red, yellow, a little orange. The black stitches crisscrossed his butt in a zigzag pattern. Sam grimaced and thought, *No wonder I'm hurtin'*.

Now sitting at his desk while the rest of the team attended the Hoffman funeral, he realized he couldn't do this all day. He could barely walk, let alone sit. He hobbled down the hall and into the classroom with the whiteboard.

Writing ideas and thoughts on a whiteboard for everyone to see didn't seem very sophisticated. Everyone in the department laughed at this arcane tradition that Jim Higgins had started. Sam had been leery of its effectiveness when he joined the investigative team, but over time, he'd realized its value. The board clarified thinking and reasoning, especially for the visual learners, which included just about everyone.

Sam stood in front of the board, contemplating the facts of the case. He picked up markers, added arrows, question marks, and motives. A couple of things bubbled to the surface. Were the two perpetrators, the bomber and the murderer of Girabaldi, the same person or two different people? Were their motives tied to the antiquities, or were they completely unrelated? And another question: Could the truck bombing and the Girabaldi murder be completely unrelated incidents?

He remembered something that had come up yesterday in their heated meeting when they were acting like a bunch of idiots. Jim revealed his conversation with Luke, the coroner. Luke thought the shooting of Girabaldi might involve someone who was ex-military, possibly a sniper. What about Girabaldi's past? Had he been in the military? If so, how long? Where had he served? The coroner said Girabaldi might have known his killer. Could the killer have been a military acquaintance of Girabaldi?

With his focus clarified, Sam pulled out his cell and dialed Emery Bushnell. A few rings.

"This is Emery."

"Emery, this is Sam Birkstein. I don't think we've met, but I'm the investigator who was bitten by Rod's dog yesterday."

"Oh, I'm so sorry about that. Rod owned big, mean dogs—the meaner, the better. How are you doing?" Sam could sense some empathy coming over the line.

"I'm sore, but I'll live," he said. "Listen, I have a question for you. Did Rod ever serve in the military?"

"Well, yes. Yes, he did. He was in the army and served in Iraq on a couple of tours of duty. Why are you asking?"

"Just standard procedure. I just wanted to verify that piece of information with you. We're building his profile, that's all. Could you send his military records over with the financial stuff?"

"Absolutely. I know right where it is."

"Great. Thanks for your help."

"Sure, no problem." Emery clicked off.

Sam went back to his desk and gingerly lowered himself into his padded chair, where he'd placed a fluffy pillow as a cushion. Firing up his laptop, he began researching Girabaldi's history, especially his military service. When he looked up at the clock, he was surprised to see it was already noon. He was feeling vindicated about his ideas. Possibilities were coming together. Things were connecting. ◉

25

At one o'clock Thursday afternoon, Jim was standing on the sidewalk in front of the La Crosse Law Enforcement Center, the backdrop for a press conference. A group of about twenty reporters shivered in the cold air. Their breaths appeared as little puffs of condensation, and they huddled together like a flock of naked birds trying to keep warm. Jim stepped to the microphone, looking smart in a dark navy wool topcoat, a blue pinstriped dress shirt, and a dark maroon tie. Paul stood at his side, his expression serious, his dark eyes somber.

"Good afternoon," Jim said. "The Sheriff's Department is releasing a couple of photos today of the suspect from the bombing which occurred last Thursday, October 18. We are requesting information from the public about the possible identity of the bomber in the explosion of a truck at the Highway 14 wayside on the day in question. We believe the perpetrator may still be in the area. Any information the public can give us will be greatly appreciated."

"Lt. Higgins?" A woman reporter named Hillary Clark punched the air with a microphone, "Can you tell us about the motive of the bomber?"

"At this time, it is not clear what the motive of the bomber was. However, the investigation is ongoing. A devoted wife and three beautiful children lost the person who was the center of their world, and we intend to provide justice for the family. This was a barbaric act of cowardice which took the life of a husband, father, and friend." Jim's blue eyes darkened with anger, but his voice exuded confidence and professionalism.

"What was the truck hauling?" a male voice asked.

"That's part of an ongoing investigation that I cannot comment on at this time. I will just reiterate that if anyone recognizes the person in the videos the department is releasing, please call us, or you may call Crime Stoppers and remain anonymous. Thank you."

Jim stepped away from the mic, and together with Paul, they walked briskly into the building. The swarm of reporters scurried after the two detectives like a batch of angry bees and continued their barrage of questions until the elevator door closed with a swish.

"Brief but to the point," Paul said quietly.

"After that funeral and burial today, I feel like tearing somebody's head off," Jim spat angrily. After a moment, in a softer voice, he said, "But that wouldn't get us very far, would it?" He gave a sideways glance at Paul.

"No, Chief. I don't believe it would."

At the same time as the press conference downstairs, Leslie was upstairs following up with Import Specialties in Galena. After some inquiries, she was directed to the warehouse.

"Yes, the shipment was picked up by Brett Hoffman on Thursday morning, October 18, at ten-thirty. Is that correct according to your records?" Leslie asked.

"A load picked up by Brett Hoffman? Just a minute while I check the log." Leslie heard papers being shuffled. A few moments passed. "Yeah. He picked up a load in the morning for Capitol Innovations in La Crosse. Left here about twelve-thirty."

"Did you change his route so that he would have been directed to a wayside on U.S. Highway 14?"

"A wayside? No. What's this about anyway?" the woman asked, sounding confused.

"Brett's truck was bombed last Thursday, and he was killed in the explosion." Leslie heard a sharp intake of breath on the line. "His wife said he'd never taken that route before to her knowledge. She couldn't figure out how he ended up at the wayside, and that's what we're trying to figure out, too. We were just wondering if you had called him for some reason, and he had changed his normal route and detoured to the wayside," Leslie explained.

Sam suddenly gimped into her office. She smiled and held up her hand in a wait gesture, her index finger pointing at the ceiling. He stood against the wall.

"No, we didn't call him. Gosh, I can't believe that happened," the woman said.

"We have a video of another person delivering a package to Brett at the wayside. You didn't dispatch someone to deliver a misplaced or forgotten package?" Leslie queried.

"No, the shipment he picked up was complete. I talk with Amanda almost every day. This is horrible. I'll have to call her."

"You do that. I'm sure she'd appreciate it. Would you check your phone records for the eighteenth and see if anyone called inquiring about the shipment? Was there anything out of the ordinary about this shipment that you can remember?"

"No, absolutely nothing. And yes, I'll check our records and get back to you," the clerk said.

"All right. Thanks for your time." Leslie clicked off and focused her attention on Sam. "How're you feelin'?"

"Sore. Very sore." He flinched but waved her concern away with a flick of his hand. "Do you have time to listen to the ranting of a newbie investigator with a sore rear end?" The ghost of a smile appeared on his lips.

"Always," Leslie said, pointing to a chair. ◉

26

That afternoon, a lab tech from the Madison ATF agency arrived on the third floor to deliver the evidence from the truck bombing scene. The Nutty Bar wrapper had been analyzed for DNA and seemed to be front and center among the gathered data.

"We got a couple of good prints," the tech expounded, scanning the report. "They ran it through their databases but didn't get any hits. If you catch him, you'll have some good evidence if the prints match. Wish we could have done more. Guess it's in your court now," he said, handing the bag and other boxes to Paul, who walked it to the locked evidence room.

Jim blew out a sigh of disappointment. He was about to walk down to Leslie's office when Emily escorted a short, compact black woman into Jim's office. Dressed in business slacks and a plaid suit jacket with a soft blouse beneath, she smiled and set a leather briefcase down. Her hair was immaculately styled, but she looked tired.

"Lt. Higgins, this is Sheila Hayes from the Chicago ICE office. She's here to meet the team and give you some direction about the artifacts from the truck," Emily said.

Jim came around his desk and reached for her hand. "Welcome," he said briskly. "Come on. We'll try and find the rest of the team."

Turning to Emily, he asked, "Would you call Paul and tell him to head down to impound? We'll meet him there. Thanks, Emily."

Jim heard Sam's voice before he saw him. He poked his head around the door frame.

"So what I'm saying is there may be two separate killers ... or not," Sam finished weakly, looking up as Jim came through the door.

"Leslie, Sam, I'd like you to meet Sheila Hayes from the ICE office in Chicago." Jim stepped aside for a round of handshakes. "Would you like coffee?" he asked Sheila politely.

"No thanks. I'm here to see your artifacts, if that's not rushing you," Sheila said apologetically.

"Not at all," Leslie said, coming around the desk. "We'll go down to the impound center on the first floor. Come on. I'll lead the way."

It didn't often happen in law enforcement, but Jim could see an immediate rapport between Leslie and the ICE official. More often than not, relations between various law enforcement agencies were competitive and territorial. Sheila and Leslie's lively conversation continued throughout the elevator ride downstairs and the short walk to impound. Jim tagged along feeling good about the rapport between the two women.

During the next couple of hours, the two women dazzled Jim and Paul with their knowledge of ancient artifacts, periods of history, world geography, and the ability to identify the country of origin and approximate ages of all the treasures. Sheila was particularly impressed with Leslie's cataloging ability and her recognition of the provenance of the antiquities.

"Lieutenant, you have a prize here in this one," she said seriously, pointing to Leslie. Leaning toward Leslie, she said in a stage whisper, "And just for the record, if you ever want a job with ICE, let me know. I could highly recommend you," she finished, tipping her head. Leslie blushed, embarrassed by the attention.

"She's worked hard learning her trade," Jim said with a smile. "And no, you can't have her." After some discussion, Ms. Hayes recommended that ICE take possession of the artifacts and see that they are returned to their rightful owners. They arranged a pickup day and time.

"Are you staying in town?" Leslie asked as the conversation wound down.

"No. I'm actually driving on to Minneapolis this evening. Stopping in to see my dad, and then I have another job in the Twin Cities tomorrow. But thanks for asking," she concluded. Looking at Leslie, she repeated, "Remember, ICE can use people like you."

"Well, that's very flattering," Leslie said modestly. "I'll walk you to your car."

Jim waved goodnight to Paul, then checked the time on his cell. Wandering through the maze of hallways on the first floor, he opened the door to the morgue. Carol was still at work, straightening her desk, finishing the day's duties.

"Hey, I'm heading home. Anything you need at the store?" Jim asked, popping his head around the door. She looked a little haggard. Her hairdo was sagging, and her makeup had faded.

Carol glanced at Jim. "No. I'm going home and heading for the soaking tub. I must be totally out of shape. This is my first week back, and I'm already exhausted."

"I'll make dinner while you soak. Deal?"

"That is a deal no woman in her right mind would turn down." Carol gave him a gracious smile.

When he got home, Jim bustled around the kitchen, opening a bottle of spaghetti sauce which he dolled up with green peppers, mushrooms, red chili flakes, and ground sirloin. With the pasta and sauce bubbling and hot garlic bread resting in aluminum foil, he poured two glasses of red wine. Then he walked back to the bathroom to check on Carol. Sneaking in, he followed a trail of clothes—heels, slacks, blouse, bra, panties. Stepping around them, he found her asleep in the tub, a cushion behind her head and bubbles up to her chin.

He leaned down and softly kissed her mouth.

She jumped, then lazily opened her eyes. "Hmm, must have

fallen asleep," she murmured, reaching up and wiping bubbles from Jim's chin.

"Hungry? Spaghetti and meat sauce. Salad. Garlic bread. Wine." Jim's eyebrows arched.

"Starving. I'll be right there." Jim offered her a fluffy towel, enjoying the view while it lasted.

Over dinner, he expressed his concerns about the team. "... and then while Sam was checking out Girabaldi's warehouse, a huge dog bit him in the butt, and now Leslie is playing nurse. She's probably falling in love with him. Then there's Paul. Being a new dad, getting in the parenting groove, realizing how much work it is to have a baby. Man, it's a regular Peyton Place."

"Peyton Place? Jim, that term is so old your team wouldn't even recognize it. Peyton Place happened in the '60s way before they were even born," Carol commented, suppressing a grin while sipping her wine.

"Hey! Easy, hon! All I'm saying is I feel like I'm living in a soap opera. All these innuendos and side remarks, secret conversations ..." His voice trailed off as he twirled his pasta on his fork, looking grouchy, his forehead frozen in a frown.

"Feel like you're losing control?" Carol reached across the table and squeezed Jim's hand. Jim looked up, his eyes wide with offense.

"What? I'm a control freak now?" he asked, his voice contemptuous, his mood still sour.

"No. No, that's not what I meant," Carol said, attempting to be diplomatic. She tried a different tack. "I'm just saying that getting together and relaxing might rebuild some of the unity that's gotten lost somewhere along the way. Maybe we could have everybody over Sunday for the Packer/Viking game, make some food, and have a fire on the patio." Her brown eyes implored him to consider the possibilities.

Jim thought for a moment. "Actually, that's not a bad idea. I could grill some brats. After the game, we could have a fire. Maybe have s'mores and hot chocolate or hot toddies." He paused, and a ghost of a smile appeared. "It might work."

"There you go," Carol said, smiling back. "Come on, let's clean this up and go to bed and snuggle. We can talk some more."

"Talk? That's not what I had in mind. Canoodling with a little extra on the side. Now that's what I'm talkin' about," Jim said as he began loading the dishwasher.

"Canoodling? Really, Jim?"

"What?" Jim said, gripping a dirty dinner plate in one hand.

"Honestly, honey, you've got to update your idioms. Who says canoodling anymore?" Carol laughed.

They finished cleaning up, loading the dishwasher, wiping Jim's mess from the countertops.

"Just so you know, when I get done canoodling with you, you won't care about idioms or anything else for that matter," Jim said, walking down the hall to the bedroom. He slapped Carol on her shapely behind as she walked ahead of him. She turned and grabbed his tie, tugging him down the hall.

"Bring it on, baby," she said, quietly closing the bedroom door. ◉

FRIDAY
OCTOBER 26

27

The next morning, the grass and weeds along Chipmunk Coulee Road were covered with hoarfrost, and the bare trees held their arms upward to a cloudless powder blue sky. Silent rows of corn stood in the fields, their pregnant golden cobs hanging limply on the stalk waiting to be harvested. Jim braked, then slowed for a combine that lumbered awkwardly down Chipmunk Coulee Road, a gravity box trailing behind. The temperature hovered at twenty-eight degrees. Jim leaned over and flicked on the truck heater. When the combine driver turned onto a field road, Jim navigated around the machine, speeding toward U.S. Highway 35.

Suddenly a pair of pheasants burst into explosive flight in front of his truck, forcing him to crank the steering wheel, careening to miss them. His heart raced from the sudden blur of birds that narrowly missed his windshield.

Since the funeral yesterday, the grief of the Hoffman family had invaded Jim's soul like a white shirt soaking up a puddle of blood. As he drove to work, the sadness percolated into righteous anger. Finding justice for the hurting family hammered in his brain with unrelenting urgency. *They deserve something more than a bottle of ashes.* He remembered the questioning look of the Hoffmans' oldest son. *Why?* His eyes were filled with tears of sorrow and confusion, anger frozen on his face. All of it was so unbelievable.

"Please, Lt. Higgins, please find my dad's killer," he'd pleaded quietly. Jim could still see the youthful innocence of his face and hear the quiet desperation in his voice, a layer of outrage lying just below the surface. *How would John and Sara feel if I was killed like that?* he thought.

"We're doing our very best to unravel this and find out who did this," Jim said somberly to the young man. "No one deserves to lose a parent this way. No one."

Paul had tenderly laid his hand on the young boy's shoulder. He looked like his father, handsome, all grown up in his suit and tie. But underneath, Jim knew the optimism and innocence of his youth had been shattered and lay like fragments of broken glass on the floor of his heart.

Jim's resolve strengthened in the face of such senseless violence, although his mind boiled with unanswered questions. What had motivated the killer? Passion must be at the core. Was it personal? Issues of abuse, intense hatred for a past transgression, bullying? Or was it political? Radicalized revenge for some societal wrong?

His first inclinations had been that the bombing was a domestic terror event. With the discovery of the Middle Eastern antiquities, the senseless violence seemed like a logical tie-in. Some radical jihadist or member of a terrorist group like ISIS making some kind of statement. But after the funeral, he wasn't so sure. Why would ISIS bother with a private trucking firm in a small midwestern Wisconsin town? There had been very few bombings in the rural areas of Wisconsin. So the radicalized terrorist theory didn't make much sense to him. The killing felt more personal than that, although he had nothing to base his ideas on, just his "gut" feeling that most cops scoffed at in this day and age. But he'd discovered a long time ago that intuition, normally attributed to women, could be just as powerful in men. More than once, he'd acted on hunches that led him down some unforeseen paths to unexpected discoveries and eventually to the criminal.

Jim considered the lone wolf hypothesis so popular with online theorists and government agencies. He knew from recent research that since the year 2000, lone wolf attacks have been on the increase. Often the people who carried out attacks like the one on Brett Hoffman were plagued by mental illness. To Jim, the lone wolf premise seemed like a more plausible explanation for what had happened.

More questions. Was Hoffman just a poor unlucky victim who happened to get caught up in someone's plan of world domination and political grievances? That seemed unlikely. Or was he just in the wrong place at the wrong time, an innocent bystander absorbing collateral damage? Maybe. Or was Brett Hoffman the target and cause of the bombing? Jim didn't know yet, and there were no easy answers.

As he settled into his office routines, he sipped on a coffee. It was piping hot, just the way he liked it. He reread his interview notes with Amanda Hoffman. Moving his finger down the pages, he reviewed them thoughtfully. *Maybe I need to follow up with Amanda again. I might have missed something.* If the bombing was personal, it might point to someone in Brett's past who had held onto a grudge. Worth checking out. Jim dialed Amanda.

"This is the Hoffmans," Amanda answered.

"Amanda. Jim Higgins here." A pause. "How are you today?" he asked, concerned.

"Oh, hello Lt. Higgins. I thought the funeral would make things easier, but I think all it did for me was make the reality of Brett's absence more real. The house is so quiet, and the kids are so sad." Her voice quivered with emotion. "He's really gone, and I feel so alone." Her soft sobs went on for a few moments. Jim waited, identifying deeply with her pain. He remembered his grief when Margie died. He understood the heart-wrenching experience all too well.

"Listen, I hate to bother you, but I realized there were a few things I neglected to ask you when we first visited. Are you up to answering a few questions?"

"I'll do my best," Amanda said, sniffling.

"I'm sure you will. Where did Brett attend high school?"

"He went to a private Catholic boys high school in Prairie du Chien called Joliet Preparatory Academy run by Father Willard Renard, I think. It's defunct now. I think the last class to graduate from there was in 1998, a year after Brett graduated."

"Did they have an emphasis of study? Like science or history? The classics or something else?"

"Not really. It was a boarding school that emphasized a well-rounded education. Their most famous graduate was Vincente Fox, the former president of Mexico. Brett lived in the dorms with the other boys even though his parents lived in the country outside of Prairie. They wanted him to have the full Catholic experience. I'm sure I have his school records here somewhere. I could look for them."

"Would you? Especially his yearbooks. That would be very helpful."

"Why do you want to know about his high school years? That was a long time ago." Amanda asked. Jim could imagine her baffled look.

"Maybe someone had a grudge against him for some reason? I really don't know where else to start. It's just an idea that occurred to me. Were you aware of anyone he ever mentioned from school that he had a longstanding conflict with?"

"Gosh, no. High school was so far in the past. We didn't really talk about it. I met Brett at tech school in La Crosse. I never even knew him during his high school years."

"Okay. Well, I've got to start somewhere. If you can get those records to me, I'd appreciate it."

"Will do. Thanks, Lt. Higgins, for all you're doing."

"Sure," Jim said, ready to hang up.

"Oh, Lt. Higgins, I forgot to tell you. I remembered something. I did get a call the morning of the bombing. I guess in the shock of everything that's happened, I just forgot about it. Whoever it was didn't identify himself, but he wanted to hire Brett to haul a load of merchandise that week. I offered to schedule it for him, but he refused. He wanted to talk to Brett himself."

"So, what was the upshot of the conversation?" Jim asked, feeling a ray of hope.

"I gave him Brett's cell number. But now I think it may have been the bomber, and it's killing me. What if I helped the bomber carry out his plan?" Amanda asked, her voice shaking.

"No, no. Don't do that to yourself, Amanda. You did what a customer asked you to do. Nothing more, nothing less," Jim counseled. "It's not your fault. Blaming yourself will not bring Brett back, and you'll only be punishing yourself for something you're not responsible for." He listened to her quiet crying. "Will you be okay? Can you call someone to come and be with you?"

"I'll be okay. I suppose you're right. Thanks, Lt. Higgins," she said softly as she clicked off.

Jim shut his phone and walked down to Sam's cubicle, where he found him standing over his desk. Apparently, sitting was still too painful.

Sam turned. "Morning, Chief," he said, giving him a hint of a smile.

"How're things on your end? No pun intended," Jim asked, seriously.

"Better. Leslie's taking good care of me." *I'll bet she is,* Jim thought.

"Good. Listen, I just caught the tail end of your idea about the possibility of two killers yesterday. Tell me about that," Jim said, sliding into a chair next to Sam's desk.

"Well, we've been assuming the bomber also killed Girabaldi, but it could be that there are two killers with unrelated motives. I guess I was thinking about what Luke said. He thought Girabaldi's murder might possibly be someone who is ex-military. So I called Emery. Rod was in the army—three tours, with two in Iraq and one in Afghanistan. I'm wondering if whoever killed Rod could possibly be military as well. That's all."

"Those are interesting thoughts. Keep investigating that angle. See what comes of it." Jim paused, frowning, then started again.

"I've also been wondering if we're not making a mistake thinking that the bomber was a terrorist and had an interest in the treasures. What if the bomber was after Brett Hoffman for some reason, and the treasures are a separate problem by themselves, or the treasures are related to Girabaldi? After all, Girabaldi did spend time in the Middle East, whereas Brett is a local boy who's never been more than a hundred miles from home," he finished.

"The problem is we don't have any proof that confirms our suspicions."

"No proof yet, but we're making some connections that may pay off eventually. We know that Rod has a connection to the treasures since they were being shipped to his warehouse. Now we know he was in the military. Once we get his business records and tax returns, we might be able to link things together. And I've got an idea I'm pursuing about Brett. We just have to keep digging."

Sam stared out the window, his face cast in anxiety. "I hope something comes to light. We need to catch these wackos before they hurt or kill someone else," he said.

Jim stood up. "Yeah, I hear you. One more thing. I want you and Leslie to go back to Jay's Antiques and check on those Iraqi vases. Find out who the seller was and if they've been purchased." Jim pointed a finger at Sam. "It's a long shot, but maybe they will tie into those antiquities on the truck."

"Will do, Chief," Sam said.

That afternoon, Rod Girabaldi's business and military records and Brett Hoffman's high school yearbooks and school report cards arrived at the office. Emily knocked on Jim's door. He waved her in as he finished a phone conversation.

"What's that?" he asked suspiciously, pointing to a thick manila folder stuffed with paper and a cardboard box overflowing with records, books, and file folders.

"Tax and military records from Girabaldi and school records from Brett Hoffman," Emily said as she dumped them noisily on Jim's desk where they seemed to form a mountain of paper. The folders began tipping, but not before Emily gracefully caught them and restacked them securely.

Jim groaned. "Boy, that was fast. I just talked to Amanda this morning."

"Well, she was in town on some other business and decided to drop them off," Emily said.

"The only good thing about this is giving half of these to Paul." He grabbed the cardboard box, handing it back to Emily. "Will you walk this down to Piano Man?" He smiled wickedly, a dimple creasing his cheek. Emily shook her head, a grin spreading across her face. "You just observed a quick lesson in delegation."

"You are such a devil," Emily said saucily.

"Nothing devilish about delegation," he grinned.

She shook her head as she left with the box.

About three o'clock, Leslie walked down the hall to Paul's office. When she lightly tapped on his door, he looked up expectantly.

"Hey, what's up?" he asked, stretching his arms over his head, moving his neck from one side to the other, loosening up the tightness.

"Just wondering if you're making any progress on that pile of stuff Emily gave you."

"It's slow. Wanna help?"

"Sure. That's why I walked over. Import Specialties hasn't shown any real promise. I've searched their company on the web, but the information is pretty general. So what have you got here?" Leslie asked, flipping casually through a pile.

Paul handed Leslie a ragged manila folder. "Actually, you'd probably be the best person to analyze these—Girabaldi's military records."

Leslie grabbed the folder and found a seat. "Glad to," she said as she began paging through documents. For about fifteen minutes, she looked through a standard collection of official military documents from the National Personnel Records Center. Absentmindedly, she rubbed the back of her neck while she read, swinging her leg back and forth in a nervous habit.

The documents were divided into two sections: Personnel Records and Health Records. Leslie sat back in her chair. These were familiar territory to her. Girabaldi's service archives were pretty standard. He enlisted in 2007 and was discharged in 2011. During that time, he was in combat operations in Fallujah and Mosul, and he received various performance awards and decorations during his tours of duty. As with many soldiers, herself included, Girabaldi suffered from PTSD, according to his medical records. Leslie knew that the degree of disability varied from person to person. He was one of the lucky ones. He had not been physically wounded or injured.

Not finding anything jumping out at her, she began studying some photos tucked inside with the more traditional records. Most were casual—buddies and acquaintances from his unit acting goofy and cutting up. But a more formal photo caught her eye. The official photograph of Girabaldi's army unit stared up at her.

Leslie was about to declare the job complete and return the photo to the folder when a soldier in the row below Girabaldi caught her eye. *No, it couldn't be,* she thought as she squinted and placed her finger under the face. A shudder of anxiety pulsed through her body. Her mind raced to understand the implications of the photo and what it suggested. How was it that Rod Girabladi and Wade Bennett had been in the same military unit and now lived in close proximity in La Crosse? Coincidence? Leslie didn't believe in coincidences when it came to crime, especially murder.

Girabaldi had been murdered execution style, according to Luke Evers. Wade was in the area. He was a trained sniper, and she knew that he had residual psychological fallout from his combat service, although he put on a good act. The thoughts shoving their way into her brain nauseated her. This did not bode well for her role in this investigation. Refusing Wade's advances would make her a target, and the last thing she wanted was the attention of her former abusive boyfriend. That was like being a rabbit hiding in a field while an eagle hovered in flight, scrutinizing your every move, zeroing in on your position, moving in for the kill. She knew all about Wade's capabilities in eliminating combatants. The chances for survival were slim to none. *I need to think about this before I decide what I'm going to do,* she thought.

"How're things going in here?" Jim asked, stepping into Paul's cubicle. His eyes met Leslie's, and he noticed her pale skin tone. She seemed startled by his presence. Her eyes were large, and she looked like she could jump out of her skin.

"Are you okay? You look like you've seen a ghost," Higgins said, his blue eyes studying her, wondering about her hyper-vigilant disposition.

"Oh, I'm fine, sir. Just fine," Leslie stuttered nervously, standing and laying the folder on Paul's desk. She began backing out of the office. "I need to go do some personal errands. I'll catch you later." She gave a little twiddle of her fingers, turned, and walked briskly down the hall.

"Was that a little strange?" Paul asked, a frown crinkling his forehead, turning his chair to face Jim.

"Yeah, it was. I'm learning that Leslie has some skeletons in her closet that maybe even she doesn't understand," Jim said, sighing softly, watching her disappear down the hall. He picked up the folder on top of the file and stared at the picture inside. *What did Leslie see in the photo of Girabaldi's unit that upset her so much?* he thought. ◉

28

Wade Bennett hunkered down in the front seat of his Chevy Silverado pickup with his Carhartt coat collar scrunched up around his ears. He'd parked a block down from Leslie's apartment, hoping to intercept her and discuss her response to his text.

What did Leslie mean—it's over? he thought. It wasn't over for him. Not now, not ever. Leslie was the girl he's always dreamed of. A Nordic blonde beauty, long and lanky with a razor-sharp intellect, and of course, sexually exciting. What more could a country boy ask for? *No, our relationship is not going to end that easily, not without a discussion.*

He thought back to their last sexual encounter some six years ago in Iraq. He was just getting ready to ship out to Afghanistan on a year-long tour. It had been a hurried spur-of-the-moment event, and in all honesty, he had to admit he was aggressive. He vaguely remembered slapping her when she'd refused. He had thoroughly manhandled Leslie until she had cried and finally conceded in giving him what he wanted. *Was that rape? Am I a sexual predator?* he asked himself.

Maybe he really did have PTSD, and it affected his relationships with women. Was he emotionally distant and cold? Was that what kept him from developing caring, intimate relationships with women—relationships built on trust? Was he unkind and cruel? He didn't think so, but he wasn't sure. All of these thoughts were very unsettling. Pondering his dilemma, he felt more confused than ever.

The evening was cold and clear. As Wade impatiently waited in his truck, dusk descended, and the streetlights clicked on, illuminating the sidewalks and houses on La Crosse Street. Little flecks of snow sparkled in the air, dancing and darting, fed by intermittent gusts of wind that occasionally moved through the branches of the bare trees. College students walked by. Some jogged, some ran. No one lingered for very long. Everyone had somewhere to go, trying to avoid the cold and thoughts of the long Wisconsin winter ahead.

By the time an hour had elapsed, Wade was thoroughly bored. His impatience tugged at him like a horse pulling on its reins. He waited another fifteen minutes, nervously jiggling his leg, occasionally letting out little puffs of air. His thoughts tumbled over one another, tangled with unfamiliar emotions.

Finally, a few minutes before six o'clock, he noticed Leslie's light blue Toyota Prius gunning down the street. She turned recklessly into her driveway. The garage door opened, and her car disappeared inside. Lights flickered on in the house. He smiled to himself. She always did drive too fast. Following closely behind, a black Jeep Patriot parked in the driveway, its engine running. A dark-haired man waited patiently until Leslie reappeared at the front door and hopped in the Jeep with him. *Mmm, a boyfriend?* That wasn't what he was expecting. But, after all, it had been six years since they'd seen each other. He supposed it would be logical that someone else would notice Leslie's Scandinavian beauty.

This could complicate things. But it would all work out. He'd just have to remain calm and unflappable like the quiet concentration that came over him when he was on reconnaissance patrol. *Well, no time like the present to use some of my hard-earned skills,* he thought. He decided to follow them. He was sure this would be interesting

SUE BERG

Inside Sam's Jeep, the mood was pensive. Leslie's emotions seemed bottled up, ready to explode. Sam had suggested a ride along the river road to Stoddard to get a bite to eat at a little place called Rocky's that served great seafood and steaks in a laid-back atmosphere.

The sun set as they drove down the Great River Road, and the sky exploded in a riot of color. Reds, pinks, and oranges swirled together over the dark, brooding Mississippi River in a kaleidoscope of intricate patterns. A flock of geese had clustered together in the backwater near the road in the fading dusk.

On the ride along the river, Leslie tried to relax. She leaned back in her seat, her mind still trying to absorb what she'd learned about Rod Girabaldi and how it might relate to his murder. Wade drifted at the edge of her thoughts, leaving her unsettled and preoccupied.

"… so I guess I have to get a few stitches taken out early next week," Sam was saying, pausing a moment. "And Donald Duck gave me strict orders that you have to take a look at them before I go into the clinic on Tuesday." He'd been performing a soliloquy of sorts since they'd driven past the outskirts of La Crosse, but he was getting negligible responses from Leslie.

"Yeah, that sounds good," she said, inattentive, miles away.

"Oh, you and Donald talked?" Sam asked, a grin appearing at the corners of his mouth.

Leslie skipped a beat. "What? Donald who?" She looked over at him, confused. "What are you talking about?"

Sam's eyes grew dark with concern. "Is there something going on that I need to know about because you're acting really weird? Have you been drinking?" Sam looked over at Leslie.

"Drinking? I don't drink except on very special occasions," she said innocently. "We seem to be at cross purposes here."

"Well, I'm glad you finally noticed," Sam said.

Leslie reached across the seat and grabbed Sam's hand. "I'm sorry. I know I'm distracted. Can we talk later? I'm really hungry, and my thought processes always get screwed up when I haven't eaten for a while." she explained.

"Sure. It's okay," Sam said, reassuring her, enjoying the warmth of her hand. He looked in his rearview mirror and noticed a Chevy Silverado making no attempt to hide. Sam's stomach rolled with anxiety. Was someone following them?

The meal was excellent, although the atmosphere was boisterous and loud. A group of local fishermen and a few turkey hunters were regaling wild tales and drinking too much, but it was refreshing for Sam and Leslie to lose themselves in good food and normal conversation. Under cover of the locals, they could spend time connecting, getting to know each other more intimately. Before they left, Sam left a generous tip.

"Ooh. You always give that big of a tip on a policeman's salary?" Leslie whispered seductively in Sam's ear, eyeing the tip lying on the table.

"She did a good job and deserved to be rewarded." Sam smiled widely. His eyes moved up and down Leslie. "You are looking very pretty tonight. Your mood has vastly improved since you downed some food."

"Nightcap? My place?" Leslie asked.

"Sure. Love to." Sam pecked her on the cheek. *Don't screw this up,* he thought.

Arriving back at the apartment, Leslie barreled in through the front door with Sam close behind. Paco greeted her with whines, kisses, and drool, but Sam got an eyeful of disdain from a distance. After a few moments, Paco eased up to Sam's side, nudging his hand. He gave him an affectionate pat on the head and some hearty thumps on his side. Paco's tail wagged limply.

"Guess I'm still getting the cold shoulder," Sam said, throwing his coat across the couch.

"It is what it is," Leslie said, hanging her jacket in the hall closet.

Sam strolled to the living room window that faced the street and slowly parted the drapes with one finger. The Chevy Silverado pickup was parked across the street from Leslie's apartment. Sam let go of the curtains.

"What are you looking at?" Leslie asked, standing next to Sam.

"Someone who's been following us all night. Who is he?" Sam asked seriously, turning toward her, noticing her blue eyes.

"Short or long answer?"

"Long enough to help me understand why you're shaking." His eyes searched her face, and he carefully put his arm around her shoulders and gently led her away from the window. She stopped and leaned against the wall, arms hanging at her side. Sighing, she closed her eyes. Her whole life had just caught up with her and slapped her across the face.

Sam stood in front of her, waiting. He was a patient man. Gazing at this very beautiful, graceful woman, he realized she was profoundly afraid of something. She was so terrified that when you got close to her, it felt as if she would explode in panicked flight and run away like a wild animal—run so far away you would never be able to stop her or catch her again.

Leslie lifted her eyes which were large and luminous and very blue. He noticed tears shining in them. He felt like a tightrope walker. The ground was a very long way down with no safety net.

"What are you so scared of?" he whispered as gently as he could.

Leslie had a moment of indecision. Finally, she said, "Wade's a very scary man. I was involved with him in Iraq."

"What do you mean by involved?" Sam spoke softly, his voice compassionate.

"I was in a relationship with him. He hurt me in unspeakable ways."

"How?" Sam asked, struggling to keep his voice even, though inside, he could feel his anger and indignation building. Moments passed. "Physically? Sexually? Emotionally? What?" Sam kept his voice low and fought the urge to speed up the confession. *Help me understand,* he prayed.

The minutes ticked by. He sensed Leslie's temptation to panic and her urge to flee—to shove everything under the rug. *Please trust me. I won't hurt you,* he brooded. Even though he hadn't said the words out loud, he hoped Leslie might sense his concern for her predicament. By now, the tears were glistening on her cheeks.

"All of the above," she said softly with downcast eyes. She let out a whimper and looked up at him, softly crying. Sam waited, taking his cues from her. "This is where you take me in your arms, kiss me, and hold me," she said, looking into his warm hazel eyes.

"Are you serious right now?" His heart flipped over. *Are you always such a nerd?* he thought.

"Yes, dead serious." She reached up and grasped the front of his shirt. She was so close Sam could feel her warm breath on his face.

He gently pulled her to his chest and held her until her shaking stopped. He tenderly stroked her hair. Leslie wrapped her arms around his waist while Sam bent his head and softly brushed her lips with his. His kiss deepened, and he made it last. He pulled away, but Leslie pulled him to her again, kissing him passionately. Finally, Sam disengaged but continued to hold her firmly against him. Leslie tucked her head against his neck. He could feel the softness of her hair on his skin.

"Do you always follow instructions to the letter?" Leslie asked, playing with the collar on his shirt.

"I do when I think someone might run away," he answered, chuckling a little. Her vulnerability made him weak in the knees. He realized with a jolt that her trust in him was a precious, delicate thing. He felt unworthy, yet the honesty of her confession moved him. *Do you know what you're doing?* he thought.

There was a sharp rapping on the door. Leslie jumped and jerked from Sam's arms. Paco let out a couple of woofs.

"It's him," she whispered, a quiet desperation in her voice. "It's Wade." She patted her leg and Paco diligently came to her side, where she held onto his collar.

"Take Paco and your cell phone. Go into your bedroom, lock the door, and don't come out until you hear five short raps. If he kills me, call the police," Sam instructed. Leslie's dilated eyes stared at him in the darkness of the hall.

"I *am* the police," she reminded him.

"Whatever. Minor detail." Some more sharp raps. "Go!" he hissed, pointing to the bedroom.

Sam walked down the short hall to the front entrance. It reminded him of a march to the gallows and walking the plank all at the same time. He swung the door open and stepped into the night air. *Be assertive right from the get-go,* he thought.

He stepped out onto the porch pulling the door shut behind him. He heard it click as it closed, and the sound felt like a signal for the action to begin. *Act I, Scene I. Birkstein's Book of Martyrs.*

Sam noticed the cool gray of Wade's eyes in the porch light. His breathing seemed controlled, but his eyes flicked nervously from side to side. There was a considerable bulge under his jacket. *Gun?* Sam thought. The hulk of Wade's muscled body made Sam feel inadequate, like an immature adolescent.

"Hello. Can I help you?" Sam asked politely, keeping his voice low-key.

"I doubt it. I want to see Leslie," Wade answered, his voice slow and low.

"That's not possible because she doesn't want to see you."

Wade blinked with reptilian slowness. His eyes moved over Sam's face. "Says who?"

"Says she ... and me. I'm speaking for her. She's afraid of you. Petrified, actually."

Scoffing, Wade asked, "Do I look dangerous to you?" He put his hand on his chest and leaned toward Sam. Sam backed away slightly.

"No, but I've met plenty of people who appeared normal but were extremely dangerous," Sam said.

"So there's no chance I can see her?" Wade asked a little less confidently. He looked down his nose at Sam. A thin grimace stretched over his perfectly white teeth. Sam thought the expression was odd, and then he remembered the glistening teeth of the dog that had bitten him.

"I'm afraid you cannot see Leslie. I'm asking you to be a gentleman and leave quietly."

"Or?"

"Or I'll have to take you into custody for trespassing and harassment. You'll spend an uncomfortable night in jail," Sam said with more confidence than he felt.

"Seriously?"

"Yes. I'm a police officer, and I will arrest you."

Wade looked Sam up and down. His hooded eyes had turned icy with contempt, and the angles of his face were hard and unflinching. He glanced over at the porch light. Slowly his eyes drifted back to Sam. He let out a little puff of air, filling the space between them with white condensation. Some kind of decision was being made. Finally, he turned around and walked down the sidewalk, crossed the street, and climbed into his truck. Sam waited until he drove away. His feet felt like they were plastered to the floor of the porch.

With shaking hands, Sam let himself back into the apartment, threw the deadbolt, and leaned against the front door. He closed his eyes, breathing hard, a light sheen of sweat on his face. As a pastor's kid, he'd prayed a lot, but this was the first time he really felt like it came from his heart. *Thank you, God, for protecting me. Help me understand Leslie.*

He walked slowly down the hallway and rapped five short taps on the door. Leslie opened it and walked into Sam's arms, clinging to his neck. He rubbed her back gently. After a moment, they separated.

"I think you better tell me everything you know about Wade," Sam began. ◉

29

Friday morning began with a flurry of winter harbingers. The brown grass was covered with a thin coating of brittle frost that crackled when you walked on it. Overnight, very light snow had fallen on the lawn, looking like a rumpled blanket on a bed. A crow clinging to an ancient bare oak branch turned a dull eye toward the horizon where the pale sun was trying to climb into the metallic gray-green sky. The bird cawed a baleful greeting. The air felt cold, dry, and crisp. Jim Higgins stood in the stillness of the early gray dawn for a moment, picked up his paper from the front steps, and returned to the warm kitchen.

In the living room, the television weatherman was attempting to paint a picture of optimism. Looking out the window, Jim thought it was a ridiculous waste of time. It was going to be a gray, cold, depressive day.

"Mornin', love," Carol said sweetly, kissing him lightly on his cheek. She could smell his faint splash of aftershave. "Love that shirt and purple tie."

Jim looked up from his perusal of the *Wisconsin State Journal* and sipped his coffee. "I'm going to invite everyone over on Sunday for the game if that's all right with you."

He watched Carol bustling around the kitchen. She looked

captivating in a pair of mocha brown dress trousers, an ivory blouse of silky fabric that formed soft folds from shoulder to shoulder and a dangly pair of earrings he'd bought her in Paris. *She's lovely,* he thought. She looked good in anything from a feminine dress to jeans and a sweatshirt or his favorite outfit—nothing at all.

Carol set her plate with a soft boiled egg and piece of whole wheat toast down on the table. She noticed Jim watching her carefully.

"Jim? What are you looking at? Is something wrong with my outfit?"

"Nope. You're just very beautiful." Jim's eyes softened, his smile subtle and filled with remembrance.

"Oh, for Pete's sake!" she exclaimed, waving a hand at him but smiling broadly.

"Just say thank you," Jim reminded her, looking up from the paper.

"Thank you," she said shyly. "Now. Back to Sunday. You just tell your crew to bring themselves," she chattered as she returned to the kitchen for a glass of orange juice. "We'll provide the food. I think your brat idea is perfect, and I'll whip up a few dips for some raw veggies. Will you make a fire outside after the game? We could make s'mores."

"Sounds good," Jim said, returning to his paper, enjoying her chitchat.

"Can't wait to see that little Melody again. She's just the sweetest baby."

"Who?" He looked around his newspaper at her.

Carol looked exasperated. "Melody. Paul and Ruby's baby. Have you met her yet?"

"Nope, but I'm sure she's adorable," Jim said, disinterested.

Finishing breakfast, Jim slipped on his wool overcoat and came back in the kitchen for a goodbye kiss. "Want to go to Piggy's tonight for dinner?" he asked, pecking Carol on the cheek.

"Oh, that would be nice," Carol said. "Pick me up downstairs about five? We can have a cocktail first."

"It's a date. See you then."

Entering the law enforcement center, Jim walked briskly to the elevator, then waited for the faint ding when it reached the third floor. He stepped out and greeted Emily, teasing her with a salute.

"Morning, sir. You have a couple of people in your office already. I let them in. Was that okay?"

Jim looked down the hall. Puzzled, he noticed his office door was slightly ajar. "Yeah, that's fine." He gave Emily a confused look.

"Just Leslie and Sam." In an exaggerated whisper, she said, "They came in *together* this morning. There's something going on, Chief. I can sense these things."

Jim whispered back dramatically. "My advice—don't go there." He lifted his eyebrows, tilting his head. Using his normal voice, he continued. "But thank you for letting them in. I always defer to your judgment when it comes to office etiquette." He rapped on her counter, turned, and walked down the hall.

Jim breezed into his office and hung his coat behind the door. Walking around his desk, he plopped down in his black swivel office chair. He laid his arms on the armrests and leaned back, studying the two detectives.

"Morning. What's goin' on?" he said politely, looking at them both. He had a brief flashback to another morning last June when Paul had sat dejectedly in the corner and told him Ruby was pregnant. He'd played counselor for over an hour. He hoped this was about something else.

"Good morning, sir," Leslie began quietly. "I have a confession to make."

Jim groaned inwardly. *Not another pregnancy,* he thought apprehensively.

"All right. Let's hear it," he said, praying for a reprieve.

"I may have impeded the investigation of the Girabaldi murder when I neglected to tell you about the picture I found in his file yesterday." Leslie looked at Sam, whether for a boost of courage or moral support, Jim wasn't sure. He recalled the odd behavior Leslie displayed yesterday when she'd held the picture of the army unit in her hand.

"You were acting a little strange," Jim replied. "Keep goin'," he said, leaning forward and placing his elbows on his desk.

Leslie took a big breath and began. "When I was on my last tour of duty in Iraq in 2011, I got involved with a guy named Wade Bennett. By involved, I mean a relationship. It ended very badly for me, but I came home and reinvented myself and tried to forget what happened. The other day I got a text from Wade telling me he was in the area and wanted to hook up, whatever that means," she said sarcastically. Her flawless forehead creased with a frown. She gathered her thoughts and started again. Jim noticed Sam was especially somber.

"The thing is, sir, Wade is a trained U.S. Army sniper," Leslie continued to explain. "He's deadly with a rifle or any weapon you put in his hands. He has formidable skills in concealment, reconnaissance, and wilderness survival."

"He's a killer!" Sam snarled loudly. Jim looked alarmed at the uncharacteristic response. He sat up a little straighter, focusing his full attention on Leslie's story.

"He's unstable," Leslie calmly answered, continuing her story. "I'm pretty sure he suffers from some degree of PTSD. He appeared on my doorstep last night, insisting he be allowed to see me. Sam stopped him." She looked over at Sam, and her gaze softened. "But I know he won't give up. He has a relentless, stubborn nature. He's a dedicated warrior, sir, and he's still on a mission, if you get my meaning."

During Leslie's explanation, Jim was watching the two of them closely, his blue eyes burning with interest, his brain racing. *Where was this conversation going?* he thought.

"Here it is in a nutshell," Sam said irritably, hijacking the narrative. He'd lost his patience with Leslie's unperturbed assessment of Wade's personality. Sam leaned forward and brushed his dark hair away from his face. His intensity surprised Jim. It was unnerving and entirely uncharacteristic.

"Wade Bennett and Rod Girabaldi were in the same unit in Fallujah in 2011, and their association could go back even further than that. Leslie didn't know Rod in Iraq, but in that photo of his unit that Leslie found in Girabaldi's file, they're both in the picture. What are the chances they both served in Iraq and then ended up living in the La Crosse area?"

Jim shrugged nonchalantly. "Could happen, I suppose."

"Pretty slim chance, I'd say," Leslie said, contradicting him, picking up the story again. "Rod is from Albany, New York, and Wade is from Viola, Wisconsin. Worlds apart. And here's the other thing. Rumors were flying around the base at Fallujah at the time of their service about a lucrative black market being run by American troops. They were siphoning off our fuel and selling it to local Iraqis and contracting companies, then pocketing the profits. This happened at quite a few bases and later at the U.S. military base in Basra. Military leaders there caught wind of it and investigated. They were successful in prosecuting a number of soldiers, but a lot of them were never caught."

"How much money are we talking about?" Jim asked bluntly.

"In one well-known case that made it to court, the thefts involved $15 million worth of fuel that was eventually sold to Iraqis for over $52 million. That's a huge profit. When the crime was finally uncovered, the charges included theft, bribery, and contract-rigging. It was a huge problem that cost our government billions of dollars, and some military personnel seemingly escaped without charges or convictions."

"So, let me get this straight," Jim said. "You think Wade and Rod may have been involved in an illegal fuel operation in which they made millions of dollars?" he asked, somewhat skeptically.

Sam spoke up again. "We have a theory about the antiquities

and Rod's murder."

"Go ahead, lay it on me. I'm all ears," Jim said, sitting forward in his chair. *This is getting interesting*, he thought. *Improbable, but interesting.*

"Just listen for a minute, Chief. Here's my theory," Sam said. He began talking energetically, using his hands to emphasize his points.

"Wade and Rod become friends in Fallujah and get involved in the gasoline black market where they make millions of dollars. They deposit their earnings in offshore accounts until they come home. Once here, they hook up again and begin to use their money to buy Middle Eastern art from dealers in Europe, which they import to the American market. When the truck is bombed at the wayside on Highway14, and the antiquities are discovered, they know their treasures could be recognized as stolen booty, especially if Leslie is involved in the investigation. Plus, the millions they earned illegally overseas may possibly come to light. Things begin to sour. They get in an argument—or something—and Wade kills Rod, or he kills Rod to shut him up about the money. Either way, at the end of the day, he is a trained sniper and an expert in reconnaissance. Killing Rod would have been a piece of cake for him. Now he's after Leslie. He's dangerous and unstable. Maybe he wants to get back together with Leslie so he can figure out our next move."

Or he's still in love with her, Jim thought. Instead, he said, "Sounds logical to me. But where's our proof? Evidence, people. Evidence."

"We need to comb through Rod's business records. Specifically, we need proof of offshore bank accounts or other large sums of money coming into his accounts from unknown sources," Leslie said. "We need to check Rod's telephone records to see where he was calling. That may lead to European or Middle Eastern dealers who are selling the antiquities. And we need to find out where Wade lives so we can bring him in for questioning. That won't take long. I've got an app on my phone I can use to locate him."

"Wait a minute," Jim said, suddenly energized. He stood up, propping his hands on his hips. "You," he pointed at Leslie, "are to

SUE BERG

be extremely careful when investigating this Wade guy. Obviously, he has more than a passing interest in you. People can be very possessive, especially if they have a history of mental illness. You said he has PTSD. Combine all of that with affection, and you get a very dangerous individual."

"Point taken," Leslie said, locking eyes with him. She felt his fatherly concern and male defensive sensibilities. Jim noticed Sam looking at her like a caged lion, protective and menacing. *Their relationship has already reached the tipping point,* he thought.

Jim continued. "Paul's been going through the financials. Let me talk to him. Meanwhile, I want you two to go back to Jay's Antiques and check out the two vases. See if there's some connection to the shop in Galena," Jim ordered. "I'm also going to talk with Luke about the autopsy results. Then I'm giving you free rein to check into the other stuff you mentioned. You got that?"

"Yes, sir," they both responded together.

"But be extremely careful about this Wade character. Many women have been killed by a former lover. You understand?" Jim asked, wagging his index finger back and forth from Sam to Leslie.

"Gottcha," Leslie said, her eyes wide with concern. Sam and Leslie left for Jay's Antiques, and Jim walked to Paul's cubicle.

"Hey, how's it goin'?" Jim asked, walking in and sitting down across from Paul, who looked bleary-eyed and exhausted.

"I'm tired. Melody had a bad night last night. Didn't get a lot of sleep. What's up with you?"

"I remember a few nights like that. The perils of fatherhood," Jim sympathized.

"She's worth it," Paul said, smiling wearily.

"What are you finding out about Girabaldi's finances?" Jim noticed Paul's desk was stacked with ledgers, taxes, and financial statements sorted into various piles. He could see Paul had given the records a significant amount of time, thought, and energy.

"Well, I'll preface this by saying I'm not a financial genius. What I do find surprising, though, is the amount of property he owns."

Paul grabbed a pile of papers, rifling through them. "Here we have two substantial warehouses—one 6,000 square feet, the other 4,000 square feet. He has five storage facilities, none of them smaller than twenty units, some larger. He owns two McDonald's and one Subway, all on the south side. Plus, two car washes, just like Emery said. Furthermore, he purchased land out by Valley View Mall a couple of months ago. Fifteen acres for $225,000 to build a proposed car wash and more storage facilities. The plans are right here."

"Makes sense so far." Jim nodded. "Keep goin'."

"So my burning question for which there is no answer is, where did he get the money to purchase and build all this stuff? He's relatively young, late-thirties, yet he has property that would take someone a lifetime to accumulate. He didn't have any higher education beyond high school, except for some military training. Granted, he seemed to be good at business management. Some people are just naturals. I get that. But he didn't have any substantial inheritance or other sources of income that I can see, yet he's probably worth $10 to $15 million just in real estate. And I haven't even gotten to his checking and savings accounts yet." Paul threw the papers back on his desk with a flourish. "So where's the capital and cash flow coming from?" he asked, frowning.

"I'm glad you asked that question," Jim replied, holding up an index finger. "Hold that thought, and let me go get you a cup of coffee. I'll explain Sam and Leslie's theory about that. And then, we need to get a search warrant and investigate his bank accounts. Maybe we can find some offshore accounts somewhere."

"Offshore accounts? How'd he get those? *Why* would he have those?" Paul quizzed.

"I'll explain Sam and Leslie's theory," Jim said brusquely, leaving to get the coffee. ◉

30

Once again, Sam found himself at Jay's Antiques & Curiosities on Grand River Boulevard, but Leslie was no longer interested in playing husband and wife this time. She smelled the prey. Posing as someone other than Officer Brown was not an option. She fully embraced her role as a policewoman and detective, no questions asked.

Entering the huge building, Sam and Leslie found a clerk. They flashed their IDs.

"We'd like to know if the two Iraqi tenth-century vases that were here a week ago are still available for sale?" Leslie began, her voice businesslike.

"I'm not sure. Could you show me what area of the store they were in?" the young female clerk asked. Leslie frowned. The young clerk continued to explain, "I work odd hours between my university classes, so I'm not familiar with all the merchandise yet."

Leslie and Sam began walking into the cavernous area on the main floor toward the back where they'd last seen the vases.

"They were in a showcase back here," Sam said, taking the lead, talking over his shoulder. He came to a sudden stop. "And it seems they've been sold," he said, looking into the showcase. The vases were gone.

"What we really need to know is who offered them for sale and who bought them," Leslie said.

"I'm not sure I can tell you that, even if I knew that information," the clerk said nervously.

"Then we'll need to speak to the manager, please," Leslie said, straightening to her full height, her body language uncompromising.

"Just wait here, and I'll see what I can do," she replied, backing away, then turning and climbing the stairs to the second floor.

"Why is it that nobody knows anything when the police start asking questions?" Leslie complained, clasping her gloved hands in front of her.

Sam smiled at her. "You've got your mojo on today. You'll find out what you want to know, I'm sure." Leslie cocked an eyebrow at him.

After a few minutes, a harried middle-aged man appeared at the top of the steps. The young clerk followed closely behind.

"Hello. I'm Greg Lawson. I'm the manager here. Is there a problem?"

"We need to know the seller and buyer of the tenth-century Iraqi vases that were for sale here last week. We believe they are at the heart of an investigation we're conducting," Sam explained reasonably.

"Oh, yes. Please follow me upstairs. I can look that information up for you." He motioned them up the staircase as he led the way. Entering the office, he went to a filing cabinet and pulled out a list. With his finger, he ran down the paper, stopping and starting until he came to what he needed.

"Yes, here it is. The seller is listed as Import Specialties out of Galena, Illinois. The buyer was a Mrs. Jeanette Anoli from La Crosse." He looked up from his paper, pleased with himself, smiling.

"Are you sure it was Import Specialties?" Leslie asked.

"Absolutely. I have the booth rental agreement right here and the date the merchandise arrived."

"When was that?" Sam asked, taking notes.

"We signed an agreement with them on September 1 of this year."

"Do you have an address for this Mrs. Anoli?" Leslie asked.

"Hmm ... yes. 2397 Bluff Side Road. I believe that's up by Grandad Bluff. Is that helpful?"

"Yes. Thanks for your time." Sam smiled sincerely. He turned to go but stopped abruptly. "Were there any other items in the shop from them?"

"Well, we were expecting a whole shipment this week, but somebody said the items had been destroyed in a bombing. That seems hard to believe, doesn't it?" the manager said incredulously.

"Not really," Leslie said. Seeing the manager's confused expression, she added, "Crazy things happen every day." ◉

31

The Benedictine Center for the Aged on Victory Street on the south side of La Crosse featured large one- and two-bedroom apartments occupied by retired priests and nuns of the Catholic faith. In a market saturated with elderly living choices, the Benedictine stood out from the rest of the offerings. Its spacious, airy apartments, Mississippi River vistas, and a stimulating variety of activities for its residents were popular features that appealed to those who had sufficient income. In addition, vespers were held each afternoon at four o'clock in the elegant chapel near the facility's main entrance.

A few minutes after four o'clock on Friday afternoon, Father Willard Renard knelt on the cushioned kneeling pad in front of his pew and began his evening prayers as was his custom each day. The brilliantly colored stained glass windows gleamed like jewels as the late afternoon sun passed through them.

"Bless me, Father God, for I have sinned and fallen short in the eyes of Christ. Forgive me, I pray, not for my sake, but for the sake of the sufferings and death of our blessed Savior, Jesus Christ," he intoned in his weak tenor voice, lifting his rheumy eyes upward to the large cross positioned above the ornate altar. The candlelight flickered warmly in the sanctuary and transported Father Renard backward in time to his memories as spiritual leader of Joliet Preparatory Academy.

He was proud (God forgive him) of his general overall good health despite his 83 years. His knees hurt sometimes, and his hips had been replaced. He was slightly overweight, a little flabby around the middle. Nevertheless, he was able to walk one mile on the treadmill in the recreation center each day. For that, he was most humbly thankful.

After vespers, he dozed in his favorite Lazy Boy chair in his cozy living room, his empty teacup resting on a small table nearby. Earlier in the day, he had searched his impressive collection of books and found the 1997 Joliet Preparatory Academy yearbook, which at this moment lay sprawled open on the coffee table in front of him, its pages yellowed and worn.

An odd phone call from one of the JPA students requesting a visit with him this evening had come as a complete surprise. He hadn't seen or heard from any of his "boys" for many, many years. In preparation, he had ordered sugar cookies from the facility's kitchen and brewed a pot of strong coffee for the guest. He didn't recognize the name of the man who called, nor did he find his name in the yearbook, either. Drew Phillips? *I guess my memory's not as sharp as I thought it was,* he mused.

His grandfather clock chimed six bells. He started with a jerk when a sharp, loud knock interrupted his little cat nap. Straining to stand from his comfortable chair, he shuffled to the door, turning the knob slowly. As the door opened, Father Renard studied the person in front of him. Medium height, late thirties, clean shaven—a face that most people would describe as average—dark wavy hair, nicely dressed. No bells of recognition went off in his brain.

"Good evening, son," he said with the utmost politeness. "Please come in."

"Thank you, Father Renard. It's been a long time, hasn't it?" the stranger said, smiling weakly.

"My, yes," Father answered. He turned and pointed his guest to an upholstered armchair near the Lazy Boy. "Please sit down while I get some refreshments."

The stranger made himself comfortable, folding his hands calmly in his lap. Father Renard ambled to the small kitchen and prepared a tray with freshly brewed coffee and a small plate of cookies. All the while, he was racking his brain, hoping he'd remember this person since he had a fondness for the academy students. Memories of them still warmed his heart. Carrying the tray into the living room, he set it on a coffee table between the two chairs.

"There now," Father Renard said, handing a mug to the guest. "Please help yourself to a cookie." Moving around him, the aging priest situated himself in his chair until he was comfortable. Then he turned his kindly face toward the visitor. His white hair was neatly combed, and within his wizened face, a pair of blue-green eyes blazed with a curiosity born from a career of nurturing and loving people.

"I'm afraid my memory isn't quite what it used to be," Father Renard began. "I apologize. Who did you say you were again?" His eyes, once clear and discerning, had become cloudy with confusion and momentary memory loss. Frustrating as that was, he was still an astute and careful listener. He focused his attention on his guest, sipping on his cup of hot coffee.

"Oh, my name isn't important. I just have such memories of the days at Joliet. They were quite something, weren't they?" The visitor's eyes seemed especially intense. He looked carefully over his coffee cup into Father Renard's face as if challenging his sputtering memory and aging body.

The elderly priest had a momentary chill of apprehension. A prickle of goosebumps crawled up his arms. He dismissed the feeling as the foolish figment of a weak old man's imagination. Then he said, "As I recall, we ran a pretty tight ship. The boys at the academy were like one big, happy family."

The stranger hesitated, his smile fading. "Your memory fails you, Father. Not everyone felt they belonged to your big, happy family," the man said, his voice taking on an antagonistic edge. "Do you happen to remember Brett Hoffman?" he asked, taking a different tack. He made the slightest movement, placing his right hand inside his coat pocket. He let it rest there.

"Brett Hoffman? Yes, I remember him as an average sort of kid," Father remarked.

"Too bad about what happened to him. Did you hear about that, Father?"

"Yes, what an absolutely horrible thing. I don't think they've figured out who the bomber is yet. But that detective. Hmm, what's his name?" His memory stalled, and he tapped his chin as he thought. Then his eyes cleared. "Higgins. Yes, Jim Higgins. He's that detective who was on the TV the other night. Maybe he'll figure out who the culprit is."

"Father, do you remember the things Brett used to do?" the stranger asked, irritated by the rabbit trail the conversation was taking. "What he did to some of the other boys? Do you remember that?"

"Well, now that you mention him, he was something of a hoodlum, as I recall. Seems he was in my office a lot, and it usually involved one particular student. Something about being a bully and the dirty tricks he played. That type of thing."

The stranger felt a wall of rage building inside him which threatened to overwhelm him. Father Renard didn't remember him or recognize him. How could that be? All the more reason to give him what he deserved. *He was supposed to protect me, take care of me, be the dad I never had.* Wasn't that why his mother had sent him to Joliet in the first place? "To come under the care and spiritual influence of other men and boys." *What a joke.* Instead, he'd been unfairly tormented and goaded, unable to physically defend himself against the brutish antics of boys who were older and much stronger.

"You don't remember me, do you?" the stranger asked, his voice a mix of regret and pity. *The story of my life. Average, dull, always standing in the shadows.* His hand tightened around the pistol in his pocket.

Father Renard looked confused as he studied the stranger. Then slowly, a light of recognition showed in his eyes. "Well, I'll be—"

There was a rustle of fabric and the quick movement of a hand. The gunshot penetrated Father Renard's chest with an explosive bang. The stranger observed Father's expression—a combination of confusion and shock and then remembrance. "Jordan," he whispered. His head lolled to the side, he made a gurgling sound and slumped forward, the front of his pale shirt turning a brilliant red.

The acrid smell of gunpowder drifted uneasily in the tastefully furnished apartment. Moving efficiently around the room, the shooter wiped down his coffee cup and the doorknob. He wrapped the cookie carefully with a paper napkin and stuffed it in his jacket pocket. He'd take the piece of paper off the lens of the surveillance camera in the hallway when he left. The stranger looked down at the slumped, graying figure in the overstuffed chair. For a moment, he almost felt remorse and regret.

Almost.

"I'll bet you'll never forget me now." He closed the apartment door quietly and was gone. ◉

32

Jim Higgins navigated the Suburban into the tight parking space just a block away from Piggy's restaurant. The river lay dark and quiet in the dusk, ripples meandering with the flow of the water. Despite the steady, unrelenting drizzle that enveloped the city, a few couples walked hand in hand under bright umbrellas at Riverside Park, and the ever-present joggers were out and about.

Inside the familiar restaurant, Jim and Carol were shown to their favorite table, one that provided a beautiful view of the river. The atmosphere was quiet with an undercurrent of bustling efficiency. Low lighting and small votive candles illuminated each table. New and repeat customers were pleased with the expertise of the wait staff.

"I'll have an Old Style Light, and my wife would like a brandy old-fashioned sweet, please," Jim said, smiling to the pert, enthusiastic waitress.

"Actually, I'll have a glass of Lambrusco, please," Carol said, catching the waitress' eye.

"Sorry, hon. I should have asked," Jim said apologetically.

"It's okay. You know me well, but it's a woman's prerogative to change her mind. And I can think for myself."

"That's true. You sure can. By the way," Jim said to Carol,

"everyone's coming Sunday, about three." Carol looked up from her menu. "We can get the food tomorrow, and I'll stack some wood outside for the fire."

"Oh, great! That should be fun," Carol commented, her eyes wandering down the menu. She noticed a distinct improvement in Jim's demeanor. "I hope it's all right that I asked my sister and brother-in-law, too. Vivian said that Craig doesn't get into football so much, but he needs to get out socially. Work is driving him nuts. He needs some downtime. John and Sara can't make it. They have other plans."

Back home on Chipmunk Coulee Road after dinner, Jim sank into the deceptively comfortable black swoopy chair despite its goofy design. He reclined and flipped through the channels on television, all 225 of them, then turned it off and picked up a new C. J. Box novel. After an hour or so, Carol appeared next to his chair. She'd changed into capris and an oversized shirt. She wore a puzzled look. Between her thumb and index finger, a half sheet of wrinkled notebook paper dangled as if covered with invisible germs.

"Jim, look at this." She gingerly handed the note over to him. "I just walked out to the mailbox, and this was lying inside on top of the mail. Should I be worried?" A frown creased her brow, and her brown eyes were dark with apprehension.

Scrawled across the half sheet in crude letters were the words,

WHO'S NEXT, HIGGINS?

Jim felt a hard knot of anxiety in his stomach, and his chest tightened with uneasiness. The note suggested someone was dead, and there would be more deaths to follow. Whoever it was knew where he lived. His mind raced with the implications. He looked up to find Carol staring at him, her hand resting on her chest, her eyes wide with unanswered questions. Jim quickly got up and took her in his arms. She stiffened and pulled back slightly. She repeated her question.

"Should I be worried?"

"Listen, we have excellent locks on all the doors of the house." An unreadable expression crossed Carol's face.

"You mean there is something to worry about," she said, her brown eyes searching his face.

Jim struggled to reassure her. "No, no, not necessarily. My first thought is this might have something to do with the truck bombing." The note flapped around in Jim's hand as he made gestures. "You know, I had that news conference which showed images of the bomber." Carol's eyes nailed him to the wall.

Despite her look of skepticism, he continued his sputtering rationalizations. "Maybe someone is playing a practical joke," he said weakly. In his gut, though, he knew this was no joke. He lowered his hand, the note dangling like a limp dishrag.

Carol pulled away and began pointing her index finger at him. "Jim, don't patronize me." Her voice was angry, and her eyes flashed. "When we got married, I knew there would be moments like this when your cases might come home to roost and spill over into our personal lives. You're failing me miserably if you expect me to accept that bullshit answer."

Her voice had risen in volume, and she stood in front of Jim, challenging his authority. She crossed her arms over her chest and waited. Her face was a stony mask, and Jim noticed her nostrils flaring, her breathing coming in irregular puffs. The silence seemed deafening after her tirade.

"Well?" She was not backing down. "Jim?"

"Okay, you're right." Jim held up a hand, surprised at the audacity of her challenge. "But I don't know what it means yet. It's obviously a threat, but how it ties into the case, I'm not sure at this point."

Carol seemed to calm down a notch. She lowered her arms until they hung at her side. Her face softened a little. Jim continued. "Really, that's the truth, honey. You just gave it to me one minute ago, so I haven't had time to think it through ... or investigate."

She let out a pent-up little sigh. "You're right. That wasn't fair.

You haven't had time to investigate. I can live with that." She crossed the room and pulled the heavy drapes closed. Turning back toward Jim, she gauged his reaction.

"Come here," he said, holding out his arms. Carol walked across the room, and Jim wrapped her in a hug. "I'm sorry. My bullshit meter must be malfunctioning," he said softly. Carol grinned and gave him a soft punch in the ribs. But immediately, her expression turned serious again.

"Listen, I know you'd protect me with your life," she said, leaning back and gazing into his blue eyes, "but promise me you'll tell me when something you're working on could harm us, okay?" Jim looked frustrated and rolled his eyes, tipping his head back to stare at the ceiling.

"Damn," he whispered.

"I know, I know," she said impatiently, placing her hands on his chest. "It goes against your protective male instincts to bother me with the gory details of your cases, but I think I deserve to know, especially when it threatens the security of our home."

He brought his gaze back to her, arguing with himself. Her confrontation was laden with concern. He sensed an unsettling disquiet between them, and it made him very uncomfortable. He pulled the corners of his mouth down in an expression that looked like defeat. "That's fair. You've got it. Sorry." Kissing her lightly on the forehead, he flipped his phone open and dialed. "I'll call Paul. He might have some ideas about this." Carol untangled herself and walked to the kitchen.

"Hey, Chief. What's up?" Paul asked. Jim could hear little gurgling sounds.

"Are you holding Melody?" he asked.

"Yeah. Ruby ran to the store for a few groceries. Melody's being good. So far."

Jim continued. "I need to run something past you. We just got home from dinner at Piggy's, and Carol found a note in our mailbox." He described the note. "It says, 'Who's next, Higgins?' What do you think about that?" A few moments of silence ensued.

"You thinkin' it's the bomber?"

"Yeah. I'm ninety percent sure it's him."

"Run it down to the lab tomorrow and put an order in to have them check for fingerprints and DNA. But my guess is it'll probably be clean," Paul suggested. "It's worth a try, though. Other than that, it's a moot subject until we get more information. Or the bomber makes another move." He paused, sensing Jim's frustration. Then he asked, "How'd Carol react?"

Jim strolled into the living room toward the windows that overlooked his backyard, well out of earshot of Carol. In an intense voice, he said, "Well, she's ticked. But I think I talked her down. She was feisty, though."

"The home is where a woman should feel the most secure," Paul said. "This moron, whoever he is, messed with her sense of safety and well-being." Jim thought, *Boy, you've come a long way in your understanding of women.*

Paul continued. "Maybe you should install a security camera near the entrance of your driveway. Might help her feel a little safer. You're gone at odd hours sometimes, so she'll be there alone. That might be the issue."

"Yeah, you're probably right. I suppose I could do that," Jim mused, sounding distracted.

"Just saying. It might be worth it until we get this case wrapped up."

"Good idea. Thanks. See you Sunday."

Jim walked to the kitchen and retrieved a baggie. He placed the note in it, but their prints were embedded all over the surface by now. While he was standing there, he had another thought. *It could just as well have been a bomb in our mailbox.* The thought made him grab the edge of the countertop. He leaned his forehead against the upper cabinet, his breathing rapid, his heart taking on a panicked rhythm. If that had been the case, Carol could be dead right now or, at the very least, seriously injured. So in a sense, the note was a death threat. *Who knew what this creep would do next?*

With that thought, anger toppled his logical reasoning and calm disposition like a wrecking ball smashing a sturdy building. Three words scrawled in pencil on a piece of paper had scaled the walls of their security and happiness. His wife was alarmed and intimidated. That was unacceptable. He went to find Carol.

The bedroom lamp next to their bed was turned low. Carol was flipping through the latest issue of *House Beautiful.* She looked distracted and tense, turning a page noisily without reading it. Jim walked in and sat down on the bed next to her. He gently removed the magazine from her hands and laid it on the bed.

"Are you okay?" he asked her softly, giving her a kiss and clasping her hand. He noticed her lacy nightgown and the soft swell of her breasts beneath the fabric.

"Yep. As long as you're here with me, I'm fine," she said, but the tension beneath the words was like a taut fiddle string. She studied his handsome face. *What would I do if I lost him?* she thought. She continued. "I may have overreacted a little bit, but I don't want to ever take our happiness for granted. And when some idiot strolls in and runs roughshod over the security and love of our home, it gets my dander up." Her nostrils flared, and Jim could see tears forming in the corners of her eyes. "Jim, I've waited all my life to find someone like you. And here's an FYI for you. I'm not willing to lose you to some friggin' nut." By now, her breathing was rapid, and her cheeks flushed. A tear escaped and ran down her cheek. She brushed it away angrily.

"I hear you," Jim said gently. "You have every right to be angry." He was still coming to grips with the strength of her reaction. The anonymous note had certainly jump-started her fight and determination.

"Come on. Let's have a cup of tea and try to relax. We'll make a plan," he finished, grabbing her hand and pulling her out of bed in the direction of the kitchen.

After tea, they crawled into bed. Jim reached over in the darkness and pulled Carol close. She snuggled her head on his chest, and they laid like that for a while. Finally, Jim spoke.

"I'll get going on that security camera by the driveway." He paused a moment. Carol stayed quiet. "Are we good now?" he asked in the dark.

"We're good now. Thanks for listening." Carol said sleepily as she rolled to her side of the bed.

"All right then," Jim said, but Carol was already snoring softly. He spooned up against her, but sleep did not come until later. ◉

SATURDAY
OCTOBER 27

33

Walking the aisles of Home Depot the next morning, Jim scanned the home security section for outdoor cameras. The selection was considerable, so he wandered some more until he found a sales assistant. After listening to multiple spiels about each one's quality and wonderful features, Jim opted for a higher grade camera with a wide-angle lens, crisp night vision in black and white, and a simple SD card. The salesperson recommended that Jim use online assistance to get his IP address up and running. He laid down $200 and went home with a very nice camera that he hoped would restore Carol's confidence in him.

When he got home, he covered the lens with paper and spray-painted the camera a dull brown to match the tree. Then he mounted the camera about eight feet high on a large oak twenty-five feet from his mailbox. He aimed the camera at the driveway entrance and made sure it was in clear view of the mailbox, although he doubted that the bomber would contact them again with a note.

"Now, let's see if it's working," he said to Carol after he'd been online and clicked through the setup. A beautiful clear image of their driveway flipped on the screen. "Looks good. How's that make you feel?" he asked Carol.

She leaned over him and wrapped her arms around his shoulders, kissing his neck. "Thank you, honey. It seems kinda stupid, I know, but just having that camera there makes me feel like we've put up a big sign that says STOP before you come in here and do something illegal."

Jim stood and faced her. *If someone wants to hurt us, a surveillance camera is not going to stop them,* he thought. But maintaining his ability to protect her was important to him.

"Listen, that's not stupid, and I'll worry less if I know you're safe when I'm out at night or gone out of town," he said. Looking into her brown eyes, he reiterated, "It's not stupid." He kissed her lightly.

"Thank you. I feel better already. Lunch in fifteen minutes?" she asked sweetly.

"Absolutely."

Jim and Carol were enjoying soup and grilled cheese sandwiches when Jim's phone buzzed.

"Higgins."

"Jim, it's Kelsey Waterman, City Police. We're on the south side at the Benedictine Home for the Aged on Victory Street. Someone called because Father Renard didn't show up to walk on the treadmill in the gym. They opened his apartment and found him in his chair shot through the heart. Figure it happened last night between six and eight o'clock. Luke said to call. He said you might have a connection to this guy?"

"Wait a minute. Father Willard Renard? The former administrator at Joliet Academy? That Father Renard?" Jim asked, sitting up a little straighter. Carol's eyebrows went up a notch.

"Yeah. You know him?"

"Not personally, but I've been studying the history of the academy in relation to the bombing case. He was the administrator there before it closed. I'll be there in half an hour. Tell the crime scene crew I'd like access to the scene, if possible."

"Sure, no problem. Luke Evers is already here. See you in a while," the policewoman said.

"Something up?" Carol asked.

"Yeah, I'm going to run into town for a bit. But I'll be home for dinner." Jim finished his lunch quickly, put on his insulated ski jacket, and headed into town. He called Sam on the way.

"Sam Birkstein."

"Sam, can you meet me over on Victory Street in a half hour? There's been a murder at the Benedictine Home," he said.

"Sure. I'll be waiting for you. I'm at Goodwill right now. That's only a couple blocks away."

When Jim arrived at the nursing home, two police squad cars and an ambulance were parked in front, but there were no flashing lights. Jim met Sam in the lobby, and they made their way to Father Renard's apartment. Snapping on blue latex gloves and booties, they entered the apartment and found Luke examining the victim.

"Hey, we've got to stop meeting like this," Luke said with a deadpan expression, reciting the worn-out one-liner.

"What do you think happened?" asked Sam, kneeling in front of the victim. Father Renard had slumped forward in a pose, not unlike that of someone in fervent prayer—head bowed, body bent low, face still and serious. *Maybe he was praying when he died,* thought Sam.

Luke looked up at Jim. "Victim apparently let the killer in. No signs of a struggle. Looks like they may have had a conversation over some coffee and cookies. Shot in the chest at close range with what looks like a small-caliber gun of some kind. One strange thing, though. I don't think he died right away. Tough old bird. It looks like he pulled this old yearbook across the coffee table toward himself."

Pointing to the bottom of the open page, Luke continued with his analysis. "Some blood here indicates he opened it to this page of student pictures. Was he trying to tell us something? Is his killer on these pages?" Luke shrugged. "Might be something to get you started," he finished, looking up at Jim and Sam.

Jim was writing the page numbers from the yearbook in his little memo pad. "I've got Brett's yearbooks in my office." He turned to Sam. "I'm going over there to get those. I'll study them this afternoon.

I'll bet the killer is connected to Brett Hoffman somehow."

"You mean the victim from the bombing?" Sam asked, a quizzical look on his face.

Jim stared at the floor and ran his fingers through his gray-blonde hair. "Yeah. Father Renard was the second one on the list," Jim said, his face lighting up with understanding. "That's what the note meant."

"What note?" Sam asked, confused. "You're not making sense, Chief."

Jim pulled the cryptic note encased in the baggie out of his pocket, handing it over to Sam and Luke.

"Carol found it in our mailbox last night."

"Whoa. That's not good," Sam said grimly as he read the scrawled message.

"No, it's not. Carol was torqued," Jim shared, grimacing as he remembered her stance in the living room, her finger wagging at him. He called Carol.

"Jim? Everything all right?" she asked, a hint of angst in her voice.

"I'm going to run down to my office to pick up some stuff that I need. I'll be home in about an hour."

"Why are you calling me? You don't usually do that."

"We've got another murder." Jim could hear Carol's gasp over the phone. He hoped she wouldn't go off the deep end. "It's not a bomb this time. Someone murdered a priest. Shot him in the chest. I think he's the second victim. The first was Brett, the driver of the truck."

Carol's response surprised him. "Be careful. I'll be waiting for you." Carol's phone clicked off.

Gray and damp, the day had turned out to be a weather disappointment. October was making its exit, and November was arriving. Today was a reminder of that. November was Jim's least favorite month, along with March. Looking at the stark landscape as he crossed town to his office, he knew why. The trees looked raw and darkly etched against the backdrop of a metallic sky. Jutting into the cold air, the beige bluffs were devoid of any color of autumn foliage. *Brown. Everything's brown,* he thought.

A couple of runners, dressed only in leggings and light sweatshirts, jogged with determination down the wet sidewalk, passing him in a flurry, their breath vaporizing into thin clouds. The air chilled Jim to the bone as he hurried into the investigative complex on Vine Street.

He took the elevator to the third floor. The office was eerily quiet without Emily's friendly face, the background noise of ringing phones, and the pool of busy secretaries. He took the note from his pocket and walked it into the locked evidence room. He returned to the office and flipped through the Brett Hoffman files until he found the Joliet Academy yearbooks from 1996 and 1997. He took them out, had second thoughts, and decided to take the whole box. He could spend the afternoon in his study going through the material.

He breezed home quickly since the Saturday afternoon traffic was light. When he came in from the garage, Carol was surrounded by family photos scattered on the dining room table along with a collection of photo mats, scissors, a ruler, and coordinating frames.

"Hey, whatcha doin'?" Jim asked. "Looks like some kind of project." He was holding the box of school stuff from the Hoffmans.

"Remember? I told you I was going to make a display of our family pictures in the hallway. This is it." She swirled her hands over the table as if they were magic wands that would complete the task for her. "I decided to bite the bullet and get it done. We'll have dinner later—lasagna."

"Mmm. Lasagna, one of my favorites."

Jim walked down the hall and entered his study. Dark walls, deep bookcases, and his father's antique desk made the room feel like a sanctuary to him, a repository of the treasures of his life. The hours he spent here reading, thinking, and relaxing gave him a sturdy foundation on which to build his world. He glanced at the books that filled the shelves, like C. J. Box, Louise Penny, and Tony Hillerman mysteries; the Bible in many different translations; books on Martin

Luther and Aquinas; American history, especially those written by David McCullough; *Foxe's Book of Martyrs*; crime scene textbooks; and some psychological volumes like *Reading People* and *Raising Cain*.

He thought if he listened carefully, he could hear the authors' voices giving him advice. The photos on the walls and his desk reminded him of his life with Margie. He was thankful Carol had embraced the twins, John and Sara, so warmly. Of course, they knew her as Margie's lifelong friend, so Jim's second marriage had been smoothly accepted by his children. *God, you've been so good to me,* he thought.

He shook himself out of his trip down memory lane and began to unpack the box of high school memorabilia from Amanda Hoffman. He sank into his padded chair, switched on his reading lamp, and spread the contents of the box on top of the antique desk.

After half an hour of perusing the material, a picture of Brett Hoffman began to gel. Report cards indicated Brett was an average student. Nothing too revealing there. A student handbook of behavior and academic expectations from Joliet Academy was interesting, but it didn't give specific insight into Brett Hoffman. Photos of football and basketball teams suggested he was athletic and enjoyed participating in sporting activities. A typical kid. Comments from instructors on his quarterly report cards included things like "more effort," "polite," and "needs to apply himself." *All things that could have been said about me at that age,* Jim thought.

It wasn't until he cracked open the yearbooks that odd references began to appear. A group called the "Nasty Nine" had signed off in every yearbook. A large number nine was drawn somewhere in each annual, and nine student names were listed under or around the number. Jim began making a list. Going on the internet, he researched and found each member. Three resided in California, two lived on the East Coast, one was deceased, and three were within the Tri-State area: Matt Fowler in southern Iowa, John Hesselink in the UP of Michigan, and Cory Barstad in Arlington Heights, a suburb of Chicago. He decided to call only the three who resided within a

SUE BERG

reasonable distance to the La Crosse area. The danger to them was more immediate. He called information, hoping they each had a landline. They did. He began calling.

As he talked to each of the three former JPA students, Jim outlined the bare facts of Brett and Father Renard's tragic deaths. They all were upset to hear about the violent way in which they'd died. He asked for input and ideas. In each conversation, Jim warned the classmates to be extra cautious about their movements and surroundings.

"Just be aware when you're out in public. Keep track of your kids. Communicate with your wives about your plans and where you're going. It's probably best not to go anywhere alone—just until we get this figured out," Jim advised. Of the three friends in relatively close proximity, only one, Cory Barstad, had traveled from Chicago to Brett's funeral.

"Man, he has a beautiful family," Cory reflected. "What a damn shame."

"Yes, it's very sad for them. Listen, I've been looking through the JPA yearbooks to see if anything jumps out at me. What's this group the "Nasty Nine" about? I saw references to that in Brett's annuals. You were a member. What kind of nasty stuff were you responsible for?" Jim questioned.

Cory became quiet. "Well, in this day and age, with all the emphasis on bullying, I guess you might say we were a gang," he softly confessed, seeming ashamed. "We were guilty of some pretty bad stuff during our four years at Joliet. You know, we lived at a private school with no parental input or discipline. We had dorm counselors, but many of them weren't equipped to deal with a bunch of rowdy teenage boys let loose on the world. There was structure, but boys could find all kinds of trouble to get into after curfew. So we often got into situations that today, when I look back on it, were probably pretty damaging to our victims."

"Like what?" Jim asked. "Can you tell me about some of the stuff you did to other students?"

"Oh, let's see ..." He took a minute to gather his thoughts.

"Crapping in somebody's shoes, tying kids up, then lowering them out a window and threatening to let go of the rope, giving a kid a swirly in the toilet bowl. Stuff like that." He paused a moment. "And there was the more subtle stuff. Following kids, giving them certain looks, sneaking in their rooms and standing over their beds during the night, threatening them if they told on us—intimidation stuff."

"That could be pretty disturbing to the victims," Jim said. "Can you think of any one kid you singled out to bully who would have held a grudge all these years?"

For a moment, Jim thought their connection had been lost.

"Cory? Are you there?" Jim asked.

"Oh, my God. I think there might be one kid, but I don't remember his name. Wait, Jason? Jared? No, Jason. Shit! I don't remember. We tended to pick on him more than most. I don't know why. I guess he was easy to intimidate, and he was a tattler. Always running to Father Renard's office. Do you think he might be the bomber?"

"Jason or Jared? Okay, that could be helpful." Jim added to the notes he'd already taken. "Do you remember any other details about this kid? Physical description, where he was from, that kind of thing?"

"He was kinda short, dark hair, shy and quiet. A whiner, always griping about something. I think he may have been from Arcadia or somewhere close. In that vicinity anyway."

Jim thought about the stolen license plate in Arcadia. A little chill ran up his back. "Okay, Cory. One more thing. When Father Renard was shot, he propped open his yearbook before he died. We think he might have been trying to tell us who his killer was. I don't see a Jason or Jared on these two pages or anyone with a name that resembles Jason. Do you have a yearbook at home anymore?"

"Oh, if I did, I wouldn't have any idea where it would be," Cory said. "We've moved five times since we were married, and with every move, we pitched out more stuff. Less to pack in a moving van. Sorry."

"What if I scan the class pictures and send them to you via email? That might help us get started. Could you do that?" Jim asked.

"Absolutely. Anything to help." Cory gave Jim his email address, and they exchanged cell numbers.

"If you think of anything else, please call me anytime," Jim advised. Cory hung up.

For the next half hour, Jim scanned the class photos from the four yearbooks of Joliet Preparatory Academy into a document and shot them off in an email to Cory Barstad. Maybe something would come of it. *We're close—really close,* Jim thought.

As he worked on the copying, Jim wondered how many adults he knew who had been intimidated or bullied over something. He thought back to his school days. He'd been bullied, but it hadn't led to any serious repercussions or emotional problems. He was sure Sara and John had been teased, and he was a cop, for Pete's sake. Bullying has been going on for centuries, but what was the tipping point that made some kids unable to tolerate it and then turn to violence? He didn't know. But by any standards, the bullying that had gone on at JPA was extreme and persistent. He hoped the clues he was collecting would point to someone soon. A killer was preparing to strike again—someone with a list and a plan. ⊙

SUNDAY
OCTOBER 28

34

By three o'clock Sunday afternoon, Jim and Carol's home on Chipmunk Coulee Road was filled with Packers fans, a few Vikings fans dressed in purple and white jerseys, and some who couldn't care less about football. With the game blaring on the wide TV screen in the living room, Carol served drinks and made sure the brats and other food flowed freely.

"Looks like everybody's having a great time," Jim said, smiling warmly, standing in the kitchen.

"You sound surprised," Carol answered, "but I knew they'd loosen up. They just needed to take a chill pill. Screaming at a bunch of overgrown men running around in tights seems like a fun distraction to me. It's probably some kind of therapy, but you'd have to ask Vivian about that." Carol giggled. Vivian was Carol's psychologist sister, whom she consulted about problematic situations in her life from time to time. Reaching to pick up a tray loaded with veggies, dips and chips, Jim intercepted Carol's attempt.

"Gimme that," Jim said. "You've done enough. Go sit down and kick back."

Carol wandered into the living room and found a seat next to Ruby. Paco, ever vigilant, hovered around Ruby and Melody, sniffing and laying his big head in Carol's lap. Finally, reassured that everyone was safe, he sprawled on the rug in front of the couch.

"She's such an adorable baby," Carol commented, clasping Melody's little hand in hers. A shout went up when the Packers scored a touchdown. Melody jumped at the outburst, pouted, and began to cry. "Let me take her so you can enjoy the game."

Ruby carefully transferred Melody to Carol's arms. Carol snuggled Melody close, her face taking on a peculiar radiant glow.

Across the room, Jim was watching Carol. She had a funny look on her face, one he hadn't seen before. He was having a hard time interpreting it. Joy? Longing? Regret? He didn't know. *Oh, boy. She's really fascinated with that baby,* he thought. *She better not be thinking what I think she's thinking.* Jim's thought was disrupted.

"Hey, Chief. That Denzelle Harris is some running back, huh?" Paul said in Jim's ear, happy and carefree. He grabbed a carrot stick and swiped it in some dip.

"Yeah, they finally got their act together so that they could score," he said, disinterested. He set the tray on the coffee table.

Paul thumped Jim on the shoulder. "Thanks for doing this. We needed some downtime."

"My pleasure. It's nice to have the house full of friends and family again." Paul followed Jim's gaze across the room to Carol. "Haven't done this since before Margie died."

"Boy, Carol's sure fascinated with Melody, isn't she?" Paul remarked, watching Jim's reaction.

At that instant, Carol looked up, and her eyes met Jim's. Her expression left him feeling a touch of wistfulness, panic, and concern, all at the same time.

"Too bad she didn't have a chance to have a baby of her own," Paul said, still watching Carol. He took another bite of carrot.

Jim's stomach did a little flip. "Don't even think those thoughts," Jim scolded Paul, his eyes clouding with worry.

"What thoughts?" Paul said, surprised at Jim's irritation. "Jeez, Chief, I didn't mean anything by it."

"Never mind. It's way too late for that anyway."

"Never say never, Chief. You're talkin' to an expert in that department." He began ticking off his fingers as he talked. "Never gettin' married, never havin' kids, never livin' in La Crosse, never gonna be a cop. I could keep goin'."

"Don't." Jim cut him off and went to the kitchen, returning with a box of matches in one hand and newspapers in the other. "I'm going out to build a fire. There'll be s'mores outside when the game is over," Jim informed him."You're in charge of getting everyone out to the patio."

The weather cooperated for the final campfire of the season. After the game, everyone meandered out onto the terrace in the lingering twilight. Finding a chair or cushion, they gathered around the warmth of the coals in the fire ring. The sky had turned into a swirling mass of reds and oranges as the sun sank in the western sky. Carol passed out s'more ingredients along with roasting sticks. As the marshmallows melted and turned golden brown, everyone topped the sweet goo with a Hershey bar and smashed it between graham crackers. It was the perfect ending to a great afternoon of fun.

Jim looked across the smoldering red hot coals to see Sam and Leslie quietly talking, their shoulders touching, eyes intensely focused on each other. Sam made a comment, and Leslie playfully punched him. The attraction was so obvious. *I can understand Sam's fascination with Leslie,* Jim thought. *Beautiful but damaged.*

"Those two work with you?" Craig asked, pointing his s'more at the couple across the fire from them.

"Yep. And they're both very good at what they do. Young with lots of enthusiasm."

"Looks like their enthusiasm right now is focused on each other."

"Yeah, I noticed. I hope they can keep it together at work."

"Romances at your place of employment are not usually a good thing." Craig sighed. "Don't even get me started." He made a wry face. Craig was Carol's brother-in-law and the founder of a startup company that specialized in the development and manufacture of intricate medical equipment used in the treatment of diabetes. "We've had to fire more than one employee for consummating an affair on the premises."

"Really? People do it at work?" Jim looked incredulous, and Craig nodded reluctantly. "Man, that must have been rough, walkin' in on that," Jim said, glancing over at him.

"You have no idea. My mental picture of the draftsman's table in the engineer's office has been changed forever. You don't want to go there unless you have to, but sometimes, you have to."

A half hour later, although Melody was bundled up warmly, she began to fuss. Ruby gave Paul a glance that meant it was time to depart. Everyone traipsed through the living room, gathering dishes and glasses and placing them in the kitchen. After everyone left through the front door, car doors slammed, thank-you's were shouted, and the caravan disappeared down Chipmunk Coulee heading toward La Crosse.

Jim and Carol cleaned up the remnants of the party. When they were done, Jim flipped the TV off, settling on the couch with the Sunday *New York Times.* An hour later, Carol peeked her head around the corner.

"I'm going to soak in the tub for a while. You could join me," she said, her brown eyes inviting.

"Tempting, but I'll pass. Going to bed?"

"Yeah, you coming?"

"In a while."

Later as Jim and Carol lay snuggling together, Carol laid her head on his shoulder, with her arm flung across his chest.

"Mmm, Jim, the finer points of making love are not lost on you, and I get to be the recipient." She sighed and dozed off, her breathing soft, her snores barely audible.

Just before Jim started to drift off to sleep, the expression from Carol's face when she was holding Melody drifted back into his mind. His eyes suddenly flew open.

"Carol? Sweetheart? Have you been using any protection?"

Carol lifted her head sleepily, her hair tousled and mussed. "What? Protection? You mean like the pill? No, but you haven't used anything either." *She's right about that,* Jim thought guiltily. She rolled off his chest. "Never mind. I don't think we have to worry about it. I'm starting menopause. I hardly have my period anymore."

Jim felt a gush of relief. "Okay. That's good." Suddenly he was very tired and happy. He cuddled up to her back, feeling her lovely body next to his. "Love you," he whispered in the dark. ◉

MONDAY
OCTOBER 29

35

EARLY MORNING

The cold penetrated the dark wooden box where Leslie was imprisoned. Despite wiggling her toes now and then, her feet felt like frozen blocks of wood. She shivered uncontrollably in her lightweight jacket and jeans. Reaching up in the darkness, she tentatively moved her fingers across her face. Her left eye was swollen shut, and she was sure a couple of teeth in her lower jaw were loose. The blood in her mouth tasted salty and metallic. A pounding throb radiated in her head and, although she'd never had a migraine, she now empathized with those who suffered with them. Hugging herself to keep warm, she winced when her hand brushed a couple of ribs that were undoubtedly cracked or broken from the impact of Wade's boot as she groveled on the floor, begging not to be raped. His concession on the sexual front had not prevented him from physically working her over. Leslie was sure he wasn't done yet.

Lying imprisoned in the dark, she lost track of time. How long had she been in here? Was it Monday yet? After the game at Higgins' house, Sam had dropped her off and drove away. When Leslie entered the garage, Wade grabbed her from behind. With a gun poked in her side, they crisscrossed dark lawns in her neighborhood until they reached his truck. Wade had stuffed her, restrained with duct tape, under the front dashboard on the floor on the passenger side of the truck. Scrunched in a ball, she recalled the intense fear she'd felt when she tried to visualize Wade's plans for her. It felt like her heart had stopped beating. Terror threatened to seize her by the throat and choke her to death. The ride in the truck filled her mind with the life-threatening possibilities that faced her. Rape? Probably. Beatings? Most likely. Death? She tried not to think about it. At that moment in time, her future ceased to exist. Now it was all about survival.

Now in the confines of a plywood box after her beating, nothing else mattered except her moment-by-moment survival. Wade was a misguided warrior, she thought. Someone who was trained to eliminate combatants, eradicate the threat, take no captives.

The silence that followed the violent beating was almost as terrifying as the abuse she'd endured. As if magnified, her hearing picked up every insignificant sound until all she could think about was Wade returning to do her in. She lost track of time when she passed out from the pain.

Regaining consciousness, she realized the locked wooden cage offered no decent chance of escape. Despite her attempts to break out of the box over the last few hours, she realized she wouldn't be leaving this man-made hell any time soon. Instead, her efforts to kick the door open had ramped up her discomfort and left her crying with thudding pain.

Her biggest fear was Wade's return. Wade was cruel and violent. When Leslie fiercely fought him off as he tried to rape her, his eyes burned with the realization that their relationship was really over. That she could never love him was a constant reminder to him of his failure with women. Rejecting his sexual advances seemed to give Wade a perverted permission to move to the next step. In his twisted line of reasoning, Leslie was sure he had crossed the rubicon. She did not harbor any doubts that he would put a bullet through her brain when he returned.

SUE BERG

Her thoughts drifted to her recent conversations with Sam. *Was she in love with him?* At times, she wondered if she was capable of loving another man. She felt so scarred, so calloused from her turbulent past with Wade. Her trust factor was at an all-time low.

But Sam had given her a glimpse of a loving, respectful relationship. He was the first man in her life who had really tried to understand her hopes, fears, and dreams. He had fought for her and protected her. She was damaged, but Sam held out hope that she could heal. Now this. Where was hope now?

Maybe I should pray, she thought. But for someone who doubted God's existence, that seemed even stupider than trying to beat down the door of the box that entombed her. Sam had listened empathetically as she opened up about her deep doubts and questions about God's existence. Did He really know about everything that happened on earth? What about evil? Why did that exist? Did God really have a plan for her life? Sam had quoted that verse: "For I know the plans I have for you; plans to give you a hope and a future." He seemed to believe that about his life. Did she believe it about hers?

Leslie liked the fact that Sam didn't preach at her. He listened. When he didn't have an answer, he didn't fake it. He just said he didn't know. They'd talked about forgiveness. What did it mean to be forgiven? What was the responsibility of the forgiver? Now in the darkness, another question plagued her mind. Could she ever forgive Wade for what he'd done to her?

She didn't have answers. But in the darkness of her imprisonment, in her pain and isolation, she decided she had absolutely nothing to lose. Her circumstances had backed her into a corner.

Desperation ruled the day. So she did something she thought she'd never do. She prayed.

God, I don't know if you exist or if you even care about me. But I need your help ... ◉

36

By nine o'clock Monday morning, Sam was having fits of anxiety. He paced in his small office cubicle, occasionally sitting in his chair, then jumping up to pace some more. He'd offered to stay with Leslie last night, but she'd refused him. To top it off, his butt was particularly sore—again.

"I'll be fine," Leslie said. "I have Paco and my phone. If Wade shows up, I'll stay inside and call you." She turned and gave him an alluring kiss. "You can come and rescue me again."

"You aren't making it easy to leave, you know," he said. He could still feel the impression of her lips on his.

"Gotta keep you interested." Opening the Jeep door with a jerk, she slid out and ran to the side garage door, where she turned and waved. Sam sat in his Jeep, an involuntary shiver crawling up his spine as he thought about Wade. A locked door would not be a deterrent from what she'd told him about Wade's training and abilities. Still, Sam didn't want to alarm Leslie. Against his better judgment and ignoring the alarm bells clanging in his head, Sam had driven off to return to his own apartment.

Now sitting on the edge of the desk with the phone to his ear, he heard the voicemail greeting again. "You have reached Leslie Brown. I'm unable to answer the phone ..." Why wasn't she answering?

Was she in trouble? When Sam thought about the threat of Wade running loose on the landscape, his blood ran cold.

Regardless of the situation, he was a police officer, and he had to display certain professional behaviors. But his thoughts were running ahead of his reason, and he wasn't feeling very professional right now. *Where are you, Leslie?*

"Oh, what the hell," he mumbled to himself as he walked down the hallway. He found Jim sitting at his desk, clicking through his emails. He knocked lightly on the door. Jim looked up, signaling him in.

"Sam, come on in. What's going on?" he asked briskly, deleting some more messages.

"I don't know, Chief. Something's wrong," he started hesitantly, fidgeting in front of Jim's desk. *Oh boy, not another real-life confession. I should have been a pastor,* he thought. Instead, he looked expectantly at Sam. "What's the matter?" he asked, slightly irritated.

"I dropped Leslie off last night about nine-thirty. She hasn't come to work, and she doesn't answer her phone or texts. That's not like her," Sam said. Jim thought he looked scared. Maybe this was what Craig meant when he warned him about in-house romances.

"Let's go out and talk to Emily. Maybe she knows something," he suggested, although in the back of his mind, he thought, *I don't have time for this hullabaloo.* They walked out to the lobby area, where Emily was chatting with another secretary. Jim caught a whiff of Chanel No. 5.

"So you need to type the report in this format. That's the way the sheriff likes them to be done." Emily finished giving instructions to the secretary and glanced up at Jim and Sam.

"Yes, Jim? What do you need?" Emily asked. Her eyes were bright with the anticipation of being helpful.

"We're wondering if Leslie called in this morning. She's not here yet, and she's not answering her phone." Jim repeated Sam's version, picking up some of his anxiety.

Emily's brow wrinkled, and her eyes clouded. "Well, no, she hasn't called. I just thought she was probably out on some assignment and would be in later." Her eyes traveled back and forth from Jim to Sam. "That is strange. She's always very dependable."

"Maybe she's checking on those vases at Jay's Antiques," Jim suggested, glancing at Sam.

"Already did that," Sam reported in a monotonous tone.

Jim turned to go down the hall.

"Go and get Paul," he said. "We need to check out Leslie's apartment, and it better not be some wild goose chase."

Paul and Sam arrived in his office in record time. They piled in Paul's F-150 Ford pickup, zipped down Lang, and hung a right on La Crosse Street, arriving at Leslie's duplex in less than ten minutes. Her front drapes were closed as they had been last night. The residence seemed especially quiet. Sam jumped out of the truck and ran up to the front entrance. He rang the bell and beat on the door. Inside, he could hear Paco barking. The side door of the garage was locked, so Jim looked in the garage door window. Leslie's little blue Prius was safely parked inside.

"Is there a back door?" Paul asked, looking over Sam's shoulder toward the backyard.

"Yeah. Let's try it," Sam said. They both jogged around the building to the back entrance. Jim calmly followed them. It was locked, so Paul jammed his shoulder against it, jiggling the knob at the same time. After a few attempts, the door popped open, and they rushed in. The only noise was Paco's frantic barking in the bedroom. The apartment smelled stale with a slight hint of dog. Sam hurried and opened the bedroom door. Launching himself up on Sam's waist, Paco licked and whined, his tail wagging furiously. Paul noticed the bed was still made, and it looked like Leslie hadn't slept there last night. Jim came up behind Sam.

"Paco needs to go out and pee," Paul said. "I'll take him." When Paul returned, Jim and Sam were still standing in the bedroom trying to get a handle on the situation.

"Looks like she's gone," Sam said. He turned to Jim, his eyes reflecting full-blown panic. "Damn! Wade's gotten to her."

"You don't know that for sure," Paul said, trying to calm him down. Jim looked peeved.

"Like hell, I don't! You didn't talk to him the other night," Sam snapped angrily. "That guy would slit your throat and never think twice about it!" He wasn't yelling yet, but he was working himself into a full-blown rant. "I've worked with enough criminals to know that much."

"Let's not rush to judgment," Jim said in a fatherly tone.

"All right, let's make a plan," Paul said calmly. "Going off half-cocked is not gonna help."

Looking around the bedroom, Sam noticed Leslie's phone resting on her nightstand. He walked over and picked it up from the charger. Holding up the phone, Sam looked over at Jim and Paul, his head angled to one side. "Well, now we know why she didn't return her calls."

"Do you know her password?" Jim queried. He was starting to get a little nervous. All the signs seemed to suggest an abduction. He continued petting the top of Paco's head. The dog let out a sharp bark, walking in a circle around Jim's legs. He tipped his head, looking up at Jim, barking again. It was clear Leslie's absence perturbed him.

"No, I don't know her password, but I know she would never leave behind Paco and her cell phone."

Paul had a sinking feeling in the pit of his stomach, and he let out a frustrated sigh. "Well, it would help if we could see her calls from last night after you dropped her off. Maybe she called Wade or texted him."

"Negatory," Sam responded firmly. "She was literally petrified of the guy. You'd be too if he were let loose on you." Jim and Paul stood still, exchanging a stony-faced glance. "Believe me, you don't want to know all the history," Sam continued. "It's not pretty."

Bending over Leslie's phone, Sam's dark hair hung over his forehead. Sitting on her bed, he persistently tried a variety of passwords. He knew she'd have an uncommon one. She was way too savvy to have some generic code for her phone. Racking his brain, he finally stopped himself. *Settle down. Think.* What had she said to him that first time he'd been here? He stared off into space, zoning out, taking himself back to the night of the bombing. Paco nudged Sam's leg. He felt the dog's warm breath on his hand, and he absentmindedly stroked his ear. *Paco. He's my number one protector.* It was worth a try.

Sam typed in "#1protector." Bingo. The phone chirped a greeting, and he was in.

"How'd you do that?" Jim asked, watching Sam scrolling through Leslie's messages.

"Don't know," he shrugged, the blue light from the screen illuminating his worried face. "My higher power must have placed the thought in my head." He sounded dead serious.

"Happens," Jim agreed, his hands in his pockets.

Paul sat down next to Sam on the bed, peering intensely at the messages. "Wait. Go back. Go to history and look at her searches. Remember, she was going to try to find out where Wade lived."

"Yeah, that's right. I forgot that." Scanning her searches, they noticed one for Wade Bennett. Opening it, the search revealed an address: Wade Bennett, 1455 Oneida Drive, Rockland, Wisconsin.

"Got it, sir," Sam proclaimed excitedly. "We need to get over there." He stood up as if he was reporting for military service. Jim almost expected him to say, "Reporting for duty, sir!" and salute.

"Whoa, hold on a minute!" Jim said rapidly. "We need to get our vests and weapons. You're the one who keeps telling us Wade is a killing machine. Remember? If that's the case, with his training, we need to be prepared. Hopefully, together we can handle him. Everybody needs to be dressed warmly in case we have to chase this guy through the woods, or he leads us on some wild survival odyssey." Jim started toward the door, then turned around when he realized nobody was following him.

"Come on. What are you waiting for? Aren't you coming?" he asked annoyed, turning back to face them.

"Aren't we forgetting something?" Paul asked.

"What?" Jim barked. Offended, he stared at his two partners. *So much for leadership,* he thought.

"Paco," Sam and Paul said simultaneously, looking down at Leslie's faithful companion.

"If anyone can find her, he can," Sam informed them. Paco woofed in agreement. Sam shook his head. "I swear he understands what we're saying."

"Okay, okay. Let's take him with us then," Jim said, studying the black Lab. "Whaddya say, Paco?" As if on cue, Paco barked loudly, whining and running in circles around the living room.

"Wait a minute. He needs his leash and vest. When he puts that on, he knows he has to work."

Sam ran to the back hallway and grabbed the items. Searching through Leslie's coat pockets, he found Paco's kangaroo chew toy. "Okay, now we're ready."

"It's about time," Jim said impatiently. "Let's meet back at my office as soon as we get organized," Jim said as they headed for Paul's truck. ◉

37

By eleven o'clock, Jim had consulted with Sheriff Davy Jones and told him about Leslie's absence from her apartment and their plan to head to Wade Bennett's place in search of her. Jones promised backup support if and when they needed it.

"Who is this guy? Some nut?" Jones asked brusquely, rubbing his neck.

"Yeah, you might say that. He's also a trained military sniper," Jim told him.

"That's all we need—a firefight with a whacked-out soldier. What else is going to happen?" he complained.

The atmosphere in Jim's office was somber. The team had reassembled wearing jeans, heavy ski jackets, hats, and gloves. They clamored out to Jim's Suburban and threw in their bulletproof vests and weapons. Then they loaded up and began the drive to Wade's farm. Paco sat on the back seat with Sam, whining occasionally, drooling on the immaculate upholstery.

The weather had turned nasty, the temperature plummeting to twenty degrees. Heavy dark clouds were moving in from the west. The local forecast called for an unusually early snowfall, six to eight inches with a hard-driving wind.

Jim clamped his flashing light on the top of his Suburban. Driving way too fast, he flew down Highway 16, dodging traffic until they connected with Interstate 90 toward West Salem. As they approached Rockland, Paul yelled out directions using the GPS on his phone.

"OK, Chief. You've got to take the exit for County U. Go about two miles, and Oneida Drive veers north," Paul instructed.

Jim exited off I-90 onto U, then flew past the turnoff for Oneida. He doubled back. Once they found the farmette, Jim drove down the road about a quarter mile to a slight rise in the land. He pulled the Suburban onto the shoulder of the road, parked, and grabbed his binoculars off the front seat. The property looked deserted and quiet.

"It looks like nobody's home, but we don't know that for sure. Let's park the truck in that little swale to the north of the barn. There are some evergreens that will give us some cover. We'll get out there and get organized," Jim said briskly.

They rumbled over the frozen field in four-wheel drive until they were behind the cover of the young bushy evergreens. Parking, Jim hopped out and opened the back door. He grabbed Paco's collar, snapped on his leash, and handed him over to Sam. They threw on their Kevlar vests, adjusting their clothes over the top of them. Each of them carried their police-issued pistols, and Jim carried a high-powered 30-06 rifle.

"Paul, you're with me. We'll clear the house and garage. Sam, you clear the barn first. Then let Paco work. Got your radios on?" Jim asked.

Paul and Sam nodded. The snow had started to fall in little hard pebbles that stung their cheeks. The sky was darkening, and the wind had a sharp, biting edge. The heavy precipitation was on its way.

"We got everything?" Jim asked. Sam and Paul nodded. "This weather's going to be on us pretty quickly. Let's hope to God Leslie's here somewhere. Sam, you're in charge of Paco. Ready?" Jim's blue eyes were somber under the bill of his Badgers hat. "Move slow. Be careful," he said softly but firmly.

Jim and Paul started off at a trot toward the house. Using trees and shrubbery as cover, they entered Wade's residence through the front door and began searching, guns drawn.

Sam carefully entered the darkened barn, his pistol drawn, cautiously creeping through the gaping structure. Paco was intensely alert. With his vest secure and buckled snugly, he was ready for action. Sam wasn't sure if this would work, but he'd seen Leslie give commands. He'd taken Leslie's nightshirt from the apartment, and now he let Paco sniff it. Pushing his nose deep into the fabric, the black Lab looked up at Sam, his brown eyes alert.

"Paco, find Leslie," Sam said seriously. Paco tilted his head, and he whined.

Sam repeated, "Paco, find Leslie."

Paco stood at attention, his head erect, his nostrils moist and quivering. Lifting his nose in the air, he suddenly trotted farther into the darkened barn, tugging Sam along. He was amazingly focused, and his urgency surprised and pleased Sam. Entering the gloom, Paco worked from side to side, sniffing and inhaling scents that drifted in the dusty cavernous building.

Jim and Paul had just cleared the house and garage when their radios crackled.

"Chief, Paco's going nuts! You need to get up here!" Sam said, his voice laced with panic.

"On our way," Paul said as he blew through the front door and began jogging up the driveway toward the barn. Jim followed in pelting snow that was rapidly blanketing the lawn and buildings. They ran into the unlit barn. Scents of baled hay and cow manure floated in the cold air.

In the back corner, under the hayloft floor next to an outer wall, Paco sat alerting in front of a locked plywood box lying on its side. It was about the size of a refrigerator. Old pitchforks, shovels, and rakes had been carelessly thrown against the box along with a few hay bales, all of it a hurried attempt to camouflage the container. Paco barked insistently, whining and snuffling at the base of the container, pawing at the hay, knocking over a fork. Suddenly from inside, Sam heard a cry and several knocks.

"Leslie, is that you?" Sam yelled. More knocking. Sam threw the hay bales aside.

"Quick, we need something to cut off this lock," Sam commanded, his eyes desperate.

"I've got a hacksaw in my truck." Jim ran to the Suburban and returned in a few minutes carrying the saw. Paco continued to alert, barking and creating a major ruckus. Sam began frantically cutting away the hasp on the box. When it finally broke off, he threw the lock aside and propped the door open. Jim and Paul knelt down and held the makeshift door up. Sam crawled inside, but Paco squeezed in ahead of him. Leslie was crammed in a corner. When she felt Paco licking her face, she began sobbing uncontrollably. Sam grabbed her hand. She was shaking from cold and shock.

"Sam, is that you?" she whispered, her speech jumbled, violent shivers racking her body.

"Yeah, it's me. You're going to be all right now, Leslie." He turned and yelled, "Call 911. Get an ambulance out here. We need a blanket and some water!" he shouted. Gently, Sam slid Leslie toward the edge of the box, but her screams of pain were more than he could stand, so he stopped. He stroked her hair and kissed her bruised cheek. "An ambulance is on the way," he whispered to her, taking her hands and blowing his warm breath on them.

"I prayed, Sam. I prayed," she mumbled, tears wetting her cheeks.

"That was the best thing you could have done," Sam said, choking up.

Jim arrived with a blanket, and he covered Leslie with it. Carefully, Sam lifted her head and gave her a drink of water. He gently laid her back down. She closed her eyes, weakly stroking Paco, who was riveted to her side. Jim found a piece of two-by-four and propped the box open. Sam ducked out of the box and stood next to Jim. Paul leaned in and held Leslie's hand, talking quietly to her. Sam was shocked at the sight of Leslie's injuries and hypothermic condition. His face was white, and he was breathing in little puffs.

"It's bad, sir. She's really beat up. She must have been out here most of the night," Sam said, his voice cracking with emotion.

Jim grabbed him. He engulfed him in his arms, pulling him close to his chest. He detected a faint smell of aftershave and maybe a hint of toothpaste. Jim thought of his son, John, in his depressive state after Margie died. Even grown men needed hugs once in a while.

"It'll be all right. She's tough. She'll hurt for a while, but she's going to be okay. She's got us. We've got her back." Sam pulled back, looking into Jim's blue eyes. He wanted to believe him, but he knew this trauma would further deteriorate Leslie's precarious emotional state. Her sense of security was already trashed. Sam stood rooted to the spot in the corner of the barn, his mind screaming with outrage at what Wade had done to her. She was lucky to be alive. The whole situation threatened to undo him. He turned and knelt next to Leslie again, holding her cold hands, softly reassuring her.

They all looked north when they heard the faint wailing of an ambulance screaming down Interstate I-90. The snow was falling heavily now, obliterating the dark woods to the north of the farmstead.

"Let's get the door off this box, so they can just lift Leslie out," Jim said, grabbing a small crowbar. They pried the hinges off and laid the door to the side.

"Ambulance is coming," Paul said, turning back to Sam. "A few more minutes, Leslie. Just hang on," he encouraged.

Jim sat on his haunches, talking quietly to Sam. "I'm just so glad we found her before Wade came back. Listen, you go with Leslie in the ambulance. Paul is putting out an APB on Wade. We'll need to ask Leslie some questions, but that'll come later when she's able to talk. She might need some surgery, so you stay with her. Call her parents in Decorah."

Sam nodded, regaining his normal calm composure. He looked back at Leslie. She was quiet, her hand on Paco's neck. The ambulance rolled up, and Jim met the EMTs. They did a quick assessment in the barn and then expertly loaded her into the vehicle. Sam explained that Paco would need to come, too.

"That's impossible. We don't transport dogs," the EMT said firmly.

Jim interrupted, his voice irate and loud. "Well, this will be your first time then, because this dog just helped us find this young woman. He's a hero, so he *is* riding in this ambulance." Jim's eyes were blazing, the authority in his voice intimidating. "Sam, you're in charge of Paco when you get to the hospital."

"But sir, I might lose my job because I failed to follow regulations," the young EMT argued, his eyes widening.

"I'll take care of that with a phone call to the ER," Jim said with a final flourish. "The dog goes!" he insisted, jabbing his finger in the air for emphasis. The ambulance attendant complied, shrugging his shoulders, a look of resignation on his face.

Another attendant signaled to Jim through the open back door. "Lt. Higgins, Ms. Brown would like to talk to you."

Jim jumped up into the ambulance and knelt by Leslie's side, grasping her cold hand in his. Her face was bruised, her eye swollen shut, and a little trickle of blood had run down from her mouth onto her chin. Her lips were swollen and purple from the cold. Jim blanched at the sight of her.

"I just wanted to thank you for finding me, sir." Her speech was slurred, but she continued haltingly. "Wade would have killed me when he came back. I know he would have," she finished. She grew pale from the effort to talk. She began crying again.

"Shh, shh. Don't talk. You're safe now. Sam and Paco will go with you to the hospital. And just so you know, Paco found you, not me. Sam helped, too."

Leslie nodded in understanding. "He's a good dog, isn't he?" she said, garbling her words slightly.

"The best," Jim said with a shadow of a smile.

"One more thing, sir ..." Leslie's hand tightened around Jim's. "He didn't rape me ... this time." The words hit Jim like a punch in the gut. He bowed his head briefly, vowing to hunt Wade down for what he'd done. He clasped his free hand in a fist, fighting the urge to punch something. Getting to his feet, he leaned over and looked into her eye.

"You're safe now," he whispered, touching her hair lightly with his big hand. He leaned down and kissed her forehead. Leslie closed her eyes as the morphine took hold. Jim jumped out the back, waving to Sam and Paco as the ambulance door slammed shut. Standing in the driveway in the swirling snow with his hands in his jacket pockets, he watched the flashing lights recede.

"Hey, Chief. I think you better come back to the barn," Paul said close to Jim's ear. Jim jumped involuntarily.

"What now?" he asked, backing up a few steps. "You call it in? We're gonna need some help out here."

Paul pointed toward the highway. "Jones' team just arrived."

Jim looked down the driveway and saw the La Crosse Sheriff Department CSI van coming, its headlights barely visible in the storm.

"I found some keys hanging on a hook by those cabinets in there. I opened a couple. They're filled with Middle Eastern artifacts, and some of them look really old. Maybe priceless. Of course, I'm no expert."

"No, you're not. Our expert is on her way to the hospital," Jim said curtly. He turned and followed Paul through the accumulating snow.

"You okay, Chief?" Paul's eyes reflected worry. The men stopped momentarily, facing each other, the falling snow billowing around them.

Jim's blue eyes revealed deep anger and frustration, his face frozen in anguish. "No, I'm not all right. I'm never all right when a member of my team gets beaten to within an inch of her life. When I finally find Wade, he's gonna remember my name," he snarled, his lips pulled tight in a grimace as he felt tears welling in his eyes. Pulling the rim of his Badgers hat down farther against the falling snow, he stomped into the barn. Paul walked in behind him, his chest tight with tension and worry. Opening some of the cabinets,

Jim was astounded by the variety of the antiquities.

"Holy cow," Jim whispered, temporarily putting his anger on hold. "These items look like they're thousands of years old. I can't believe this."

He carefully removed a gold and silver statue of a ram caught in a thicket. The workmanship was superb. The ram was carved from lapis lazuli, the gold and silver branches of the thicket hammered and woven together to resemble the vegetation of a desert shrub.

"This is a representation of the ram God provided for Abraham when he was going to sacrifice Isaac," Jim said, awestruck. "Boy, you're a long way from home," he said to the statue.

Paul stared wide-eyed at Jim. The guy never ceased to amaze him. Although Paul's biblical knowledge was limited and spotty, he recognized the names. "How do you know that, sir?"

"Well, the patina looks a lot like the other artifacts we found in the Hoffman truck. These articles are probably from Mesopotamia— modern-day Iraq. God provided a ram for Abraham as a substitute when he was going to sacrifice Isaac. The ram was caught in a thicket and couldn't get away, just like this sculpture shows." Jim continued to carefully assess the priceless object, rubbing the lapis lazuli ram with his thumb and stroking the twisted pieces of the metallic thicket with his fingers. "This is amazing. These are high-quality museum pieces," he concluded. He carefully replaced the statue in its wooden stall, then he turned to Paul and shifted his focus.

"We need to call Sheila Hayes at ICE and get her back up here as soon as possible," Jim said to Paul. "She's the only other person I know besides Leslie who can identify these artifacts and help us connect them to some larger operation."

"Right, sir. Sheila knows her stuff." Paul recalled the session with Leslie and the ICE expert. Her knowledge and expertise had wowed him earlier last week. "I'll call her when we get back to the office."

Jim removed his cap, running his hand through his hair. "Wade's all tied up with the antiquities. He's in this thing up to his neck. We need to call Galena police and advise them to get over to Import

Specialties and begin a thorough investigation—and be on the lookout for Wade."

By three o'clock, Jim and Paul had handed over the premises of Wade Bennett's farmstead to the La Crosse Sheriff's Department crime scene technicians. Traveling back to La Crosse, Jim and Paul drove to Gundersen Lutheran to check on Leslie.

The third-floor waiting area was packed with people. Some scrolled on phones, one harried young woman chased her screaming toddler across the carpet, and another pair of teenagers had retreated to a corner to play a quiet game of chess. Jim scanned the room and saw Sam sprawled across two chairs he had pushed together to make a type of bed. Lying under the chairs, Paco had collapsed on his side, his leash hooked under a chair leg. He was gnawing on his kangaroo toy. Walking over to Sam, Paul nudged him with his knee. His eyes popped open. Paco lazily lifted his head, then stood, stretched, and yawned.

"Oh, hi guys," Sam said sleepily, rubbing his eyes briefly. His clothes were rumpled, and he had thrown his boots in a nearby corner. He slowly sat up, disoriented and groggy.

"What's the update on Leslie?" Jim asked tersely. Paco put his muzzle in Jim's hand, looking for some affection. Jim leaned down and thumped his side, scratching him behind one ear.

"First," Sam held up a finger, "I called Leslie's folks. They were both going to pack a few clothes and drive up. They thought they'd be here by early evening. Second, the doctor—I forgot his name—is still assessing her injuries. A couple of cracked ribs, a few loose teeth, and a ton of bruises and hematomas. He seems to think she might have broken her right wrist, but an X-ray will tell the story. That's about all I know right now. Everything's still up in the air."

"We found more antiquities in Wade's barn. Actually, a whole lot more. We're calling in ICE to work with us. Can you stay with Leslie until her parents get here?" Jim asked.

Sam nodded. "No problem."

"We'll check back later," Paul said, thumping Sam on the back. ◉

38

"There's no evidence of DNA or fingerprints?" Jim asked, resting his elbows on his desk after returning to his office.

"No, the note you found in your mailbox doesn't have any DNA traces. Sorry, Higgins," the voice said apologetically. "What I can tell you is the paper was taken from a common spiral-bound notebook, the words written in a number two pencil. Other than that, it's a dead end for any evidence that might lead to the bomber."

Jim groaned. "Thanks." He'd no sooner hung up than his phone buzzed again.

"Hey, Jim. Luke here. Gotta minute?"

"Yeah. You have some news about the Renard murder?"

"Well, there's not much. The murderer used a small-caliber pistol, a compact semiautomatic. They're favored by women and first-time handgun users. I found chest trauma from a high-velocity shot at close range. The bullet entered the left side of the chest, shattering the sixth rib and passed through the left lung. The bullet's trajectory changed when it bounced off the sternum, entered the heart's right atrium, then passed through the left atrium. The bullet lodged itself in the muscle under the arm. The damage to the heart was catastrophic. Even with immediate medical attention, he couldn't have been saved."

"Too bad for the old man," Jim said. "Anything else?"

"Not right now. I'll let you know if I find anything else," Luke finished. He clicked off. A few minutes later, Higgins' phone beeped again.

"Hey, Lt. Higgins. This is Stephanie Klaus downstairs. Thought you might want to know what we found at the Renard apartment."

"Go ahead," Jim said briskly.

"There were surveillance cameras in the hallway by Father Renard's apartment, which the killer had covered with cardboard and masking tape."

"Yeah, we saw the camera when we came in. His method was crude but effective," Jim commented.

Stephanie continued. "When we watched the tape, everything was blacked out from 5:32 p.m. on. He must have covered the camera before he went in to visit with Father Renard. Might have had someone inside the nursing home help him with that. I don't know. The cup he drank from was wiped clean. If he ate a cookie, he must have taken it and the napkin with him. He was pretty careful. Door knobs were wiped clean, too. Doesn't look like there's much to go on. Sorry," Stephanie said dejectedly.

"Well, let me know if anything else turns up, and thanks," Jim said.

He leaned back in his chair and rubbed his eyes. Despite the distracting phone calls, he could still conjure up Leslie's battered and bruised face, the desperate and haunted look in her beautiful blue eyes. Eyes that now reflected the terror of a crushed spirit and a broken heart. *I should have listened to Sam when he told me about Wade,* he thought bitterly.

Carol rapped lightly on his door. She walked in and came around the desk. Jim stood and turned toward her. Wrapping her arms around him, she kissed him lightly.

"I just heard about Leslie," she said softly. "How awful. I'm sorry."

"Yeah, it is pretty awful. I thought Sam was going to lose it when we found her. He seems better now. The doctors are still assessing her injuries."

"Are you done here? I thought we might get a bite to eat and stop at the hospital on the way home," Carol suggested.

"Not quite. I've got to check on a few things. Give me an hour, okay?"

"Sure. Pick me up when you're ready."

After Carol left, Jim walked down to Paul's office. He was listening intently on his cell, his face in concentration mode, making a few notes on his desk pad. He hung up and looked at Jim.

"IRS. I found out that Rod Girabladi does have a couple of offshore bank accounts. The tax people have been working with the banks, one in Italy and one in the Cayman Islands, but they're just getting started, and the process can take a while. For the time being, we can assume he was probably trying to evade some major taxes, especially if he has significant amounts in the accounts."

"So what do we do in the meantime?" Jim asked gruffly.

"The IRS recommends we get a search warrant so we can have access to the transactions when the account information comes through. Without a warrant, we can't look at anything."

"I can get something ready tonight so we can have it tomorrow," Jim said. "Oh, one more thing. Verizon called. Girabaldi had been making calls to France and Italy on a regular basis every couple of weeks. Probably his broker for the antiquities in Europe. They're working on trying to pinpoint the location. They'll let us know more when they know more. And I also put a call into Sheila at ICE. She's going to catch a plane to La Crosse in the next few days to help coordinate the identification of the treasures we found at Wade's."

"Sounds good. That's some progress anyway," Paul said.

"Any progress is better than no progress," Jim said. "Carol and I are going to get something to eat and head over to the hospital. What about you?"

"I'll check on Leslie and pick up Paco. We're going to keep him until Leslie gets home and settled." Paul said. "Call me with updates."

Jim nodded, turned, and waved. "Catch you tomorrow."

The rattle of a metallic cart loaded with meal trays being pushed down the hallway penetrated Leslie's woozy brain. Glass plates and cups clinked together, the sound slicing through the muted atmosphere of the hospital room. Sam tiptoed to the door closing out the irritating hubbub. The lights were dimmed, and the drapes were drawn over the large window allowing just enough light for Leslie to make out the shadowy presence of Sam through her swollen eyelids.

"Hey, how are you doin'?" Sam whispered, leaning on the metal bedrail. His wavy dark hair was tousled, and his hazel eyes reflected deep concern.

Leslie groaned. "I've been better," she mumbled. She shifted her right arm restlessly on the mountain of pillows propped beneath it. The cast and its unfamiliar weight felt clumsy. She moved her legs and flinched.

"Your parents went to get something to eat. Doctor Harrison set your wrist in a cast. That's why it probably feels weird," Sam told her in a soft, compassionate voice. He readjusted her arm on the pillows and pushed a lock of blonde hair away from her forehead, running his fingers gently down the swollen side of her face.

"It feels good to be warm ... and safe," she muttered softly through a medicated haze. "Where's Paco?"

"Paul stopped by and took him to his apartment. He'll keep him until you're up and around."

Sam noticed Leslie studying his face. He wasn't sure what she was looking for. Her gaze made him feel uncomfortable.

"What?" he asked her. "What's worrying you?"

"Wade. Did you find him?"

"No. But that's not your problem. Lt. Higgins has made that his mission, believe me. Right now, you just need to be quiet and heal."

"Me, quiet? Are you kidding?"

"No. I'm not kidding." Leslie's eyes closed. She was exhausted from the brief exchange. In a few more minutes, soft snores emanated

SUE BERG

from her swollen lips. Clasping her hand, Sam continued his vigil.

He heard a rustle behind him. Carol and Jim slipped in next to the bed. At the sight of Leslie, Carol gasped, lifting her hand to her mouth. Tears welled in her eyes. Jim nodded somberly, then crooked his finger at Sam and Carol and pointed to the door. They followed him out into the hallway.

"What's the prognosis?" he said, his blue eyes searching Sam's face. He wanted to grab the nearest doctor and nail down the injuries and Leslie's recovery time.

"Her right wrist had a hairline fracture, so they set it in a cast. Her eye that's swollen shut will be okay; it's just bruised. She has a couple of cracked ribs which are going to give her a lot of discomfort. Over time, the hematomas and bruises will heal." Sam completed his injury discourse and leaned against the wall. He let out a sigh at what wasn't being said and had to be faced. He went on.

"But the worst is the damage to her peace of mind. It wasn't good to start with, and now ..." His words drifted away. He fought back tears, shaking his head back and forth.

"Oh, Sam! I'm so sorry this happened," Carol blurted. She grabbed his hand and squeezed it. "But I know what it's like to lose your sense of security. After my attack last June, every little sound made me jump, and I didn't sleep well for a long time. But Jim surrounded me with attention and love. That's what Leslie's going to need, too—someone who's there for her because she'll be scared and jumpy." Carol's brown eyes seemed like liquid pools of love.

Sam nodded, afraid to speak for fear he'd lose it. Instead, he bit his lower lip until it hurt. In the awkward silence that followed, Jim pulled Sam to him and briefly hugged him.

"Carol's right. Things will get better in a while. The waiting will be the hard part," Jim said.

Sam gave a quick nod. *Sheesh, any more nodding and I'll turn into a bobblehead,* he thought. Finally, he found his voice. "Got it, Chief. I'm in it for the long haul as long as Leslie lets me."

"Atta boy. We're always here as a sounding board. Trust me, it'll be worth it," Jim said, stepping back. "I want you to stay with Leslie until she gets home and can move around without too much pain. You going to be okay?"

"Yeah, Chief. I'll be fine," he said, turning back to the room.

Grabbing Carol's hand, Jim pivoted, and they started down the hall.

"I'll check back tomorrow," Jim said with a wave of his hand.

Wade Bennett sat on a hillock a short distance from his Rockland property. It was a haven for deer and rabbits, thickly populated with wild blackberry brambles, sumac, and buckthorn shrubs, although none were here now. Dressed in his Cabella brown and green camo insulated pants and jacket, he was invisible to the naked eye. From a distance, he imagined he might look like a rock or some shrubbery. He was prepared. His insulated boots, stocking hat, and long johns kept his core warm. Lightweight gloves stretched over his large hands gave him the flexibility to shoot, observe with his binoculars, or take a drink of water.

When he approached his property, he could see the commotion of the police presence at the farm. He quickly drove past the farmstead a couple of miles farther until he came to a two-wheel dirt trail leading into a thickly wooded area. Parking his Chevy truck on the backwoods logging road, he spent a few hours in his vehicle, stretched out on the front seat comfortable in a thick down sleeping bag, trying to stuff the panic that reeled in his gut. Then, he jogged on foot and circled around his neighbor's field to this sheltered lookout on a small hill.

Now he watched the methodical procedures unfolding at his property. The jig was up. He could already imagine the DNA rising from every surface. Everything he'd touched was imprinted with his unique make-up, and the cops would use it to hunt him down with unmerciful resolve.

He'd have to go underground for a while until he could safely get out of the country. The next twenty-four to forty-eight hours were crucial. He would rely on his survival skills, keeping a low digital profile—going dark. He had a number of spots where he could hunker down, quietly existing until the heat at the farmette dwindled back to normal. If he could keep ahead of the cops, he might be able to escape arrest and prosecution.

Right now, he was lying on his stomach in the newly fallen snow, watching the cops comb through his farmette from about three hundred yards away. He could see the yellow crime scene tape fluttering in the bitter wind. Several La Crosse County law enforcement vehicles were parked near the barn. Officers were loading up cardboard boxes into the back of a Ford van—the Middle Eastern antiquities. Wade groaned in disappointment. *Everything's comin' apart,* he thought. *First, Leslie—now this.*

He'd only planned to be gone an hour. The cops must have arrived shortly after he left for West Salem to get some fruit, water, protein bars, and cheese. He'd planned on loading up Leslie when he returned. With her out of the way, he'd pack up the treasures and head to Galena. Well, that was Plan A. This was Plan B.

His future wouldn't be pleasant. It was certainly not the one he had planned. Since his early days growing up on the farm near Viola, he'd enjoyed the outdoors and the camaraderie of hunting with his dad and brother. His dad had been the consummate sportsman. Wade had been taught the ethics of hunting from an early age, and now at this crucial juncture of his life, he could hear his dad's voice, "The animal should not suffer. One shot and done. Instant death is the most humane way for an animal to die, whether it's a rabbit, turkey, or deer."

Lying in his lair, hidden from view, he wondered where he'd taken a wrong turn in his life. How was it that he could apply the one-shot rule to humans and not think twice about the life he'd taken. He realized his duties in Iraq. Hunting down insurgents and eliminating them had changed him in a significant and fundamental way. He'd crossed an invisible line somewhere that had blurred his core beliefs about the value of human life. Was that why he could snuff out people and not feel anything? When had he changed so dramatically? What had happened to his heart?

He did have feelings for Leslie. She was a beautiful creature, but she'd become a liability. When Wade tried to analyze what went wrong, he became confused and angry. He couldn't afford to waste any more time on her. She'd already caused him enough trouble when she led the cops to him. She wasn't worth it. Hell, no woman was worth it.

Resigned to the failure of his operation, Wade carefully crept backward from the small hill until he could stand without being seen from the farm. Using small patches of undergrowth along the fence line for cover, he made his way back to the truck, cutting cross-country. Most people would mistake him for a bow hunter instead of the fugitive he'd become. Returning to the section of woods where his truck was hidden, he got in his Silverado, started the engine, and disappeared down the road in the early evening dusk. ◉

TUESDAY
OCTOBER 30

39

Paul Saner came home Monday night with Paco trailing behind him. Ruby expected the worst when she saw the trusty canine walking dejectedly next to Paul. Leslie would never leave Paco. Something must have gone badly.

Paul cracked open a beer, then explained how things had played out. Ruby had a hard time wrapping her head around it. She couldn't imagine how devastated and terrified Leslie must have been—exposed, beaten, locked in a box, and left for dead.

Now in the early light on Tuesday morning, she heard the click of Paco's claws on the ceramic tile in the kitchen. She turned away from the window and patted the side of her leg. Paco came shyly, his tail barely wagging.

"Hey boy, how're you feelin'?" she crooned to the black Lab. "Takin' care of you is the least we can do for Leslie." Paco yawned and groaned. His brown eyes seemed dull, and his majestic head drooped forlornly.

"How about a stroll in the park, eh?" Paco's eyes brightened, and his tail swayed in a quicker rhythm.

Grabbing her jacket, headband, and gloves, she descended the three flights of stairs with the lab on a leash. He huffed and woofed his excitement when the bracing cold air hit his lungs. Ruby trotted him across the street. Grasping his leash loosely, she let Paco set the pace. He was surprisingly focused, content to run and investigate the river's edge. A few cardinals and blue jays dashed from the low arborvitae bushes scattered throughout the park. Flitting and teasing, the ever-present squirrels skittered around the trunks and branches of the tall oaks and maples, always just out of the dog's reach.

Returning to the apartment after the run, Ruby found Paul standing by the kitchen island in a white T-shirt and boxer shorts talking on his cell. He flipped his phone shut.

"Cold out there," Ruby shivered. She kissed Paul, pulling him close. He looked beat up and tired. Just then, she heard Melody's familiar wail. "I'll get her. You have some coffee." ◉

WEDNESDAY
OCTOBER 31

40

South of La Crosse on Chipmunk Coulee Road, Jim and Carol were going through their morning ritual. Standing in front of her section of the closet, Carol fussed. She stood in her bra and panties, rifling through the hangers, shuffling the colorful garments like a deck of cards.

"Don't tell me you don't have anything to wear," Jim chided her, selecting a dress shirt and tie from his side of the closet. He chose a pair of trousers and matching socks. "You better get with it, babe. Time's a-wastin'."

"Nothing appeals to me today. I guess I'll have to do some shopping this weekend. Everything's starting to look the same."

Grabbing a suit jacket from the closet, Jim walked quickly from the bedroom through the house to the front door. He picked up the morning edition of the *Wisconsin State Journal* from the front porch and poured a cup of coffee. His phone buzzed.

"Jim Higgins," he answered, rather brusquely.

"Is this the famous detective Jim Higgins?" a hushed voice asked.

"This is Lt. Jim Higgins of the La Crosse Sheriff's Department. Can I help you?" He scanned the headlines of the newspaper as he halfheartedly listened.

"No, you don't understand," the voice continued, breathy and low. "Father Renard told me you're a rather famous detective in these parts. So, since you're so famous and all, I was wondering if you've figured out *who's next?*"

If the floor was still holding him up, Jim didn't notice. He let go of the page of newsprint, and it settled back on the table silently. A stab of anxiety in his chest momentarily took his breath away, and he felt his heart begin to race. Clenching the phone in a steel grip, he hoped he wasn't having a heart attack. His knuckles began to turn white. He cleared his throat nervously.

"Honey, how does this—?" Carol stopped abruptly when Jim stepped quickly toward her, taking his finger and covering her lips, shushing her. Her eyes widened, puzzled at this strange gesture.

The caller laughed quietly. "Who's that with you? Is that your pretty little wife, Carol? That's her name, isn't it? My, she's a looker, isn't she?"

"What is it that you want?" Jim asked, hoping his voice sounded reasonably calm.

"Tonight. Grandad Bluff. Ten o'clock. After all, it is Halloween. Come alone."

"Tell me—" but the line had gone dead. Jim looked up, his phone suspended in mid-air. Carol had brushed Jim's finger away, and now she held his hand firmly.

"Jim? What's going on?" She could see there was more trouble brewing on the horizon. "Jim? Tell me. Remember—no secrets."

"I just have to meet someone tonight, rather late. It's nothing important. I just couldn't hear very well when you interrupted the conversation," Jim told her, his tone accusatory. *Don't blink. Look right in her eyes, or the jig will be up,* he thought.

Pausing, Carol stared at him. Jim could see her red flags popping up.

"Okay, what time should I expect you home?" Carol asked. Her voice had taken on a wary edge. Jim felt the guilt of his deception like he'd been hit in the chest with a baseball bat. *So much for vulnerability,* he thought.

SUE BERG

"Probably not 'til midnight."

"Fine. I'll most likely be sleeping when you get home anyway. Are you ready then?"

"Yep. Let's hit the road."

After a brief stop at Kwik Trip for coffee and bagels, Jim pulled into the snowy parking lot of the law enforcement complex. Carol's icy demeanor had put a damper on the drive into town despite the gorgeous sunrise over the Mississippi. Jim tried to make small talk, but it fell flat. His frustration ramped up. His actions this morning after the phone call were suspicious at best, deceptive at the least, and downright sinful at their worst. The last few days were the first time Carol had been anything other than sweet and reasonable in their marriage. He'd always been proud of the fact that he was a straight shooter. Now he had lied to her. He didn't blame Carol for being upset and feeling betrayed. He wasn't all he was cracked up to be, and the realization made him squirm with discomfort.

Grabbing his coffee, he started to get out of the truck, trying to avoid the whole situation. But Carol leaned over and tugged on his jacket sleeve.

"Wait a minute. I just want to say one thing," she started. Jim froze. Their eyes met, but Jim looked away. Carol noticed his silhouette was tense. He seemed ill-tempered and unsettled.

"Go for it," he said testily, biting down on his teeth, his coffee cup warming his hand.

"I know you're doing something risky tonight. Not telling me is what you've decided to do to protect me. I don't like it, but I'm trusting that it's coming from a place of love." She waited. She stared straight ahead through the windshield.

"That's more than one thing," Jim said sarcastically, ashamed of himself after he said it.

"Minor technicality. I'll wait for you at home," Carol said evenly.

"I'll be home ... later." He blindsided her with a quick kiss on the cheek and tromped into the building. His curt one-word greeting to Emily left her wondering. *Lover's quarrel?* She watched him huff down the hall to his office and slam the door.

The morning passed in a blur of phone calls, interruptions, and information gathering. Michelle from Import Specialties in Galena returned a call to Leslie, which was transferred to Paul in her absence.

"Someone called here the morning of October 18 inquiring about Brett Hoffman," Michelle, a secretary at the company said, explaining her discovery. "Whoever it was wouldn't identify himself. He just wanted to know when Brett was scheduled to pick up his load."

"And what did you tell him?" Paul asked.

"I don't specifically remember the exact words I used, but I'm pretty sure I gave him the general time frame."

"Did you give him Brett's phone number?"

"No, but I believe Amanda gave the number to someone who called her home that same morning. It probably was the same person who called here. You'll have to ask her about that," Michelle finished.

Paul walked down the hall looking for Jim. He found him leaning over the counter in the reception area, conversing with Emily. His face was uncharacteristically somber.

"... wondering if Sprint verified or identified that call Amanda received on the morning of the eighteenth," Jim said. "Did you get a return call from them?"

"Yes, they called yesterday. I have it right here," Emily answered, leafing through a pile of memos neatly stacked on a corner of her desk. "They said the call came from an Arcadia number— someone named Julia Huntley."

Jim copied the number and name in his memo pad. "Thanks, I'll check it out." Turning to walk to his office, he practically tripped over Paul.

"What?" Jim asked curtly, his expression grumpy.

"Import Specialties said Amanda gave out Brett's number," Paul began.

"Yeah, she did. She told me that the last time we spoke, and we've got the number the bomber called from. I've got it right here. Sprint finally came through with the trace. A Julia Huntley from Arcadia. Here's the number. Why don't you track her down and see what you can find out."

"Right, Chief."

Jim walked to his office. It was already eleven o'clock, and he hadn't had time to return a call to Sheila Hayes from ICE headquarters to coordinate the treasures found in Wade's barn. His phone buzzed again.

"Jim Higgins," he said crisply.

"Lt. Higgins. Cory Barstad here," a friendly voice said.

"Cory. I hope you've got some good news for me."

"Depends on what you consider good, I guess."

"Let's hear it then," Jim said tersely.

"I studied the pages from the yearbooks—all the class photos. There was a boy named Jordan Lagerton. I knew his name started with a J. His picture is in the 1996 yearbook. He was a junior then. We did a lot of crap to him, and all I remember is he went to see Father Renard a lot. Tattling and stuff like that."

While Cory talked and filled in details about their escapades, Jim leaned over and retrieved the 1996 JPA yearbook. He flipped through the pages until he came to the photo of Jordan. He studied it intently, memorizing the boy's features, trying to imagine how his looks would change over the decades into adulthood.

"I'm looking at him. You're sure he's the one?" Jim asked.

"Well, I'm not positive. Maybe eighty percent. We picked on a lot of kids, but him more than most. So if it's anyone from JPA, I think he'd be the most likely candidate."

"Great. This is really helpful. Thanks, Cory. And ... be careful."

Jim hung up, but his phone buzzed again.

"Higgins," he said, still gazing at the Joliet Preparatory Academy yearbook picture of Jordan Lagerton.

"Lt. Higgins, it's Leslie," a soft voice said.

Jim sat up straighter. "Leslie. Are you home?"

"Yes, sir. My parents just left. Sam's here. But I'm afraid I'm still very stiff and sore."

"Well, take your time. Is Sam taking good care of you?" Jim asked gruffly.

"Oh, he's been wonderful." A pause. "I know this might sound crazy, but I had a dream," she said timidly. "And I thought you might want to know about it."

"Okay," Jim began hesitantly, "although I'm not into dream interpretation or anything." *Where is this going?*

"In my dream, I was back at Brett Hoffman's funeral. I locked eyes with a guy in the narthex. I think it was the bomber." She let out a huff of frustration. "So maybe I didn't have a real dream. Maybe it was more like a flashback."

"Well, it's odd you should call right now. I just got a phone call from a former JPA student, and he believes a guy named Jordan Lagerton may be our bomber. What did this guy in your flashback look like? Do you remember?"

"Shorter, dark kinda curly hair, a slightly upturned nose, dark eyes. Maybe brown?"

Jim felt a little chill run up his arms. "Could be the same guy," he remarked dryly.

"That's all, sir. I thought it might be helpful, even though it sounds a little crazy," she replied wearily.

"You sound tired. Get some rest. Thanks."

Jim opened his cell and scrolled through his contacts, then dialed.

"Family Counseling Services, Jan speaking. How may I help you?"

"This is Lt. Jim Higgins at the La Crosse Sheriff's Department. I have a rather urgent matter to discuss with Vivian Jensen. Is she in?" Jim asked in a professional tone.

"Just one moment."

Jim leaned back in his chair and turned to face the window. He crossed one foot over the other and propped them on the low windowsill, watching the traffic churning down on Vine Street. A few snowflakes drifted in the air. The sky was studded with gray stratocumulus clouds, although the sun peeped intermittently through the cloud cover. The weather reflected his bumpy, uncertain, and unsettled mood.

He was still struggling with the conflict he'd had with Carol this morning. He'd never forgive himself if some pervert hurt her. His responsibility to protect her weighed on him like a heavy cloak, depressing his normally upbeat attitude. He blew out his breath noisily while he waited.

When she answered, Vivian's voice held a nervous twinge. "Jim? Is something wrong? Can I help?"

"Well, I'm counting on it. I need advice on a couple of fronts. One professional, one personal."

In the next few minutes, Jim laid out the framework of the bombing incident. He explained the bullying that had gone on at Joliet Preparatory Academy, where Brett Hoffman had been the ringleader of the Nasty Nine gang. He mentioned Jordan Lagerton, a JPA student who the gang had routinely targeted. A profusion of particularly disgusting and demeaning pranks and attacks had been perpetrated on him. Jim believed the evidence that he'd accumulated from Cory Barstad and the videotapes pointed to Jordan as a strong suspect in the murders of Brett Hoffman and Father Willard Renard.

"The problem I'm having with all this is that it doesn't seem believable that bullying could cause somebody to snap and commit murder," he said, doubt reflected in his voice.

"Oh, I believe it could," Vivian quietly disagreed. "I can tell you that prolonged, intense bullying can lead to severe lifelong problems if it goes untreated," she continued to explain. "The symptoms can be similar to those of people suffering from PTSD—soldiers, for example, who have survived intense combat situations—anxiety in social settings, panic attacks, negative self-image, depression, loneliness, and feelings of isolation. The list is long and bleak."

"I know a few people who suffer from PTSD, so that sounds familiar. There's another aspect to all of this that is a little more personal."

"What do you mean?"

"Oh, I think I really blew it with Carol," Jim huffed impatiently, his agitation spilling over in his voice. He leaned back and stared at the ceiling. "Some storm clouds have appeared on the honeymoon horizon."

Taking on her counselor role, Vivian said, "Oh, I'm sure it's not that bad."

"Wait 'til you hear about it before you jump to conclusions." He paused, then started to explain. "With Margie, we had an understanding. She listened to me unload about my work when I needed a sounding board. Other than that, she stayed out of my cases. She did her job with the house and kids, and I did my cop thing. With Carol, it's different. She's a professional and has her own identity. She doesn't have children, and although she's a great cook and decorator, the heavy household chores are relegated to Maria, our cleaning lady. Plus, she works in the same building as I do, which gives her access to information and situations Margie was never even aware of. On top of all that, I feel I've failed to help her understand the danger I sometimes confront in my job, and now it's come home to roost in this bombing case." He felt like he'd dumped his load on her all at once.

"What do you mean 'come home to roost'? Tell me what's going on."

"It all started when the bomber left a note in our mailbox last Friday night after he shot Father Renard to death in his apartment. At least that's our theory right now."

"Oh my! I can see why that would be unsettling," Vivian said.

"Yeah, it was upsetting for both of us. And then the bomber contacted me at home this morning on my cell. That's why I called. Carol was very upset about the note. I talked her down on that one. Even installed a security camera by the driveway. But this morning, when I got the weird phone call, I hid that it was the bomber, which ticked her off. She knows something's up. It's just better if she doesn't know everything I'm involved in right now. I've frozen her out, but I don't want her to worry." he finished dejectedly. "God, I can't believe I did that."

"Deception in any relationship is never good, but I won't preach. How can I help?" Vivian said compassionately.

"Could you come by Carol's office at the end of the day and take her out for dinner?" Jim asked. "Maybe go back to your place in Holmen and play a few rounds of Scrabble or whatever it is that you two do when you're together? I have a rendezvous with someone at ten tonight, and I want Carol out of harm's way. Since the bomber knows where we live, I don't want her home by herself. Criminals can be unpredictable so—"

"I'll help in any way possible," Vivian interrupted. "I'll try to make my appearance seem spontaneous."

"Isn't that deceptive?" Jim asked.

"Yes, but the intentions are good. Just as yours have been." Vivian paused. "A word of caution, Jim. Like most women, my sister, Carol, is very intuitive—indecisive at times—but you've got to get up early in the morning to pull something over on her. When this blows over, sit down and talk. You're both adjusting to each other and your unique work. A little conflict is normal. The love you two have for each other is obvious, and in my opinion, love and good communication can conquer a multitude of problems."

"Thanks. I can see why Carol asks for your opinion now and then. I owe you."

"I'll bill you for the psychological advice concerning your suspect, but the rest of it is free and confidential, for what it's worth. And be careful."

With Vivian's information and pointers rattling around in his head, Jim began preparing for his meeting on Grandad Bluff at ten o'clock. He had a strong suspicion he'd be confronting Jordan Lagerton. What his motives were, Jim couldn't guess. Whatever was coming, he knew he had to follow the request of the caller. *Come alone.* ◉

41

"So you're telling me, Mrs. Huntley, that you don't remember calling someone named Brett Hoffman on the morning of October 18?" Paul asked impatiently early on Wednesday afternoon.

"Well, young fella, I hardly remember who I called yesterday, so remembering who I called last week is a stretch, to put it bluntly." Mrs. Huntley's voice was pleasant if somewhat high-pitched. Paul thought she sounded like someone was pinching her.

"Okay. Did you have any visitors who may have used your phone?"

"Visitors?" A pause. "Well, most of my family is dead, so the only visitors who come to see me are the people from Helping Hands."

"Helping Hands? What do they do?" Paul asked impatiently, his swivel chair creaking under his weight. *Is this what it's gonna be like when my parents get old?* he thought.

"They come to clean my house and take me to get my groceries."

"Would one of them have used your phone?"

"I suppose they could have. I probably wouldn't have noticed if they did," she commented.

"Do you remember who cleaned for you on October 18?"

"No, I'm sorry. I don't. But I'm sure the agency could tell you."

"What agency is that?" Paul asked, taking notes.

"They're a part of Golden Years Senior Care Nursing Home in Arcadia," Mrs. Huntley said.

"Thanks so much, Mrs. Huntley. Sorry to have bothered you," Paul said politely.

After he hung up, Paul leaned back and stretched his arms over his head, then walked down the hall for a cup of coffee. Returning to his desk, he flipped his cell open and dialed Golden Years. He introduced himself and began peppering Tammy Mason, the manager of the service agency, with questions.

"So tell me, Miss Mason, who cleaned Julia Huntley's apartment last Thursday?"

"I'm not sure I can release that information. It depends on how you're going to use it," she said rather defensively.

Paul's voice hardened. "Listen, we're investigating the murder of two individuals in the La Crosse area, and we believe one of your employees may be involved," he rattled off brusquely. "I need that information from you. I'd prefer not to have to get a warrant."

A long silence followed. Paul could hear papers shuffling in the background.

"According to the schedule, Jordan Lagerton was there that day. Does that help?" she asked in a huff, her voice cold and distant.

"Jordan Lagerton? Yes, thanks. Can you tell me where he might be today?"

More shuffling papers while moments passed. "Today he's in town at a number of residences," Tammy said. "Do you want the addresses?" she asked, becoming a bit more cooperative.

"If I need them, I'll call you back. Listen, this is very important. Do not, under any circumstances, reveal to Jordan that we talked. I will contact you again if I need more information. Do you understand?" Paul said as he drummed a catchy rhythm on his desk with his fingertips.

"Yes, I understand. Am I in danger?" In his mind, Paul imagined her panicked look.

"No, just continue your duties as you normally do, and you

should be fine. Thanks for your help." He wrote the name on a sticky note and walked down to Jim's office. Approaching his desk, he laid the note down in front of him just as he was finishing his conversation.

At the sight of the name, Jim visibly paled. "So, tell me what this is about," he said, taking the note. It dangled from his index finger as he fixed his blue eyes on Paul, who fidgeted and shifted from one foot to the other.

"The phone call from Julia Huntley? You told me to follow up, so I did," Paul rubbed the back of his neck.

Jim nodded pensively without saying anything. He continued to stare at Paul, waiting for his explanation. "Let's hear it," he said.

"Apparently, Ms. Huntley has a home care service that comes to help her clean her apartment. She says she had no other visitors other than the people from Helping Hands. That guy," he pointed to the note, "was there on the eighteenth and used her phone to call Brett Hoffman. Julia doesn't remember it, but she sounded ancient, so that's not surprising," Paul finished bluntly, hiking up his pants.

"Just remember, you're going to get old someday, too, so watch who you're callin' ancient," Jim snapped, irritation beneath his words. He stood abruptly. "Get your vest and gun. Be back here in ten minutes. I need to make a phone call to the Arcadia police."

In ten minutes, they were exiting the law enforcement center, and Paul was weaving through traffic on U.S. Highway 53. Heading north, they hooked up with Highway 93, a straight shot to Arcadia. Driving close to eighty miles per hour, they made record time and entered the outskirts of the city a little after one o'clock. During the drive, Jim called Tammy Mason at Golden Years Helping Hands.

"Do you have a current address for Jordan Lagerton?" he asked after identifying himself.

"Just a minute. It's in his files," Tammy said. After a moment she came back. "Yeah, he lives on the south side of town at the Evergreen Trailer Court on Belvedere Road. His trailer lot number is 109."

"Thanks, that's helpful. Also, where is he scheduled to work this afternoon?"

"He's at one of our senior high rises, Spacious View Apartments on Highland Avenue. He cleans for residents in apartments 112 and 342 this afternoon. He might be between jobs. Sometimes he goes home for lunch, but he's usually done by four o'clock."

"Great. Thanks." Jim shut his phone. Using his truck's GPS, Paul drove to the Evergreen trailer park on the edge of town. As befitting its name, the park was bordered on the north by a row of large blue spruce evergreen trees. Paul parked the truck in the shadow of the pines. Presently, an Arcadia police cruiser pulled up beside Paul's truck.

"Vest on?" Jim asked Paul as he struggled into his, grunting and flailing until he had it secure.

He adjusted his shoulder holster.

"I'm ready," Paul said, his voice tight, climbing out of the truck.

Jim walked up to the driver's window of the cop car.

"You the guys from La Crosse?" the officer asked.

"Yeah. We're going to check out this guy's trailer. You might want to stick around in case we need some assistance," Jim suggested.

"No problem. We'll be right here. If somebody starts shooting, we'll back you up."

Jim turned to Paul. "Let's walk to his lot. That way, if he's home, he won't be as likely to get spooked by an unknown vehicle."

They began walking along the pine tree border. Eventually, they came to a lane that veered off the main road like a spoke on a wagon wheel. The mobile homes along the lane were numbered in the 100s. They walked slowly down the double-track dirt road, finally coming to a white trailer with faded sky-blue shutters. A post near the driveway had the number 109 imprinted on a metallic tag. Rust seemed to be growing from the undercarriage of the mobile home, creating a dark orange stain that kept spreading upward. A few ragged curtains hung crookedly in the front windows. An ancient oak spread its branches over the rumpled tin roof, casting ominous shadows over the lot. It was quiet. No sounds of a TV or pets came from inside.

"Watch the back door while I knock," Jim said to Paul.

Paul nodded and walked to the back of the mobile home's rear door. Jim stepped on the rickety stairs leading to the entrance door, unsure if they would hold his weight. He hammered his fist repeatedly, beating a steady rhythm, but there was no response.

A voice made them both turn around.

"Looking for Jordan?" a young woman asked. She was skinny—so skinny her spandex pants hung slack on her legs for lack of flesh. She wore a dirty purple Vikings sweatshirt splattered with red paint, and something dried and brown stained the front of the shirt. Stringy, dirty hair framed a pockmarked face absent of teeth. Her nervous, twitching demeanor told Jim all he needed to know. *Meth. Advanced addiction.*

"Do you know where he is?" Paul asked, walking toward her until he got a whiff of her.

"Probably workin' like always," she said. Her attention to Jim and Paul drifted away. She turned and wobbled down the street, walking crookedly, weaving toward some unknown oblivion farther down the road.

Jim and Paul jogged briskly to the truck. The Arcadia police car led them across town to the Spacious View Apartments on Highland Avenue.

The building, the invention of an uninspired bureaucratic architect, seemed to rise like an ugly scab on the city landscape. Its pale cream-colored brick and white window trim were lackluster and screamed for a hint of color. Inside the lobby, the tired country decor and threadbare carpets were worn down with an attitude of dirt and age.

Jim and Paul walked in. The smell of disinfectant and window cleaner saturated the atmosphere. Finding the manager's office, they flashed their IDs and explained their purpose for being there.

"We're trying to track down Jordan Lagerton," Paul began. "We're wondering if you've seen him today."

"Yes, he came in about two hours ago. He should be cleaning apartment 112. Should I call and ask him to come down?" the young gal asked.

"That would be very helpful, but don't tell him we're waiting for him," Jim warned.

Jim and Paul stood off to the side while the girl conversed with someone about Jordan.

"Oh, really. That's rather odd," she said after a few moments of small talk. "When did he say he was going to return?" She finally hung up the phone after the rambling conversation and crooked her finger at them.

"I'm so sorry. You must've just missed him. I called 112 and then 342, but both residents said he canceled today. He didn't give a reason." She shrugged and made a wry face. "Sorry," she said again.

"Do you know what kind of vehicle he drives?" Jim said.

At that moment, an older man with a friendly face walked into the office. Giving off an affable vibe, he was armed with a tool belt fastened around his waist that dangled with a variety of small pliers, screwdrivers, and hammers. A cart that carried household cleaners, dusters, and a ream of paper towels was parked in the lobby.

"Jake, what kind of car does Jordan Lagerton drive?" the young receptionist asked.

Jake frowned, trying to spark his memory of the vehicle. "Well, he used to drive a gray Mercury Marquis, but he ditched that and got some used piece of junk. I think it was a little Ford Focus. Older model, maybe a 2005, 2006?" Jake said, his frowning concentration turning into a smile.

"Color?" Jim asked.

The custodian rolled his eyes upward, then focused them back on Jim, "Umm, as I recall, it was kind of a shitty mint green with a whole lot of rust. Ugly little car. Very ugly."

Jim alerted the Arcadia Police Department and surrounding counties of Jordan's missing green Ford Focus. An APB was issued, including a warning that the driver may be armed and dangerous.

All Jim could hope for now was a break and that Jordan would show up for the rendezvous at Grandad Bluff.

"Let's get out of here. It's a dead end: Lagerton's already gone," Paul said. They walked back to the truck and drove quickly back toward La Crosse.

The weather had brightened considerably since the morning hours. The corn stubble in the fields was sprinkled with a powdered sugar dusting of light snow. The temperature was cold, hovering at thirty-three degrees according to Paul's dashboard digital thermometer.

"Seems later than October, with the snow and all," Paul said, attempting to draw Jim out with some easy conversation. Something had gotten Higgins' cork out this morning, and he had no idea what set him off. Reading the chief's mood and body language was easy for Paul most of the time. After three years of working cases with him, Paul found him to be stable and predictable, intentional in his actions and thoughts. Jim's irritable responses lately were completely out of character. Something was eating at him. Paul admitted he still struggled with nonverbal cues occasionally, but that was improving. Being married and having a baby helped.

"Looks more like late November. Must be something to do with global warming," Jim said, his voice neutral. His internal struggle to tell Paul about the meeting with the bomber on Grandad Bluff at ten this evening pitched him into indecision. He knew Paul's comment was a fishing expedition—an attempt to expose the burr under his saddle—and he appreciated his efforts. After all, who was always harping about being a team? What about unity? What about having each other's back? Vivian's words came back to haunt him. *Deception in any relationship is never good.*

Jim blew out a noisy sigh and started. "Listen, Paul. I'm sorry about this morning," he said. They looked at each other, and Paul shrugged nonchalantly. When Jim mentioned the bomber's note and explained the phone call to his house, Paul sat up straighter. Jim continued looking through the windshield as he shared his fears and concerns about Carol.

"I really don't want Carol to know what I'm doing at work, but she's pretty perceptive. I'm finding out I can't hide much from her. If she's constantly worried, wondering what I'm doing, wondering if I'm going to come home safe, it'll really strain our relationship. I just don't know how I'm going to protect her and keep her safe."

A deep frown crinkled Paul's forehead. "You can't," he said rather brusquely.

"Can't what?" Jim asked, feeling stupid like he'd just tuned into the conversation.

"Protect her. I mean, yes, in a literal sense, you can. You can beef up your house until it looks like an armed fortress. You can buy every alarm system and security camera the world has to offer, but you can't be on guard duty twenty-four-seven unless you're going to pitch a lawn chair in the driveway and sit there with a loaded 30-06 day and night." The ridiculous picture Paul described began forming in Jim's mind. "Nobody can do that. The only person who can really protect Carol is God, I guess."

Jim gaped at Paul. *How could I be so stupid?* he thought. He could almost imagine God looking down on him lamenting, *Oh ye, of little faith. That would be you, Jim.*

Once again, he has been brought up short—his stubborn superiority on full display. He'd been playing God, the Great Protector. No wonder Carol was confused and angry. He shook his head in frustration and let out a soft groan.

"You know, you're right. You're absolutely right. I can't protect her from everything that might come down the pike. I never could." Then he whispered, "I just *thought* I could."

They drove along in silence for a while, the white snow-covered fields a kind of balm to their tattered nerves and frank conversation. By now, dusk was beginning to fall, and the city seemed hushed and subdued despite the frenetic pace of the traffic. Paul whipped into the McDonald's on Frontage Road, ordering cheeseburgers, fries, and Cokes. Both men were famished. They ate silently on the drive across town, enthusiastically finishing their meal in the Vine Street parking lot.

"About tonight—" Jim started, wiping ketchup from his mouth with a napkin.

Paul interrupted. "You're not going alone. That's total bullshit. We need to come up with a plan." He dipped a fry in some mayo. "Besides, how's the bomber going to know whether you're there alone or not? It's a public park, for Pete's sake. There's no guarantee that other people won't be there, is there?"

"That's true. But some star-crossed lovers might want to take a romantic look at the city, especially with the newly fallen snow," Jim said, smiling wickedly.

Paul stared wide-eyed at Jim, his mouth slack at the suggestion. "Oh, no. You couldn't possibly be suggesting *that,* sir," he said, wondering at the unconventional proposition he was alluding to.

"Why not? Remember Sam's drag get-ups? He could pass for your girlfriend very convincingly. Whatever happened to teamwork?" Jim raised his eyebrows suggestively. "Besides, it worked before."

Paul groaned. "There's got to be something better than that, Chief," he whispered. "Anything's better than that." ◉

42

Carol sat at Huck Finn's on the Water near French Island at a table with Vivian that overlooked the backwaters of the Mississippi River near North Bay Marina, Pool 8. One of the city's finest, the restaurant was moderately busy for a Wednesday night, the waiters and waitresses trying to accommodate their customers' wide-ranging cuisine preferences and drinking whims.

Carol picked at her Caribbean chicken, chasing a pea around her plate, her eyes wandering to the marina. She was withdrawn and quiet, tired after a stressful day in the coroner's office. A traffic accident involving a gravel truck and a small mid-sized sedan had resulted in the deaths of a young mother and her eighteen-month-old toddler. Carol had counseled the husband in a quiet room off the morgue, holding his hand until he felt strong enough to identify his lovely wife and precious little boy. She could still feel his racking sobs as he collapsed in her arms, reeling in disbelief as his world unraveled.

Vivian's surprise visit to Carol's office at the end of the day was a godsend.

"Hey, are you up for dinner with your sister?" she'd asked perkily, noticing the dark circles under Carol's eyes and her pale complexion.

"Wow! You're a welcome sight. I'd love dinner. Just let me finish a few things," she'd said.

Now, as Vivian watched Carol across the table, she felt a stab of concern. Her sister's bubbly disposition and confidence were conspicuously absent, and she could see the weight of the world had settled on her shoulders. Reaching across the table, she placed her hand over the top of Carol's. "Earth to Mars. Nano, nano, nano. Anybody there?" she said softly, attempting a bit of *Mork and Mindy* humor.

"Oh, sorry. A bad start to the morning and a very tough case today," she said, clasping Vivian's hand. "Nothing a hot toddy, a long soak in the tub, and ten hours of undisturbed sleep won't cure," she said, her eyes wistful. "Maybe a heart-to-heart with Jim."

"Anything I can help with?" Vivian asked, tipping her head in sympathy. "Chocolate? Wine? A snifter of brandy? A sympathetic ear?"

"No, not really. I'll work it out. It'll be fine ... I think."

They finished their meal in relative silence, then left the restaurant.

"Are you up for some Scrabble?" Vivian asked as they settled in the car and buckled their seat belts.

"And let you win when I'm at a disadvantage? Never!" she blurted out. She hesitated, then said, "Actually, could you do me a big favor and drive me home? Jim's working late, and I really need to crash."

"Only if you let me stay with you for a while. I hate to be blunt, but you look awful."

"Sure, I'd love to have my big sister take care of me. Deal?"

"Deal."

While Carol soaked in the tub, Vivian fixed a tray of dark chocolate sea salt caramels she'd picked up at Finnottes downtown on Main. She poured two small glasses of cream sherry and waited for Carol to appear. On a whim, she texted Jim: "Change of plans. At your place with Carol. Will stay with her 'til you get home. Vivian"

"Oh, that was heavenly! I feel so much better," Carol crooned, snuggled in her velour robe and slippers. Her eyes spotted the treats and drinks on the tray. Selecting a caramel from the tray, she asked, "Ooh, chocolate and?"

"Cream sherry," Vivian answered. They clinked their glasses and retreated to the living room.

Chitchatting sister-style, Vivian shared the ups and downs of Craig's rapidly expanding small business and the increase in clients at her counseling service. Carol analyzed the changes in the lives of Jim's young colleagues and the recent violent incident involving Leslie. Finally, at eleven o'clock, Carol yawned for the umpteenth time and excused herself to bed. Vivian made herself comfortable on the couch, cuddling under a downy quilt determined to wait out Jim's clandestine operation. *Lord, whatever Jim's up to, keep him safe,* she prayed. ◉

43

A mild breeze fluttered the U.S. flag on the illuminated seventy-five-foot pole atop Grandad Bluff at the summit of Bliss Road in La Crosse. Up here, the sandstone bluffs rose over five hundred feet above the long, skinny river town. Stunning views of the city and the big blue bridge arching across the river attracted thousands of visitors each year. After the first powdery snowfall, the beige bluffs were dusted with white, their formations rugged and craggy. The frigid temperatures had swept the air clean, and the crisp, invigorating smell of pine wafted in the air.

Jordan Lagerton stood in the shadows of a stand of old oak trees that lined the wide, gently winding sidewalk leading to the open-railed overlook. For once in his life, he felt the setting provided an appropriate theatrical backdrop for the spectacle that he'd planned, now just a little more than an hour away. The vista from here was impressive. The city and Mississippi River unfolded below like a miniature diorama, complete with streets, houses, churches, and factories all in elfin size.

As he waited in the shadowy undergrowth, he hoped the detective would show. It would make everything so much more interesting and dramatic. Jim Higgins was a worthy opponent. His reputation preceded him. Jordan had spent considerable time researching his many accomplishments in the La Crosse law enforcement community: several promotions as a city police officer, numerous community service awards, and his rise to chief investigative officer in the sheriff's department. The resolution of several difficult, puzzling cases by his team had resulted in statewide and even national recognition. Tough cases seemed to gravitate to him like lightning to a high point on a steep mountain.

Jordan had cut out of work early, spending most of the day avoiding police and highway patrol officials on his trip from Arcadia to La Crosse. Driving the back roads, he ditched his Ford Focus in an alley below the bluff next to a small, dilapidated garage. He threw a tarp over the car, hoping no one would discover it until later. Jordan spent the day scrambling over rocks and small outcroppings using some of the hiking and climbing trails below the bluff until he finally crawled to the south end of the bluff and over the precipice early in the evening. The park was largely deserted now. Residents below were busy answering doors and stuffing bags with candy and treats for Halloween revelers. He found a bench along the trail, waiting for Higgins' arrival.

Back at Jim's office, Paul secured a small digital recorder to Jim's chest with a velcro strap. The slight bulge in his jacket pocket looked like a wallet or a phone.

"Put a couple of strips of tape over the strap so it doesn't slip," Jim instructed.

"Boy, this better work, Chief, or we'll be the butt of some pretty bad jokes around the department," Paul complained, ripping a piece of tape off the roll with his teeth, securing a section of the strap.

"Been there, done that. How bad can it be?" Jim waved his hand in a dismissive gesture. "Besides, I don't see anybody else trying to apprehend this guy. If somebody's gotta do it, it might as well be us. You done yet?" he asked crossly, his uneasiness increasing by the minute.

Paul checked the recorder, tugging on the strap. "Looks good," he said confidently.

Jim walked to the door of his office and yelled down the hallway. "Sam, are you ready?" he asked, pulling a T-shirt over his head.

"Just about. Give me another five minutes," he shouted.

Jim's phone buzzed. He picked it up and saw it was a text from Vivian. He read it and groaned. That was not the plan, but it was too late to change it now.

Driving across town, Paul zipped out to Losey Boulevard, then hung a right on Main. When he got to the base of the bluff, he pulled over to a city squad car. Jim hopped out and talked a minute, then got back in the vehicle.

"They ready?" Paul asked.

"Yep. As soon as we call, they'll assist," Jim said quietly.

Paul worked his way up Bliss Road, coping with a series of switchbacks until he came to the Alpine Inn near the top. Parking the F-150 in the lot, the team continued the hike along Grandad Bluff Road on foot. The wind had picked up. Raw dampness saturated the air leaving the three men cold and chilled despite their warm clothing. A crescent moon peeked through a bank of clouds in the velvety night sky.

What was it that Mark Twain said about the moon? Jim tried to remember as he huffed up the wet asphalt road in the dark. Finally, it came to him. "Everyone is a moon and has a dark side which he never shows to anyone." Unfortunately, Jordan Lagerton had shown the dark side of his personality when he bombed the hell out of Brett Hoffman's delivery truck. Jim thought about the suffering Jordan had endured at the hands of his classmates. But that faded into the background when compared with the chaos and sorrow he'd caused in exacting his revenge. The guy was unhinged and extremely dangerous.

"Hey, Chief," Sam whispered as he stopped ahead of Jim. "We're almost there."

The bare tree branches swayed in the night wind, creaking and bending. The men stood huffing, their breath coming in jagged gulps. Jim felt a cramp of apprehension at what awaited him. His shoulder harness and his Glock 22 semi-automatic pistol were tucked securely under his arm beneath his jacket. He mentally settled himself, said a silent prayer for protection, and sent his love to Carol and his kids. He turned to Paul and Sam and gave them final instructions.

"Okay, you know the plan," he said in a hoarse whisper. "You'll have to wait until he shows himself before you can move in. Stay undercover. Don't reveal yourselves too soon. I have no idea what he's going to do, so we'll have to be flexible. Don't try to be a hero," Jim instructed, "and try not to do anything too risky."

"This whole damn thing is risky, Chief," Paul said softly. In the pale moonlight, Jim picked up the anxious expressions frozen on the two men's faces.

"Easy, guys. I got this," Jim said, more confidently than he felt. He turned and began to walk alone toward the hilltop park.

At the end of Grandad Bluff Road, Jim entered the perimeter of the park. Walking purposefully, he could see the glow of the city lights at the end of the winding cement sidewalk that led to the overlook. No one was there. His footsteps echoed on the pavement. As he approached the overlook, he felt exposed and vulnerable, like a walking target. Carol's words came back to him. *I'm not willing to lose you to some friggin' nut.*

"Good evening, Lt. Higgins," a smooth, calm voice said behind him. Jim stopped walking. His heart thumped unsteadily in his chest. The voice continued, "Keep walking. Move to the overlook. Don't turn around."

Jim heard the set of footsteps behind him as he moved forward, and then he felt a hard poke in his back. A gun? With a steady pace, he pressed on until he came to the circular overlook. The panoramic beauty of the view jolted him with nostalgia and wistfulness. Grandad Bluff had always taken his breath away. This was his city, his home. He had a deep abiding love of the people here. As he thought about that, inexplicably, his eyes filled with tears. Below to the north, Miller's Coulee lay dark in the shadows, and Forest Hills Golf Course spread out just below him. He felt weak in the knees at the incongruity of his predicament.

"So, Higgins, did you figure out who's next yet?"

Jim hesitated for just a second. "Well, Jordan, if you think it's me, you're badly mistaken, son."

There was a long, tense pause.

"You know who I am?" he asked, astonishment in his voice.

"Of course. Jordan Lagerton, Class of 1997, Joliet Preparatory Academy, Prairie du Chien."

Jim's eyes swept over the scene before him—the twinkling lights of the city, the dark ribbon of the river in the distance. "You were exposed to a series of intimidating, unfair incidents when you attended the academy—incidents in which you were harassed and tormented. A terrible business. I'm sure that was very disturbing and must have left you feeling powerless and defenseless."

"Screw you! Don't play the psychologist with me!" Jordan sneered. "I'm way beyond that. No psycho babble! I intend to deliver the final installment of my revenge. I. Will. Have. Justice. One way or another, this ends tonight."

"Don't do this, Jordan," Jim said. It was a command, not a plea. "I can get you help. Two people are already dead. Nobody else has to die."

"Shut up, Higgins! Besides, I have other plans for you. You're going to be my witness tonight. Some unbelievable things are scheduled to happen. You'll have a bird's eye view of some of the most spectacular events in La Crosse history that will live in your memory forever. Events that will help my legacy live on."

By this time, Jim had turned and was staring into the face of Jordan Lagerton. He was just as Jim had pictured him all along. The man who stood in front of him now was true to the photo in the JPA yearbook. Medium build, dark wavy hair, a slightly upturned nose. But to Jim's shock, his eyes were totally devoid of any human feeling or expression. It was like looking into the stone-cold, heartless eyes of a marble statue, without human feeling or emotion. Jim had no doubt this was the man who had killed Brett Hoffman and Father

Renard.

Jim's breathing quickened, and he swore he could feel his heart knocking against his rib cage, beating desperately beneath his jacket. A cold sweat of fear glistened on his forehead. At the same time, he realized his sympathies had been misplaced. This man was a despicable creature, absent of moral integrity or human compassion. One who had taken lives without a hint of remorse. One who had probably enjoyed it and found a hideous pleasure in it. Anger raged within Jim, his chest tightening, his body tense.

"You were right about one thing, Higgins. You won't be the next victim tonight. Oh, no. My plans tonight include keeping you alive. You, the man of faith, the good husband and father, the famous detective," Jordan sneered. "Even the great Detective Higgins will not be able to prevent what is going to happen tonight." Jordan spat the last words in Jim's face.

From beneath his jacket, Jordan reached in a pocket, removed a cell phone, and opened it, its blue light illuminating his stony face. Jim watched in horrified fascination.

"I've been busy makin' plans. Building bombs and hiding them at places around the city. Stores, businesses, and yes, even some churches. Oh, when we start activating these bombs, just think of the chaos and confusion that will occur. Fireworks of humongous proportions." His face crinkled with a hideous smile. "And we'll have a front-row seat. Won't that be something?" He laughed quietly, then became serious again.

The insanity of Lagerton's plan left Jim speechless for a moment. In desperation, Jim moved toward Jordan in a threatening motion, grabbed him by his shirt collar, and jerked him up to his face.

"If you think for one minute that you'll get away with this, you better think again—over my dead body," Jim yelled, his lips pulled back in a sneer that marred his handsome face.

"I wouldn't resort to threats if I were you," Jordan said calmly, peering into Jim's startled blue eyes. "Your number is already programmed, and all I need to do is push SEND. Now, let's be reasonable, shall we?" He slowly turned the screen so Jim could read the address. In the diffused light of the phone, Jordan's face reflected a sardonic smirk.

Jim's eyes slowly pivoted from Jordan's face to the phone screen. He felt like a puppet suspended on strings that a madman was now controlling. His grip on Jordan's shirt loosened, but he didn't let go. If the world was still turning, if the moon was still shining, he couldn't care less. His voice dried up, his throat parched.

"That's my home," Jim croaked hoarsely, his eyes wide with horror. "That's *my* address." He thought of Carol and Vivian waiting for him there.

Suddenly, a couple of male voices began singing. Jordan nervously looked down the lane. Jim's gaze swiveled toward the sidewalk path, his hand dropping limply to his side. *About time you guys got here,* he thought.

The famous song by Queen reverberated throughout the darkened woods.

"We are the champions, we are the champions, we are the champions of the world," Sam and Paul belted out drunkenly. They were hanging on each other, staggering down the sidewalk, aiming for the overlook. Sam tripped clumsily and grabbed Paul's shoulder. He straightened up briefly, then brushed Paul away. Swaying precariously toward their destination, Paul and Sam approached the overlook and leaned against the metal railing.

"OMG, look at this view! This is incredible!" Paul shouted obnoxiously, sweeping his hand dramatically over the city scene. Holding an Old Style beer bottle in the other hand, he turned and shouted to Sam, "Do you believe it?" Beneath his leather jacket, his shirt was rumpled and partially hanging outside his jeans.

"Hey, La Crosse! Anybody down there?" Sam screamed, pulling out a joint and lighting up. A baggy trench coat hung limply over his sweater and jeans. *Another Goodwill special,* Jim thought. Sam inhaled deeply on the joint. Turning awkwardly, he noticed Jim and Jordan hunched at the side of the overlook. Incredulous, Jordan stared unblinking at the two revelers. Jim, equally speechless, watched his two detectives acting like a couple of drunken goons. Glancing over at Jordan, he thought, *So far, so good. This might work.*

"Hey, we got company, Paul," Sam said, his speech slurred as he turned his attention to Jim and Jordan. "Looky, here. Maybe they wanna join our little party. Can't find a better party town than La Crosse."

Sam lurched over to Jim, slapping him roughly on the shoulder. "Man, you look pretty uptight. Why don't you take a hit? Might make you feel a little better." Sam held up the smoking joint. *Nothing like some drunken entertainment to ease the tension,* Jim thought.

Jim looked at Sam, then moved his eyes in Jordan's direction. Paul had stumbled over, and suddenly he tripped, clumsily knocking into Jordan, grabbing him with both arms. Jordan temporarily lost his balance. Jim moved swiftly, tackling Jordan to the ground, pinning Paul underneath. Fists flew and legs churned as Jim fought to retrieve the cell phone from Jordan's hand before he hit SEND. Sam cursed and jumped on top of the pile while Paul muscled his way out from underneath. Jordan took a well-aimed swing at Sam and connected. Sam cursed and grabbed Jordan's arm.

"Turn him over! Turn him over!" Paul shouted. With some effort, Jim and Sam restrained Jordan, flopping him on his stomach like a piece of beef. With a satisfying click, Paul cuffed his hands behind his back. All three men sat in a heap, breathing hard, Jim holding up the phone.

"Take this and bag it as evidence." He handed the phone to Paul. "There are addresses in the phone of places where bombs might be planted." Jim started to get off the ground.

"Not *might* be; they *are* planted. The bombs are already in place. They're all there," Jordan shouted furiously, his face scrunched into the frozen grass.

"Shut up!" Sam hollered, cuffing Jordan across the back of his head. Groaning loudly, he moaned, "My butt is killing me."

SUE BERG

Jim flipped open his cell phone, called for La Crosse City police backup, and dialed the sheriff's department.

"Dispatch. La Crosse Sheriff's Department, Heidi speaking. How may I—"

Interrupting, Jim ordered, "This is Jim Higgins. I need a squad car to get out to my house at 1760 Chipmunk Coulee Road and evacuate my wife and sister-in-law from the premises. I believe a bomb has been planted somewhere on my property. Also, we're going to need the bomb squad from Fort McCoy in Tomah to get here as soon as possible. There have been a number of explosives hidden throughout the city that are cell phone activated. Alert and engage La Crosse Emergency Management. We need all personnel to report to the law enforcement center on Vine Street immediately! This is an emergency! Do you understand?"

"Yes, sir. I copy. Anything else?"

"Yes, call Sheriff Jones. I'll meet him at the center in fifteen minutes." Jim clicked off. He bent over, his hands resting on his knees. His breathing began slowing, and relief washed over him. He turned to Paul and Sam. They heard the familiar shrill of a police squad car heading up the winding, treacherous bluff road.

"Well, this incident will forever taint my view of Grandad Bluff," Jim growled. His face softened. "Nice work, guys. I was wondering if you were ever going to get here. And whose idea was Queen?" He looked back and forth at Sam and Paul. "Queen? Really?"

"Worked, didn't it?" Paul said, grinning. ☉

44

T he persistent banging continued on the front door of Higgins' house. With a start, Vivian jerked awake, vaguely aware of the desperate pounding that continued unabated. Throwing the blanket on the floor and flipping on lights as she went, she stumbled to the front entrance, disoriented and confused. When she reached the door, she could see flashing red lights in the driveway. She grabbed the deadbolt, turned the knob, and whipped the door open.

"What in the world is going on?" she asked in a panicked voice. The thought of Jim's clandestine operation filled her with foreboding. "What's happened?"

Officer Mike LeLand stared at her.

"You're not Carol. Where's Carol?" he asked, pointing at her chest. "I need to talk to Carol."

"I'm right here, Mike. What's wrong?" Carol said, her voice amazingly calm. She pushed past Vivian and stood in front of the officer, barefoot in her velour robe.

"Jim's fine. Everybody's fine, but he wanted someone to come and evacuate you to a safer place. They captured the bomber, but he's planted a series of bombs at various places around the city, and he mentioned your place." Mike was speaking rapidly, his voice articulate and strong. "So, I need you to get dressed. Jim wants you at the office downtown as soon as possible."

As Leland recited his orders, goosebumps crawled up Carol's arms. She stood as if she were a tree whose roots were embedded in the flagstone of the entry.

"Carol? You need to throw something on and come with me," Mike repeated. "Now!"

Carol jerked as if she'd woken from a deep sleep. "Okay, okay. Just gimme a minute. I'll be ready as soon as I can find a pair of jeans and a sweater," she said, turning and jogging back to the bedroom.

In ten minutes, Carol and Vivian were seated in the back seat of the city squad car, racing through the south side of town. Vivian reached across the seat and grasped Carol's hand.

"Are you all right?" she asked quietly.

"Yep. As long as Jim's okay, I'm okay," she stated matter-of-factly.

The law enforcement center and jail facility on Vine Street was always busy with activity during the day, but now near midnight, it was bustling with extra officers and squad cars. Lights were blazing inside the building, and phones were ringing off their hooks. City police officers, members of the sheriff's patrol, National Guard personnel, and emergency government officials were scurrying in and out of the building. Everyone wore a serious, uneasy expression. Accompanied by Officer Leland, Carol and Vivian rode the elevator to the third-floor investigative wing. Stepping off the elevator, they found Emily at the helm.

"Yes, I'll put you through. Just one moment, please," Emily said politely. When she caught Carol's eye, she motioned her over, her gesture hurried yet poised.

"Jim's in the large classroom with the sheriff's staff and city police," Emily began explaining, covering the phone receiver with her hand. "They're trying to figure out exactly where the bombs have been placed. Fort McCoy is sending their bomb squad, but they're not here yet. The sheriff has called up the National Guard to help search the targeted buildings. It's going to be a long night. What can I help you with?" she asked.

"Sorry. Mike Leland said Jim wanted me here, but I don't know if that's the best idea," Carol said, apologizing for the interruption, her eyes darting nervously down the hall to Jim's office. Emily's phone rang again. She held up a finger. Three more officers stepped out of the elevator.

"Down the hall, guys. Room 341," she whispered, noticing their Vernon County Sheriff's shoulder patches on the arms of their department uniforms. "Carol, I think you should just wait in Jim's office until the meeting breaks up. They've been in there an hour already, and I expect they'll be done soon. They need to start conducting searches of the buildings. So just wait in there, and then you'll be able to talk to Jim."

"Sounds like a good plan," Carol responded. She winked at Emily and whispered her thanks. Carol and Vivian walked down the hall and tried to make themselves comfortable in Jim's office. They conversed quietly until they heard Jim's voice in the outer hall. Carol stood, waiting apprehensively. "... so you go with one of the sheriff's teams." Jim turned and walked into his office. "Oh, you got here." His voice sounded calm, but Carol could see the worry and panic in his eyes.

Tears formed in Carol's eyes. "I'm here," she said simply.

Vivian excused herself to get a cup of coffee. "I'll be down the hall if you need anything," she explained, slipping by Jim.

Jim softly closed the door. He strode across the small office and pulled Carol into his arms, hugging her tightly. Talking into her hair, he stuttered, "I'm so glad you're safe."

"Jim, I was wrong," she began. She pulled back enough to look into his eyes. "We have a lot to talk about, but I just wanted to apologize."

"Shh, not now." He leaned down and kissed her. Her lips felt warm and inviting. There was a ruckus outside the door. It was flung open.

"Hey, Chief. What am I supposed to do with—" Sam stared at the chief and Carol kissing unabashedly, fully in the moment. Jim stopped the kiss and looked at Sam.

"Right. I'll catch you later," Sam said, quietly shutting the door. He smiled. *Nice to know there's still a little romantic passion left in the world,* he thought.

Inside the office, Carol pulled away. "What's the plan?" she asked, her question breaking the silence.

"I'll be here most of the night, at least until we secure the four buildings. So when I'm almost done, I'll call you. Why don't you go to Vivian's? Once they clear our house, we'll be able to go home. How does that sound?" Jim watched her closely, trying to read her thoughts.

"Home. That sounds good," Carol said. "I'll wait for your call." ◉

THURSDAY
NOVEMBER 1

45

Leslie was having a nightmare. In the dream, it was brutally cold. Steady driving snow blurred the outline of trees that crept up the slope below the ridge. The landscape seemed to recede into a gray and indefinite mass. The wind whipped through Leslie's hair, turning her face blotchy and red. Her whole body felt numb and frozen, yet she was sweating from terror despite the freezing temperatures. Leslie threw off her jacket. Rivulets of sweat ran between her breasts. The fatigued muscles in her legs screamed for relief as she fled. Running. Running.

Wade was somewhere close. Even now, she could sense his presence behind her, advancing relentlessly. Leslie heard the swish of his snowshoes as he whisked expertly through the icy woods gaining on her. She knew he'd come to kill her.

Paco whined. He nudged Leslie's hand, then frantically began licking her palm. Jerking awake, she pulled her hand away. The room slowly came into focus. She let out the air she'd been holding in her lungs. Relief flooded over her in waves when Paco planted his cold nose in the crook of her arm. She was home in her apartment. Safe in her bed. Paco was here. Cradling his furry face and ears in one hand, she whispered to him. He responded with more kisses and a few groans and woofs. Leslie became aware of the cast on her wrist.

It felt heavy and clumsy. She rolled on her side, moaning from the sharp pains radiating from her rib cage. The clock on her nightstand read six-thirty. The sun was just barely up, the dark dispersing as rays of light peeked over the horizon. Slowly with great care, Leslie sat up on the side of her bed, slack-jawed and sleepy. Everything hurt—her ribs, the bruises on her back and stomach, her blackened eye, and her broken wrist.

She heard a rustling at the bedroom door. Sam stood there, dressed in his nighttime garb—sweats and a T-shirt. He looked at her, watching her face. Then he yawned and stretched his arms over his head in a kind of yoga pose. Secretly, Leslie enjoyed a moment admiring his muscled torso.

"I heard you shuffling around in here. Need help?" he asked kindly, lowering his arms. His hair was disheveled, his eyes sympathetic. He looked tired, like he'd been out all night.

"Yeah, I do." She held out her hand.

Sam tenderly took her hand in his, supporting her cast with the other. He stood in front of her as she pulled herself to a standing position. Her face turned a shade whiter.

"Just take it slow," he coached. "Deep breaths. I'm right here." Sam pivoted, standing next to her, his arm supporting her back while he held her hand.

After Leslie used the bathroom, he helped her hobble to the couch. She felt shaky and weak. Sam settled her, covering her with the quilt he'd used. Leslie could still feel his body warmth in the folds of the blanket. The kindness and attention he'd given after her parents had left was so unselfish it overwhelmed her, and she felt hot tears sliding down her bruised cheeks.

Sam knelt down next to her. "Hurting?" he asked softly, finding her hand and kissing it.

"Yes, in more ways than one. But I have a question."

"Shoot."

"Why are you doing this?" Her blue eyes penetrated his. Sam felt his stomach cramp. *Be careful. Weigh your words,* he thought. *She's not ready for what you're feeling.*

"Orders," he said cockily, brushing tears from her cheeks.

"Orders?" She tipped her head to one side. "What do you mean?"

"Higgins' orders. I'm to stay and watch over you 'til you're on your feet again," he explained in a formal tone, giving a mock salute. "At your service, ma'am."

"Is that all? Just orders?" Leslie said, disappointment coloring her voice. "Kinda like when I watched over you when you got bit in the butt?" Sam nodded. "Any other reasons?" she asked, the question obviously a probe at something deeper.

Sam looked at her then, scrutinizing her for what seemed like an eternity. She felt as if he were looking into her very soul right down to the bottoms of her feet. Her bruises and injuries seemed to fade into the background, leaving her very essence on display.

"Yes, there are other reasons, but I'm not sure you're ready to hear them." His face was somber, and the lilting humor had disappeared.

"Think I can't handle it?"

"Something like that." He looked away for a moment, and then his eyes drifted back to her. "How about some coffee and breakfast first, and then I can fill you in on the capture of the bomber at Grandad Bluff last night."

"What?" She jerked forward and suddenly stopped, her face scrunched in pain. "Ooh. Wrong move," she said, carefully lying back down on the pillow. She grimaced and held her hand over her rib cage. She took a few shallow breaths, then asked, "Pancakes and bacon?"

"Comin' right up," Sam said, lightly kissing her cheek.

The aroma of brewing coffee and frying bacon brought normalcy back into Leslie's life, which seemed to border on the surreal. Was it really only four days ago that she'd been shoved into Wade's truck and kidnapped? It felt like eons since it happened, yet he stalked her dreams and upset her equilibrium daily. She knew she was giving him the power to disrupt her life, but right now, she didn't know what else to do. *One day at a time,* she thought. Then she corrected herself. *No, one hour at a time.*

Sam was sitting on the old coffee table directly in front of Leslie, amusing her with his version of the Grandad Bluff capture. He took another bite of pancakes and crunched on some bacon. Although it hurt to laugh, Leslie couldn't help it. The caper Sam described went beyond anything she could imagine doing.

"And you should have seen Higgins' face when I offered him a joint. It was a classic moment in the annals of undercover surveillance," Sam laughed. "As the saying goes, it was priceless."

"Maybe you should start a new reality series—Cop Capers?" More laughter. "You really enjoy doing that stuff, don't you?" she asked. Sam's eyes were bright, enjoying Leslie's smile and suggestion.

"Once in a while, you've got to step out of your comfort zone. Makes life interesting."

"You wore your vest, didn't you?" Leslie asked seriously.

"Oh, sure. Higgins is a stickler about that," Sam reported. His voice took on a more somber tone when he said, "No kidding, though, that dude planned to do some serious destruction in La Crosse. He's one bad boy. If Lt. Higgins wouldn't have met him on Grandad Bluff and gotten his phone, we'd be looking at a very high death toll. He targeted four places in the city and then built cell phone bombs and planted them at each one. It's hard to imagine the number of people who would have been maimed or killed."

"So where is this bomber guy right now?" Leslie asked.

"He's in the La Crosse County Jail and faces arraignment today in front of Judge Benson on multiple charges—two counts of murder and endangering public safety. The list is long and horrendous. After we all get some rest, Higgins is going to interview him. That should be interesting. Lagerton is obviously deranged and suffers from some kind of disorder. He's a pretty damaged individual. What a lunatic."

Leslie giggled again. "Is that your professional opinion? Lunatic? It does sound like it might apply to this guy." Sam nodded, remembering the scene on the bluff. Her eyes softened. "Thanks for breakfast, by the way."

"My pleasure," he said sincerely. He began gathering the dishes. "Refill?" he asked, holding up her coffee cup.

"Yeah, just a smidge, please."

When Sam returned, he handed Leslie her cup, which she took and set on the end table. Then she grabbed his other hand, pulling him down in front of her.

"You never told me your other reasons for helping me," she said, her eyes searching his face. His hair was wild and curly, framing his features with a tenderness she found extremely alluring. The humor suddenly dried up and blew away.

"Show or tell?" he asked, leaning forward. He let his lips find hers. They were warm and still slightly swollen. She responded immediately, letting out a little groan telling him this was what she'd wanted all along. After a bit, he pulled back.

"Now," he said, his voice husky with emotion, "do I need to tell you, too, or was that enough?" He lifted his eyebrows and tilted his head, challenging her to ask for more.

"Message delivered loud and clear," she said, grabbing his T-shirt, pulling him toward her so she could deliver another long, lingering kiss. ◉

46

By six o'clock Thursday morning, the various law enforcement teams had searched for homemade bombs at the La Crosse establishments selected by Jordan Lagerton—McDonald's on Losey Boulevard, the Barnes & Noble bookstore at Valley View Mall, Target in Valley View, and Cathedral of Saint Joseph the Workman downtown on Main Street. A thorough inspection of Jim's residence and outlying property on Chipmunk Coulee Road came up empty. The camera by the driveway provided ample proof that no one other than Vivian Jensen had approached the house. However, four phone-activated homemade bombs were recovered from the other places selected for destruction by the bomber. The bomb squad from Fort McCoy neutralized the bombs, loading them up to be deactivated and analyzed at their facility in Tomah, Wisconsin.

"I'm going home to get some food and sleep. I may come in later today and question Jordan. Or maybe not," Jim said wearily to Sheriff Jones.

"Sounds good. I'll want a full report on how all this went down later. Right now, you need to go home. You look like death warmed over," Jones said. He turned, waving blindly to Jim as he entered the elevator on the third floor.

Jim grabbed his coat, stumbled to the elevator, and in twenty minutes, he was winding up his driveway. He hit the garage door button, parked the Suburban, and climbed out. Hanging his jacket in the back hallway, he tossed his shoes by the washer and dryer.

"Jim, is that you?" Carol asked from the depths of the living room.

"Yeah, it's me. I'm headin' for the shower," he yelled as he hung a left and ambled into the bathroom. He began stripping down, whipping his T-shirt off over his head. The velcro strap was still taped to his chest and back. During the hectic race against the clock during the night, he'd completely forgotten that Paul had plastered him with sections of medical tape to secure the recorder.

"Carol, can you come in here?" Jim said loudly, staring in the mirror at his predicament.

Carol appeared at the bathroom door and looked in.

"What?" she asked.

"I need help getting this stuff off." He picked the edge of a piece of tape and yanked it hard.

"Ah! There went half my chest hair," he said, frowning at the unpleasantness of the task.

"Poor baby," Carol said, ripping another one off his back, a hint of a teasing smile on her face. With the last remnant of tape removed, he stepped into the shower. The hot water and fragrant suds relaxed him, and he stood under the stream for ten minutes.

Walking into the kitchen in a pair of jogging pants and a T-shirt, Jim grabbed the cup of coffee Carol had set on the counter. She turned to the stove and flipped the sausage patties, preparing to crack eggs into the pan.

"No, you don't," Jim cautioned, coming up behind her, setting his coffee cup down. He kissed the back of her neck, then took the spatula and laid it on the counter. Carol turned toward him, and Jim gave her a deep, passionate kiss holding her face in both of his hands. Pulling away, he said, "You've hardly said a word, hon." His blue eyes reflected concern. *Are we going to be okay?* he thought.

"I know. Right now, I don't have any words. I'm just so tired. We had a really tough case yesterday. A young mom and her little boy were killed in an accident. Hit by a gravel truck." She stopped, a shadow of sadness passing over her face. "It was really bad, Jim. So, let's eat and get some sleep and then we'll talk, okay?" she asked, her brown eyes imploring, wanting his understanding and patience.

"Sorry, honey. I guess we're both pretty beat up," he said, kissing her temple.

They ate in silence, then walked quietly down the hall and fell into bed. Both were asleep instantly, the long night finally spent. Outside, the sun was blazing a trail over the horizon, the promise of a new day. ◉

FRIDAY
NOVEMBER 2

47

Jim stretched his long, lean frame in one smooth continuous movement, coaxing out the kinks. He was still in bed, the stress leaking away. It was barely dawn, and sunshine was just beginning to curl around trees in the yard. He raised his head from the pillow, the covers falling away. The drapes were open, and the day promised to be sunny and bright. According to the meteorologist's report last night, it would be unseasonably warm today in the mid-forties. The snow that had accumulated would melt by noon.

He laid back and rolled on his side, studying Carol in the soft grayness of the morning. Some people didn't look so great when they slept. They tended to be puffy and bloated, their flaws more pronounced—wrinkles, random facial hair, blemishes. But that was certainly not true of Carol.

Jim found her so enticing. A pink hue barely colored her cheeks. Maybe it was her great skin or the dark brunette hair, her delicate eyebrows or the button nose. Whatever it was, the effect was one of otherworldly beauty that was immensely pleasing to his masculine senses. He thought of that country-western song. *She don't know she's beautiful.* Although he cringed at the improper grammar, he agreed with the gist of it.

Quietly, he hauled himself out of bed, pulled a T-shirt over his head, and slipped on a pair of boxers. He shambled out to the kitchen and hit the start button on the coffee maker, appreciating the quiet gurgling and the promise of a mug of fresh, piping hot brew. As he retrieved the *Wisconsin State Journal* from the front steps and settled into the swoopy black chair, he replayed the conversation with Carol last night.

Their discussion had been an epiphany for both of them. They woke up in the late afternoon on Friday, and after a light supper, they'd retreated to the living room. Jim got to the couch first and made himself comfortable, stretching casually along the length of it. Carol snuggled between his legs, leaning up against his chest. When Jim wrapped his arms around her, he noticed the tightness in her body. She was still wound up and nervous.

She sipped on her glass of sherry, and he savored his two fingers of brandy. Eventually, they both started to wind down. Carol's body was warm against his chest. He leaned back and thought again about how stupid he'd acted. For quite a while, they were silent, but the deepening darkness outside and the cozy crackle of the fire in the little Franklin stove seemed to provide the atmosphere needed to discuss their emotional tangles.

"Listen, let me be first to apologize for the way I acted yesterday morning," Jim began softly, staring at the flickering flames of fire, gently kissing her neck. Carol began to protest, but Jim grabbed her hand and held on. "No, no. I was wrong on a number of fronts," he began. "I was rude and petty. I lied to try to protect you, and—"

"Jim, stop." Carol ran a finger lightly along his arm. "I have just as much to apologize for. I haven't adjusted yet to all the stress that the demands of your job put on a relationship, so I have some work to do, too." Her voice was soft and forgiving. She turned around then and sat with her knees pulled up, hugging her legs as she faced him.

"You're the one I never thought I'd find. It'll take more than the events of the last few days to ever change my mind about you. There're going to be rough patches, but as they say, love will find a way." Her brown eyes were warm and tender. She leaned forward and kissed him lightly.

Jim nodded, thinking about what Vivian had said. *Love and communication can solve a lot of problems.* "That's good to hear." He felt a happy release like a tugging in his chest that told him they were on the way to a resolution.

"But I really need to say this," Carol started up again. Their eyes locked, but it wasn't combative. Jim listened. *Just shut up. You're not so smart you can't learn something,* he thought.

"I'm not the delicate rose you'd like to think I am," Carol continued. "If anything, I'm really more of a steel magnolia. As endearing and charming as your protective instincts are, I'm not totally helpless in the face of danger. Remember Gordy?"

"How could I forget that?" Jim asked, a little irritated. *That SOB.*

"Well, all I'm saying is that you can be straight with me about your work, and I promise I won't have a breakdown or melt into a puddle. After all, I deal with tough situations almost every day in my job."

"That's true. You're right," he said, nodding his head, watching her face. He swirled the brandy in the glass. "In all honesty, I'm trying to figure this out, too. I promised myself I wouldn't bring up Margie, but I need to for just a minute." Jim's eyes softened at the mention of her name. He took a sip of brandy and continued.

"Margie took care of the home front, and God knows, she was good at it. But a lot of times, she was alone and lonely. We made it work, and in no way did I think less of her because she didn't have a career. Her career was our family, and that's why we had a happy home. That's not always true for cops. The job is demanding, people disappoint, it's dangerous, and sometimes the rewards don't equal the risks." Jim stopped, realizing he was going off on a tangent. He looked at the ceiling, letting out a pent-up sigh. "Sometimes your partner burns out. There are a lot of marriage problems and divorce in our profession. But Margie stuck with me, and I'm a better man for it."

Carol grabbed his hand. "I hear you. I'm listening." She could see that remembering Margie and their life together was still difficult for him.

He continued. "You, on the other hand, have a career, and that's different for me. You know more about my job than most other cops' wives do—certainly more than Margie knew. So, I'm adjusting, too. We'll figure it out as we go, I guess." He took her hands and pulled her onto his chest, gently rubbing her back.

"I overreacted to the note and phone call," she said. "I'm sorry."

"Don't be sorry. It was threatening, so let's not minimize it."

"That's true. But dangerous people are part of your job. I have to accept that, although I don't like it very much, especially when it lands on our doorstep."

"I agree. One more thing. I realize I can't always protect you." Carol sat up, waiting for the rest. "But I want you to remember this," Jim said as Carol nodded. "I *want* to protect you. And please let me do that." She looked about to interrupt, and he impatiently waved his hand. "I know, I know, I'm not Superman, but it's important to my moral sense of things. I'm your husband, and protecting you is what I want to do. But you have to let me do it when I can." He ran his hand through his hair. "Boy, that sounded convoluted, but you know what I mean, don't you?" His blue eyes begged for understanding.

"Yes, it's part of your innate maleness. It's programmed in your DNA. You have an instinct to protect those you love and don't apologize for it, although most people would probably scoff at that idea today."

Jim's eyes opened wide, amazed at Carol's insight. "Yeah, you get it. It's what makes me such a dinosaur." He grinned, his dimple denting his cheek.

"No, that's what makes you a man, honey. A good man," Carol finished.

Then he said seriously, "Of course, I know that ultimately it's God who protects you ... and me," he finished. Waiting a minute, he said, "So ... are we good now?"

"Yes. I love you."

"Mmm, I love you more." Jim felt a weight lift, the anxiety breaking free.

"You wanna fight about it?" Carol smiled, then giggled.

"No, but there is something we *could* do about it."

Now in the shadows of the morning on Saturday, Jim smiled, the memory warming him inside. The coffee pot was in its last flurry of gurgling. He got up and walked to the kitchen. Reaching for a mug, he poured some coffee. He heard Carol call his name. He poured another mug and walked briskly down the hall.

"Morning," he said cheerfully, setting her coffee on her nightstand and leaning down to kiss her. "You were very beautiful this morning in the predawn light."

"You were watching me sleep? Yuck!"

"Nothing yuck about it." He noticed her mussed hair and the beautiful curve of her neck.

"Well, I guess it's all in the eye of the beholder," she said.

"You got that right," Jim agreed. "So, what do you have planned for today?"

"You know, I think I'm going over to see Leslie and take her some food," Carol said, sipping her coffee, her bare shoulders exposed beneath the sheet she'd wrapped under her arms.

Jim was still standing next to the bed. "Hmm, that's a nice gesture. Mother her up a little bit."

"If she'll let me. What about you?" she asked, gazing up at him.

"I'm heading to the jail to interrogate the bomber. See what he has to say for himself." Jim's eyes drifted to the window. "Oh, and by the way, I'm cooking tonight. A little surprise to get us in the mood for other festivities later." Jim grinned, watching her reaction.

Carol laughed. "Festivities? I've never heard sex called that before," she mumbled.

"You have now," Jim said, a smile creasing his face.

SUE BERG

Avalanche in Vernon County was a widening of County Road Y where Tainter's General Store, now defunct, stood dark and abandoned. Population: 16. Scattered within the confines of the tiny town were a couple of four-square homes, cube-shaped structures that boasted a pyramidal roof and central dormers. A wide bridge spanned the west fork of the Kickapoo River. That was about it. If you blinked, you might miss it.

If you turned left on County Road S before the bridge, you'd end up in Bloomingdale, another unincorporated town with a slightly larger population of 45. If you crossed the bridge and turned right on County Road S to the south, you'd eventually come to State Highway 82 and Brush Hollow, which wasn't a town at all. People living along the road were friendly, and there was a unique community vibe among them which extended to strangers. If you continued on County Y up the hill, you could follow a number of roads along steep ridges that overlooked deep valleys on your way to the village of La Farge.

The exquisite landscape, filled with craggy, striated bluffs alternating with plains of oak savanna and thickets of white pine, had a drawing power that got under your skin. In recent years, it had become a premier destination for avid outdoor enthusiasts who agreed the scenery was arresting to the senses and just a little bit on the wild side.

Paddlers in canoes navigated the languid Kickapoo in the temperate months, and bikers swarmed to the area, bewitched by the twisting, hilly terrain and the slow pace of nearby Amish communities. In winter, snowmobiles raced along groomed trails through deep woods, and cross-country skiers raced between the hills and flat valleys. Sportsmen enjoyed the bounty of whitetail deer, ruffed grouse, and pheasant. Some of the finest trout fishing streams in the country were located here. Flowing southwest through Avalanche, the Kickapoo—dubbed as "the crookedest river in the world"—meandered lazily through farm fields dotted with weathered barns and abandoned tobacco sheds, grazing cows and flocks of wild turkeys, and charming Amish horses and buggies.

Chet Boyer and his twelve-year-old son, Rusty, were ambling along a ridge above Avalanche, scouting the terrain looking for a good place to build a hunting blind. The air smelled sharply of pine and the musty scent of rotting leaves. It had warmed up to a comfortable forty-two degrees, and the sun broke through the stratocumulus clouds at alternating intervals. One minute it was sunny and pleasant; the next minute, the clouds pouted, and it looked like rain.

Opening deer season was only a few weeks away, and this was a tradition Chet had started with his son. Father and son walked in about three miles from the main road, climbing through stands of oaks and maples, easing their way up to the top of the ridge, marking a few choice spots along the way. They entered an area of public hunting grounds recently set aside by the DNR. Chet had never been this far along the ridge before. A slight breeze ruffled some straggling oak leaves still clinging to rough branches. The leaves made a little whisking sound above them as they walked.

An opening among the hardwood trees overlooked the valley below. Tapping Rusty's arm, Chet pointed to a group of whitetails browsing in an open field in the valley. He brought his binoculars up and scoped the surrounding landscape. Noticing a wisp of smoke along a little creek below them, he zeroed in, adjusting his focus. He was surprised to see a small cabin, not more than two rooms, maybe only one. Smoke curled in shiftless swirls out of the fieldstone chimney, twisting in the air currents and then diffusing into the atmosphere. The area around the cabin was neat. A stack of split firewood was piled along a gnarled rail fence twenty feet behind the cabin. Whoever stacked it was particular. The cabin site was quiet but obviously occupied.

Rusty noticed his dad's intense focus. "Dad," he whispered, "what are you looking at?"

Startled, Chet shrugged. "Thought I saw a buck. But it was just a couple of does." Chet couldn't explain his reaction to the discovery of the unknown cabin, but something wasn't right. It was just an intuitive suspicion—a disquieting feeling about this setup. But he wasn't quite sure why he felt uneasy.

Once more, he held the binoculars up and looked at the camp below. That's when he saw a well-muscled lean man walk out onto the cabin porch. He had shoulder-length hair, a trimmed beard, and mustache. Something about him captured Chet's attention.

Whoever he was, he was no city slicker. His self-assurance suggested a reliance on basic skills that had been honed to survive. His clothes were sturdy and adequate, not fancy or expensive. The attire suggested a modest approach to life and a talent for fitting in with country folk. He had a rigid yet confident bearing. Military? Survivalist? Militia?

Another thing. Where was his vehicle? There didn't seem to be one, not even on the other side of the narrow man-made footbridge that crossed the creek. And Chet hadn't noticed a vehicle parked along the main road on a side turnout. So how'd the guy get here? He looked comfortable like he'd been here a while and was planning on staying.

"Come on, son. We better be heading back. Your mother expects us for lunch," Chet said in an undertone, making a mental note of his bearings.

"Ah, come on, Dad," Rusty said, disappointment lacing his voice. "We haven't even found half of the places where we could build a blind on this ridge," he complained.

"Another day, son. Another day," he said quietly as he turned back and began making his way to the highway and the car. Throwing his arm over his son's shoulder, he said, "You know how Mom is. She'll be worried about us." ◉

48

Jim Higgins sat at his desk, buried in a flurry of paperwork, phone messages, and other police bureaucracy. Sitting back in his creaky office chair, he rubbed his eyes, his fatigue still throwing a disorienting cloud over his thoughts. He was considering the mounting evidence stacked up against Jordan Lagerton when Sam breezed into his office late Saturday morning, offering to assist in the interrogation of the bomber.

"We need to review our evidence first," Jim started, "before the interview." He noticed Sam's outrageous attire but decided not to comment.

Sam started. "Well, we've got the two videos, one from the trail cam and the other from the parking lot at Beaumont Furniture, which pinpoints Jordan's locations before and at the time of the bombing. That should be pretty convincing to a jury," Sam said, placating Higgins' ongoing emphasis about collecting evidence.

Jim cleared his throat. "Should be. But I wish we could really zero in on both videos and get a clearer image. They're both pretty grainy. Of course, we do have the nursing home staff who will testify that Jordan was driving a Mercury Marquis at the time of the bombing. We need to find that car," Jim said, distracted, shuffling more paper into piles.

"Do we know what was in Jordan's trailer home yet?" Sam asked.

"The Arcadia police and the Trempealeau Sheriff's Department are working together to go through the trailer today. We'll have to wait and see what shows up there."

"What about the Nutty Bar wrapper?"

"We have fingerprints from Jordan now. The lab is working on that," Jim said. "The charges facing Lagerton will put him away for his lifetime. Cory Barstad's ID from the JPA yearbook paid off big time." Jim leaned back in his chair, pushing himself away from his desk. "Can you believe that whole bombing scheme? Man, that would have put us on the national map for a long time in a really bad way." Jim paused and studied the traffic out on Vine Street. "I'd like to get him on tape admitting to the murder of Father Renard, but that probably won't happen. Finding the pistol would be another great piece of evidence that would help, but I'm not setting my hopes on that, either."

Sam crossed one leg over the other and shifted in his chair. "Not to steal Jordan's thunder, sir, but what about Wade Bennett? Anyone come forward with information? Anyone spot him?"

"No. I wish something would shake loose. That guy is another seriously deranged individual." Jim brushed his hand across his face. Both men paused in the conversation, lost in their own thoughts. Jim spoke first.

"How's Leslie?"

"Well, it's hard to tell sometimes. I'm not sure how severe her PTSD was from her military service, but after her incident with Wade, she's ... well, she's very needy, if you get my meaning."

"Needy like how? Sexually, emotionally, what?" Jim watched Sam closely. Sam blushed. *Like I'm going to tell you about my sex life. Not,* Sam thought.

Instead, Sam said, "All of that—and more." He blew out a sigh. "She's a tangled up mess. Sometimes she acts tough as nails like none of it bothers her. You know, that military hero stuff, but then at other times, she gets all clingy and weepy." Sam stared over Jim's shoulder. Jim had no idea what he was thinking. Sam went on. "I know one thing. She's not ready for a committed relationship. She's really screwed up right now. Her emotions are all over the place."

"You have a steady, dependable personality," Jim advised, shifting to counseling mode. "That's what she needs from you—stability and compassion. You know her history and how she suffered when she was with Wade. People locked in those kinds of relationships don't always realize how imprisoned they really are. Abuse isn't easily overcome without professional help. She'll need continuing counseling. Meanwhile, you just practice your listening skills and bite your tongue."

"Oh, you mean like married couples do?" Sam grinned.

"And what would you know about that?" Jim asked skeptically, raising his eyebrows. Sam's grin disappeared. "All I'm saying is be sensitive to her fears and insecurities. And although it's probably not the modern thing to do, at some point, you may have to fight for her." *Another dinosaur idea,* Jim thought.

"I already did that once," Sam answered darkly, slouching in his chair.

"Yes, you did, but frankly, if I were you and Wade was still drifting at the edges, I'd be very worried. It isn't over yet."

"No, it's not. He's out there somewhere," Sam said, hostility shadowing his voice. Jim gave him a blue-eyed stare, and said, "Yeah, I know. That's why I worry."

Jordan Lagerton was seated at a table in an interrogation room on the first floor of the law enforcement center on Vine Street. He was exhausted, having slept very little after being processed into jail late in the early morning hours. His orange jumpsuit itched, and despite the warmth of the room, he felt cold and clammy. Dreading his questioning with Lt. Higgins, he'd eaten very little. Now his stomach growled ominously. He felt like the walls were moving inward, squeezing the air out of him.

Being captured was a risk he'd been willing to take, but now he was disgusted that he hadn't been more careful. Jail sucked. He was sure prison would be a lot worse. He hadn't given Higgins enough credit. When he'd actually shown up at Grandad Bluff on time, Jordan was surprised. He'd come alone and seemed fearless. The guy had balls.

Down the hall, outside the interrogation room, Jim stopped walking and turned to Sam. Out of earshot of the jail attendant, he asked Sam, "Where do you come up with these get-ups?" His eyes traveled up and down Sam's lean frame, his head wagging in disbelief at the poor taste and ridiculous ensemble displayed by an officer of the law.

"Hey, Chief! Come on! I'll have you know these Air Force 1 sneakers cost over $100, but I got them at Goodwill for twenty bucks. Besides, it's Saturday. I'm officially off duty."

"Well, when Jones jabs me for not enforcing the dress code around here, I'll just tell him you were off duty at the time, even though you're in the law enforcement center and are assisting in an official interrogation. How's that sound to you?" Jim wore a frown, but Sam could see he was suppressing a grin forming around his mouth.

"I appreciate your support, sir. But I can't afford to dress the way you do with $200 pairs of pants and $75 ties." Sam shrugged nonchalantly. "Out of my league, especially on my pay."

"Yeah? So now you're turning this into a request for a raise?"

"Worth a shot."

"Not happenin'. You'd just buy more crap at Goodwill," Jim said brusquely as he turned and whisked down the hall. He stopped at the door of the interrogation room and turned the doorknob. The door clicked and swung open.

Jim Higgins and Sam Birkstein entered the room, making eye contact with Lagerton. To Jordan, Higgins seemed taller, his large frame imposing itself on the cramped space of the tiny room.

Higgins was more threatening than he'd remembered from his brief encounter last night. He dressed professionally and wore a crisp, blue dress shirt, dark gray Ted Baker wool trousers, and an Italian Ferragamo silk navy necktie sporting frisky, white dogs with red bowties. His eyes were very blue, something he hadn't noticed last night. If he was dressing to impress, it was working. Higgins pulled out a chair and sat down.

Who the hell is this guy? Jordan thought, sizing up Sam. Baggy gray sweats hung loosely around his legs. A bright lime-green T-shirt peeked out from under a purple LSU Tigers sweatshirt. Sam leaned casually against the wall, crossing his feet. His dark hair curled around his face, a lock hanging loosely over his forehead. His feet were decked out in a pair of lemon yellow Nike Air Force 1 sneakers. He was casually scrolling on his phone. Jordan wondered if this was Higgins' way of intimidating him, making him jumpy and off-kilter.

Inside the room, Higgins pushed the button on the mounted video camera and the inquiries began after Higgins' baritone voice recorded the initial information and recitation of Miranda Rights.

Sitting calmly across from Lagerton, his hands clasped in front of him, Jim rested his elbows on the table. Jordan's eyes roamed over Higgins' face.

"So Jordan, how'd you sleep? Get some rest?" Higgins began.

"Why should you care how I slept?" Jordan asked, sneering sarcastically. His eyelids were at half-mast, anger and resentment bubbling to the surface.

"Just a friendly question. We want you to be comfortable."

"Well, you sure weren't worried about that last night when you body slammed me into the ground!" Jordan snapped.

Jim calmly continued. "Sorry about that, but you have to admit your activities last night were rather threatening to a large portion of the La Crosse population."

Jordan shrugged, unresponsive.

"How's the food? Have you gotten enough to eat?" Jim asked.

"Yeah, they brought me pancakes, bacon, and scrambled eggs

this morning. It was okay, I guess."

"What kind of food do you like?" Higgins asked, his fatherly tone coming through.

Jordan's eyes moved to Sam, then refocused on Jim. "I'm kind of a junk food junkie. I really like Little Debbie Nutty Bars. That's what I usually eat for breakfast." Sam's eyes locked with Jim's.

Jim was thrilled with the lead-in, then said, "Nutty Bars, huh? That's kind of an interesting coincidence."

"Oh, you like them, too?" Jordan was warming to the snack food theme.

"We found a Nutty Bar wrapper at the scene of the bombing on Highway 14. Can you explain that?" Jim's eyes bored into Jordan's.

Suddenly the air felt like it had been sucked out of the room. Jordan blew out a few breaths, then nervously scratched his head. More thinking, his eyes drifting upward. *Well, I walked right into that one,* he thought.

"Jordan? Can you explain that?" Jim repeated, watching him closely.

"Lots of people like Nutty Bars. What makes you think I was there?"

"Your fingerprints were on the wrapper," Jim answered in a deadly calm tone. The room had become so quiet you could hear the unobtrusive whirring of the video camera.

Jim waited, studying his fingernails. "Where were you, Jordan, on the afternoon of October eighteenth?" Jim asked.

"That was more than two weeks ago. You expect me to remember that?"

Jim slammed his hand down on the table in front of Jordan. Jordan's eyes widened at the display of anger, and he sat up straighter. Jim snarled, "When you planted a bomb on the seat of Brett Hoffman's truck, then yes, I would expect you to remember that!"

Jordan leaned forward, cradling his head in his hands. His confident, piss-ant attitude was quickly receding. Jim waited for a response, leaning forward, dipping his head so his eyes met Jordan's. His voice crackled with emotion. "Brett had a lovely wife and three beautiful children. They're alone now. Brett's gone. They'll never see him again," Jim said quietly, his voice intense and clipped. He continued, rolling out the evidence before Jordan.

"We have you on a wildlife trail camera at the wayside above Ten Mile Hill on Highway 14. It shows you getting out of a gray Mercury Marquis, walking to the truck with a package you placed on the front seat. Then you walked back to your car and drove away. Fifty-six seconds later, the truck exploded." Jim shifted back into his chair. The quiet that descended in the room unnerved Sam, who'd been observing the interrogation. He shifted uneasily next to the wall. Seconds ticked by.

"He deserved it," Jordan said softly, his eyes downcast, his head bowed.

"What did you say?" Jim asked, leaning forward again.

"He deserved it!" Jordan yelled, bringing his fists down on the table. His face was red, spittle flying. "After all the suffering he put me through as a kid, he got exactly what was coming to him."

With these guys, it's always someone else's fault, Jim thought. *Poor little ol' me.*

Jordan looked up into Jim's eyes. The chill of his dehumanizing stare gripped Jim again, throwing his heart into palpitations. Jordan's litany began.

"Why don't you tell us about it?" Jim said gently.

"It all started at JPA when I was a freshman, and my dad left my mom for another woman."

The interview rambled on until three o'clock. Once Jordan got started, he didn't seem to be able to stop. When it was over, Sam and Jim were relieved that Jordan confessed to the shooting death of Father Renard, but he wouldn't reveal the location of the pistol.

Sam headed out, and Jim returned to his office to retrieve his coat. He was surprised to find his daughter, Sara, waiting patiently in a chair. She'd been reading the newspaper, and she stood to greet him.

"Hi, Dad. I stopped at home, but nobody was there. I thought you'd probably be down here," she said casually.

"Hi, sweetheart," Jim said, embracing her in a hug. He pulled back and noticed her green eyes. She smelled of something peony-like. "You're looking lovely. New boyfriend?"

Sara waved her hand dismissively. "Dad, you've got to quit trying to marry me off. Remember? I'll do it my way!" she said, grinning.

Jim laughed heartily. "Okay, okay, I hear you. So what's up?"

"Nothing much. I just haven't talked to you in a while, and I miss you," she shrugged.

Jim immediately felt guilty. Since their return from Paris and his caseload at work, Jim and Carol had neglected the twins. The Tuesday date night he'd always had with Sara since Margie died had dried up. Now he felt terrible about it.

"I'm sorry. How can I make it up to you?" he asked sincerely, loosening his tie.

"Brunch tomorrow at the Guadalupe Shrine? John and Jenny will join us. Ten o'clock?"

"Sounds great," Jim answered.

"I'm heading out to the mall. Oh, congratulations on catching the bomber, Dad." She turned the newspaper's front page toward him. He scanned the front-page headlines: BOMBER CAUGHT, DISASTER AVERTED. "What a nutcase! Everybody's talkin' about it on Facebook. Gotta go!" she said, leaning in for a kiss on the cheek. "Love you," she yelled as she disappeared down the hall, leaving the newspaper crumpled in the chair.

Her floral scent lingered a moment in the air, filling Jim with nostalgia. He could still remember the years when Sara thought perfume was stupid and girly even though she was a girl. Go figure.

He smiled, his heart lighter at seeing his daughter. *Funny how they still need you even when they are all grown up,* he thought. He made an effort to straighten up his disastrous desk. He finally gave up and grabbed his coat, shutting off the office lights as he went. He had some shopping of his own to do. Tonight was going to be *memorable.* ◉

49

"I've been having these nightmares about Wade. They're so real, I wake up in a cold sweat," Leslie told Carol, a shiver running up her arms. "They don't seem to be stopping."

Carol was sitting next to Leslie on the couch, holding her hand. She was concerned. Leslie's injuries had been substantial. Physically, she seemed to be moving around with greater ease, and the pain was subsiding each day, but her emotional state was delicate. Paco looked up at her with worried eyes, lounging at her feet near the sofa.

"Have you seen your therapist?" Carol asked, noticing her bruised eye.

"Not yet, but I have an appointment on Tuesday."

"Good. Keep it. What about Sam? Has he helped?"

"Oh, Sam has been wonderful. He's so kind. But—"

Carol sensed the other shoe was about to drop. "But what?" she interrupted.

Leslie struggled to maintain her self-control, but soon tears were coursing down her cheeks, and her shoulders jerked with sobs. Carol put her arm around her and let her cry. Paco stood and laid his big head in her lap, whining empathetically. After a few moments, Leslie took the tissue Carol offered and blew her nose loudly. She began again.

"I feel so unattractive and *used*, like an old shoe with manure stuck on the bottom," she lamented. "I'm not beautiful anymore. I'm just a bag of broken bones and broken emotions." She stopped and wiped more tears. "Sam deserves someone who can at least give him something, and it feels like all I'm doing is taking. I can't give him anything."

"Who says he's expecting anything right now? He seems to be pretty happy to be with you and help you recover. What's wrong with that?" Carol asked, rubbing Leslie's back.

"I don't know. Maybe there's nothing wrong with that. It just feels unfair, like I'm not holding up my end of the deal." Carol stayed quiet. "And I don't know if I can give myself to him when the time comes. Right now, there's no pressure, but eventually, he'll want to have sex, won't he?" Leslie looked over at Carol anticipating her answer.

"If you stay together, I'd say yes, he'll want that. That's what normally happens. But back up the train. Do you love him?"

"Oh, I want to," her voice was throaty with emotion, more tears falling. "I want to feel all the wonderful feelings that go with love. And Sam deserves to be loved by somebody special. I'm just not sure that's me."

Carol leaned in, her voice soft and motherly. "Here's my advice. Stop worrying about where you're going and start appreciating where you are. I happen to know from Sam's reaction to your attack that he has deep feelings for you." Carol paused and pushed a bunch of stray hair away from Leslie's face. She looked so vulnerable and raw.

"Relationships are a dance, not a business contract. Love is a feeling, but it's more of a decision." Leslie looked confused, so Carol continued explaining. "Things are not always even-steven in a relationship. Sometimes one person gives more than the other to meet a need. I'm sure that's what Sam is doing. Give yourself time to heal before you worry about the sexual stuff. If you love him, then your responses will most likely kick in at the right moment. Just be patient with yourself. You've been through hell and back."

"Don't I know it," Leslie said grumpily. They sat silently for a few minutes. Carol noticed the descending darkness outside the windows. Against her better judgment, she gave one last snippet of advice.

"Listen. Take a long bubble bath this afternoon. Indulge yourself a little bit. Spritz on some of that perfume I brought you and put on a little makeup. Get dressed in something comfortable but pretty, and enjoy your dinner with Sam tonight. Think about the way he fought for you when Wade showed up on your doorstep. That was pretty brave. Leave the feelings of guilt behind and see what happens. okay?" Carol counseled.

"OK, but if it doesn't work, I'll have you to blame," Leslie said, pouting.

"Blame away," Carol said, smiling.

Jim drove up his driveway on Chipmunk Coulee Road with his Suburban loaded with groceries, wine, and cheese. He unloaded the bags on the kitchen counter then changed into jeans and a comfortable sweater.

Coming back in the kitchen, he dressed an organic chicken with lemon slices, garlic, thyme, and olive oil, popping it into the oven to roast. Filling the wine bucket with crushed ice, he set two bottles of French wine in it. He hoped the gal in the liquor aisle at Festival Foods knew what she was talking about when she'd recommended the wine. He'd picked up some crispy baguettes and three kinds of soft, spreadable cheeses to munch on with the wine. Baby red potatoes mixed with olive oil, salt, and pepper were set aside in a pan on the counter. Bright greens, tomatoes, and sweet onions were mixed in a chilled salad bowl. He'd make a quick vinaigrette closer to the meal.

Whistling as he worked, Jim went about setting up the romantic atmosphere. Retreating to the guest bedroom, he opened the closet door and found two fluffy quilts, which he took to the living room and placed in front of the little Franklin stove. Gathering wood, he built a fire and turned down the damper once it was roaring. He found the portable disc player and scrounged around in his study until he located *Favorite Parisian Melodies* that he'd bought in Paris. Turning the recessed lighting down low, he lit a few candles Carol had scattered around the house, positioning the dozen yellow roses in the crinkly paper next to the chilling wine bucket and glasses. He stepped back and scanned the room. Voilà! Paris on rewind.

He retreated to his study until he heard Carol come in through the garage. Walking out, he met her in the dining room.

"Something smells divine," she said, kissing him lightly on the cheek.

"Ready for a little picnic in Paris tonight?" he asked, grabbing her hand, his eyes sparkling.

"What are you up to?" Her brown eyes shimmered with anticipation.

"Come and look," he said, pulling her to the living room.

Carol's eyes took in the scene. "I can't believe it. It does have a Parisian feel to it." She pushed one side of her hair behind her ear. Jim could see that the scene had triggered memories for her. "Jim, this is déjà vu! Just like that day in the Tuileries Garden. Remember the Louvre and that little stand where we bought lunch?"

"Well, isn't it obvious I remembered?" Jim bowed deeply from the waist. "Madame, get comfortable, and I'll serve some appetizers," Jim said, enjoying Carol's wondrous expression. The evening passed with laughter, wine, and good food eaten picnic style on the thick, soft quilts, and charming music floated in the background. An hour later, Jim served velvety chocolate mousse and hazelnut coffee.

"So, did you enjoy Paris on rewind, sweetheart?" Jim asked.

Carol's eyes softened. "You are the most amazing man, and you're all mine."

"You got that right. I am all yours," Jim said scooting up to her. Sitting cross-legged, they talked some more. Carol shared her concerns about Leslie, and Jim filled her in about Jordan's interrogation.

"Oh, by the way," Jim interrupted, "we're supposed to meet the twins at the Guadalupe Shrine at ten tomorrow morning for brunch."

"Oh, that will be fun," Carol said pleasantly. Jim took Carol's plate and cup and delivered them to the kitchen. He reappeared in the living room, standing above her, holding out his hand.

"Time for the fireworks," he said as he pulled her up to him.

"Fireworks? You have fireworks, too?" she said, remembering the light show they'd enjoyed at the Eiffel Tower. She looked up at him with an expectation that took his breath away.

"Not that kind, baby. But they'll be just as good," he said, leading her to the bedroom. ☉

SUNDAY
NOVEMBER 4

50

Dusk was just beginning to fall in the isolated valley east of Avalanche. Wade Bennett had ridden over the ridge on his ATV. Hiking on foot into another valley, he'd worked up a sweat climbing the steep hills thick with trees. The Kickapoo River flowed gracefully beside Highway 82, then veered off into a stand of yellow birch, the ragged bark looking like broken plates of armor. Outcroppings of limestone jutted in cliff-like structures which overlooked the quiet ripple of the stream.

Along the shadowy edge of the river, Wade hurried to the rendezvous point, a flat tabletop rock hanging about six feet over the waterway. Since Wade and Royce had been young boys, this portion of their grandfather's land had been their playground, and the rock was their secret place where dreams and fantasies had been carved out during their childhood days of play and imagination.

As he approached the spot, he whistled the cardinal's song, *Cheer, Cheer, birdie, birdie, birdie.* Almost immediately, his brother, Royce, returned his call. Climbing the sides of a deep gully, Wade crested the top of the rock where he found Royce lying prostrate, a timid grin pulling at the corners of his mouth.

"Hey, you're late. It's going to be dark soon," Royce chided.

"Sorry, got carried away cutting wood. You got my supplies?" he asked, barely out of breath.

"Yeah, I brought a plastic sled and lashed everything down. You should be able to pull it to your four-wheeler, then head for the cabin. When are you leavin'?" His ruddy face reflected worry.

"Soon. No more than a couple of weeks or so. I need to go into La Farge one day and send some emails at the library on their free WiFi. Once I get everything arranged, I'll be gone for a long time. Probably a couple of years. Maybe head down to Mexico or over to France. Money's not an issue," Wade explained.

"What should I tell Mom?" Royce asked, the anxiety coloring his words.

"Anything but the truth. Tell her I enlisted again, and I'm going undercover. She'll believe that."

The two brothers climbed down from the outcropping, slipping and sliding to the bottom. Wade nodded his approval at the supplies compactly secured on the plastic sled. He reached down and grabbed the rope handle, then turned to his brother. He pulled Royce into a brief hug.

"Take care of Mom. I'll send you money now and then. Thanks for helping me out. I hope someday I can return the favor." His eyes misted over, and he looked awkwardly at the ground.

"Be safe, brother," Royce whispered, his voice cracking.

In the gathering darkness, Wade turned and pulled on the sled. Snow began softly falling as he retraced his steps back to his ATV. Royce watched him recede and disappear.

"Take care, brother. Take care," he murmured again, his cheeks wet with tears. ◉

WEDNESDAY
NOVEMBER 7

51

Since the capture of Jordan Lagerton, things had slowed considerably for Jim and his team. They kept busy, though, with desk work. The collection of evidence from the bombing continued unabated. Paul and Sam were following leads that had been called in about Wade Bennett after a news release requested the public's help in locating him. In addition, they were wading through Rod Girabaldi's financial records trying to make connections.

Jim was on his way downstairs to meet with Sheila Walsh from ICE. After several delays, she had finally arrived to begin classifying and sorting the antiquities found in Wade Bennett's barn.

"Hello again, Lt. Higgins," Walsh said, extending her hand to Jim and giving him a friendly smile. She was at work in the impound center where rows of tables were set up. The antiquities lay spread out in long lines awaiting her expert opinion. This time, her attire was less formal. She wore jeans, sneakers, and a black vest emblazoned with ICE on the back. Her demeanor was just as professional and restrained as before.

Jim grasped her hand firmly in his big palm. "We meet again."

"You won't get rid of me if you keep finding more treasures." She waved her arm over the layout behind her. "I understand they were confiscated in a raid at a local farm? Is that right?"

SUE BERG

"Yes, after you left last time, we uncovered them on a farm in Rockland of all places. But the man who supposedly owned them, Wade Bennett, has disappeared. We're looking for him, but we're not having much luck locating him," Jim said downheartedly, staring at the variety of relics on the tables.

"Well, don't feel like you've failed. These smuggling rings can be very complicated. Some of my colleagues are working on the Galena end of this scheme. We're pretty sure that's how Girabaldi fits into this deal. It seems the treasures have been coming into New Orleans from overseas, then up the Mississippi where they're being taken by private boat up the Galena River to Import Specialties. Our agency is still trying to track down all the players involved. They've had a few interesting confrontations in boats on the water at night." She made a wry face. "Damn! I missed out on that!"

Jim shrugged. "I like the water and boats, but I wouldn't want to chase criminals on a river at night. Although, it'd make for some good stories if you survived." Getting back on the subject, he asked, "So can we assume these artifacts are genuine Middle Eastern treasures?"

"They most likely are. There may be a few fakes, but they look right to me."

Seeing Jim's questioning look, she began to fill him in on the background of the Middle East antiquities operation.

"The looting in Syria and Iraq has escalated at an alarming rate over the last few years due to ISIS activity in that area of the world. We believe that the profits ISIS makes from the sale of these treasures have increased their coffers substantially, making them one of the richest terrorist groups on the face of the earth."

"That's not a comforting thought," Jim said seriously, his hands propped on his hips.

"No, it's not," Sheila said. "The whole Middle Eastern area is just one huge archaeological site that is now the playground for a bunch of thugs. Studying maps of different areas, we can see places that have what we call 'pockmarks' or sections that have been stripped clean of their cultural heritage. Everything from cuneiform writing tablets to cylinder seals to important sculptures, like that one of the ram in the thicket you found, has been looted and sold to the highest bidder. It's the equivalent of selling off our Declaration of Independence and Betsy Ross' hand-stitched American flag on eBay."

Jim cringed at the thought. Then he said, "So ISIS digs up the treasures, and then what?" Jim felt like a fifth-grader in history class, and he squirmed uncomfortably at his ignorance.

"Then the artifacts are sold wholesale on the black market. The thieves work through a broker, someone they know who has a connection to world markets. Individual dealers purchase the stolen goods from the broker and provide false provenance to collectors of the antiquities. The dealers often claim the pieces have been in a family for a long time, and the family wants to remain anonymous. But in reality, there are no written records to accompany most of these pieces. It's simply word of mouth and trust. Since the paper trail is not authentic, hunting these pieces down and prosecuting the people involved is hard. In the end, dealers are convinced they have done nothing wrong in purchasing the merchandise and then offering it for sale in their shops. It makes the recovery challenging, to say the least."

"And people are eager to buy this stuff?" Jim asked, fascinated by this new information.

Sheila nodded vigorously. "Oh, very much so. Wealthy patrons and collectors, museums anxious to upgrade their collections, auction houses and online sites enthusiastically purchase items every day not knowing what they're doing, or worse, turning a blind eye to the fact that a portion of their money is supporting a worldwide terrorist organization. That we've found an active group doing a brisk trade in the Midwest is very alarming."

Jim shook his head in amazement. "I know. I thought it was crazy, too," he commented, pausing a moment. "So, what do you need from me to help you get started?"

"I'd love to have Leslie's assistance if she's available," Sheila said, her face hopeful.

Jim's face turned somber. "Oh, I guess you didn't hear about her abduction," he said.

"What? What abduction? When did this happen?" she asked, the questions coming in a flurry. Sheila searched Jim's face for an explanation. "Is she okay?" Despite her professionalism, Jim could tell the news rattled her.

"She's recovering slowly. It's been about ten days since she was kidnapped. Fortunately, we were able to locate her quickly. Her physical wounds are healing, but she's pretty beat up emotionally." Jim's voice had become thick and husky, his eyes misting over.

Sheila's attention drifted to the door of the impound center and stayed there. Jim turned and watched Leslie slowly make her way over to them. She was tentative in her movements, her face withdrawn and pale. She came and stood in front of them.

"Speak of the devil," Sheila said softly, making eye contact, her eyebrows arched.

"Lazarus resurrected—or at least healed ... sort of," Leslie said, smiling shyly. "I heard you were back and might need a little help."

Jim touched her arm. "Are you sure about this?" Leslie nodded. Lifting her arm, she said, "My cast will make things a little awkward." A vexed look crossed her face.

"But if I sit one more day in my apartment, you'll have to visit me in the psych ward, sir."

"All right then," Jim said, grinning. He patted Leslie gently on the shoulder as he turned to go. "I guess you've got your wish, Sheila. Have at it," he said as he pointed to the treasure trove on the tables. ◉

52

Chet Boyer and DNR warden Jim Stensrude were hunkered down beneath a clump of red cedar trees that were clinging precariously to a hillside goat prairie southeast of Avalanche. They had climbed to the high barren slope which overlooked a wide valley. The coulee below them was peppered with clumps of hardwood stands, white pine thickets, and red-tipped sumac. A sinuous creek made its way southwest, where it eventually dumped into the Kickapoo. The thin ribbon of water occasionally sparkled like diamonds against a burlap sack.

Chet pushed aside clumps of grama grass and foxtail, clearing a view for his binoculars. He was glad he had marked this location a few days ago when he and Rusty had tramped up to the top of the ridge in search of an ideal deer hunting stand.

Warden Stensrude cleaned a flat spot on the ground for his spotting scope, brushing away an unmelted clump of snow, pebbles, and crusty frozen vegetation. Lying prone on his belly, he zeroed in on the rustic log cabin a quarter mile down the wide valley. This area was inaccessible by road and was recently set aside and designated as a public hunting area by the DNR. An ATV could easily maneuver among the wooded landscape and shallow trout streams that wandered here and there.

"Yep, I got the cabin in my sites. Nice little cabin, probably an original settlers cabin," Stensrude commented dryly. "It's been here a while. Somebody's there now. Smoke's comin' outta the chimney."

"Nothing wrong with having a nice little cabin on an isolated piece of land unless you're a fugitive wanted by the law," Boyer said nervously, stroking his beard. "And you're trying to avoid capture," he added as an afterthought.

"So you think this guy might be this ... what'd you say his name was again?"

"Wade. Wade Bennett. Saw a picture of him on the news the other night. Supposedly he's involved in some big Middle Eastern art heist, and he also kidnapped a female detective from the La Crosse Sheriff's Department a couple of weeks ago."

Stensrude looked over at Boyer, his frozen mustache white with frost. "They find her?"

"Yeah. He beat the shit outta her and locked her in a box in his barn. Her dog found her, I guess," Boyer whispered.

"How do you know all this stuff?"

"My brother-in-law works at the La Crosse jail. He knows just about everything that's goin' on—in law enforcement anyway. He's a regular male gossip," Boyer said sarcastically.

Straining to focus his spotting scope, Stensrude suddenly said, "Hey, I think I see him. Tall, lean, mustache? Looks like he could take on a couple of guys?"

"Yeah, that's him," Boyer said, watching through his own binoculars as Wade hauled in an armload of wood. "He's in his prime. Used to be a sniper in Iraq and Afghanistan. I'm sure he's deadly with a rifle." Boyer felt a chill run up his back. "Not someone we want to take on alone." He looked at Stensrude, glanced at the pistol on the warden's belt, and fidgeted uneasily.

"For sure. We need to get back to the sheriff's office and report this," Stensrude said. They watched Wade a while longer. Finally, Stensrude began packing up his scope. The men heaved themselves off the ground and began the hike back to their vehicle.

While the men were watching him, Wade was splitting wood, stacking it carefully along the fence. He suddenly felt an alarming shiver as if someone was spying on him. He supposed a hunter could have discovered him, but he was back in some pretty thick country. In his stay at the cabin, he hadn't seen one person yet, and he'd been here a little over ten days. But he'd learned from his military service to listen to his own paranoia. It usually proved accurate.

What are the chances someone could have spotted me? he thought. Slim to none. So far, his experience back in Wisconsin had proven to be terribly unlucky, though. Things seemed to come out in the other guy's favor. Maybe it was time to move along. He knew how to travel light. An urgency came over him as he began the next stage of his plan. Hopefully, it would turn out better than the other endeavors he'd attempted.

Chet Boyer and DNR Warden Jim Stensrude sat opposite Vernon County Sheriff Clyde Cade, rolling out their tale of the discovery of Wade Bennett's hiding place.

"You found this Bennett guy where?" Cade directed the men's attention to the map on the wall to the right of his desk. "Show me on this wall map where you found that cabin," Cade said, getting up from his desk chair and stopping in front of the Vernon County map.

"Okay, you see where Highway 82 and Vance Hill Road kinda form this Y here," Boyer said, pointing at a location on the map that was southeast from Avalanche. "The cabin is right about here," he said, looking over at Sheriff Cade.

"Is that the new DNR land?" Cade asked Stensrude.

"Yep. That property actually belonged to Wade's grandfather, Charles Bennett, at one time, but he sold it to the State of Wisconsin about two years ago, and the department decided to make it a public access hunting area," Stensrude explained. "I'm assuming the cabin was probably an original settlers cabin that's been maintained by the family for hunting purposes. That's where this Wade guy is hanging out."

"How come no one else ran across him?" Cade asked.

"I don't know, but not too many people know about that area. It was just designated last spring. And it's pretty rough country," Boyer replied. "Most hunters now want easy access to their hunting land. They don't want to walk up and down the hills searching for deer when they can find a spot a half mile off the road with a nice blind."

Cade walked back to his desk and flipped open his cell. "That makes sense, I guess. I need to talk to Davey Jones up in La Crosse and Jim Higgins. Thanks, guys, for the information."

"No problem," Boyer said, standing up to leave. "Hope you catch the guy." ◉

53

"You mean he had a joint overseas bank account with Wade Bennett? In the Cayman Islands?" Paul asked, surprised at the discovery.

"You are inquiring about a Mr. Rod Girabaldi from La Crosse, Wisconsin, are you not?" the British-accented voice reiterated.

"Yes, that's what the IRS criminal investigation is focused on. They suspect that Rod Girabaldi has hidden his profits from an international military gas smuggling operation in an account in your overseas bank."

"We reported his balance in his account to the IRS in November of 2016." The voice had lost its friendly quality, and in its place, a hint of hostility was riding on the clipped consonants.

Paul picked up the change. *My ear for music comes in handy at the most inopportune times,* he thought.

"Yes, I realize you must report the account because of FACTA. My question for you is this: Were you aware that Mr. Girabaldi and Mr. Bennett were involved in an international smuggling ring that is helping to fund ISIS terrorist groups around the world?"

No, sir," the British banker said. "We are only required to report the existence of the account to the United States division of the IRS. We never question the origin of our clients' funds. That would overstep

SUE BERG

our authority and threaten the confidence that our investors have in us. What the IRS decides to do with that information is up to them," the voice said, ratcheting up in tension.

"Right. Thanks for your assistance, sir," Paul said. *That was a dead end,* he thought. He hung up the landline and stood up. Stretching backward, he worked out the tight muscles in his back. Then he strolled down the hall to Jim's office.

Jim had been talking with Sheriff Tom Waverly in Trempealeau County. He was learning more about Jordan Lagerton's bomb-making capabilities when Paul walked in and sprawled in a chair in front of his desk. Paul studied the ceiling, letting out a noisy sigh.

"So you're telling me he might have had some assistance in his bomb-building spree?" Jim asked, shrugging his shoulders at Paul. "Any idea who that might be?" Jim continued to listen, scribbling and doodling as Waverly talked.

"Mike Walsh, Kreibich Coulee? Yeah, it's not too far from where I live. We'll check it out. Thanks." Jim laid the phone in its cradle.

Paul asked, "Who're you talkin' to?"

"Sheriff Waverly up in Trempealeau. They found bomb components in Jordan's trailer, which is no big surprise. But the Dane County Bomb Squad thinks that someone with rather sophisticated munitions knowledge may have helped Jordan construct the bombs he planted around La Crosse. Somebody named Mike Walsh." Jim looked down at his sheet. "Sounds like a nut. Got his address so let's go over and talk to him. See what he says."

"A nut? Whadda ya mean?" Paul asked, alarmed, his brow furrowing into a scowl.

"Well, I talked to Jones downstairs. Apparently, there've been some problems with the neighbors. Davy's sent a couple of officers out to his place multiple times. He likes to regularly blow things up—on his own property, of course. That sounds pretty crazy to me." Jim said. He paused, then asked, "What'd you find out about the IRS probe on Girabaldi?"

"The account in the Cayman's is a joint one with Wade Bennett."

Jim eyebrows arched in surprise. "Joint? That's unusual, isn't it?" he asked.

"Yeah, although the bank executive I talked to didn't seem to be concerned about it." Paul made a rude noise. "Go figure. The British." He got back to his explanation. "The IRS is now officially conducting a criminal investigation into the financial account of Girabaldi and Bennett. I'm pretty sure they'll tie it back to the antiquities and the black market gasoline sales in Iraq. It'll be a huge paper trail that's going to involve the military and maybe the FBI. It's way bigger than we ever realized," Paul concluded.

"Wow. Well, if the FBI is involved, then we're out of it. We'll have to let the big dogs handle it now. We're just gnawin' on bones," Jim commented, walking around his desk and grabbing his coat. "Let's go out and talk to this Walsh guy."

Driving south out of La Crosse on U.S. Highway 35, Jim took in the beauty of the Mississippi River valley spread out before him. The snow had disappeared in the latest temperature hike. Only a few white mounds remained on north-facing locations. The hills were brown again, scattered with thick dark brown groves of hardwoods, punctuated with clumps of evergreens. The western sky was beginning to cloud over, and the promise of more snow was in the forecast.

Turning on County M, where Marmon Creek ran parallel to the road, Jim wound his way through the valley until he came to Kreibich Coulee. He drove down the gravel road through the woods until he came to a small fire number on a post labeled 1389. Jim turned the Suburban up the lane and eventually came to a small farmstead which included a leaning, run-down barn pockmarked with missing boards and windows and a newer red metal pole shed next to it. The house was a log cabin affair, small but adequate. A conglomeration of broken-down cycles, rusted shells of cars, and a Farmall 200 tractor stood silently scattered around the yard, reminders of better times. A dog barked in the backyard, but otherwise, it was quiet.

Jim and Paul climbed out of the Suburban. Paul pulled his jacket back, his police-issue pistol loaded securely in his shoulder holster.

Jim noticed, nodded, and took several long strides toward the cabin when the door flew open unexpectedly.

"Who're you?" a mountain man yelled. Sporting a full beard and wild unruly shoulder-length hair, Mike Walsh wore a red, buffalo-plaid flannel shirt topped with a dirty gray Carhartt vest and a pair of grungy, off-white long underwear. He was barefoot even though the temperature hovered around forty degrees.

Jim flipped open his ID and held it up. *A little paranoia?* he wondered. *Anti-social behavior?* Mike bumped down the stairs and quickly came up to Jim, eyeing his badge with an eerie kind of bravado. Paul stepped forward a few feet, calmly holding up his ID, too.

"We don't mean any harm," Jim said with a forced calm, his heart thumping in his chest. *This is how cops get shot,* he thought, upbraiding himself for not wearing a vest. "We'd just like to ask you a few questions." Jim continued to walk up to him slowly, kind of like you'd approach a wild dog or frantic horse. Calm. Intentional. Confident.

"Questions about what?" Mike demanded rudely. Jim noticed his intelligent blue eyes, just a bit on the turbulent side, distrust just below the surface. Mike was carefully backing toward the porch as Jim advanced.

"Can we come in for a minute?" Jim asked politely.

"Whatever I got to say can be said right here," Walsh said in a quiet, threatening tone, pointing downward at the ground. He'd backed up on the steps. The red flags from Walsh's behavior made Jim tone down his rhetoric.

"That's fine. We can talk here," Jim said. He shifted on his feet and put one foot on the bottom rung of the stairs. Mike backed up to the top step. "Do you know Jordan Lagerton?"

"Only know what I read in the papers," Mike said, looking over the tops of their heads.

"And what did you learn about him in the papers?" Jim continued, watching Walsh's eyes.

"Guess the cops think he killed that truck driver up by the wayside," Walsh said, shifting uncomfortably in his bare feet.

"I understand you know quite a bit about munitions and bombs. Can you tell me about that?" Jim said, his voice deep and calm.

"Learned it in the army. Served in Nam, then came home and worked for the government building federal dams and stuff." Walsh eyed Jim suspiciously, then his eyes drifted to Paul. Paul felt the urge to squirm but forced himself to stand still.

"I've heard you've had some trouble with your neighbors," Jim said. It was more a statement than a question.

A grin spread across Mike's features. "Some. They don't have an appreciation for the work I do."

Paul stepped forward. "Can you tell us about your movements the last week or so? Where you've been, what activities you've been engaged in?"

"I've been here every day. Argued with my crotchety neighbor over a tree. Made a few trips to Walmart. That's about it."

"Do you live with anyone? Have a wife?" Jim asked.

"Whadda ya think?" Walsh replied sarcastically. "Look at me? You think some woman is gonna wanna live with me?" Mike cocked his head and swooped his hand over the front of his body. "Really? A wife?" he finished, shaking his head, grabbing a fistful of his shirt.

Jim smiled in spite of himself. "Did you help Jordan Lagerton build four bombs in the last two weeks and then help him plant them in buildings around La Crosse?"

Walsh stared at Jim, his eyes unblinking for a long moment. Finally, he answered, shaking his head as he spoke. "Now I've done some rather questionable things—on my own property, of course— but I've never done anything *that* dumb."

Jim turned to leave, talking over his shoulder. "Thanks, Mr. Walsh. We may ask you to come down to the law enforcement center on Vine Street sometime for more questioning."

"Damn bureaucrats," Walsh whispered under his breath.

As they crawled into the Suburban, Jim turned to Paul, catching his eye.

"Well, we didn't learn much, but you've got to admit, *that* was entertaining."

Paul nodded, his heart banging unpredictably in his chest. He sure hoped that it would slow down and go back to its normal rate on the drive back into town. ◉

MONDAY
NOVEMBER 12

54

Sam Birkstein huffed alongside Paco as he jogged the Rotary Vista Trail in Hixon Forest in the early morning light. Coming up over a rise in the trail which snaked along the edge of the bluff, Sam felt a slight buzz—something he always attributed to a good workout. In the distance, a couple of miles off, he saw the Mississippi River through a haze, a low-lying fog hovering just above its surface. During the overnight hours, the humidity in the air had created a rime frost. Clinging to the crooked branches of hardwood trees and brushy undergrowth, the frost transformed nature into a storybook world of lacy, crystallized foliage. Evergreen needles were flocked with white, their brownish-black trunks in stark contrast to their adorned branches. This morning, there was a quiet, majestic beauty in the silent forest as cardinals and blue jays flitted among the frozen vegetation. *The glory of God,* Sam thought.

As he ran, Sam contemplated the raid they'd be making this morning near Avalanche where Wade Bennett had been discovered. He'd run the details of the operation over and over in his mind. Their plan had been carefully designed and analyzed, equipment had been gathered, and maps of the area were marked up with arrows. The group of eight men had argued strategy yesterday and had finally come up with a workable plan. But Sam knew the best-laid plans could go awry, especially where Wade was concerned. His stomach churned at the thought of confronting Bennett again. Anyone who hadn't looked into his eyes could not begin to understand the alarming effect he could have on your mental health. Sam shook his head and tried to forget the image of Wade on the front porch of Leslie's apartment. He shivered involuntarily.

Paco ran ahead in his excessive dog exuberance, then doubled back to bark fitfully at Sam. Finishing the two-mile loop over switchbacks and bluff vistas, Sam clicked Paco on his leash, and they cooled down, walking quietly back to Leslie's on La Crosse Street. The sun was just peeking over the horizon.

Reaching the apartment, Sam leaned down and unhooked Paco's leash. He ran ahead and waited at the back entrance until Sam caught up and unlocked the door. In the apartment, Sam heard the shower running. Bolting through the house, Paco barked and fretted until he finally came to a stop perching on his haunches outside the bathroom door.

Sam walked into the kitchen and started the coffee maker. Opening the refrigerator, he took out orange juice, yogurt, eggs, and bacon. After a few moments, Paco stuck his head around the corner of the kitchen door, then looked back, his tail wagging. Leslie appeared in her bathrobe, combing her wet hair. Sam messed around getting out a couple of frying pans and bread for toast.

"Hey, thanks for taking Paco on his run," Leslie said, leaning against the door frame. "He's had a hit-and-miss exercise schedule since I got hurt. Without his exercise, he gets difficult to handle. Too much energy."

"Kinda like me." Sam smiled, noticing the clean soapy smell of Leslie. *What would it be like to wake up beside her every morning?* he thought, immediately chiding himself. *Too early for that.*

"I can't imagine you're ever very difficult," she commented, her eyes watching him separate bacon strips and lay them in a cast-iron skillet.

"I can be." *You're about to find out,* he thought.

"That sounds like a bad omen," she said, suddenly suspicious. "Something going on?"

He turned toward her, leaning against the kitchen counter, stopping his cooking preparations.

"Yeah. A couple of hunters spotted Wade hiding out in some ancient log cabin in the woods down by Avalanche yesterday. Way back in the woods." Leslie stopped combing her hair and fixed him with an intense stare. "They figured he's been there since he disappeared from his farm. We're wondering if he's getting some assistance from a family member," he finished, watching her reaction. His chest tightened. He felt his breathing quicken.

"He's got a brother around La Farge, I think," she said calmly, combing her hair again.

"We're going down to assist in his capture this morning."

"Who's we?" she asked, leaning over to pat Paco's head, absentmindedly stroking his ear.

"Higgins, Paul, Mike LeLand from city police, and me, plus some guys from Vernon County. They're runnin' the show." He placed his palms on the countertop behind him.

"Sounds dangerous," Leslie said, her voice taking on a worried tone.

Sam scoffed. "One against eight?" He looked agitated. "He can't be that tough, but you're the expert when it comes to Wade." Sam's voice had taken on a flinty tone. "If he's as dangerous as you say, we'll be ready for him."

Leslie stared at him until he squirmed. Sam was feeling anxious about facing Wade again. As he talked about it, his nervousness made him feel like he was confined in a small cage. He stood a little straighter, staring at her.

"I'm not playin' this game, Sam," she finally said quietly.

"What game?" he asked sardonically, a frown creasing his brow.

"The game where you get to go kill Wade and come back like some conquering hero." Her eyes had turned hard. Paco sensed the tension, whined, and pressed his muzzle against Leslie's leg.

"Game? Is that what you think this is about? Me being a hero? Well, don't let your thoughts about him cloud your judgment. The guy murdered Rod Girabaldi in cold blood, and he would have finished you off if we wouldn't have found you!" Sam's voice had climbed in volume. He gripped the edge of the counter behind him, his knuckles turning white. He felt combative and feisty, but immediately he regretted his words.

"What?! Are you kidding me?" She huffed, her eyes growing big. "Really? Do you actually believe I have one ounce of affection for that man?" She pointed her index finger at Sam, jerking it up and down as she talked. "That was a low blow, Sam. I have news for you—women who get raped don't have affectionate feelings for the rapist." Her voice was shaking with rage. She pulled her finger into a fist, then lowered it slowly to her side in the silence that followed.

Suddenly, the gulf between them seemed enormous. *Well, that didn't go well, you idiot,* Sam thought. He dropped his arms to his sides and walked across the small space between them. Leslie backed against the wall, her eyes wide with apprehension. *If looks could kill, I'd be dead,* he thought. He remembered a Bible verse his mother had taught him. *A soft answer turneth away wrath. You better give it a try,* he thought. He inhaled a long breath. "I didn't mean to suggest you had any kind of affection for him," Sam said, talking softly and shuffling uneasily from one foot to the other. "I'm sorry. That was a really stupid thing to say."

Leslie continued to stare at him, her face shut down, her emotions in check. Finally, she asked, "Are you nervous about this mission?"

Sam grimaced at the military term. He wiped his hand over his eyes, his hair still sweaty from his run. "Nervous doesn't begin to describe it," he confessed, letting out a gush of air. "Will you forgive me?" he asked, his hazel eyes contrite.

Leslie remained cold and aloof. He started again, moving his hands up and down like he was pushing his emotions down into a box. "I'm not angry at you. It's just that when I think about what

Wade did to you, well, I have a hard time."

Leslie was surprised to see tears forming in Sam's eyes. He stopped, looked away from her, struggling to gain control of his racing thoughts. "I have to admit that when I'm near you like this, I have trouble staying focused." *Especially when I know what's under the bathrobe,* he thought. "You're just so incredibly beautiful. You've been treated very badly, and someone should give you the love you deserve. That's all." Quiet pervaded every corner of the kitchen. Paco sat at Leslie's side panting, looking up at Sam as if to say, *Way to go, big guy.*

"Someone like you?" Leslie asked, searching his face, her tone softening.

Sam sighed, leaned in and tenderly kissed her. *I love you, even though I know it won't be easy,* he thought.

"Maybe we should start over. Ya think?" whispered Leslie. She grabbed his hand.

"When I'm nervous, I can really be a nerd," he said, a grin shadowing his mouth.

"I noticed. You're forgiven," she whispered back. She pulled him into a gentle hug. "Eww, you don't smell so good," she said, crinkling up her nose.

"My heart's in the right place, though. Breakfast?" Sam asked into her wet hair.

"Sure, I'll help," she replied, pulling back and looking into his eyes. "One thing. Did you mean that? About me being beautiful?"

"I meant every word." ◉

55

By ten o'clock, the La Crosse team had gathered in Jim's office and taken inventory of their equipment and weapons. Each man was dressed in practical duck pants or black jeans, flexible waterproof footwear, a Kevlar vest, and warm tactical fleece-lined jackets. The mood was somber. Jim felt the situation with Wade was one of the biggest challenges his team had ever faced. *Maybe we'll all be wrong. Maybe Wade won't try to kill us all. Maybe he'll surrender peacefully, and no one will get hurt,* he thought. He huffed to himself. Paul looked over at him.

"You say something', Chief?" he asked, glancing over at him.

Jim shook his head. "No, no. Just thinkin'," he responded. *Maybe he'll surrender? Not a chance on God's green earth,* he thought.

The day had started with sunshine snaking through the branches of the huge maples outside Jim's house throwing crooked shadows on the brown grass. Jim stood outside on his front porch in his stocking feet, the morning newspaper in hand, pondering the complicated set of challenges it would take to capture Wade Bennett. He shook his head when he thought of all the different scenarios that could take place. None of his thoughts were the least bit comforting. Wade Bennett was highly trained, supremely determined, and desperate. Jim couldn't shake the uneasiness he felt. The bad feeling he'd had

SUE BERG

earlier was still there, stronger than ever. He hated it when he had those kinds of misgivings.

After breakfast, he'd given Carol an especially tender kiss and embrace when he left. She hadn't asked what it meant, and he hadn't told her. Perhaps they were both becoming a little wiser.

As the four men loaded the Suburban in the parking lot of the law enforcement center on Vine Street, a bank of purplish clouds lay low in the southwestern sky, looking threatening and ominous. A gray haze was rapidly replacing the vibrant morning sunshine. The temperature hovered at about twenty-eight degrees, and Jim thought it would be snowing by late afternoon or evening.

"Anybody hear the forecast today?" he asked, trying to alleviate some of the tension.

The subdued conversation from the team told Jim the weather was the least of their concerns. Quietly scrolling on his phone, Paul snapped the device shut with a sigh, slipping it into his jacket. He stared blankly out the windshield. Sam fidgeted in the backseat, his leg jiggling nervously until he caught Jim's eye. He'd been trying to visualize Leslie's image, thinking it might bring him some comfort and ease his anxiety, but it wasn't working, which bothered him. He made an effort to bring his edgy demeanor under control. The city cop, Mike LeLand, was selected to assist in the capture since he'd been taking classes at the technical college and recently finished his Principles of Investigation course. Plus, he'd volunteered. Jim knew as soon as he was qualified, he would be applying for openings on the investigation team.

"Mike? You okay?" Jim asked from the driver's seat, his eyes scanning Mike's face in the rearview mirror.

"Just fine, sir," he said quietly, but Jim could tell he was jumpy. He kept tapping his fingers on his pant leg, and more than once, he breathed in deeply, then let his air out in a rush.

Jim drove to the U.S. Highway 14 turn off on the outskirts of La Crosse and headed southeast toward the Vernon County Sheriff's Department in Viroqua. In forty-five minutes, he was driving into the small city, past the north side Kwik Trip, pulling up outside the Vernon County Law Enforcement Center, an impressive brick and glass structure.

Parking the Suburban, the team jumped out of the truck and fidgeted nervously, getting the knots out. They walked into the cavernous building, and a woman officer led them to a classroom in the back. Sheriff Cade greeted them, and then they got down to business. A county map was tacked on a cork board, and the eight officers gathered around.

The Bennett cabin was located in a valley between County Road S to the southeast and Highway 82, which ran east to west. The roads formed a lopsided V shape. Steep wooded hillsides surrounded the cabin, and small groves of hardwoods and pines were dispersed throughout the valley. A trout stream twisted and snaked throughout the low-lying area.

Plans included driving four ATVs in from a central starting point along the county road. As they crossed the terrain, each ATV would veer off at different points to get as close to the cabin as possible from different angles. When they were within a couple of hundred yards of the cabin, the officers were instructed to proceed on foot, using trees and shrubbery to stay undercover and hidden, basically forming a noose around the cabin that would tighten as they moved forward until they were in close quarters. Stealth and quiet communication would be required to take Wade alive.

"You need to be aware that Wade most likely will not surrender," Sam spoke up, his voice spiked with authority, his eyes taking on a hard glitter.

The men turned to look. Sam felt their street smarts and experience evaluating him.

"Bringing him in alive is our top priority," Sheriff Cade repeated, his eyes a dead calm, the message unmistakable.

"I understand the mission and objective," Sam said, adjusting his tone to meet the challenge in the sheriff's voice. "I'm just saying, he's a warrior, and we are the enemy. I doubt that he will accept defeat, and he would consider being captured defeat."

"We hear you. Message delivered, loud and clear," Cade said quietly. He made eye contact with the officers as he talked. "Remember everyone, cell phones on vibrate mode. We'll be texting our positions and readiness when we are in place and have made visual contact with the cabin. Any other concerns or questions? Jim?" Cade asked, looking over a few heads to where Jim was leaning against the wall.

Jim had been listening carefully. He stood up straight and said, "It's a good plan. I want to reiterate that everyone needs to be aware of the capabilities and desperate nature of the perpetrator. From every indication we have, he's already killed one person. And Wade seriously injured one of my officers and would have killed her if we had not found her first. Do not underestimate his skill set. He will be armed, dangerous, and more than willing to do the hard things to escape capture," Jim lectured. His eyes floated over the men in front of him. A few nodded. The seriousness of the situation was not lost on them. Sam met his eyes and silently agreed, giving him a quick nod.

"All right. We've got it. Let's move out," Sheriff Cade said solemnly.

The caravan traveled north on Highway 14 for a few miles, then east on County Y until they descended into the valley. Driving out of Avalanche, they drove south on County S until they came to the edge of a farm field. They parked their vehicles and trailers under a grove of towering white pines. The sky had turned a metallic gray color, and dark blue clouds scudded along the horizon. The moisture had been building in the air all morning, and now tiny bits of snow were falling, pushed by a steady, raw easterly wind.

The officers unloaded the four ATVs and teamed up. Since the land they'd be on was owned by the DNR, a phone call to the local warden had given them the permission they needed to proceed with the arrest and capture of the fugitive. Jim hoped they wouldn't be too late.

Jim and Sam partnered up, and Paul agreed to ride with Mike

LeLand. Everybody mounted their ATVs and entered the wasteland, branching out at different points to eventually pull the drawstring of capture around the cabin.

Sam expertly drove the four-wheeler over the rough ground, driving through oak savannas and into more open country, finally cresting over a small rise on the valley floor, then dipping down into a swale. A bald eagle soared effortlessly above the valley floor, watching for the movement of rodents in the high, brown grasses. Sam crossed a narrow neck of a trout stream and stopped. Jim jumped off and pulled out his binoculars. Standing under the branches of a red pine, he surveyed the scene.

"We're getting closer. Our point of reference is Tainter Rock. I can see it on the hillside over there," Jim pointed in the distance, "so we're good. Let's go a little farther and find someplace to hide the ATV. Then we'll go on foot," he finished.

About a quarter of a mile farther, Jim tapped Sam's shoulder and pointed to a small area of undergrowth. Sam parked the vehicle and hopped off. They began walking northeast in the direction of the cabin, not knowing for sure where it was. As they walked, Jim pushed thoughts of Carol and the twins from his mind, vowing to concentrate fully on the events at hand.

Suddenly, Sam held up a hand and knelt down in the shelter of a small copse of sumac and dried grasses. Jim slowed his pace coming up alongside him. Through the trees and random undergrowth, the weathered cabin lay peacefully next to the creek two hundred yards away.

"That's the place," Sam whispered, his anxiety just below the surface.

"Smoke from the chimney," Jim said very quietly. "He must be there." Despite the calmness in his voice, Jim felt his heart rate pick up, and he swiped his hand across the side of his face.

"Checking in," Sam said as he popped open his cell and texted Sheriff Cade. "Have arrived at site. 200 yds. out. Awaiting instructions. Jim and Sam."

Sam kept his cell phone in his hand. Jim monitored the cabin through his binoculars. Sam's phone vibrated. A text arrived. Sam read it.

"Three teams ready. Wait for signal to move forward. Cade"

Sam texted back. "Waiting for further instructions. Sam"

"Any movement, sir?" Sam asked, leaning in and looking over Jim's shoulder.

"Nothing yet, but I'm sure he's there—or at least in the area," Jim whispered.

Suddenly from behind them, a soft yet confident voice spoke. "Good afternoon, gentlemen. Kinda far from home, aren't you?"

Sam felt his stomach clench in a violent cramp. He slowly stood up and turned. The cool gray eyes of Wade Bennett stared at him. Jim pivoted in a quick jerk.

"Easy, old man," Wade continued, pointing his SIG Sauer handgun at him. "We don't want anyone to get hurt, do we?"

Jim's eyes gravitated to the gun, the little "o" of the barrel filling him with dread. Wade's face, though ruddy from the cold, was like a chiseled mask of granite. Flicking his eyes to Sam, he said, "And how is Leslie doing these days?" A lazy slow grimace stretched over his lips.

Sam cursed. "She's recovering slowly. There's one thing I'm sure of," he said, meeting his gaze.

"What's that, lover boy? Have you bedded her yet? Take it from me; it's very enjoyable." Sam's jaw worked furiously as he bit down on his teeth. Jim put a protective grip on Sam's arm.

"Easy, Sam. He's not worth it," he said quietly. You're better than that." Casting a gaze on Wade, Jim asked, "So what's your plan?"

"You tell me. You're obviously not here alone," Wade responded briskly.

Jim took stock of their situation. "Actually, we are alone," he lied. "A couple of hunters spotted your cabin a few days ago and reported your presence in this valley. We were just verifying you were actually here."

Jim studied Wade with a cool calmness. After an intense moment under his scrutiny, Wade began to squirm and fidget. While Jim was engaging Wade, Sam had turned off his phone and slipped it in his pocket. He could only hope Sheriff Cade would interpret his silence as a glitch in their plans. All of his worst nightmares were materializing right before his eyes. Wade being let loose to wreak havoc with his insane plans, whatever they were, filled Sam with cold, raw fear.

"Well, here I am—in the flesh," Wade said. But then he began protesting. "Don't tell me you're alone. I don't believe that. You can't be."

"Why not?" Jim asked, staring Wade down despite the spike of anxiety he felt.

"You'll never take me alive. You do realize that, don't you?" Wade's gray eyes wandered across Jim's face. Jim met his gaze with one of his own.

"That's up to you. Dead or alive, you're responsible for the death of Rod Girabaldi and the attempted murder and assault of Leslie Brown. I'll see that you pay the price for your crimes," Jim said roughly. Sam shuffled on his feet.

Brandishing his pistol, Wade ordered, "Weapons. Take them out of your jackets. Slowly. Throw them on the ground." His tone was belligerent. Jim and Sam carefully reached into their jackets and removed their pistols, throwing them on the ground at Wade's feet. He kicked the guns into the scrubby brush. Then he made a sharp gesture with his gun toward the cabin. "Get movin'!" he snarled. "Toward the cabin. Let's go!"

Jim and Sam turned simultaneously, stepping through the dense undergrowth and out into the open prairie habitat. With Wade trailing them, they headed toward the cabin. Jim's mind raced with the implications of their predicament. Nothing about this situation looked promising. He glanced at Sam, whose face was a pretense of calm. *God, he's such a good kid.*

As they trudged over the frozen ground, snowflakes began falling, landing on their heads and shoulders. A crow cawed prophetically from a tall red pine, his screech echoing above them, drifting out over the open field. Jim was filled with foreboding. The needles of the pine swished in the faint breeze. That they could possibly escape their fate seemed foolish beyond any practical calculation. Still, Jim continued to hope beyond hope that the other officers might come up with a plan of attack or some kind of intervention. They had the cabin surrounded. Sheriff Cade must be aware that something had gone wrong. Then a random thought came to him. *Do what you can, where you are, with what you have.*

The small cabin loomed before them across the rippling creek. From a distance, it had seemed quaint and charming. Now, as Sam and Jim walked over the hand-hewn log bridge that spanned the water, Jim felt the ominous implications of being held hostage within its walls.

They slowed and stopped walking, standing under a towering white pine. Pine cones crackled under Wade's feet as he approached them from behind. In any other circumstance, Jim would have enjoyed the sharp, intense scent of evergreen that wafted in the air.

Jim wasn't a believer in clairvoyance, but in an instant, as he bent over to tie his shoe, Sam seemed to read his thoughts. A glance and a moment in time presented itself. A hefty stick that had fallen out of the huge pine lay on the ground within Jim's reach. He grabbed it, and as he swung around to face Wade, Sam dove at Wade's feet, tackling him to the ground. Unfortunately, instead of hitting Wade, the branch missed its mark and flew helter-skelter past the target, leaving Sam in a death grip, the life-breath being choked out of him.

"Stupid choice, old man!" Wade hissed. He pointed his gun at Jim and pulled the trigger. The blast, deflected by Sam's desperate swipe, went wide, hitting the huge pine, ripping the bark loose from the trunk, sending splinters into the air. Wade and Sam continued in a do-or-die tumble, rolling back and forth on the ground, the gun still in Wade's grip jerking aimlessly in the scuffle.

Just at that moment, Jim noticed Paul in his peripheral vision, running full bore into the encampment.

"No! No, Paul! Stay back!" Jim warned, his voice loud and strident. He waved his arms wildly, his hands gesturing in a pushing motion.

Two gunshots rang out. Paul went down, screaming and flailing on the ground. Jim dove on top of Wade, wrenching the pistol from his grasp, throwing it several feet in the air. By this time, the other officers were arriving, guns drawn. Mike LeLand knelt beside Paul. Sam and another officer subdued and handcuffed Wade.

Horrified, Jim ran over to Paul.

"Paul! Paul!" he said, taking his hand. "Hang on, buddy. Help's on the way." He looked over Paul's body, noticing the tear in his pants leg, blood pouring out of his thigh onto the ground. "It's a leg wound." Jim looked at Mike. "Call the MedFlight crew from Gundersen. Give them your GPS coordinates. If we don't get help quickly, he's going to bleed out."

While Mike called 911, Jim tore his jacket off, ripping the string out of the casing on the hood. He tore open Paul's pants, his hands shaking. Using the string, he tied it around his thigh above the wound. Paul screamed in pain.

"Help me, Chief! Help me!" His eyes were wild with shock and pain. He began shaking, sweating profusely, clutching his leg.

"What should I do?" Mike asked, his eyes wide with terror.

Jim unzipped Paul's jacket, then pulled up his shirt. He hadn't realized it, but Paul had been shot twice, once through his right leg and another through his right side. Jim could see blood steadily seeping from it. By now, Sam had joined Jim, kneeling next to him.

"Need something to make a compress," Jim instructed in a tight voice. Sam felt in his jacket pockets. Nothing there. Jim eyed Sam's T-shirt.

"Take your T-shirt off, fold it and hold it against this wound," Jim ordered.

Sam threw his coat on the ground and whipped off his shirt. With trembling hands, he folded the shirt and rolled Paul on his side. Pressing hard, he held the compress on the wound. Paul groaned, then seemed to pass out.

"He broke rank, Chief," Sam said through a grimace.

"He did his best. End of story," Jim answered gruffly.

The officers under the huge pine tree struggled to subdue Wade. He shouted a string of obscenities, wrestling against the restraints that had been placed on his wrists. Helping him stand, Wade glanced at Jim, locking eyes with him.

"How's that for justice, Higgins? One of your own bit the dust," Wade yelled sarcastically. An officer next to him said something to Wade, and he was taken up the hill toward the ATVs that had been hidden behind a group of pines.

Running up to the La Crosse team, Sheriff Cade asked, "Whadda ya need, Jim?" Resting his hands on his knees, he hovered over Paul.

"We need a blanket or something to keep him warm." Jim wiped his arm across his forehead. The shock of seeing Paul incapacitated left him breathless. Sheriff Cade peeled off his jacket and laid it across Paul's upper body. "Copter will be here in twenty minutes."

In the chaos that followed, Jim lost track of time. He sat next to Paul, holding his hand, talking quietly to him although he was sure Paul couldn't hear him. He seemed to be drifting away. Sam held the compress on his wound. "How am I going to tell Ruby?" Jim said to no one in particular.

"He's going to be all right," Sam said. "All right. He's going to be all right."

After several minutes, they could hear the *whump, whump* of the helicopter blades churning the air, coming in from the north. Soon the MedFlight helicopter appeared over the crest of the hill like a giant insect hovering above a flower. The machine hovered in the air, and then the pilot lowered it to the ground. Dust and dry grass rose up around the machine forming a swirling grimy cloud. Technicians jumped out carrying a board.

"Over here!" Sheriff Cade yelled, waving his hand in the air. "Over here."

The next minutes seemed surreal and dreamlike as the EMT crew worked on Paul and strapped him to the board.

"You riding along?" a young woman attendant asked Jim, looking up at him where she'd been kneeling by Paul.

"Sure," Jim answered. "Wait." Motioning to Sam, he grabbed his arm and said, "Take my Suburban back to La Crosse. I'll meet you at the hospital. Call Leslie. Have her get Ruby. She shouldn't hear the news alone. I'll call Carol."

The attendants were already loading Paul, and Jim jogged quickly to the copter. As it rose into the air, Jim waved to Sam. As the wooded hills receded. Jim closed his eyes and felt the tears come— tears of relief, tears of sadness. He leaned back against the seat, suddenly exhausted. *How am I going to explain this to Ruby?* he thought for the umpteenth time. ◉

56

T he lights of the surgical waiting room at Gundersen Lutheran Hospital were dimmed. Outside, the sky had darkened to a deep purple as the sun set below the bluffs on the west bank of the Mississippi River. Small groups of people were huddled here and there, some sleeping, some quietly conversing. Someone went to the window and drew the shades. The computer monitor blinked regularly with patient numbers and updates. People sipped on coffee and soft drinks. Cardboard pizza boxes, fast food containers, and crumpled napkins were scattered on several tables.

Carol made her way through the parking ramp outside the hospital, walking briskly toward the hospital entrance through the cold November air now laced with gently falling snow. Checking in at the desk, she learned that Paul was already in surgery. She climbed the stairs and made her way to the corner where the team was sitting. The news of Paul's injuries had spread among the law enforcement community. Over twenty off-duty officers had joined the detective team and were crammed in the corner awaiting news about Paul's condition. In the corner, Ruby cuddled Melody while Leslie and Sam sat next to her quietly talking. Ruby stood and burst into tears when she saw Carol. Rushing forward, Carol hugged her. Leslie came up and gently rubbed her back.

"Do you know anything yet?" Carol asked sympathetically, brushing a few locks of Ruby's hair from her face. Her eyes were panic stricken, and she looked ready to take flight like a captured bird.

"Not yet. Just that he's still in surgery. The doctor will be out when he can give us more news," she said through her tears.

"Listen to me." Carol grabbed her hands, making sure she had her attention. She looked directly into her eyes. "Paul's young and strong. The doctors here are very good. Let's stay positive. Are your parents coming?"

Ruby nodded her head. "Yeah, they should be here within an hour. They're going to take her back to our apartment while I stay with Paul."

"Good. Come on. Let's sit down," Carol said, guiding Ruby to a chair. The three women huddled in the corner together, thankful for the distraction of Melody's infant antics.

"Anybody hungry?" Sam asked after a bit. "I could order pizza." Carol noticed his weary look and his dirty clothes. Leslie softly brushed his hair away from his face.

"Pizza sounds good," Leslie said.

While they were eating, Carol noticed Jim climbing the stairs wearily. She got up quietly and met him. He looked exhausted. His eyes were dull, and he was unshaven and disheveled. Carol enfolded him in her arms. When she pulled back, she could see the tears forming in his eyes.

"How's Ruby doing?" he asked in a hoarse voice.

"She'll be fine. She's got a good support system. How're you?"

"I'm glad we got him." He was trying hard to remain impassive, but with Carol so near, he couldn't hang on to it. The tears spilled onto his cheeks. "Damn! I tried to warn Paul to stay back."

"Hey! We're not doing this," Carol warned sternly, shaking her head. "Paul did the best he could. Do you have any news about his condition yet?"

Shaking his head, Jim pulled out his phone and checked the

time. "He's been in surgery about two hours. There should be some news soon," he sighed. He felt like this day was never going to end.

"Hungry?" Carol asked.

Jim paused a moment. "Yeah, I guess I am," he said, surprised. He hadn't had any time to even think about eating.

They walked over, and Jim embraced Ruby.

"I want you to know Paul did everything right," Jim said. "His timing was perfect." Jim gave Sam a look. *Shut up. It's not important now.* "Sam and I will always be grateful for what he did," he finished.

"That's good to hear," Ruby said, her eyes glistening through more tears.

Finishing up their pizza, everyone listened as Jim reviewed the details of the capture. Sam contributed more, explaining how the shooting had gone down. Satiated with food, everyone grew quiet. Sam stretched out on a loveseat and promptly fell asleep. Ruby's parents stopped, got an update, and took Melody home to the apartment. Jim and Carol held hands and talked quietly. Finally, a nurse strolled over to Ruby.

"Are you Paul Saner's wife?" she asked politely. Ruby nodded.

"Paul's out of surgery. He's in recovery and will soon be sent to a room in the intensive care unit. The doctor would like to meet with you. Is there anyone you want to come with you?" the nurse asked, looking over the motley crew. *Guess police work isn't as glamorous as it is on TV,* she thought.

Ruby looked over to Jim and Carol.

"Would you come with me?" she asked them.

They stood. "We'd be honored," Jim said solemnly.

Later on the drive down Chipmunk Coulee, Jim sat in the passenger seat of the Suburban, exhaustion threatening to shut down his brain. Silently he reviewed the doctor's report in his mind.

"Officer Saner sustained two gunshot wounds, one in his lower right thigh, which fractured a portion of the femur bone about six inches above the knee," Dr. Rashad explained. "During the surgery, we cleaned the leg wound and inserted a rod in the bone shaft, which will help stabilize what remained of it. The body should regenerate bone around the rod as it heals, but these kinds of wounds are notoriously messy and heal slowly. The other bullet passed completely through the muscle in his right lateral side, miraculously passing between the two lowest ribs without shattering any bone. We cleaned out the wound thoroughly and closed it up. It should heal fine." He paused, waiting for questions.

"How long will his recovery take?" Ruby asked.

"We'll keep him in the hospital for three or four days to ensure no infection sets in. He lost a lot of blood; we gave him four units. He'll be weak for a while, but he's young and strong, and he'll regain his strength quickly. I think that healing will take six to eight weeks. We'll do some physical therapy when the pain and soreness subside. He should be back to work on light duty in a couple of months."

The conversation drifted away somewhere out of Jim's brain as he fluttered in and out of sleep during the drive home. Carol came around the car as the garage door closed and opened Jim's door. He jerked awake at the sound.

"This is a little backward, isn't it?" Jim asked, unfolding his large frame and climbing out of the Suburban.

"I only do this for dinosaurs and in the privacy of the garage where no one else can see," Carol teased. She grabbed his hand and led him to the hallway, where she hung up his coat.

"To the shower," she said, crooking her finger over her shoulder. Jim followed her down the hall to the bathroom. She turned on the water. "Clean up and then straight to bed," she ordered.

Jim saluted. "Aye, aye, captain," he mumbled.

After the shower, he put on boxers and a T-shirt and ambled into the bedroom. Carol had already climbed in and was waiting for him. She gently patted the quilt, turning back the sheets. Jim crawled in, and Carol pulled the covers over him, kissing him good night. He was quietly snoring in less than a minute. She turned out the light. *Thank you, God, that I still have my husband.* ☉

THURSDAY
NOVEMBER 22

57

Carol hummed quietly as she mixed ingredients for the Thanksgiving turkey stuffing. Smells of onion, sage, thyme, and butter filled the house with delicious scents. While she peeled potatoes and stuffed the bird, Jim set the table with her best china and silverware. The wine glasses sparkled, and the horn of plenty centerpiece was filled with miniature pumpkins and squash, apples, pears, and assorted nuts. Candles glowed warmly on each end of the dining room table.

"Wow! You sure know how to entertain, honey," Jim said, scanning the beautiful table setting. "Everything looks great. When are the kids coming?"

"I told them we'd eat about one so we can watch the ball game later or maybe play some games," she said from the depths of the kitchen.

"Sam and Leslie coming, too?"

"Yes, they decided to forego a trip to Decorah." Jim walked into the kitchen and stood by the sink, helping cut up the potatoes. "Leslie didn't think their relationship was far enough down the road for a weekend with the parents yet." Carol looked over at Jim and raised her eyebrows tellingly. "Honey, you're not matchmaking, are you?" Jim asked, concerned, grasping a potato.

Carol turned to him, her mouth ajar. A little huff escaped her lips. "Me? I had nothing to do with Sam and Leslie getting together," she said, holding the potato peeler in her hand. "Besides, it's a little too late for that. If you want to blame someone, look no further than yourself."

"Me? You're going to blame me?" he asked, placing his free hand on his chest.

"Wait a minute," Carol said, laying the peeler down by the sink and holding up her hands. "I call a truce. I happen to think Sam and Leslie make a beautiful couple. I'm sure lots of people had plenty to say when we got together, and that didn't stop us, did it?"

Jim gave her an amused look. "No, I guess you're right. It started a whole new chapter for both of us," Jim admitted. He grabbed her hand and pulled her to his chest. He looked softly into her brown eyes. "I will unabashedly tell anyone who asks that you are the greatest thing that's ever happened to me." He dipped his head and kissed her tenderly.

As Carol leaned back, she frowned and rubbed her stomach. "Ooh. Something's rumbling down there," she said uneasily.

"Are you getting sick?" Jim asked, worried. "I knew this would happen. You've been workin' like a dog getting everything ready."

"No, no. It's just a little indigestion. I'll be fine." She pecked him on the cheek and aimed him toward the living room. "Now, get out of here so I can finish getting this meal ready."

By one o'clock, the table was heaped with food, and the guests were seated. Leslie and Sam, John and Jennie, Sara, Vivian and Craig, and Jim and Carol oohed and aahed at the abundance of the cuisine on display. Jim asked for quiet and reverently read Psalm 100, saying a prayer of thanks. After the wine was poured, John rose unexpectedly to make a toast.

"Well, everyone, I'm not as good at speeches as Dad," his eyes found Jim's and stayed there for an extra moment, "but I wanted to say how thankful I am for the family I have. I know we all miss Mom, but I wanted to be the first to welcome Carol into our Thanksgiving celebration and our family." Carol's eyes misted over with his words, and under the table, Jim caught her hand and held it tightly. "And I wanted to introduce you to a future member," he reached down and pulled Jennie from her chair. "I've asked Jennie to marry me, and she said—"

"Yes!" Jennie interrupted. John leaned over and kissed her sweetly. Everyone erupted into applause. Jim got out of his seat and hugged John and kissed Jenny on the cheek.

"Wow! I'm so happy for you, son," Jim said, holding back tears. Sara beamed at her brother.

"Thanks, Dad. I knew you would be," John said, his voice cracking with emotion. Suddenly it was quiet. Jim turned to everyone, and with a flourish of his hand, he grabbed his wine glass and said, "Well, let's eat!"

Later, as the girls admired Jenny's diamond and talked wedding plans around the dining room table, the men retreated to the living room and gathered around the TV for the game.

"Jenny's a lucky girl, Jim," Craig said. "You've raised a great son."

Jim watched Jenny, her expression ecstatic as she revealed the plans for her upcoming nuptials. "Yeah, I'm pretty proud of him. He's a hard worker, and he'll be a good provider. And Jenny is beautiful."

"Before you know it, you'll be a grandpa," Sam said, joining in the conversation.

"That's all right by me. The more, the merrier," Jim said, his dimple showing.

Suddenly as Carol stood, she tripped and grabbed the edge of the table. Jim rushed to her side, catching her before she fell.

"Carol! Are you okay?" Jim asked, supporting her around the waist.

"Ooh. I just felt a little nauseous and dizzy." She laid her hand near her throat. Everyone stopped and stared. "I'm fine," she stammered. "I think I'll just go and lie down for a bit."

"Come on. I'll help you," Jim offered, leading her down the

hallway. Pulling off Carol's shoes, he removed her pearls, cashmere sweater, and dress slacks. He noticed her pale complexion and the faint circles under her eyes. Comfortable in her bra and panties, he tucked her into bed and pulled the quilt over her.

"Jim, this is ridiculous. I have a houseful of company. I can't go to bed," she argued, trying to fling off the bedspread.

"Yes, you can," he said, covering her back up. He held up his index finger. "No arguing. You are going to rest a little bit." Carol settled back on the pillow. He continued. "The meal was fabulous. And lest you forget, I whipped up a Parisian picnic, so I'm sure I can serve the pumpkin pie and whipped cream. I'm no dummy. So just chill. You take a nap, or at least close your eyes for an hour or so," Jim reasoned. She started to argue, but then the exhaustion from the preparations caught up to her.

"Okay. One hour. But you wake me up," she insisted while Jim closed the shades on the bedroom window.

"Shh. You rest," he said, kissing her forehead. He snuck out and quietly closed the door. Vivian met Jim in the hallway. Her calm demeanor didn't fool him.

"Is she okay?" she asked, her eyes anxiously scanning the bedroom door.

"You know how she is. Everything's gotta be just so. She's just tired," Jim said with a wave of his hand.

"Well, maybe," Vivian said dubiously. "But promise me you'll make her go for a checkup. She seems exhausted lately."

"I promise. Don't worry. You girls are from good midwestern stock. Besides, we've had a lot on our plate with this last case of mine. We're both exhausted. But I promise I'll get her in to see her doctor."

"Good. Now, let me help you serve that pie," Vivian said with a smile. ⊙

THURSDAY
DECEMBER 6

58

Colonel Michael Bogdonovich stretched and slowly opened his eyes. His flight from New York via Chicago and finally on to La Crosse was preparing to land. Fortunately, the predicted winter storm slowly building to a fury in the western states hadn't arrived here yet. But within the next three days, it promised to hit the Midwest with a wallop of nine to twelve inches of snow, hurricane-force winds, and bitterly cold temperatures. However, being a resident of Upstate New York, winter didn't rattle his cage. He just hoped he could get back home by this time tomorrow night before the promised storm hit and sidelined him in Wisconsin.

During his flight, he'd reviewed the document that outlined the details of the discovery of the Middle Eastern antiquities smuggling ring in southern Wisconsin. The subsequent recovery of $2.2 million of Middle Eastern Iraqi treasures and the capture of several operatives involved in the black market illegalities led the national director of ICE to recognize Higgins and his team for their accomplishments. Bogdonovich was here to represent ICE and the two countries that were continuing their cooperation in recovering the artifacts.

In the final analysis, Wade Bennett had taken center stage, but not for his brilliance in passing off the antiquities, but rather for his reckless abandon in eliminating Rod Girabaldi and his assault and attempted murder of Detective Leslie Brown. Despite the formidable odds against them, Lt. Jim Higgins and his team had managed to break open the case.

The smiling flight attendant walked up and down the aisles, collecting garbage, reminding passengers to lock their trays securely in front of them and buckle their seat belts for landing. As Bogdonovich deboarded in the small airport terminal, he spotted Sheriff Davy Jones standing quietly at the edge of the crowd. Jones raised his hand in greeting, acknowledging the colonel's presence.

"Colonel Bogdonovich, welcome to God's country," Sheriff Jones remarked enthusiastically, holding out his hand. His hazel eyes seemed self-satisfied, and his demeanor was typically understated —a nonchalant midwestern attitude. He grabbed Michael's overnight bag.

"Flight okay?" the sheriff asked.

"Yeah, just glad the storm hasn't arrived yet," Michael said. "Let's hope I'll be winging my way back home this time tomorrow." They began walking through the terminal to Jones' waiting car. "I've reviewed all the details of the work you guys did uncovering this smuggling ring. Pretty impressive."

Jones waved his hand at nothing in particular. "We're just glad to see justice served. After all, we do get paid for what we do, although it's not enough," he added as he swung the bag into the back seat.

"I hear you," Michael said, climbing in the car.

Swinging into traffic, Jones worked his way through the north side of La Crosse to the riverfront. Pulling in front of the Charmant Hotel on State Street, Jones got out and accompanied Bogdonovich to the front desk.

"This place is impressive," the colonel commented, his eyes taking in the gleaming maple floors, wooden beams, and exposed brick and wrought iron accents. "Very nice."

"Yeah, they call it an independent boutique hotel. Used to be a candy factory back in the late 1800s. I guess Charmant was the name given to a premier line of chocolates the factory produced, so the owners decided to use it as the name of their establishment."

The front desk clerk turned to the two men, offering a high wattage smile.

"Room for Michael Bogdonovich," the colonel stated.

The young woman offered her hand across the desk. "It's such a privilege to meet the 'Bulldog of Baghdad,' sir," she said proudly, leaning toward him over the check-in counter.

Michael's face registered surprise as he shook her hand. "Well, how'd you know my nickname?"

"Our owner is a Vietnam vet and has a soft spot for all of our military personnel. He's followed your career for a while. It's a distinct pleasure to have you visit our city."

"Well, thank you so much," Michael said sincerely.

"You'll be in the Chateau King Suite for the evening. Just proceed right down the hall and take the elevator up to the fourth floor. You'll have a great view of the river and all the Christmas lights at Riverside Park," she said.

Interrupting, Jones said, "Hey, I better get home and get slicked up. The wife is all excited about meeting you. See you around six-thirty for drinks."

By five o'clock that evening, Jim and Carol were in the throes of dressing in their finest evening wear. Carol primped in the bathroom mirror.

"Hell, I wish this was over," Jim complained, his face crinkled in a frown as he flicked his fingers through his damp hair.

"You're much too handsome to wear such a sour face," Carol admonished him, evaluating his grumpy demeanor in the mirror. "What's the matter anyway?"

"I don't know. It just seems wrong to get an award for doing your job. We took the thugs off the street. That's what we're supposed to do, for Pete's sake." He slammed the hairbrush down on the counter.

"Well, your team paid a high price to bring down these smugglers, and the Iraqi and United States governments wanted to show their appreciation. Recovering millions of dollars of priceless treasures and returning them to Iraq doesn't happen every day. I think it's a rather nice gesture between the two countries," Carol said, defending the award ceremony.

"Maybe you should work for the State Department," Jim said sourly.

Carol sighed. "You'll have to at least pretend to appreciate the efforts that everyone has gone through to give your team this special night, Jim. Bogdonovich is no slouch. I've read about him. He's famous for the work he's done in returning priceless artifacts to their proper owners—countries— whatever," she finished with a wave of her hand. "He's known as the Bulldog of Baghdad."

Jim wasn't really listening. Instead, he noticed Carol's warm brown eyes and her lovely cheekbones.

"Have you changed your hairdo?" he asked, tilting his head, looking at her in the mirror.

"No. What makes you think that?"

"I don't know. You just have a sort of glow lately that I can't explain, but I like it," he said, leaning down and kissing the back of her neck. His stomach was flip-flopping in nervous anticipation of the awards ceremony. He'd rehearsed what he was going to say about a hundred times in his mind. He hated these public events where everyone gushed on about how fabulous they all were. Blah, blah, blah. He was dreading the entire evening.

"Jim, you are acting very strange," she said, concerned. "I think I know what you need." She turned, reached up, and gave him a passionate kiss.

"Whoa, baby, we don't have time for that right now," Jim muttered in a panic. "Later ... maybe," he said as he left for the bedroom to get his shoes.

Across town, Leslie was studying herself in the full-length mirror. She ran her fingers along her cheekbone. All evidence of bruising seemed to be gone. She'd splurged on a special dress. She hoped it wouldn't be considered too risqué for the event. The floral A-line silhouette dress in a luscious cream color was embellished with delicate blossoms embroidered on overlaid silk. The scoop neckline was accentuated with her mother's pearls, and the scalloped hem played up her lovely legs. She'd spent extra time applying her makeup. She felt special, and she hoped Sam would notice. Sometimes he seemed so dense.

At Grandview Apartments near Riverside Park, Paul showered and dressed in his best gray suit. He wore a baby blue percale shirt, a Salvatore Ferragamo silk tie adorned with elephants and a blue flag motif. Ruby had found it online for $100 and had presented it to him as an early Christmas present. Even with his crutches, he was still very handsome.

She hoped their peaceful truce would last. Lately, they'd had a lot of stupid, inconsequential spats. One had been whether Melody should have a pacifier, and another was about what kind of food Paul should be eating to promote the quickest healing of his injuries. Such blather.

Recently after another mind-numbing ruckus about money, Ruby had shouted, "Are you going to remember this conversation a month from now? Huh? Are you?" Her face was red, and tears stung her eyes.

"Whadda ya mean?" Paul shouted back, his face flushed. "I'm just trying to keep a handle on our finances."

Ruby took a deep breath. "We're spending all our time arguing about stupid stuff that, in the end, will never change anything. It's garbage! It's crap! It's a bunch of bullshit!"

The silence that followed was deafening. Paul looked at the ceiling, closing his eyes, letting out a groan.

"You're right. We've got to stop this," Paul finally said, grabbing her hand. Not talking about what happened during the shooting undermined everything they believed about each other and their marriage. So they started discussing the shooting incident. The fear.

The timing. The horror of being wounded. The surgery. The recovery. The nightmares. And finally, as the days went by, they arrived at a place of acceptance and peace, tentative as it was.

Now it seemed another argument was about to erupt.

"Ruby, we can't afford ties like this," he said in a frustrating tone, touching it as he spoke.

"Shh. I got a bonus at work, and when I saw it, I just wanted you to have it. Please be happy about it. Okay?" her green eyes pleaded. Their struggles overcoming Paul's situational depression and financial concerns seemed far from over. It was like a holding pattern they couldn't seem to escape.

"Come here," he said, his voice softening. He was leaning against the granite counter of the kitchen island. She sidled up to him, and he gathered her in his arms. "Thank you for wanting good things for me," he whispered softly into her hair. She looked especially lovely in a cashmere ivory sweater and smoky gray tulle skirt. Her red hair was piled on her head in a mountain of curls, and her skin was soft and luminous.

"I do. I do want the best for you," she said somberly, looking into his hazel eyes. "You've had a tough time after this shooting, and I want you to have a special night tonight." She kissed him tenderly.

"All I can say," Paul finished, "is when I've recovered my natural lionized state, you and I are going to have a weekend of lovemaking that will threaten to stop your heart, baby."

"I'll be ready, my king," she said, smiling eagerly.

"By the way, you're going to wow everyone in that outfit."

"Well, cops' wives can be classy, right?"

"Absolutely." The buzzer for the elevator rang.

"That's Mom and Dad. I'll buzz them up."

Across town, Sam had driven up to Leslie's apartment on La Crosse Street. He reached across the seat and picked up the dozen yellow roses he'd selected at Festival Foods. He made sure he ripped off the supermarket sticker. *This is not the night to reveal what a cheapskate you really are,* he thought.

He walked into the apartment through the garage, where Paco woofed at him affectionately. He leaned down, pounded his side, and fluffed his ears. As he looked up, Leslie came out from the bedroom. His heart skipped some beats. His mouth fell open.

"Sheez, Lez. You look gorgeous," he whispered. The roses hung limply from his hand until he remembered he was holding them. He thrust them at her in a nervous gesture. *Yellow for friendship, not red for passion,* she thought.

"Thanks," she said carefully. "I'll just put them in a vase, and then I'm ready. You look … good."

He shrugged his shoulders and stood modestly in front of her. He had resurrected his navy blue suit and added a soft yellow dress shirt accented with a narrow blue striped tie he'd found in his roommate's closet. Leslie appeared from the kitchen, opened the closet, and put on her coat.

"Let's hit it, then," she suggested.

Throughout the cocktail hour, Jim nervously played with his tie and ran his hands through his hair. *Why can't people just let us do our job without all this hoopla?* he thought. He felt a gentle tugging on his arm. Carol pulled him close to her.

"How're you doing?" she asked, her voice husky and warm.

"Fine, I guess," Jim mumbled. He looked at her closely. She'd decided to wear a light gray wool merino sweater with ruffled sleeves accompanied by a black sequined skirt that hugged her wonderful figure. She wore a crystal and silver necklace and earring set Jim had bought her when they were engaged. Her dark brunette hair shimmered, and her brown eyes were warm.

"You do realize that everyone is staring at you, don't you?" Jim asked quietly, his blue eyes softening.

"Don't be ridiculous. Have you seen Leslie and Ruby? They're gorgeous. I'm just a pretty bauble on the tree," she said, downplaying his remark.

"By the way, did you make that doctor's appointment I asked you to?" Jim asked, scanning the crowded room.

"Yep. Next Thursday, the thirteenth. It's on the calendar."

Colonel Bogdonovich made his way through the crowd toward Jim and Carol as the dinner seating began. Extending her hand, Carol pulled him in as he approached them.

"Colonel Bogdonovich, this is my husband, Jim Higgins," she said graciously.

"Pleasure to meet you, Jim. You must be very proud of your team," he said, pumping Jim's hand. Jim gave him a dimpled smile, but his eyes flitted nervously around the room.

"I'm almost always proud of them. They're young, and they've got a lot to learn, but they have really good investigative instincts. And they're one enthusiastic bunch," he finished, picking Leslie out of the crowd.

"Well, fellas, how about you accompany me to dinner?" Carol asked, hooking her arms in Jim's and the colonel's.

"Can't turn down an offer like that," Michael grinned. Jim rolled his eyes but gave Carol a dimpled smile.

As the festivities wore down near eleven o'clock, Jim began to relax. Being in the spotlight was not something he relished. He was most comfortable at home, existing in anonymity. The plaque of recognition was tucked under his right arm as he made his way through the crowd.

"Hey, Chief," Sam slurred. "Quite a night, huh?"

"You make sure someone else drives home," Jim warned. "We don't need you getting a DUI."

"Leslie doesn't drink, so she can drive." Jim noticed Leslie and Colonel Bogdonovich in an intense conversation across the room.

"Good. I'm heading out. See you tomorrow morning," Jim said.

"Sure," Sam mumbled. Then he grabbed Jim's arm. "She looks really great tonight, doesn't she, Chief?" Jim noticed the soft glow in Sam's eyes. *The guy is totally in love,* he thought.

"She does look fabulous. And you better respect and appreciate her, or I'll have your ass," he said, with the crook of an eyebrow.

Sam looked over at him, shock registering on his face. "Always, Chief. Always." ◉

THURSDAY
DECEMBER 13

59

Jim was working quietly in his office catching up on bureaucratic paperwork related to the Middle Eastern antiquities smuggling case while Sam investigated alleged rumors of a prostitution ring at a local massage parlor up on the north side. Leslie was tying up loose ends with Sheila Walsh at ICE. Jim had talked to Paul by cell. He was resting comfortably at home, going to therapy to strengthen his leg. Suddenly, a familiar voice wafted into Jim's office from the lobby.

"Merry Christmas, Emily!" Jamie Alberg said loudly. "Is the chief in? I really need to see him and congratulate him."

Jim heard Emily calmly engaging the archeologist in quiet conversation. Jim leaned back in his chair, rubbed his eyes, and groaned at the prospect of the visit. Jamie Alberg had assisted him in a previous case of a lost gold coin shipment stolen from Fort Crawford. Although he'd helped move the case forward, the snags he'd gotten himself into had complicated the case and brought him close to being murdered. Recently, he'd been studying forensic archaeology in Egypt. Jim supposed he was home for the holiday break.

Emily appeared at his door. "I did everything I could to discourage him from interrupting you, but you know what a stubborn little twit he can be," she said quietly, not telling him anything new. "So, should I bring him in?" she asked, her eyebrows raised, expecting a grumble of protest.

"Yeah, I'll talk to him," Jim murmured, frowning at the interruption. "At least we're not in the middle of any cases we need his assistance with," he finished, continuing to sort through the piles on his desk.

Jamie clomped through the door in his snow boots, leaving a trail of water stains along the threadbare carpet. He appeared confident and greeted Jim with a warm handshake.

"Hello, Chief. I've been reading about your latest caper. Middle Eastern antiquities? Smuggling? Murder? How in the world does this stuff always get dropped in your lap?" he asked, his eyes wide with wonder. "Your name is being discussed in some very high places."

Jim shook his head in disbelief. "I doubt it, Jamie. And I don't know how this stuff keeps falling in my lap. Just seems to happen," Jim commented casually. "So, how's Egypt these days?"

Jim studied Jamie carefully. He seemed to have gained weight and matured physically, but underneath he was the same mildly autistic pain-in-the-butt he'd always been. But he had to admit he had something of a soft spot for the kid.

"My studies are proving to be challenging. I'll return to Egypt at the end of January and finish up in June. Then I'll need to find a university where I can complete my degree," he informed Jim in a businesslike tone.

"You should talk to Leslie. She's quite the expert on anything archaeological."

"Oh, she's so hot I couldn't possibly ask her to help me with that," Jamie said, blushing. He fidgeted restlessly on his feet, his cheeks flushing red. Jim tried to control the chuckle bubbling up in his chest, but it escaped, much to his chagrin. He laughed out loud.

"Oh, she's hot but very approachable," Jim said, grinning madly. "Just walk down the hall and poke your head in her office. I'm sure she'd love to give you a few pointers."

"Really?" Jamie asked, his mouth askew.

"Worth a try, don't you think?"

With those encouraging words, Jamie stomped off down the hall, searching for Leslie.

"Great. Now I can get something done," Jim sighed.

The late afternoon sun was losing its power. Outside the office window, its rays were fading rapidly, and the shadows of dusk were falling across the parking lot at the Women's Reproductive Health Clinic on Clinton Street.

"I hope you're joking, Dr. Lockhart," Carol said, panic rising in her chest. She was seated in the doctor's office after having a thorough physical examination.

"I never joke about a pregnancy, Carol." Her eyes were serious. She watched her patient closely, not knowing what kind of response to expect. Dr. Lockhart had seen every possible reaction from older women who found themselves pregnant—surprise, shock, disbelief, anger, joy. You name it; she'd seen it. She continued to wait.

Carol looked away. Then slowly her eyes drifted back to the doctor's face as if the reality of her condition was just beginning to dawn on her. It was like watching the first rays of light begin to illuminate the morning sky.

"There's no way this could be a fluke?" Carol quietly asked as she laid her hand over her abdomen.

"No."

"When am I due?"

"Best estimate—late May, early part of June."

Carol sat, remembering the lovemaking with Jim. So many. *What is Jim going to say?* she thought. *He'll blow his stack.*

Dr. Lockhart leaned forward across her desk, folding her hands, carefully watching Carol's face. "Is there something I can help you with? You seem totally surprised by this turn of events," she counseled.

Carol looked embarrassed. "Well, Jim and I have been very ...

SUE BERG

enthusiastic, and I just assumed ..." Her voice trailed off. Words eluded her. Instead, her thoughts were hurling themselves backward over the last few months. *I must have gotten pregnant in Paris.*

"Listen. I need to establish one thing before we go any further. Do you intend to keep the child?" Dr. Lockhart questioned.

"I'm sorry—keep the child?" Carol asked, even more confused.

"Yes, you're not planning to abort, are you?"

"Oh, my heavens, no! No! No!" she said forcefully, sitting up straighter. "Jim and I will figure something out," she finished tentatively.

"All right then. Let's discuss your risks and your prenatal care," Dr. Lockhart said in a professional tone, grateful they'd gotten over that hurdle. "I want you to know I specialize in pregnancy in older women, and I will give you the very best care available. Now let's talk about what you can expect in the next few months."

By seven o'clock that evening, a winter storm warning was blanketing the entire southern half of Wisconsin. At least a foot of snow was predicted to fall overnight, followed by blustery winds and frigid temperatures. Jim stepped out on the front porch to check his barometer. The air felt heavy with humidity, and a few lonely snowflakes were beginning to tumble from the sky. The needle plunged toward UNSETTLED on the dial when Jim tapped the barometer with his finger. Somehow the word seemed to crawl into his mind like a premonition of things to come.

"Well, I think we're in for it," he announced, returning to the living room in his stocking feet. "My dad always said if the barometer is still falling when the storm hits, it's gonna be a big one." He looked over at Carol, who was lying under a quilt on the couch. She seemed to be fixating on a point on the ceiling. He'd noticed her subdued disposition at dinner.

"Honey, did you hear me?" Jim asked curiously.

"Yeah, I heard you." Carol rolled on her side. "Listen, when are we going to get a Christmas tree? If we don't get one pretty soon, the season will be over."

"We can cut one out in our woods if you want. Might be kind of an adventure. Strap on the snowshoes and take a little hike tomorrow back by the creek. There are some nice smaller trees back there. How's that sound?"

"Good," she said, smiling wanly. "Actually, that sounds like fun."

When Jim and Carol woke the next morning, the house had a hushed feel to it. Jim climbed out of bed, walked to the bedroom window, and pulled the drapes open. Carol rose on her elbows, her hair mussed, her eyelids swollen from sleep. Overnight, the heavy snow had turned the backyard into a spectacle of white whirling snowdrifts that rose like small mountain ranges across the lawn. The evergreens seemed to be bending in worship. Everything was still and quiet.

"Wow! Guess we won't be going to work this morning." He looked back at Carol lounging in bed, pillows propped behind her. "How come you always look so beautiful in the morning?" Jim asked, getting back in bed and pulling her over to him.

"Oh, *pa-lease*, honey. That's just your way of getting a little something extra."

"Hey, that was a compliment of the first order," he said, feeling hurt.

She didn't laugh. Instead, she sat up a little straighter and continued staring out the window. She sat like that for a few minutes. When Jim tore his eyes away from the outdoor scene, he noticed the tears silently falling on her cheeks.

"Carol? What's wrong?" he asked, his stomach clenching in alarm. He'd forgotten to ask about the doctor appointment she'd had yesterday. He would never forget the day when Margie had told him about her breast cancer. *God, this can't be happening again, can it?*

By now, she was openly crying. "I don't know what I'm supposed to think or feel. I just didn't expect it! It's a total, complete surprise," she vented. Jim went into a full-blown panic at her look of utter helplessness.

"What's wrong?" he asked tensely. "Was it something you found out yesterday at the doctor?"

Carol nodded her head. "Yes."

"Well, what's going on?" Jim asked, holding her hand. His blue eyes met hers, and she began crying again.

"I'm pregnant," she said softly.

He sat staring at her as if she had said she was turning into an elephant and would soon grow a trunk. His eyes seemed to dilate, and he went somewhere deep inside himself. He stayed there trying to take in this news. His thoughts returned to the conversation he'd had with Paul when Ruby turned up pregnant. Then he thought of the lectures he'd given his young team on the word *assume*. How if you assumed certain things, you might come out looking like an ass. All of this passed through his mind in a matter of milliseconds.

He plopped back on his pillow still holding Carol's hand. She laid her head on his chest and let out a long sigh. At least she'd stopped crying. That seemed to help.

She's forty-two. I'm fifty-two. We're going to have a baby. He thought back to the Bible story of Abraham and Sara. What had God said? "With me, nothing is impossible."

"Jim? Say something," Carol said simply.

"There are no words," he whispered.

Carol started to cry again. "I've always dreamed about being a mom," she said through her tears. "Now I'm pregnant with someone I love so much. I want to be over-the-moon happy about this, Jim, but I can't be unless you are, too."

"I can understand that," he said softly. "But you'll have to let me wrap my mind around this whole thing. I need a little time."

"OK. That's fair. How about some breakfast? I'm starving," Carol said, wiping the tears with the backside of her hand, climbing out of bed.

Over scrambled eggs, bacon, toast, and coffee, Jim continued to absorb the news of the pregnancy like someone inhaling the first breath of spring air. He breathed. He thought. He breathed. He meditated and breathed some more. Gradually the tight ball of incredulous surprise began loosening. He supposed he was returning to a more normal state of mind.

After breakfast, Jim went out to the garage and plucked the snowshoes from the wall. Carol had settled down, and now they bundled up and ventured into the winter wonderland at their door. Jim pulled a plastic sled with his tree saw rattling inside it. The ice-bound world seemed to soften the shock of the news, and Jim felt himself relaxing. It seemed to him that they were the only two people on Earth lost in a frozen tableau of freshly fallen snow. He looked over at Carol and grabbed her hand. She gave him a tremulous smile. Silently they wandered back to the creek, snowshoes settling slightly in the deep drifts. The only sounds were the swish of their movements in the frozen landscape and the caws of some blue jays in a nearby tree.

"Oh, Jim. Look! There's the perfect little tree," Carol said, pointing toward the creek. Jim walked over to it. The tree was about Jim's height, and its branches were bent downward with snow. It was the perfect shape.

"This is a beautiful tree," Jim said, digging down to find the base of the trunk. He began sawing the trunk, and then he loaded it into the sled. They turned back toward the house. As they walked, Jim was suddenly overwhelmed with wonder. He stopped. The sled bumped into the back of his legs. Carol looked over at him, and he pulled her close.

"You're pregnant," he said with a sense of awe. She looked up at him with a grin. "I'm pretty experienced at this dad thing, you know. And you'll be a wonderful mother." He kissed her cold lips tenderly. "I love you, and that's the way it is," he finished.

"Let's get this tree in the house," she said. His blue eyes gazed at her with such love that it felt like warm sunshine after a fierce storm.

SUE BERG

"Sounds like a good plan," Jim said as they slowly trudged to the house. He stopped and faced her again. "One more thing," he said firmly. "If it's a boy, then we should name him Henri—like H, E, N, R, I," he spelled, emphasizing the I. "You know, the French spelling. And if it's a girl, Claudette. Remember that girl we met at the Eiffel Tower? Her name was Claudette. Whadda ya think?"

"Well, this baby was probably conceived in Paris, so a French name would be perfect." That evening as they decorated the tree with white lights and ornaments, Jim thought of Michael Smith's new Christmas song. He heard it on the radio a number of times lately. The words seemed to fit.

All is well. All is well. Angels and men rejoice.

For tonight darkness fell into the dawn of love's light.

Sing a-le. Sing alleluia.

THE END

If you have enjoyed this book, I would be so grateful if you would consider writing a review. I love hearing from readers who enjoyed my stories, and reviews play a big part in other readers discovering my books. If you bought a book online from Amazon or Barnes & Noble, you may leave a reader review there. Otherwise, you may message me on Facebook (Sue Berg-Luepke) or at my email: bergsue@hotmail.com

ABOUT THE AUTHOR

Sue Berg is the author of two previous novels, Solid Roots and Strong Wings, a family memoir which was written in 2011, and Driftless Gold, the first book in the Jim Higgins Driftless Mystery Series published in 2021. Sue resides in the Driftless area near Viroqua, Wisconsin, with her husband, Alan. ◉

COMING IN
AUGUST 2022

JIM HIGGINS'
ADVENTURES
CONTINUE...

Look to the opposite page for
an excerpt from *Driftless Deceit*.

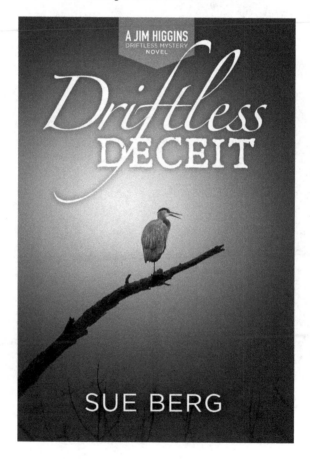

1

FRIDAY EVENING, MAY 10

T he orange sun was sinking toward the horizon airbrushing the blue sky with swirling masses of orange, pink and red. The Mississippi River flowed silently in the distance, a dark brown ribbon snaking its way south, meandering here and there, picking up speed and power as it traveled. Barges and boats moved noisily, horns blaring with intermittent blasts. The temperature grew cooler, and Juliette pulled her dirty loose sweater tightly around her shoulders. She dreaded the dark hours of night ahead with her small granddaughter, Lillie.

Here in Tent City, the center of the homeless population on the northern edge of Riverside Park in La Crosse, Wisconsin, they were relatively safe, although outbursts and arguments from other vagrants sometimes punctuated the hours of darkness.

"When are we going to find Bapa?" little Lillie intently questioned her grandmother, Juliette, while they rested on one of the park's benches. "Does he know we're here? When will we get to see him?"

"Oh, hush now, Miss Lillie. We just arrived yesterday," Juliette reminded her. Her illness heightened her sense of insecurity and filled her with a deep, dark despondency. She began coughing, the dry rasps filling the night air. Shivers prickled her skin as chills racked her body. The pain in her lower back built to agonizing spasms, leaving her weak and shaken. Although it seemed horribly selfish, she prayed that her death would come swiftly and soon.

"I'm hungry, Grandma," Lillie whined. Her vivid blue eyes were large with want and malnutrition. Her T-shirt was smudged with yesterday's dumpster food, the sleeves covered in grime. The little girl's ringlets of blonde hair were dark with grease and sweat from the weeks they had been on the road traveling to La Crosse. With her flip-flopped feet dangling from the bench, she looked like a poster child from a third world poverty-stricken country.

"Here, here now," Juliette groaned, trembling from her coughing spell. She pulled a discarded sandwich from the pocket of her sweater. She'd found it lying on the cement near the back entrance of a nearby restaurant. With quivering hands, she handed it to the innocent child. Lifting a bottle of water from her tote bag, she screwed off the top, offering Lillie a drink. The child gobbled ravenously at the stale sandwich, gulping drinks of water between bites.

"Come on, now," Juliette said, her gutteral voice laced with pain. She gently took Miss Lillie's hand and led her into the wooded area beyond the International Gardens where they had spent the day loitering and resting. "We need to find a place to sleep for the night."

Lillie began crying, a pathetic whimpering that Juliette hated to hear. It was hard to bear the suffering of such an innocent child when she was all alone and desperately ill. All she could hope for now was that she could find her brother, Jim, before she passed away.

She was convinced her death was near. She'd been sick too long without medical care, and everything seemed to be crashing down around her. Still, without Lillie to care for and defend, she was sure she would have died months ago.

Last night a vivid dream of an angelic being came to her, and she found the comfort more welcome than she cared to admit. In the velvety darkness of the night the angel sang to her. *I am a poor wayfaring stranger, traveling through this world below. There is no sickness, no toil, nor danger, In that bright land to which I go.* The resonance of the

SUE BERG

heavenly voice soothed Juliette like a mysterious balm. For just a few precious moments she was pain-free. The haunting notes lifted her to another world that was filled with hope and light. An assurance that the Lord had not forgotten their desperate needs washed over her, easing her agony and freeing her from the incessant loneliness that weighed her down.

One more night, Lord. Just one more night so we can find Bapa, she prayed silently.

They found a patch of tall grasses near the jogging trail that skirted the homeless community. Juliette fell into it, patting the grass into a kind of natural mattress. She was so tired. In her last act of kindness for her precious Lillie, she pulled a thin blanket from her bag and pulled her granddaughter close to her, groaning in pain as she covered the little waif with the blanket. The inadequacy of her provision for the child filled her eyes with tears. As darkness descended, they fell into a restless, wounded sleep, praying for the morning and another chance for hope.

2

SATURDAY, MAY 11

The fishing lure plopped on the surface of Timber Coulee Creek and floated gently along the rippling current, bobbing and dipping in the stream. Lt. Jim Higgins, Chief Investigative Officer at the La Crosse Sheriff's department, was reveling in the uninterrupted solace of nature. The wooded foliage on the hillsides and along the creek was just beginning to pop with green, and the heavy, sweet scent of lilac filled the air.

Racing over exposed rocks in the stream, the sound of the gurgling creek filled Jim with a deep sense of contentment. He noticed the sting of sunburn on his nose and forehead as he adjusted his Ray-Ban sunglasses. Fumbling around in his backpack, he found the sunscreen and swabbed some across his face, ears, and arms. He found a hat and plopped it on his head.

Jim continued to amble down the creek in his camo waders, his Badger hat shading his striking blue eyes from the intense morning sunshine. Moving athletically, he climbed up and down the banks casting and retrieving his line with a casual expertise that belied his recent conversion to the sport of fly fishing. As he maneuvered in and out of the clear, cold water, he thought back to the morning events and his wife, Carol.

Dawn was just beginning to find its way into the darkened recesses of the bedroom on Chipmunk Coulee Road. Carol, now her in her ninth month of pregnancy, slept sprawled on her side, her nightie barely concealing her expanding tummy. Jim smiled at the prospect of a baby. When he thought about it, it seemed so absurd. Carol had been divorced for over twenty years and Jim lost his wife to cancer two years ago—this was the second marriage for both of them. Carol was forty-two; he fifty-two. Never in any world they'd inhabited in their imagination or in the bedroom had they expected to find themselves pregnant.

Believing that Carol's perimenopausal symptoms would make pregnancy impossible had been their first mistake. Her pregnancy had taken a considerable amount of time to adjust to. There'd been a few arguments, a weak attempt to lay the blame at one another's feet. Gradually, though, as the months passed, the disbelief and bewilderment had turned to joy and now, in the past few weeks, excited anticipation.

This morning, Jim had tried to get out of bed and dress quietly. He wanted to get an early start fishing near Coon Valley where some of the best trout streams in Wisconsin offered unparalleled relaxation. But Carol's ears were tuned to him and his movements. Opening her eyes, she rolled on her back in a lazy motion.

"Hey. You headin' out already?" she asked, her voice raspy with sleep. "Kinda early, isn't it?"

Jim leaned over for a kiss, but she pulled him down beside her. They cuddled up together, and Carol rested her head gently on his shoulder.

"I can't sneak away from you anymore," Jim said in his deep baritone voice, nuzzling his nose into her brunette hair. "Your ears are fine tuning for this baby. New mothers hear every squeak and squawk their babies make."

Carol grabbed his hand and held it to her swollen belly. Jim could feel the urgent kicks and tugs rippling under her skin.

"Active little thing," he said, giving her a tender kiss on the temple.

"Just like his daddy," she said. "When are you going to be home? Dr. Lockhart told me at my last check-up that she thinks I might go earlier than June. I'm measuring farther along than she thought. And I wouldn't want you to miss out on the whole event," she said, anxiety lacing her words. Her brown eyes scanned Jim's face as she ran her fingers through his blonde hair, now flecked with graying streaks.

"Honey, I'm going to Coon Valley, not the moon. I'll have my cell," he said seriously, "but don't call me except in an emergency, okay?" Staring into the cool blueness of his eyes, she felt the rising panic in her chest subside. Those eyes tugged on her heart strings like no other.

Kissing him passionately, she said, "Well, there's a little something I need before you go."

His eyebrows arched, and he grinned.

"That's the reason you're in the condition you're in right now," he teased, responding to her with a kiss of his own. "You better settle for a nice back rub and a shower."

"Oh, come on. I miss our little early morning romps," she said impishly.

"You are such a devil," Jim said, grinning. "But I think we better shelve that idea," he said, running his hand over her taut tummy.

Now standing in the creek, Jim reached for his phone, deciding his hours of relaxation in the verdant greenery of Spring Coulee would have to come to an end. Patting his pockets, he groaned when he realized he'd left his cell in the truck. He'd promised Carol the new crib for the nursery would be assembled by evening, and he knew better than to upset her organizational mojo. Glancing at the position of the sun in the sky, he knew it was time to go if he was going to be home by noon.

Loading up his gear in the back of his Suburban, he swung onto the road from the designated turn-out for fisherman, working his way over the gently rolling hills of the Driftless Region of southern Wisconsin near La Crosse. After several weeks of cold, rainy spring weather, the sunshine had finally arrived in force. It's strength increased daily, warming the earth until the temperatures consistently hovered around seventy. Puffy cumulus clouds leisurely floated against the powder blue sky. Jim powered down his window, leaned his arm on the frame, and drew the clean air deeply into his lungs.

Hooking up with County Highway K, he breezed around a huge tractor and corn planter, waving out the window while negotiating a wide berth. A female bobwhite and her brood fluttered hurriedly across the road disappearing into a patch of brush. Farther along, he noticed Gladys Hanson hobbling to her mailbox. He slowed, pulled up beside her, and rolled down his passenger window. Gladys gave him a quick wave of the hand and a mannerly smile.

"Beautiful day, huh?" Jim commented smiling, a dimple denting his right cheek. He leaned toward her.

"Shouldn't you be home with Carol? She's due any day, isn't she?" Gladys said with a put-on sense of indignity, her wide bosom filling the truck window. Her flowered dress was covered with an apron that looked ancient and was speckled with flour. Snow white curls framed her wrinkled face, and she wore an expression of someone who had no interest in pretense or social posturing.

"I'm heading home right now," Jim said, feeling like he was reporting to his mother.

Hiding a grin that was fighting to get to the surface, she asked, "You been fishin' again?"

A guilty look crossed Jim's face. "Might be my last chance in Timber Coulee for quite a while."

"Does Carol know you're fishin'? she asked persistently.

What is this—the Inquisition? he thought. "Absolutely. She's all for it," he stated, feeling like a kid who got caught with his hand in the cookie jar.

"Well, you let me know when she has that little one." She pointed at her buxom chest with her index finger. "I don't do Facebook and all that other nonsense. A phone call from you will do," she said seriously.

"You got it, Gladys. I trust you'll spread the word to the other ladies at Hamburg Lutheran Church when the event happens," he said, pointing a finger at her.

"Those old windbags can find out for themselves," she said abruptly.

Jim threw his head back and laughed. He could always trust Gladys to give him her honest opinion with a twist of humor. Then turning serious, he asked, "Can I count on your prayers?"

"Always. Been praying ever since I found out about this... *expectation*," she said, her face flushing pink. She looked at Jim with her attentive hazel eyes. Her voice softened. "I'm praying every day."

Jim nodded his head, and his blue eyes softened. "As I thought you would. Thank you, Gladys. Gotta go!"

He lifted his hand in a good-bye and sped down the blacktop. Driving up Chipmunk Coulee Road, he turned into the driveway. Carol was on her knees in a flowerbed by the front entry, digging in the dirt, transplanting perennials. She glanced up expectantly when he rolled up to the garage. Jim climbed out and walked up to her.

"Hey, whadda ya doing?" he asked casually.

I'm sweating. That's what I'm doing, she thought irritably. Her garden gloves and the knees of her jeans were covered in black dirt. She stuck her trowel in the soil, leaned back, and placed her gloved hands on her jeans, her swollen belly resting on her thighs.

"Well, I'm trying to get some gardening done before this baby comes. By the way, did you realize your phone is turned off?" she asked, giving him a frazzled look. Her brunette hair, normally carefully coiffed, was in disarray. She took a gloved hand and pushed a few loose strands away from her face.

Jim reached in his pocket. "Well, I guess I didn't notice," he said sheepishly, retrieving it from his jean pocket.

Carol gave him a sideways glance. "Really?" she asked sarcastically, tipping her head.

"Honestly, I didn't know it was off," he said, holding out the phone.

"You're supposed to call Luke at the morgue," she said. Jim gave her a puzzled look. "He wouldn't tell me a thing, and I didn't ask," she finished. She made an effort to stand. Jim reached out and pulled her up.

"Ooof. It's getting harder to do that," she complained, a frown creasing her forehead as she laid a hand on her distended belly. "I'm heading for the shower. Would you be sweet and make some sandwiches while I clean up?"

"Sure. No problem."

"Don't forget to call Luke," she reminded him as she waddled down the hall to the bathroom.

"Then this afternoon you've got to get that crib put together."

Jim began rummaging through the refrigerator searching for sandwich fixings, placing them on the counter. In the middle of grabbing the mayonnaise and mustard, his phone vibrated in his pocket.

"Jim Higgins."

"Chief, it's Luke down at the morgue. Just wanted to let you know a jogger found a dead individual this morning in Riverside Park. It's a set of unusual circumstances. I want you and Carol to come down here in the next couple of hours. Can you do that?" he asked, his voice taking on an anxious tone that Jim found unusual.

"Why Carol?" he asked, confused.

"It's hard to explain over the phone. Can you promise me you'll come down, say by two o'clock?" he asked again, more impatient this time.

"Can't you just tell me right now and save Carol the hassle of the drive into La Crosse?" His voice had taken on a brusqueness of its own. "She's pretty uncomfortable."

"No, you both need to come down—by two or so," Luke ordered, his own voice echoing Jim's tone.

"All right, if you say so. We'll be there." He stood in the sunlight of the kitchen wondering what could have happened that would require both of them to head to the morgue. *Maybe it's Matt. Probably wandered into the park after a gig and died of a massive coronary,* he thought.

Matt Donavan was Carol's ex. He was known throughout the area for his country/rock band *Mississippi Mud,* a wildly popular tri-state entertaining act. He was also notorious for his hard partying and escapades with women. Jim shook his head. *Who knows what happened. Sometimes life is stranger than fiction.* He started making a couple of sandwiches.

Over lunch, Jim explained the odd request from Luke Evers, La Crosse County Medical Examiner, who happened to be Carol's boss.

"He wants us both to come down?" she questioned, making a wry face. "I've got a million things to do, Jim."

"Yeah, I tried to tell him that, but he was acting really weird," Jim commented, taking a bite of sandwich. Carol frowned and pushed a lock of hair behind her ear.

"Can't imagine what that could be," she said suspiciously.

"Me, either," Jim finished. "I have no idea what this is about. I'm not even going to speculate." *I just hope it isn't something about Matt,* he thought. He couldn't imagine any other reason that Carol's presence would be required. His sense of uneasiness grew. *This is not what Carol needs when she's about to deliver a baby.* ◉

ACKNOWLEDGMENTS

Publishing my first novel was like standing on the edge of
a diving board, looking down at the cold, clear water below
knowing that the dive would be frightening but, at the
same time, completely exhilarating.

I have felt so fortunate in this journey to be supported
by so many friends and family—thank you.

To my first readers and those published authors who so
generously read my books and were gracious and kind
in your remarks—thank you.

To the many friends I met throughout the spring,
summer and fall months of 2021 at art fairs, bookstores,
book clubs and online through Facebook who took time to
read my first book, *Driftless Gold* and post reader reviews on
Amazon and Barnes & Noble—thank you. You encouraged
me to continue writing and not give up.

To Phil Addis—master photographer who captures the spirit
of the Driftless region's geography and people in his iconic images
and provides me with great book covers—thank you.

As always—thank you, Alan, my love of 44 years. He hasn't read
one of my books and probably never will, but he's always proud of
me and encourages me in all of my interests. How precious is that?

"Whatever you do, do it heartily as unto the Lord and
not men, knowing that from the Lord you will receive
the inheritance as your reward."
Colossians 3:23

CPSIA information can be obtained
at www.ICGtesting.com
Printed in the USA
JSHW050857060822
28922JS00003B/14